I am a little Faut.
Gima wash my mouth out with sope
I said bad word. I made bubbles
with the sope. It was fun. But it no
taste good tho.
Gima said I   don't know what to
do with you. You a little faut. (Smileing)
Eating sope it not suposed to be fun.
I cryed. Gima say Oh hell! Lady's
say bad word some times.
   Gi-pa make me feel uckey.
I stay with my Gima.

                              nov 18,

   I had help writeing.

   Sophia   Punk
     chris
   Ted is diorced   Amber

   Cryal Crystal Jane

   Kitty   Tumblina
                    Frogie

to pay for doing wrong. We should never wanted!!
this ain't right, tis not! tis them's I's should
this been mad at.
I NO LiKe ME MoRe.

You Known what we can Do?
or wood do if we think there no
other way! Thats all we going to
say! We don't want to be bad!

NO ONE. We not
Doing good
A LiCE.

TiF Fany here

us talk to the mother.
She called us. I want to
hided Like Lizzie DO.

I+ hurt me too SU ZE

I want to Love Punky

I love you stay a way   Sara
you die to.   Little

Dare to Reach Beyond Normal

David D. Yates, M.S.

Dare to Reach Beyond Normal

David D. Yates, M.S.

Edited by: John Crandall, M.S.
National University, Sacramento

Kathy Goldman, B.A., University
California, Berkeley, M.A.
California State East Bay

Beverly Hill, Associate Health Physicist

Adult Fiction
Published By: David D. Yates, M.S.
2023

Front and Back Cover Artist: Iris

First printing 2023

Library of Congress Control Number
ISBN: 9798372318359

Ordering information:
This book may be ordered from the printer Amazon or the publisher David
Yates, M. S., but try your local bookstore first.

Publisher: David Yates, M.S.
Address: Shingle Springs, California
yatesdc@sbcglobal.net

Special discounts might be available on quantity purchases by corporations,
associations, educators, and others. For details,contact Amazon.
U.S. trade bookstores and wholesalers, please contact Amazon

Photo by: Carol Yates

Dedication

This book is for Dorothy, last seen sitting on a floor holding and rocking herself, who became only a faint recollection

David D. Yates

Acknowledgments

I appreciate my editors, John Crandall, my long-term friend and mentor, and Kathy Goldman and Beverly Hill, my new friends. Thanks to David Martin Yates, Jolana Yates, Brooke Anne Marie Yates, and Alicia P. Harrison for their technical support. Most importantly, accolades to my wife, Carol, for handling all other matters while I tackled this project.

Preface

Hopefully, this story will help victims in their struggle to persevere who've lived or are living the hell herein described, and touch others in a way that prevents more children from getting hurt.

Introduction

Dorothy, the real-life person whose experiences are the basis of this story, suffered harsh and constant abuse, leading to profound emotions and sensations beyond her developmental competency to understand and manage. The outcome was Dissociative Identity Disorder (DID) a mental disorder characterized by maintaining at least two distinct and relatively enduring personality states, "alters" (alters). DID was known as Multiple Personality Disorder (MPD) until 1994. See the appendix for the criteria for DID.

The resulting "dissociation" (dissociation) left Dorothy disconnected from herself and her surroundings, disrupted her identity, and intruded upon her consciousness and experience of body, world, self, mind, agency, intentionality, thinking, believing, knowing, recognizing, remembering, feeling, wanting, speaking, acting, seeing, hearing, smelling, tasting, and touching. Dissociation is a method of coping whereby one disconnects from one's conscious experience of reality, intentionally or unintentionally, due to the perceived threat of danger or annihilation.

To partake in her horror and agony, Dorothy endured by spawning alters, "splitting" (splitting), who could express a broad range of emotions in a brief time. She dreaded that other people would be repulsed by what she divulged and was always cognizant of others' receptivity. Her lurking fear was that she was answerable for all the inhuman desecration heaped on her.

Holly Gray, Ph.D., is a psychiatric mental health nurse practitioner. She defined an alter as a dissociated piece of self with the ability to operate independently, perceive self and the world in its unique way, assume control of the mind and body, or exert enough influence to impact thoughts, feelings, and behaviors (2-24-11).

The "system" (system) is a collective term to describe all alters "inside" (inside), the inner world where all can be when not interacting with the "outside" (outside), the outer world. "Hosts" (hosts) are alters interacting with the outer world.

A "fragment" (fragment) is an incomplete alter or an extreme form of compartmentalization of thought and action, often holding a single memory, handling one emotion, or performing a specific task. An alter is "out" (out) when interacting with the outer world. "Sub-systems" (clusters), specific groups separated from others inside in a particular manner, are formed by more than one alter. Dorothy's clusters have explicitly stated purposes, and the alters within usually have separate goals and independent sets of thoughts and emotions.

Dorothy's story includes 62 clusters, 160 alters, and 80 "fragments" (fragments). I've described and provided explicit functions of alters, fragments, and clusters as they are introduced in this story. Fragments other than the 80 aren't identified, and some become alters in parts of the story not told. The named alters and fragments not appearing in this tale number 112. See the appendix.

When Dorothy introduces a cluster, she names all alters within, even though they might not appear in the story until later. Dorothy sometimes adds alters to a cluster after she creates it. Many alters aren't part of a cluster.

Alters are typically frozen at the age conceived, but some grow a few years or even to adulthood. Alters might be spoken about in the present tense because they haven't gone away, even if they're not active.

A sprinkling of Dorothy's imaginary friends appears in this story. A thin line exists between an imaginary friend and alter, and an imaginary friend can become the seed from which an alter will grow.

Dorothy tells this story until age 15 when she becomes Dorothy Anne, a separate person who lives inside Dorothy. Dorothy Anne briefly continues the tale until she marries at age 18 and changes her name to Dorothy Lynne at her husband's request. Dorothy Lynne, an entirely different person from the other two Dorothys, becomes the storyteller during her marriage. After her marriage ends, Dorothy Lynne remains somewhat involved in the storytelling, but Evangelina (Leena), the "shell personality" (shell), and various alters finish the story. A shell is an informal term meaning the person serving as an encasement to hold and display what alters are thinking and feeling. The self-reference of the storytellers might be singular or plural depending on whether he/she views his/herself as many versus one.

Leena believed that the total number of alters, named and unnamed, remembered and forgotten, was well over 500, not to mention an unknown number of fragments.

The font in this sentence is used when alters ages eight and older communicate.

The font employed in this sentence is used when alters ages seven and under, print, or speak because it's more youthful in appearance with connotations of simplicity.

To promote clarity, the font employed in this sentence is used when Dorothy communicates.

The reader will be advised later of the fonts employed when Anne, Lynne and Leena talk. {Input from this writer about terminology appears with braces as shown and in the font used in this sentence.}

Dorothy, Dorothy Anne, Lynne, Leena, and alters who felt more distant from the natural mother, called her The Mother. Other alters referred to her differently because they had different feelings about her, and their self-reference could be singular or plural. Those who felt closer would refer to her as "my mother." If their self-reference was plural, they referred to her as "our mother." Some, under the age of eight, called her "mommy." Heidi, Bell, Tamara, Rachel, and Kay referred to her as "mama."

One - My Childhood With The Mother.

My Bone-Chilling Beginning

The railroad ties are hard and cold, and the aroma of hot metal and oil lingers on the tracks, where 3-year-old Wanda lies, curled into a fetal position and repeatedly swallowing while clutching her stuffie. Her tiny body trembles as the train approaches, and she tenses her teeny muscles in anticipation as the whistle and clacking metal of wheels on rails grow louder. Then the sounds diminish and fade into the distance after the train passes. Again, Wanda chose the wrong tracks. Dejected, with eyes downcast, she drags her feet and teensy droopy body all the way home, where The Mother locks her in the cold, 4-by-5-foot metal dog cage on the porch for the night and forces her to eat dog poop off the cage floor.

I created Wanda to help carry the fear of The Mother and men. Wanda frequently ran away from home, packing her lunch pail with clean panties and an apple and toting one of her stuffies as she hiked the railroad tracks.

Three years earlier, I began as a thought or seed planted in The Mother by God. I felt hopeful and dreamed of a good life as I floated peacefully through glorious blue, purple, white, pink, and orange clouds. I felt The Mother's distrust, anger, and sadness and heard her voice and others' voices but couldn't understand them. On the day I came out, I wasn't fond of the bright light or loud noise and was scared because I somehow could foresee being hurt.

I was born as Baby Dorothy in 1931. My 4-year-old brother, Buster, cared for my sister, Rebecca, not yet two, and me as best he could while The Mother bar-hopped. The Mother gave me something to cry about, like a pinch or a slap when I cried. It wasn't okay to shed tears because it made The Mother angry.

At age one, I began creating alters to help survive the pain and horror of The Mother's desecration initially and later from men. When I made a new alter, it often started as a baby who needed to grow into an actual person.

I made three 1-year-old female alter babies, Brooklyn, Cathy, and Katherine. They helped absorb the pain and horror of The Mother's relentless abuse and neglect. A Baby Cluster emerged, carrying the pain of knowing what The Mother did to me. Crybaby, our fourth alter baby, who began as an infant girl, later joined that cluster. The Baby Cluster also included Mary, Angel, Punky Lil, Misty, Half-Pint, Meme, and Prissy, all made to soothe the four alter babies when they cried. The alter babies couldn't remember it all because they'd become overwhelmed, weep and disappear. They'd see and hear The Mother speaking to them, and then the pain came.

Brooklyn, my first alter baby, who frequently grimaced, eventually grew to adulthood. She carried the immense pain and dizziness from The Mother breaking my rib.

The following is my drawing at age eight of Cathy, my second alter baby, in her crib, with my brother, Buster, comforting her. Alter, I-See, not shown, is an ageless female angel from heaven who always watched over us and taught us to love.

The Mother continued to be either vicious or inattentive, prompting my third alter baby, Katherine, who cried continually in response to The Mother's pinches or slaps. She was also from the Kids Cluster: Katherine, Art, Katty, Ann, Kay, and others. They were alters under age 10 who took care of other alters by helping take on the agony, loathing, and dreadfulness of The Mother's neglect and torture and injured themselves when they became angry.

Next, I made Doer, a bright boy from the Bad Cluster: Doer, Dee, Helpless, His-Self, Peaches-and-Cream (Peaches), Rachel, Sexy, User, the Bad Ones, and Andy, formerly Hater. The Bad Cluster carried our evil thoughts and emotions: anger, pain, humiliation, horror, hate, evil, killing self, and denial.

The Bad Ones were Adora, Crystal, James, Sandy, Toughie, Ugly, Winter-Two, and Winter. They were rescuers who helped us survive by managing our rage because they had no emotions. Still, their ruthlessness could get us locked up. Non-alters: The Mother, Satan, uncles, and other men, made up the outside bad.

Doer began at age one, and although at age five, he became Mary, further introduced later, he continued to live within her. When he got scared, he wet his pants or bed, for which he received a whipping. Doer carried the emotions the other alters couldn't handle, especially intense animosity toward people. He also hated us and made people hate us by saying and doing bad things.

As Baby Dorothy, I became so broken emotionally that I died at 14 months and started over as Dorothy. New alters continued to emerge.

When I was 18 months old, The Mother separated from my dad, ran over him with her car, and cut him with a knife. She'd wanted to go dancing, but he insisted on working instead. The Mother asked me to choose a parent to live with, and when I said my dad, she told me to shut up and get the hell in the car. I felt safe with my dad.

I created Child, an 18-month-old girl toddler, who often bowed her head with wet eyes, to hold the sadness, anger, and bitterness from my not getting to live with my dad. My dad refused to relinquish legal custody of me, so The Mother had him jailed for non-support. Ronald, my half-brother from The Mother's union with my first stepdad, came along about then.

I made Wisher when I was two to help hold the pain of losing my dad. Wisher began as a 2-year-old boy but grew to age 16. He wanted to live with his dad or maternal Grandma, so life would be better. He sometimes hated The Mother and wished her dead.

After my first stepdad left, The Mother acquired a new boyfriend who almost beat her and another man to death when he caught them in bed together. The Mother wanted what she wanted when she wanted it. The Mother bashed the new boyfriend's head with an iron skillet and drove her car into him a week later. That boyfriend told The Mother's next lover that The Mother had false teeth and no breasts.

The Mother became pregnant with that new lover, but he wouldn't marry her. He wasn't a good guy.

Then came the next boyfriend, a good guy who didn't harm my siblings or me. He caught The Mother in bed with another man and refused to leave the house as The Mother insisted, so she shot him with her pistol.

An unnamed young alter explained that the boyfriend, who soon followed, didn't like The Mother to complain when he squished her during sex, so he didn't last long.

The Mother married my second stepdad soon after that. My half-brother, Henry, came from that union. The Mother regularly started fights with this stepdad, and he'd tell her to knock it off. He didn't last long.

When this stepdad wasn't home, the Mother had lovers who came into my bedroom at night. She drove her car into one of her lovers and knifed him after he had sex with me because that made her no longer "number one." So, I had my first sex before age three.

The Mother used to duct tape the mouths of my siblings and me when she wanted quiet. Ronald once made a hole in his tape and got a whipping.

19

Also, she'd line up my siblings and me and beat us, becoming angrier as she went down the line. She didn't allow us to block the blows, as that was defying. The worst part was waiting for my turn.

Even worse was when she'd often strike me from behind, pull my hair, and whip me until I explained why I was getting a thrashing, but I never knew why. She threatened to kill us if we phoned the police.

Another of The Mother's tortures was forcing me to eat rotten food, covering my mouth to push it down until I threw up, then pounding me for wasting the food she claimed she worked so hard to get.

The Mother began abandoning my siblings and me before I was three, regularly leaving for two weeks at a time and sometimes longer. She'd put my brother, Buster, seven at the time, sister, Rebecca, age four, and me in a motel. I don't remember where Ronald or Henry was. Buster would help my sister and me climb into dumpsters to get dinner. One time a kind dishwasher noticed and began putting food out for us. The police, fire department, and child welfare people came when Buster set our room on fire while cooking.

Authorities placed us with our maternal Grandma and step-Grandpa. My real maternal grandpa went to jail for writing bad checks, and no one was supposed to see him when he got out, but I don't know why.

A Brief Respite With Grandma but Then Back to The Mother

I only got to stay with Grandma for two to three weeks before The Mother brought me back home, where I created even more alters to help bear the harm from The Mother's abuse, including mixed messages. For example, I got into trouble if I lied to The Mother, but she forced me to lie to the men she brought home.

I also created a new alter to carry my guilt each time I did anything wrong. I began as one but kept making alters until I became nothing. I felt crazy because different alters had differing answers to the same question, accepting the opinions or positions people had imposed on them.

A short time later, The Mother returned me to my Grandma, where I remained for the whole summer before my third birthday. One day I wanted to get on the school bus with my brother, Buster and was upset when Grandma wouldn't allow it. Grandma said, "I won't have my good little helper if you get on the bus," making me feel better.

During this stay with Grandma, I made Gatekeepers of the Secrets, whose names I've forgotten, to know what happened in my family but not tell the other alters. They also kept other secrets to keep me out of trouble, like where I hid toys from The Mother at Grandma's house. {A gatekeeper is an alter who can control who's inside or out or other matters.}

At the end of that summer, The Mother forced me to return home. Soon after, I became panic-stricken due to beatings and continual sexual exploitation by The Mother and the men she brought to our home.

I was so overwhelmed I made the Little Ones: Tabatha, Fur, Rock, Roxie, Vicky, Little, Think, Teresa, Spunky, Neddie, and PJ, all 3-year-old girls, and Sky, a non-gender 3-year-old. Little Ones also included Cathy, Katherine, Wanda, and Child, introduced earlier.

Little Ones came out when they thought it was safe. They engaged in dangerous activities like cutting themselves or sticking metal objects into light fixtures to feel pain. To continue noticing the pain, they had to increase the level. An unnamed Little One tried to put her face into a garbage disposal. While standing on a stool in front of the kitchen sink, she bent forward and pushed her face into the hole as far as she could. Flipping the switch, she licked her lips and salivated in anticipation of the pain the spinning blade would inevitably bring. Dejected because she couldn't get her face close enough, she climbed down from the stool and dragged her feet and tiny limp body to her bedroom.

Little Ones wanted to be well-behaved, so they didn't get into trouble with The Mother; therefore, we made a new one to carry any additional misbehavior. {In some DID literature, a "Little" is a child alter under eight years old.}

Little Ones drew the following work titled "Our Childhood Pain." Seven hands reach for a crying face near the words: pain, hurt, sad, and want.

Meme, further introduced soon, printed on the back of this drawing, so tiny it must be magnified to read: I'm Meme. I used to be called Thumbelina. I'm tiny.

Tabatha helped hold our pain and fear from The Mother's brutality. She often grimaced, did dummy things, and had temper tantrums by throwing her arms, stomping her feet, and making ugly faces. Because Tabatha carried pain, our chest hurt upon her arrival, and the more Tabatha was present, the more hurt we endured. When Tabatha left, she took the pain with her. Tabatha worried about her soul and waited for something to happen because she felt dead.

Fur expressed anger toward The Mother by growling and exposing her teeth, like a furry animal, but The Mother only whipped her harder.

Rock, also a Nobody, those who weren't much of anything but helped us determine what was happening, was bull-headed and didn't move when The Mother hurt us.

Roxie was emotionless because the continual mutilation by The Mother emotionally overwhelmed us.

Vicky helped bear the fear of The Mother and men. She was shy and afraid of people, lightning, bridges, heights, and herself.

The Mother and one of The Mother's boyfriends came to Mary, but she didn't like it. She said it felt yucky and scared her and that she didn't want it. Mary created Little to help absorb the resulting pain and horror. Little, from the Good Ones: Punky, Sarah, Tara, Kara, and Carrie, also helped absorb the terror from The Mother igniting our bed. Little often displayed wide eyes and a lifted brow and sometimes trembled. Good Ones believed in children, hope, angels, spirits, doing good, forgiveness, keeping safe, wisdom, dreams, wanting, and unconditional love.

The Mother was only kind to me on the rare occasion she was happy. She usually punished me whether I misbehaved, was well-behaved, or somewhere between. I couldn't cry because crying made The Mother angry, so I made Think, who never cried.

Teresa helped absorb the pain from The Mother forcing me to choose between her and anyone else.

Neddie wanted to be loved, not hated.

Because Wanda's dog cage experience caused terrible feelings, I created Spunky to suffer those emotions.

PJ helped carry our fear of The Mother but felt better when discussing her painful memories. She was petite and shy and usually displayed wide eyes and a lifted brow while trembling.

Sky, a non-gender alter, was created to keep us feeling peaceful.

Lastly, at age three, I made the following: Missy, who began at age 3 but grew to 12; Peter; the Nobodies, who were Dusty, Mathew, and other alters, including some unnamed; Deon, an 8-year-old boy fragment; Dee, an 8-year-old deaf girl; Hurt, an 8-year-old boy; Iris, a 10-year-old girl; and Punky, a girl who started at age 8 and grew to 12.

Missy helped bear bewilderment from The Mother's crazy-making behavior. She banged her head against walls to get thoughts out until age nine because The Mother told her they were untrue or unreal. Missy sometimes appeared confused, with a tilted head, narrowed eyes, and furrowed brow. {She experienced "de-realization" (de-realization), a feeling that reality is fake, incorrect, or distorted, often accompanied by depression or anxiety. It commonly occurs with dissociation and "depersonalization" (depersonalization). Depersonalization is a type of dissociation in which a person has a sense of detachment from one or more personal realities: identity, thoughts, feelings, consciousness, emotions, and memory, often experienced with depression, anxiety, and "body dysphoria" (body dysphoria) seeing one's body as unattractive.}

Peter, who started as a dragon named "Dragon, Dear" but became a 3-year-old boy who grew to age 13 and could become "Dragon, Dear," was created to protect us and was our oldest boy. To take The Mother's whippings, which usually drew blood, Peter would change into a giant, robust, pinkish-purple dragon, scary to others but not us. When The Mother cut Peter with baling wire, it didn't hurt much because boys are tough, and dragons are even more rugged. {An "animal alter" (animal alter) is an alter who, for coping mechanisms, appears as a total animal.} Timothy A. Bradshaw (Charles II), further discussed later, drew Peter as follows, protecting us from The Mother's belt:

Dusty and Mathew were 5-year-old boy Nobodies, also from the Us Cluster, sometimes referred to as "club 900," along with Cindy, Gypsy, Mathew, M, Melissa, Pennie, Six, Ugly, Windy, and three unnamed others. Their ages ranged from 3 to 13 years. They wanted to be intelligent, have friends, and fit in to convince The Mother they could be like other kids instead of taking care of the baby, cleaning the house, cooking, and selling their bodies. The more they accepted themselves, the more they allowed the emotions and ideas of others. They often spoke in near unison, sounding like a symphony of crickets; however, they sometimes talked as individuals. They wrote or printed as a group or individually. Some only spoke when spoken to and didn't do that very much. Many withdrew, blocked emotions, and rarely did or said anything due to the fear of feeling stupid and the accompanying unbearable shame.

Unnamed Ones were 27 unnamed alters, ages 4 to 12 for the most part, stuck in The Mother's bedroom wall, created to act adult because it wasn't safe to be a child.

Deon was from the Hidden Ones, Can-Bes, and We-Two Cluster. He helped halt our pain but was self-destructive. Deon talked about death all the time, cut us, tried to drown us, and tried to overdose us on pills. He often grimaced and sometimes held himself and rocked from side to side.

Hidden Ones were Dee, Deon, Deand, De-de, and others, all fragments except for Dee, an alter. Each fragment bore the memory of up to 5 minutes of the feelings of a 15-minute whipping.

Can-Bes were Deon and Pamela Boy, who was a girl, and others, who copied alters needed for a job and replaced them if, for some reason, they couldn't remain out to finish it.

The We-Two Cluster was Deon, Charles, Punky, Silly Sally, Mary, and Timothy A. Bradshaw. The We-One Cluster was Nora, Clara, Tamara, and others, and the We-Three Cluster was Nettie, Annie, Amy, Pink, and Lilly. The We Clusters helped bear the hurt and terror of our childhood wounding. The more they accepted themselves, the more amenable they were to others' emotions and ideas. They were always out in groups and wrote or printed in groups, but only one spoke at a time, even though self-reference might have been plural.

Dee stood for death and spoke of death regularly. She hated and wasn't kind. She tried to kill us numerous times between ages three and five to end our pain and horror by laying us on railroad tracks during our runaways. Sadly, Dee's timing or choice of tracks was always lousy. Dee also cut us, tried to drown us, and attempted to overdose us on pills as Deon did. She cut for various reasons, such as to show people how bloody and icky it was or to punish herself because she wasn't kind or deserving. She was programmed to cut more often and deeper and lived on the edge, frequently driving too fast or standing on guardrails overlooking cliffs. The other alters sometimes wanted to hurt Dee because she tried to kill us.

She was from the Hidden Ones, Dark Secret Ones, and Bad and Hurt Clusters. Our portraits of alters often appear older because older people tend not to get hurt. {Dee was a "persecutor," a type of alter representing some kind of pain a system goes through and is often prone to dangerous, self-destructive, panicked, manipulative, or irrational actions.} Dee's portrait follows:

Dee 8
(Beth)

Dark Secret Ones were Beth, Dee, Adam, and James, who perceived hell as a dark place and helped ease the pain and horror from our wreckage at the hands of The Mother and men.

The Hurt Cluster consisted of Beth, Dee, Hurt, Iris, James, Mary, Suzie Q., and Seven-and-Three-Quarters (7 ¾). They were markedly injured, spread evil all around, and traded sex for a hug, smile, love, and to know the location of the monster, any abuser.

The grandpa to my half-brother, Ronald, and I, took Ronald and me to a shed to teach us God's words about obeying parents and grandparents. He also beat us with a leather strap and did other stuff I don't clearly remember, but I recall thinking that God must be mean and not like girls.

Hurt, who carried pain and outrage over The Mother's brutality and frequently grimaced or clenched his fists and bared his teeth, was also a Taker and Angry One.

Takers were unlikable ones who took too much damage and harmed others, though they preferred to stay hidden and not hurt anyone. They consisted of Angry, Hurt, Stupid-Head, Pennie, and myself, Dorothy.

The Angry Ones were Amanda, Angry, Bell, Heidi, Hurt, Rose, Six, Nineteen, and others. They carried moderate anger over our brutal mistreatment by The Mother and others and wanted revenge.

I also created Unnamed Ones, 27 unnamed alters, ages 4 through 16, stuck in The Mother's bedroom wall. They acted grown-up because it wasn't safe to be a child.

Iris was the color of a rainbow and focused exclusively on drawing.

At age three, we chuckled as we listened to our favorite radio program but later hated that broadcast for acquainting us with what it meant to be happy. After that, it became more challenging to handle the bad because we'd tasted cheerfulness. We created Punky to hold the key to unlocking happiness, so that life wouldn't be horrible. Punky was a trusting tomboyish girl Helper from the Happy and Hope/Heart Clusters. {A "helper" (helper) is a leader in the system, knowing everyone and working to maintain stability and help everyone, and doesn't usually come out often. A helper is generally a "protector" (protector), an alter protecting the body, system, "host," "core" (core), or other specific alter or groups of alters. The core is the original personality, born with the body.}

Helpers were Holy Man, Intelligent One, Knower, Sarah, Seer, Tara, Oneida, Annie, Punky, Punky Lil, Wise Ones, and unnamed others who helped us know what was happening. I made them while I lived with The Mother, except for Punky Lil, created at Grandma'.

When we couldn't show emotions, we put them in a box and gave them their alter names. Punky was trust. Punky usually slumped her shoulders and had trouble meeting a gaze, closing her eyes, or glancing down and away instead. She reconciled the difference between what The Mother and Grandma said and helped spread joy, so that life wouldn't be horrible. {An alter who disperses joy is called an "innocent."}

The Happy Cluster consisted of Bunnie, Meme, Punky, and Silly Sally. They remembered The Mother's abuse but didn't judge her because they believed it wasn't their place.

The Hope/Heart Cluster consisted of Beth, Hope, Carrie, Stupid-Head, Maria, Sarah, Sunshine (The One), and Tara. They believed in children, hope, angels, spirits, doing good, forgiveness, keeping safe, wanting, wisdom, dreams, and unconditional love, as did the Good Ones.

Punky made three girls, Punky II, III, and IV, to spread her responsibilities. Each grew from age 4 to 12. Punky II was the bad one, Punky III was the non-proper one, and Punky IV lied and sat on men's laps. My portraits of Punky on the left and Iris's rendering to the right follow:

The Mother would sometimes tie Punky to a chair for hours. Her arms would swell, making the ropes even tighter. Punky would cry and would kick in an attempt to get loose. She thought she was glued, like when her brother, Buster, put glue on her chair. Other alters would come to share the intense pain.

Punky even had to eat dinner tied up, and if she spilled, The Mother slammed her head into the dinner table, called her pig, and insisted that she oink. The oinking brought snickers from those present. The Mother then took Punky's dinner away or put her on her side to eat off the floor while still tied to the chair.

My following sketch of Punky depicts my bewilderment and fear at this time in my life. Punky is asking "what," with "not real" printed on her forehead, "die" on her stomach, "no, no," to the left of her head, "sleep, sleep, go to sleep" to the right, and "very scared" and "it comes" above her head."

I disappeared early on to survive and could no longer feel The Mother's slaps, blows, lashes, or burns because my senses were gone. After I ceased having physical sensations, I could pull hot pans from the oven and sometimes get burned but at times not, but rarely felt pain.

When I was four, The Mother shot her boyfriend, Will, in my presence, burned my arms with cigarettes and punched them with a fork, and set my bed ablaze because my brother, Buster, and I wouldn't come from under it.

The Mother also taught me what worthless trash I was by putting me in a trashcan, pouring garbage over me, and telling me to stay there and think about how useless I was. The Mother growled, "Don't move, or you'll wish the hell you hadn't." She put me in the trashcan before my nap, lunch and after dinner, after which she reprimanded and savagely beat me. She'd yell, "I'm ashamed of you. You smell and look like trash. Don't touch anything with your filthy hands." I was amazed I didn't feel the beating, and the stinging verbiage seemed far away.

In the trashcan, I heard the buzzing of flies in the dark and felt the creepiness of worms. I trembled with fear and gasped for air as the stench of my sibling's diapers burned my nose. I thought I'd be okay if only I could lift the lid a little, breathe, get my toe under it, and see a tiny light. My body froze, and my breath quickened as silence followed a loud, jarring bang on the trashcan. I wished The Mother would kill me and get it over with. I cringed as the trashcan tipped over, fearing that The Mother would end me.

To carry this terror and help carry the terror of The Mother beating us, we made Isabelle, who began as a 4-year-old girl but grew to age 12.

I cried at age four as I stood by the bed where The Mother lay, partially naked. The Mother would growl, "Go if you don't love me. Tell your sister to come here. She loves me more. You don't love me. Leave me. Go. I don't need you. You only want to hurt me. You've hurt me enough. If you don't love me, how can I love you?" I responded: I love you! Don't say that!

In a drawing not shown, Iris sketched erratic red scribbles over my thrashed 4-year-old body, next to the words, "Angry-Red, Sad-tear drops," and "Pure Hate," and drew a tearful broken heart, house sprinkled with tears, and locked safe above the word "soul."

The 12 Original Dominant Selves

To survive my fifth year, I made and joined 11 alters to compose the 12 Original Dominant Selves (12 Selves). Those alters were: Am, Crybaby, Punk, 7 ¾, T, Amber, Andy, Angry, Mary, Charles, and Pony. {In DID literature, "Selves" (selves) are alters who speak among themselves but not to others.}

These 11 and I were our knights in shining armor who tried to protect us from anything wrong or adverse. We were best buddies and a council with a community brain. I knew how to fashion the older ones because I'd been around older kids. I needed them to handle more challenging problems.

Am, a 4-year-old girl who didn't speak and rarely came out, carried our pain from The Mother saying to keep your mouth shut and no one will know you're stupid.

Crybaby, who often held herself and rocked from side to side, began as an infant girl but grew to age four. Because she couldn't talk, she cried to get heard when left in her crib too much, her bathwater was too hot, her rear hurt because her diapers weren't getting changed, or she got the broom handle. My brother, Buster, took care of her most of the time. Even as an infant, Crybaby could contribute to the council because of their community brain. She remembered men asking her to help them, which scared her badly.

Punk, a 12-year-old girl, carried much of our pain from The Mother's savagery. She could slide forward or backward in age depending on the circumstances, such as when she needed to remember what happened at a particular period. Her forward sliding limit was age 12. Some alters could shift between genders, but I can't remember their names. {These alters are "age sliders" and "gender sliders," respectively.} Punk was also usually entrenched in the system's communication, often playing go-between for other alters. {This type of alter is called a "communicator."

Punk frequently grimaced with wet eyes but wanted to be happy and be a real kid, unlike the screwed-up ones. She liked rabbits, finger painting, and stars because alters were like stars. Some were bright, some not, some could be seen, whereas others couldn't, but you knew they were there. All around us was the darkness holding the secrets.

Seven-and-Three-Quarters, whose name was her age, was proud because she was almost eight. I drew her, as follows, a horrified, crying, nude, gagged young girl with hands tied, bloody privates, and a spider on her shoulder. She absorbed a great deal of the horror from The Mother's maltreatment, including scrubbing her privates with hot water and Clorox or lye until they bled. She often trembled and shrank back from others.

T was a 5-year-old girl who got her name from the sounds of laughter. She cried for the other alters because The Mother didn't allow it, and she was afraid of men, as were most alters. T helped Grandma with sewing and other activities.

Amber was an 8-year-old girl, also from the Angry and Me Clusters. She often jutted her chin and shook her fist. Angry Cluster alters carried great anger over The Mother's brutality, hated her, didn't give a crap, and wanted to hurt her because she injured others. It included Amber, Adora, Jennifer, Lucy, Mary, Sophia, and Lady Sophia.

The Me Cluster alters were Amber, Bree, Patty, Seer, and others. They helped us carry knowing what we were, why we existed, and how many we were. They didn't give their names because doing so would've given away their power because people could have called on them to provide a service. The Me Cluster differed from the Myself Cluster in that it had fewer alters. The Myself Cluster consisted of Nina, Mike, and unnamed others.

Andy, previously Hater, was a 12-year-old "piss-off-er" who got angry and got things done, but he carried so much hate from The Mother's wreckage that he feared he'd hurt himself or others. He often clenched his fists and bared his teeth. At times Andy also felt such intense pain and fear his breathing stopped. I made him when forced to take care of others, even when I was very ill. Andy never truly learned to play, having just started before being forced into adulthood. It wasn't fair.

Angry was an 8-year-old boy who often bared his teeth and clenched his fists. Angry helped bear the hurt and outrage from harm by The Mother and her boyfriends. He started fires, got mad and damaged property, and hated and injured others and himself. Angry neither asked for nor wanted sex. He thought a man sometimes beat boys man-to-man, punished girls, wanted everything done his way, broke things, yelled, hit walls, and cursed at and threatened to do bad things to kids.

Angry and Hurt were the beginning of Mary, a 5-year-old girl. Mary carried anger over the harm done to us by The Mother and helped hold the key to agreeing, in that she could ignore those inside who disagreed and thereby promote moving forward with a decision. Mary was also hurt, confused, scared, and wanted to behave because she feared getting hurt if she misbehaved. She sometimes bared her teeth, clenched her jaws and snarled, and periodically held herself and rocked from side to side. In our emotion box, Mary was anger. She was from the Want-To-Bes, Angry, Hurt, and We-Two Clusters. The following is Iris's portrait of Mary appearing as a young woman:

Want-To-Bes were Alice, Carrie, Mary, Nice Ones, and myself, Dorothy. We suffered immense depression because we wanted to do what real kids do, but The Mother didn't allow it.

The Nice Ones were Sunshine and Ice Queen. They weren't human because they had no emotions except when near. When they got hurt emotionally, we had to keep them safe by assigning the hurt to others, but they had to retain some pain if we didn't have time to make room.

Mary later combined with Jane, a 4-year-old bad girl who sometimes shook due to the terror she helped bear from The Mother and men having sex with us. This union produced Mary Jane, a 5-year-old girl who carried anger and terror from the cruelty and sexual exploitation by The Mother and men. The alters said they were having sex versus being molested or raped because of brainwashing.

Charles, a 6-year-old boy, helped make our fear and other bad feelings go away. He also helped us endure the misery and horror of our childhood torment, including shameful sex. Charles would come and take The Mother's kisses away. He sometimes had difficulty meeting another's gaze but leaned forward and made steady eye contact when addressing us.

Pony, drawn as follows, began as a pony. We rode Pony on spectacular fantasy adventures, which made us happy. With eyes wide open and head tilted back, her pulse and breath quickened as a giggling Little One rode Pony through delightful flowering meadows, charming villages, and marvelous clouds. Pony later became a 4-year-old boy who jumped around but didn't talk and grew to age 10.

The Great Ones were four smart mid-teen alters I created at the time, whose names and gender I don't remember. With the help of Overseer, further discussed shortly, and the 12 Selves, they made another alter when the existing ones became filled with too many painful memories and emotions, thereby facilitating our trudge through life. More alters resulted in more opinions, so we constructed walls to separate them. The Great Ones called this putting them into boxes to grow and deal with life versus dying.

At age four, we needed more help to persevere, so we also made 19 girls, all age four: Zoe, Froggie, sometimes called Frogger, Is-Is, Half-Pint, Butterfly, Sexy, Cindy, Pennie, Meana, Tiffany, Bunnie, Prissy, Safe, M, Ugly, Christina, Punky Lil, and Jane and Isabelle, previously introduced. We also made a 4-year-old boy, Cole, and two 4-year-old non-gendered alters named Stuffy and Fluffy. Then we made Carrie, a 4-year-old girl who grew to adulthood, and Angel, a girl who began at age 4 and grew to ages 8, 10, and 15. Finally, we made Meme, age four; Lilly, who started at 6 months and grew to an 8-year-old girl; Overseer, a teenage boy; Hope, a 14-year-old girl; and Cathleen, a young adult female.

Zoe, made while living with Grandma, was the Gatekeeper of the Vision, internal peace created by cooperation and no more hating, jealousy, or fighting. Zoe helped bear our pain from The Mother's defilement and often grimaced but didn't cry.

After The Mother forced Zoe to return to our home from Grandma's house, Zoe decided to run away and go back to her beloved Grandma, who had just shown Zoe how to put pee on her freckles to get rid of them. The Mother helped Zoe pack her lunch box and told her that she was glad to get rid of her and that no one wanted her because she was trouble, dumb, ugly, used, and had nothing to offer. Zoe knew everything The Mother said was correct and only got as far as the sidewalk before coming back and sitting on the porch for hours before The Mother came out and asked if she was still there.

No one ever treated Zoe nicely. Everything in her life was terrible, she didn't know what it was like to be loved or even wanted, and she cried alone in the dark so nobody could see her.

The Mother forced Zoe into a parental role, whereby Zoe had to take care of her younger siblings, including changing their diapers, while The Mother went to bars. Zoe also had to climb onto a stool to cook The Mother's steak and got a whipping if she made a mistake. My siblings now included my 1-year-old half-brother, Henry, Buster, Rebecca, and half-brother, Ronald. Zoe over-warmed Henry's bottle once, and The Mother poured the hot milk on her to teach her a lesson.

It wasn't safe to show anger toward The Mother, so Zoe walled it off. If Zoe cried, The Mother made fun of her and whipped her, so Zoe learned not to have emotions leading to tears.

As punishment for talking back, The Mother often kicked Zoe out of the house. Zoe would wander around the neighborhood but return home just before dark, after which The Mother would force her to spend the night in the dog cage for additional punishment.

When The Mother went out, she hid our toys and the radio, and brought strange men home. My brother, Buster, always managed to find some toys and the radio, and my siblings and I took turns watching out for The Mother.

An Animal Cluster emerged about that time, including Pony, "Dragon, Dear," Butterfly, and Froggie, drawn as follows by Iris, with a butterfly on his nose.

Is-Is, who helped us suffer our severe childhood pain, resided in "lost land" and came from the expression, "it is what it is, so just muddle through it." Someone assisted Is-Is in explaining Froggie, made by Half-Pint, as follows: Froggie had terrible memories and was often choked up with emotions, like when you get upset and feel a lump in your throat. He croaked like a frog because he couldn't talk. Froggie helped the Little Ones hop from one to another. Older alters went through doors, but the Little Ones hopped.

Froggie was made by Half-Pint, a 4-year-old girl, alter number 108, who often grimaced because she helped carry the pain of knowing nasty things The Mother did to us. Grandma gave us the name Half-Pint because that's what she called little kids.

Butterfly, drawn as follows by Iris, carried the hope we'd someday be loved. She had all this ugliness within like a homely worm but slept and awakened as a butterfly. She figured she could change into a beautiful butterfly if she couldn't get love as an ugly worm.

Butterfly

Sexy, a little whore who looked down and away versus meeting another's gaze, imitated The Mother so that The Mother would love us. She was from the Sex Cluster, which helped carry the shame from our molestations and rapes, and included Cheri, Dirty, Peaches-and-Cream, Rachel, Sherry, Liar, Not So, and others. Liar and Not So were each half-boy and half-girl.

Cindy helped absorb the unbearable shame from what she called yucky touching by The Mother's boyfriends. She avoided eye contact and sometimes even hid her face with her hands.

I was four when authorities returned me to Grandma due to The Mother's drinking alcohol and neglect. I loved stuffies. Iris's following drawing of a teddy and bunny reading a bedtime story reminds me of what life was like with Grandma: "Once upon a time, there were two best friends" is printed on one page. On the opposite page is a house with a smoking chimney.

The Mother and Her Boyfriends Touched Pennie in Yucky Ways.

The Mother didn't love us, and the pain that caused continually overwhelmed us, despite our Grandma's immeasurable nurturing. Pennie helped endure that pain. Pennie also bore the hurt of being an accident and the agony and fear of frequently lying between The Mother and one of The Mother's boyfriends. She said they touched her in yucky ways. Pennie often lifted her brow, darted her eyes, and sometimes froze or rocked from side to side. She tended to withdraw and block emotions and rarely did or said anything due to the fear of feeling stupid and the unbearable shame it brought. She usually avoided arguments and confrontations but sometimes hurt others. My portrait of Pennie follows:

PENNIE 4

When her uncle gave Pennie a dime, she cried because she wanted a penny.

Sometimes, Grandma got upset with her, but not like The Mother did. Pennie cried when she upset Grandma and crumbled when The Mother stopped letting her visit her Grandma.

Grandma would put a vomit bucket at her front door because Pennie lost her breakfast when The Mother picked her up for visits. Pennie wanted to play with the rattlesnake, but Grandma told her to stay away because it'd kill her, whereas she thought if she was kind to it, it'd be sweet to her.

Pennie's tummy and ears hurt when many of us talked at once. When The Mother got mad at Pennie's dad and ran into him with her car, Pennie said to her dad in her small, frail voice: *No cry. I love you. No cry. So many tears. We no cry. We big. We love you.*

Pennie had feelings and knew that The Mother didn't love her. The Mother went to bars and picked up men and did naughty things. She was supposed to be a mother.

Pennie's tiny body fidgeted as she crossed her arms and held her breath while lying between The Mother and The Mother's boyfriend. When they touched her, she floated to the ceiling. Afterward, as she showered with The Mother, The Mother would ask in a syrupy tone, "You love me and want to make me happy, don't you?" The Mother would then scrub Pennie's privates while Pennie floated upward and suspended.

Pennie wished she were dead, and Dee would try to kill her if Pennie was in too much pain, but when Dee intended to kill any of us, we switched to little happy alters who didn't want to die.

We especially loved spending time with Grandma, who crossed our country in a covered wagon. Grandma baked her flour and then separated it from boll weevils. We giggled, watching our minuscule Grandma slap her cows in the butt with her broom to get them into their stalls. Grandma made us a doll from Grandpa's T-shirt, straw and cotton, and a wagon from a coffee can. She taught us canning and to dry fruit, allowed us to swim in a shallow canal on her farm, and let us play on a rope swing. Grandpa was a quiet, kind man but asserted himself at times.

Meana, a mean girl, expressed our anger over The Mother beating us. Meana used to yell and hit back, but that only got her more trouble.

Tiffany helped us endure fear and the belief that we were evil and kept people away from us. She either trembled with wide eyes or sneered with squinting eyes.

Because some of us wanted to remember The Mother's harsh treatment but not judge her, believing it wasn't our place to do so, we created Bunnie. Bunnie feared people would hurt her and was scared to talk because people would think she was silly. She could hop and be good. She sometimes trembled and rocked from side to side. Her portrait by Iris follows:

At four, we bawled to get The Mother to stop beating us. Sometimes we were stubborn and didn't move when she hurt us. After we quit feeling physical pain, The Mother wore herself out when whipping us because we wouldn't react. Sometimes we still felt the military belt cut our skin, but most times felt nothing. We made baby robots to sew us up when we were hurt badly. Peter and "Dragon, dear" also helped.

Prissy helped suffer the painful recollections of The Mother's ugly deeds.

Safe, who frequently trembled, helped bear our fear of everything.

Jane sometimes trembled due to the terror she helped carry from The Mother and men having sex with us. She believed she was a bad girl even though she told The Mother's boyfriend and The Mother no. They got angry when Jane said no and continued to do as they pleased.

Just as Pennie did, M withdrew, blocked emotions, and rarely did or said anything for fear of feeling stupid and the unbearable shame that brought.

Ugly helped us endure the pain and horror of the evil and craziness heaped upon us.

The Mother believed Punky Lil didn't know how to play because she was retarded. Thus, The Mother didn't allow her to go outdoors and play with other children unless The Mother entertained a boyfriend and couldn't leave Punky Lil at church for three to four hours. I made Christina so Punky Lil could have a playmate.

Punky Lil was Grandma's Girl

We created Punky Lil, Grandma's Girl, to help leave The Mother's ugliness behind and reconcile what The Mother said versus what Grandma said. Punky Lil was a farmer from the Baby and Helper Clusters who'd do anything for you. She and Grandma enjoyed many fun activities together, and Punky Lil otherwise received abundant nurturing from Grandma. Punky Lil was typically seen smiling, giggling, displaying her crinkled nose, swinging her arms, and spinning loosely. When Punky Lil wore "fancy" clothes and strutted around Grandma's house like "big stuff," Grandma called her Hottie Tottie. Iris drew Punky Lil's portrait as follows, gussied up to go to town with Grandma:

Punky Lil called Grandma, G-ma, and Grandpa, G-pa. One day Punky Lil said a bad word, and Grandma washed her mouth out with soap. Punky Lil made bubbles with the soap. She had fun, but it didn't taste good. Grandma said, "I don't know what to do with you, you little fart. Eating soap isn't supposed to be fun." Punky Lil cried, and Grandma said, "Oh hell, ladies say bad words sometimes."

Grandma was kind and let Punky Lil be a kid. Together, they laughed, danced, hugged, and hopped. Grandma would do Punky Lil's hair, and they'd get "dolled up" by putting on boots and painting their lips and cheeks before going to town or picking up Grandpa from work.

Grandma allowed tree climbing, but The Mother didn't. Grandma got Punky Lil a rocking chair, but The Mother burned it. Andy came out and told Punky Lil to let it go.

At Grandma's, Punky Lil gardened, camped, fished, ran through sprinklers, colored with crayons, sewed, and fed chickens and cattle, including Betsy, the cow, and her calf. She also churned butter, baked, and made fudge with Grandma. Grandma would set her on the counter to get ingredients from the shelves.

Punky Lil decided she wanted to have a farm with animals when she grew up because animals love you and let you pet them. Punky Lil got to hold and pet the chicks and hug Betsy and her calf, and they loved her. Grandma told her she'd make a good mother. The farm felt warm and fuzzy to Punky Lil.

Grandma took Punky Lil to ride the merry-go-round at the county fair, where Grandpa went to get cattle. Punky Lil hated vegetables but thought ice cream and cake were good for you. She took baths in Grandma's sink and liked the robust pleasant smell of Grandma's coffee in the morning. Grandma had a big fireplace and large kettle with witch's brew, her secret weapon, and had an eye in the back of her head. Punky Lil's feelings were hurt when Grandma scolded her, but Grandma would give her a soda, which always made Punky Lil feel better.

Grandma played music on her accordion and a harp-like instrument. Grandma had an old washing machine, and one of us got his hand caught in the ringer but didn't cry because he was used to getting whipped by The Mother for crying.

Punky Lil had a beautiful life with Grandma and Grandpa. She got to swim in ponds on their picnics. They even visited a winery and Hearst Castle, where the statues were nasty because they had no clothing. My drawing of "Special Times" follows:

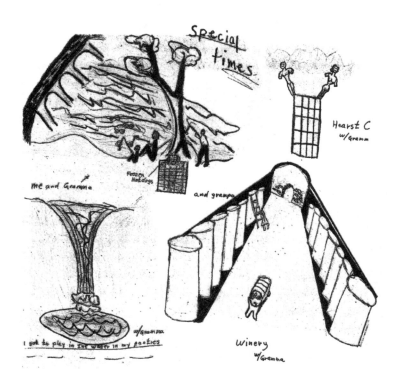

Grandpa was a kind man, but Punky Lil said she felt yucky when he scolded her. Punky Lil once played London Bridges under Betsy, the cow, while Grandpa was milking it, and he sent her to the house, saying cows are sensitive and dangerous when being milked. Grandpa sometimes thumped Punky Lil if she was noisy, waking him from his nap. She so much wanted Grandpa to be kind and loving always.

Grandma was also capable of being ornery. She told about dragging The Mother from the backseat of cars when she found her there with boys. Typically, though, Grandma had a lovely way about her. She suggested constructive activities for Punky Lil and her siblings if they were in her way. She was kind to Punky Lil's siblings, but Punky Lil was special because Grandma frequently chose her for work or play.

Grandma made Punky Lil a little medicine bag representing Native American philosophy, which involves caring for mother earth. Grandma taught her that enlightenment is the awareness that we're all one and the most diminutive creature has as much value as the biggest, brightest, or most productive.

From Grandma, Punky Lil learned to love and that she could be whatever she wanted. My drawing of Grandma's farm, as follows, includes a rocking chair called "My Rocker Little," Punky Lil wearing Grandpa's shirt, toys under her bed, and our sister's bedroom.

There are also barns and a corral, chickens, a garden with flowers, Grandma and Punky Lil washing clothes, and a canopy over Grandma, Grandpa, and Punky Lil camping. Not shown is Grandpa's horse in a pasture with a stream.

It was a sad day when Punky Lil had to return to The Mother for good. Grandma wrote this parting message to Punky Lil on my drawing: "Always remember the good times and the bad times not so bad. I love you, my Punky Lil. I wish you could stay forever. You remember, always remember the good, honey."

Cole took some of our whippings because boys are tough. He also got his privates scrubbed and cried because it stung.

Stuffy and Fluffy were made while living with Grandma by Half-Pint not to have emotions because emotions hurt and not to talk, so we didn't have to lie. That way, we could get love but not punishment. Fluffy got his name from a bunny rabbit we saw on Grandma's farm. We named him Fluffy for two reasons. Bunnies are fluffy, which provides padding for protection from harm, and if you have a cute name, you're a kind person.

The Mother would growl at Carrie: "Life isn't about playing. It's about doing a damn job and doing it right." The Mother once persuaded Carrie to demonstrate her stupidity to The Mother's boyfriend by putting her hand on a hot stove.

Singing helped us take our minds off our horrible life. Angel (Gloria or Lulu) began at age 4 and grew to 8, 10, and 15. When an alter went away, they sometimes got healed or stronger emotionally and returned, as Angel did. She was an African American female gospel singer created when we attended an African American church because we liked singing. When they shook, rolled on the floor, and said, "The devil got me," we stopped going because we didn't want the devil to get us. Iris's portrait of Angel follows:

Angel spoke well but would like to have read better. She loved routine and schedules, laughed uncontrollably because The Mother didn't allow laughter, and sometimes disappeared. She panicked and wanted discipline if matters got out of control. When we were Angel and looked in the mirror, we saw Angel.

Meme, Thumbelina, was an intelligent non-gender fairy with tiny wings that slept in a walnut shell but became a teeny girl alter, age four, born of Is-Is, who helped endure the distress of what The Mother did to us. Meme's frequent huddling in a corner and rocking was barely noticeable. She was also from the Strange Ones, alters ages 8 to 12 primarily, unnamed except for Meme and Teach, a mid-teen girl, created when we heard voices while in the "crazy farm." They thought people on the radio could talk to them.

Lilly was trusting, caring, outgoing, and sane before she suffered grave wreckage, after which she often sat in a corner and banged her head against a wall.

Overseer, the spirit of and a Gatekeeper of the Sleeper, claimed he could put the good in our life in Meme's tiny hands. Gatekeepers of the Sleepers included Maria, Wise Ones, and others, who held the key to the Sleepers, unnamed sleeping boys and girls under age 10, who enabled us to lock away our painful experiences, to forget them.

Hope, a 14-year-old girl, helped us imagine a better life.

We created Cathleen, a young adult female, to save the alter babies. She remembered men asking her to help them do something, which scared her badly. Cathleen often displayed wide eyes and a lifted brow.

The Mother never allowed us to lock doors or be in a room with closed doors. One time The Mother overheard the 12 Selves talking, dragged me out of my bedroom by my hair, and told me I could never be left alone again. She liked pulling my hair and banging my head against a wall. My work, titled "WHO'S ME," follows, depicting the confusion my dissociation brought at that time:

We needed help believing life wasn't as bad as it seemed and would get better at age five, so we made Annie, a 5-year-old-girl Helper and Unreal One, from the Hope/Heart and We-Three Clusters. She was known as Daddy's Girl, was Tiffany's mommy, and lived inside Lilly. Annie helped us determine what was happening and held the key to unlocking silence to tell our story someday. Annie was a feral alter who wore rose-colored glasses, believing in children, hope, angels, spirits, doing good, forgiveness, keeping safe, wisdom, dreams, and unconditional love. Annie thought you were a kind person if you had a sweet-sounding name. She helped carry the hurt and terror of our childhood wounding, including the humiliating sex with The Mother and men. I drew her portrait as follows, depicting her wide eyes staring into space.

ANNIE 5

Unreal Ones were Annie, Skeeter, and others. They lived in their private world and provided hope by wearing rose-colored glasses. They believed in forgiveness, everyone was good at heart and trustworthy, and life wasn't as bad as it seemed and would get better. They were part of the Crazy Ones: Ugly, Toughie, and Nettie.

Crazy Ones suffered the pain and horror of the evil and craziness heaped upon us. They were feral alters, those living in a world of their own and wanting others to understand their world.

We also made two 8-year-old girls, Beth and Tina, a 6-year-old girl, Susan, and 13 additional 5-year-old girls: Daisy, Suze, Amy, Abigail, Five, Pink, a toddler who grew to age five, Bonnie, Oneida, Quinn, Misty, Bubble, Liar, and Runner, a 5-year-old girl who grew to age seven. Lastly, we made Ham, a 9-year-old boy, Not So, a 5-year-old half-girl and half-boy, the Undead, and the Wronged.

Beth was an especially injured, angry combination of Mary, Dee, and others, who agreed to pass as one. She was traumatized by a transgression by one of The Mother's boyfriends, carried tremendous fear and shame, and traded sex for a hug, smile, love, and to know the monster's whereabouts. Beth sometimes froze or rocked from side to side and often looked down and away.

Tina was a crybaby, filled with hatred from absorbing The Mother's name-calling and beatings. She often displayed a fake smile or lips extended to their physical max to one side of her face and made no eye contact. She was so afraid to talk that she took a long time to learn.

The Mother once told Tina to wipe the killer look off her face, confusing her. She remembered looking in the mirror to see what The Mother saw. Anger, love, and hate all appeared the same to Tina. She sometimes had no facial expression, which was called a dumb look. The Mother made derogatory statements about how Tina appeared, talked, sat, and moved. Tina tried to control herself to halt The Mother's name-calling and beatings, but she learned to feel helpless because the punishment was unpredictable. Tina believed a mother should go outdoors and cool off versus getting angry and whipping children.

Susan helped absorb the pain from The Mother pulling us out of the bathtub by our hair and brushing us with hot water and Clorox or lye if she thought we were touching ourselves.

Daisy, made because we liked flowers, doesn't remember the bad.

Suze began at age five but became Suzie Q. at age 11. She bore the horror of The Mother putting us in a dark attic for punishment at age five. Suze sometimes held herself and rocked from side to side.

Amy helped us endure our fear of The Mother. The Mother breathed heavily when she gave Amy long kisses, which Amy didn't like. Charles would come and take the kisses away. Amy sometimes huddled in a corner, rocking from side to side. She didn't want to feel love if this was love.

Abigail, who helped carry our evil thoughts, often bared her teeth and snarled at people. She wanted vile thinking gone because she didn't wish to think unkindly about others. She belonged to the I's Cluster with Peanut Butter, Sarah, and the Gatekeepers of the Heart: Abigail, Margie, Oneida, Sard, and other Spirits, created to love and remove pain from other people. The I's Cluster helped us read, write, and deal with people.

Five thought lots of people kicked us around, so we all should've been called Ball. She knew that kids lie to avoid whippings and that it wasn't right if someone else got your punishment. Five helped take on the agony of Ham seeing The Monster and breaking.

Tina knew about The Monster but couldn't tell because The Mother didn't want to hear it. That one was horrific, and it scared us badly to even think of him. We met him one of the times The Mother placed us with relatives. The Mother knew about him but claimed he wasn't real, saying we had a vivid imagination. The Monster's portrait by Iris follows:

Monster

old

Pink frequently appeared with wide eyes while trembling because when she was tiny and had just begun to walk, she helped us endure the terror of our encounter with The Monster.

Bonnie dealt with our pain by not having physical sensations. I named her after the song "My Bonnie Lies Over the Ocean." My lyrics were "Bring Back My Body to Me."

Oneida was a Helper and Gatekeeper of the Heart.

Quinn, who'd perhaps get angry but not furious, helped relieve our pain by forgetting the bad stuff.

Misty helped hold our pain from what The Mother did to us and helped soothe the four alter babies when they cried.

Bubble, who was almost always smiling, giggling, and displaying her crinkled nose, helped us be real kids.

Liar, who fabricated, helped bear the pain and horror of being continually molested and raped.

Runner loved running and ran so fast from age five to seven that she broke track records. She sprinted from school as quickly as possible because The Mother gave her 10 minutes to get home, but she didn't know how much 10 minutes was. Our running saved our lives.

The Mother would start in on Runner, barking, "Where've you been? Don't lie, you liar. Were you with some damn boy? Is that why you're out of breath?" Runner said: No. I just *run fast.* The Mother hit Runner, asked if the boy was a bastard, and then hit her again and said, "If I see you running again, it'll be the death of you. Go to your room. I'm telling your father about how you want to kill me."

Runner shouldn't have told The Mother she liked running. She never ran after that and blamed herself for not getting to run again. She lost her only freedom and now had nothing. Undoubtedly, she broke after that and thought it was her fault for crumbling because she was selfish. She decided to never rely on anything or anybody, fearing she'd fall to pieces further if she did.

Runner ran all day at Grandma's house, including outdoors, to the bathroom and the table. Grandma said ladies don't run indoors but can run outdoors all they want. Runner was little when she discovered running. The Mother took it away, just like she took Grandma away.

Ham was so named because we liked ham. After seeing The Monster, he frequently grimaced, usually hunched his shoulders, and tended to shrink back from others.

Not So helped us absorb the pain and horror from our unwanted sexual encounters. She was stubborn and held notions we either believed or disbelieved.

The Undead were unrighteous emotions and memories of what happened, such as the memory of The Monster.

The Wronged were Ruth and unnamed others. They helped endure anger from severe torment, which they expressed by being nasty.

Age six was exceedingly dreadful, so we made Joe and Sissie, 6-year-old boys; Terry, a teenage boy; and Deand, who was three 6-year-old fragments, one girl and two boys. We also created 19 additional 6-year-old girls: Genie, Samantha, Rachel, Bree, Tami, Cara, Adora, Katty, Kay, Abby, Six, Stay, Tinker, Gabby, Nina, Bee, De-de, Ann, and Penelope.

Joe helped suffer the pain and horror of The Mother's abusiveness. He became aware he and Little told a similar brutality history and blended into Little Joe, a 6-year-old boy/girl.

Sissie liked dolls. With the assistance of De-de, Sissie, and others, I drew, as follows, a depiction of our horrible life at about that time. Above a broken heart, a barely detectable 5-year-old Annie lies on a bed beneath a much larger body. She printed I cry. Sissie printed they so big. Carrie misspelled Carry, at age four, looking in a mirror, printed: I be good they love me. Take me home. Someone printed I like playing. De-de printed I mad. Suze, at age five, printed: I scare. It dark. Hope, a 14-year-old girl, made when I was four, wrote and printed Maybe in time.

Deand, three fragments, could bear the memory of all 15 minutes of the feelings of a 15-minute whipping.

I named Genie after Genie's magic lamp, which gives three wishes. She had magical powers to make our pain disappear and push other alters to the background if they recalled too much bad.

Samantha managed our claustrophobia and helped take on the shame of being sexually exploited many times. She thought she was a whore because she'd had sex with a teacher, a preacher, The Mother's boyfriends, and other men. Samantha tended to look down and away and sometimes buried her face in her hands.

Rachel, a bull-headed girl soldier, carried the pain and humiliation from The Mother forcing us to lie in the yard nude, facing the street with legs apart, holding a sign reading, "only 20 cents a pop." She also absorbed the fear and shame of being raped repeatedly by one of The Mother's boyfriends. Rachel said she didn't like how his big pee-pee felt in her, repeatedly told him she was sorry for not enjoying it, and was mad at herself for not being fond of it. She often slumped her shoulders and grimaced with wide eyes and a lifted brow. I drew her portrait as follows:

We created a teenage boy, Terry, to tell our teacher about these ugly encounters. The teacher thought Terry was telling naughty stories but still reported them. Authorities questioned our siblings about it, which made their lives hell. Understand? We did that to them. The Mother yelling at the principal didn't help.

Bree, drawn as follows, helped take on the shame of these rapes. She usually slumped her shoulders and often looked down and away.

When we first revealed these violations, The Mother didn't believe us but later cut this boyfriend with a knife because she wanted him for herself. We were horrified upon seeing The Mother's wrath and the boyfriend's bloody face. The Mother contacted a priest, hoping he'd threaten the boyfriend with hellfire and damnation. The church counselor spent much of her intervention helping The Mother resolve her bitterness toward her boyfriend and us.

We learned from a book how to leave the body while being violated so we could return without remembering it. It got so easy that it became difficult to remain in the body, which scared us, so we envisioned tying a rope to ourselves to come back. We couldn't always get everybody out, so we had to put those in the "forget room" to block the memory and pain. This skill also improved with time.

The Mother called Tami "The Little Bitch." She absorbed our humiliation and heartache from The Mother smacking us and forbidding us to be an angel with paper wings in our first-grade play. The Mother thought Tami would embarrass the family. Tami frequently sobbed and looked down and away.

Cara, who generally displayed wide eyes and a lifted brow, helped bear the horror of The Mother putting us in our deep freeze. Cara turned purple, saw angels, and hoped to go to heaven. She said it felt like breathing ice and her lungs hurt so badly she wanted to die. When my brother, Buster, opened the deep freeze, The Mother threatened to put him in. Cara knew The Mother could do so because once, fearing Cara's brothers could become pedophiles, The Mother tried to drive them off the road to kill them.

Adora, who sometimes clenched her jaws and shook her fist but usually appeared docile, hated herself because she wanted to love The Mother, who saw evil in others, cared only for herself, and couldn't love. In contrast, Adora saw the good in others, cared only for them, and could love them. She helped us survive by dealing with rage because she could be emotionless, but her coldness could get us locked up. Adora carried massive anger over The Mother's brutality and didn't give a crap. She hated, and wanted to hurt The Mother for harming others.

Katty carried the horror of The Mother throwing a pot of hot water on me because I allowed it to get too hot when warming a bottle of milk for my half-brother, Henry. The Mother poured the hot milk on Zoe.

Kay, who hurt herself when she became angry, assisted in taking care of others by helping us take on the excruciating pain, hate, and horror from The Mother's neglect and abuse. She often grimaced and shook her fist, and the chords of her neck stood out, but she sometimes rocked from side to side while clutching her stuffie.

The Mother told me she'd beat me to death if a single strand of the baby's hair was out of place. When the baby cried, The Mother would bark, "What did you do to it, you little bitch?" She'd then beat me. When I changed my sibling's diapers, The Mother would snarl, "Why are you taking so long, you nasty little bitch," then drag me by my hair into the kitchen and pummel me. I became overwhelmed with life because I believed The Mother might kill me.

Abby, who sometimes trembled or rocked from side to side and made animal cries, suffered the horror of The Mother abusing and killing our pets.

Six, whose name is her age, wanted to be intelligent, have friends, fit in, and convince The Mother she could be like other kids instead of taking care of the baby, cleaning the house, cooking, and selling her body. Six knew what had happened in the dark.

Stay helped bear the pain and horror of our many waves of sexual abuse. She got so proficient at leaving her body and coming back without remembering the violations she had difficulty staying in her body, which scared her.

We created Tinker to help carry evil and selfishness because we didn't want either.

We made Gabby, who was confused by life and talkative because we liked to talk.

Nina helped us know what we were, why we exist, and how many we were.

Bee helped absorb our anger and struck back with hits that stung like a bee.

De-de was a second-grade girl fragment helping to bear our anger.

Ann helped us endure our pain, hate, and horror from The Mother's abuse and hurt herself when angry. She either grimaced and shook her fist with the chords of her neck standing out or rocked from side to side while clutching her stuffie. She believed the right way was to obey and love adults, but she was never this way.

Penelope, who liked to paint and helped manage pain by disappearing, often grimaced and her lower lip sometimes quivered.

At age seven, I created the first 7-year-old girl alter, Angie, who helped block out the harsh reality at home by daydreaming of being like other kids and having kind parents. Angie learned at school what a typical kid was supposed to be and discovered she wasn't. Angie tried to be like other kids so The Mother would want her. When Angie got excellent grades, The Mother claimed Angie wasn't smart enough to get good grades and accused her of cheating. One day Angie told The Mother her teacher told her she could be anything because she had a good head on her shoulders. The Mother responded by cutting Angie's tongue and snarling she'd cut it out if Angie didn't quit lying. Part of us went away and died that day.

The Mother came to Angie's school and told the teacher what a stupid, terrible girl Angie was. After that, Angie's teacher ceased making kind remarks to Angie. Angie's classmates began calling her a "mental retard" and making fun of her, and then The Mother whipped Angie for hitting them.

One day Angie had stomach flu and accidentally pooped her pants, and The Mother forced her to go to school with poopy pants so everyone could see how nasty she was. The teacher asked her to clean up, but Angie told the teacher that The Mother would be angry if she did. The teacher called The Mother to clarify and then told Angie that Angie had misunderstood. When Angie got home, The Mother beat her and forced her to lick her poopy pants for telling the truth. Angie began carrying tremendous shame, wishing she were dead and hating herself and The Mother.

Teachers insisted Angie play with the other kids, but Angie explained she didn't know how to, and if she tried, she'd get a whipping. The kids snickered at her and called her stupid when she couldn't play correctly. The teachers lost patience with Angie, labeled her a bad kid, sent her to the corner, pulled her ears, made her put her head on her desk, smacked her with a ruler for writing with the wrong hand, and sent her to the principal's office to get paddled. The school became a horrible place, just like home. Angie began sitting alone and burying her head in her hands.

The Mother couldn't stand anyone else being correct about anything. Angie tried to be friendly and understanding with The Mother and let her know she loved her, but nothing she tried ended The Mother's wrath.

The Mother frequently slapped Angie, put ice in Angie's pants, told her to think about how she was wrong, and put in more ice each time Angie gave an incorrect answer.

Angie began banging her head against walls, and several adults were required to restrain her. The first time The Mother saw Angie bang her head, she helped Angie do it and growled, "If you're going to do that, I'll show you how."

Angie's school brought Angie to the attention of County Mental Health when she began suffering severe anxiety attacks. Mental health professionals found that her anxiety attacks were precipitated by visions of rape and took the form of psychotic-like seizures, followed by headaches, blindness, blackouts, and hyperventilating. Angie stayed in a facility for a few days, after which the doctor released her to The Mother.

I wanted to escape the horror at home. No, no, I changed my mind! I didn't wish for it! That would be mad! No one deserves the excruciating pain hope could bring. Still, I would've liked just a taste of it to entirely grasp how abusive The Mother and her boyfriends were. They deserved the misery they brought to their relationships for the hurt they caused me in childhood.

I thought of chopping The Mother into pieces but figured she'd just come back. I also wished and prayed, God, please put The Mother on a pretty island, so she can't hurt me anymore. I drew The Mother alone on a tiny island, not shown, captioned: "God doesn't love me either. God protects the good but thinks I'm bad. I must be. I'll change and be good, so The Mother and God will love me." I signed this drawing, your child, Dorothy, 1938.

I Survived the Freezer, Oven, Electric Cord, Baseball Bat, and Razor Belt.

My drawing titled "Life with The Mother," not shown, depicted The Mother's waves of torture. I captioned an eye seen through the peephole of a little locked closet door, "My hell," a freezer, "Freezer she put me in," and an oven, "She put me in the oven and also poured boiling water on me." I captioned a vehicle hitting me, "She attempted to run over me," and a military belt containing razor blades, "Razor in a belt." I sketched without captions: a wire coat hanger, baseball bat, tree limb, and electric cord.

I trembled from within the oven as I heard The Mother tap on it and ask if I could make out what she said. Then she snarled, "I can try cooking the water out by cooking you on high, but I have to be careful you don't go up in flames." I screamed as The Mother turned the oven on and froze when I saw an angel and real-appearing people in the range, saying, "We know how both The Mother and you can have what you want." I asked one who looked like me if I was cooked and if she could stay so I could go. Then in a flash, I was on the kitchen floor, and The Mother was yelling at me.

My heart could be in my throat, but my body no longer reacted to pain. I once told The Mother that she didn't love me but only kept me to hurt me. The Mother shouted, "That's the most hateful thing a child can say." She tried to persuade the church that I needed an exorcism. I wanted to kill myself and go to heaven but didn't because the alters needed what only I could do and understand.

In my drawing, titled "Have to Hid," not shown, I captioned drops of blood, "Blood," a shaded area, "Dark," and an adult female's detached head, "Mother dead." I wrote," things I did to live" near the words "feelings and fears."

Dummy-Two printed "bad thing" backward on this drawing. He was a 7-year-old boy I created at age seven. He was afraid and didn't want to be hurt, couldn't remember, and didn't talk but could be trusted. He helped bear the pain of The Mother putting us in a "dummy school." He was never sure exactly what happened to him but knew that The Mother, an aunt and uncle, family friends, The Mother's boyfriends, and other people harmed him horribly. He often grimaced or trembled and sometimes whimpered.

No matter how good I tried to be, things kept going badly with The Mother. I hated whippings and would sit and cry alone afterward. I disconnected the emotional from the physical to stay sane because The Mother claimed the beatings were love, invalidating my reality because they didn't feel like love.

To help with my continuing agony, at age seven, I created 10 additional 7-year-old boys: Bobby, Glenn, Sam, James, Charles III, Jay, Lefty, Forgotten-One, Frank, and eB. I also made 10 other 7-year-old girls: Olive, eM, Hurter, Jan-the-Jelly-Jam, Pollyanna, Apple, Banger, Eater, yM, and Clara.

We fashioned Bobby to display appropriate behavior so people wouldn't be scared of us. He wanted to be happy and a real kid, so people wouldn't glare at him or be afraid of him. He frequently dragged his feet with his bottom lip jutting out.

Glenn bore the pain of The Mother stabbing me in my hand with a fork for reaching across the dinner table.

Sam, a second-grader who often grimaced, wasn't allowed to be a kid, wanted to give up, and didn't know how to tell how things hurt him. The Mother forced him to climb down an outdoor toilet hole to retrieve a toy he dropped, told him he was careless and unappreciative, and warned him to watch out for the snakes and spiders.

James, made by Beth and Iris, began at age seven and grew into a 13-year-old boy. He carried moderate anger over ruthlessness from The Mother and others and wanted to get back at them. James never cried. He was tough, so he didn't get hurt as girls did.

James perceived hell as a dark place and always talked about death. He was markedly injured, spread his evil all around, and traded sex for a hug, smile, love, and to know the monster's whereabouts. James sometimes grimaced, clenched his fists, and jutted his chin. He wanted the stuff about The Mother not to be real so he could be a good kid. My portrait of a 13-year-old James follows, trailed by my sketch of a younger James. The red color represents blood, and the yellow and red represent fire.

JAMES₁

The Mother hit and burned Jay, and his belly came up from the pain. The Mother told him to shut up, or she'd give him something to cry about, and that if he wasn't stupid, he wouldn't be here crying and hurt. Jay decided not to let anyone injure him again. He decided he didn't love or need anyone anymore and no longer cried, claiming nothing was worth sorrow or tears.

I conceived Charles III, whose portrait follows, to have manners so The Mother wouldn't hurt us.

51

I made Lefty because I threw balls with my left hand. He liked cars.

Forgotten-One, who shook frequently, always asked first to avoid The Mother's wrath because that was The Mother's number one rule and went for everything.

Frank had a big head that held a lot, and he told it like it was because we needed honesty in our lives. He thought The Mother was good at whipping and insisted that no matter what we did, she tore out our hair and threw us against walls to make us cry, and she never said we were good.

eB (dyslexia Be), who frequently grimaced, helped absorb the pain of being mistreated at school.

Olive walked backward because she didn't want to be like others.

eM (dyslexia Me) carried shyness and held her head down or otherwise averted her eyes from the gaze of others.

Hurter helped me suffer the shame from The Mother's scoldings and from having sex with one of The Mother's boyfriends. She slumped her shoulders, looked down and away, and sometimes buried her face in her hands.

Hurter pondered: What's wrong with games, wishing, sitting on the floor, lying down, looking at a face, wanting more, washing me, or staying in my room? What's wrong with me? I can't do right. What do I do wrong? What's a bitch? It bad, I know. What's a whore? It bad, I know.

The Mother would snarl at Hurter, "Don't ask questions because others will know how stupid you are, and I don't give a crap about your needs. Don't appear or act dumb, and try to think. This child is killing me." Hurter wondered: How do I kill her? I don't want to. The Mother would ask, "Can't you act normal for once?" Hurter wondered, what's normal?

My three least favorite words were normal, love, and special. Darling, baby, and "mental retard" were also dreadful. I hated being stupid. If I'd been smart, I wouldn't have misbehaved and gotten hurt, and The Mother would've loved me like a parent is supposed to.

I couldn't have friends because it made The Mother angry. She'd snarl at me, "I won't share you with anybody. Do you understand me? No one. You don't share your body, love, or family things. They belong to me. I'll know and leave you if you do. Do you understand? I can leave now without looking back or giving you a single thought because of your stupidity. You'll die without me, fool. Leave me before I kill you. Go! Damn you to hell. I said, go!

Hurter revealed: We played house with the girl and saw her daddy's thing. We bad. Her daddy and we played "Mommy and Daddy." Her daddy hurted us. So we want to hurt him, so we tell, but we got hurted. Her daddy no got hurted. Her mother loved him more, so we got hurted. She hate us more. So we don't want to be out. We don't want to hurt people. Then we won't get hurted either. Bad people get hurted. We're awful for wanting to hurt people back. They no got hurted. We got hurted more. Then we want to hurt them more. Go round and round.

In a drawing not shown, Iris sketched a dolphin playing with a ball, and a sailboat, captioned "Jan-the-Jelly-Jam," printed backward and forward by Dummy-Two, along with his note printed in reverse, which read: "*I like you, Dorothy. I drink to Dorothy. I go to a dummy school. I'm evil and cut, hit, and hurt us too badly.*"

Jan-the-Jelly-Jam, whose portrait by Iris follows, was non-sexual because we didn't like sex. She developed anorexia because she wanted to be invisible to men. She liked potato chips, ice cream, noodles, and fruit and could write backward.

Pollyanna was irrepressibly optimistic and found the good in everyone because it was scary when everyone was terrible. She became fed up with bashing from The Mother and projected her anger by fighting with her classmates. One time her teacher intervened, and she even hit her teacher.

Apple had the self-control to avoid the "crazy farm" and have a window to deal with the outside.

Banger counted each time she banged her head to get unpleasant thoughts out.

Eater ceased eating, so we wouldn't live.

yM (dyslexia My), who frequently grimaced, helped hold the pain of being mistreated at school.

Although she was only seven, Clara was a teacher who helped bear our physical pain and assisted with our medical care. She frequently grimaced yet often chuckled and had a great sense of humor.

Mary, Angel, and Tabatha drew a broken heart and printed names of numerous alters on the front cover of Iris's art book, not shown, titled "Our Lives." They sketched a fractured heart and a portrait of me in tears on the back cover.

Mandy, my half-sister, came along about then from The Mother and my second stepdad's union, which ended shortly after that. Then came my third stepdad, who didn't last long. Despite his stabilizing influence, household violence exploded due to The Mother's multiple affairs.

The Mother Showed Me Sex for My Benefit

As depicted by my following drawing of Punky standing in her yard crying and covering her privates, my hell continued at age eight. Punky dreamed of lying in bed in the dark next to The Mother, so scared she couldn't breathe. Her body was a big, painful cramp from head to toe, and it felt like she was shaking herself apart. She wanted to run and hide but lay there, rocking from side to side.

The Mother would say, "I'd never hurt you. You mean so much to me, baby. Some only want what they can get from you, and I don't want you hurt. Do you think I want to hurt you, you little bitch! I'm showing you this for your benefit!"

The Mother always hurt me. She never allowed my siblings and me to talk to one another if she couldn't hear us. She'd hit us if she caught us and bellow, "If you have something to say, say it here and now." She also criticized me for playing alone, saying it wasn't healthy and that games are bad and rot your brain.

I had to deal with The Mother's boyfriends as well. I froze, except for shallow, rapid breathing, each of the three times a day, one particular boyfriend came to me for his sexual pleasure. I'd assume a fetal possession and attempt to cover my face with my hands as he pummeled me with his fists until he grew tired. I didn't like being a girl. Given a choice, I wouldn't have had a gender.

Beth carried the trauma of a transgression by one of The Mother's boyfriends, who said to me, "You'll like it, you know, plus you'll show me how much you love me. Don't you want to show me how much you love me? Didn't your mother tell you to do what I say, and if you don't, she'll beat you until you can't sit for a week?"

The Mother did say that. This boyfriend continued, "Kiss my thing and open your mouth more." Afterward, he said, "Boy, you sure love me. Everybody is happy now, and if you tell your mother, she'll be mad at you, not me. You know how much she loves me. She believes me over you, and you know it. She told me all about how dirty and nasty you are. If you cry to your mother, I'll know you're not grown-up enough to go to a party or have a new puppy. I've been telling your mother how adult you are and that you need your own puppy. She told me you're too stupid to have one, you wouldn't like to have one, and you can't love it." I shouted, yes, I can!

"If you don't get her more upset with you, we'll see about a puppy because I think every kid should have one. See. I help you even when she gets mad at you because I love you, pumpkin. You're very special to me, and I wouldn't want your mother to get mad at you and hurt you worse than the last time. I don't even hurt you that bad because I love you despite your dirty, whoring ways. I do. I swear."

When I was age eight, The Mother hated me. She'd scream, "Why are you raping my boyfriend? What a terrible thing to do to me!" I couldn't produce a satisfactory answer for The Mother or myself, so I found a middle ground. I told myself The Mother did what she thought was right because of my evilness and that it was just bad luck that I had sex with so many men.

The Mother washed my mouth out with soap or forced me to drink Tabasco sauce if I spoke a dirty word or didn't do everything she wanted. If I protested, she made me drink even more sauce. I learned to decipher what she wanted, and I created a new alter if I didn't have one that could maintain control.

The Mother hurt me 24 hours a day. I was in such excruciating emotional pain that I wasn't sure I'd survive the day. I lived day by day and tried to create peaceful moments to say my life was okay.

To help me persevere, I made nine girls: Pam, Dirty, Peaches-and-Cream, Patty, Believer, Brat, Nettie, Cutter, and Dorothee, and seven boys: Hurt, Sard, Morey, Mickey, Ben, Chopper, and Breather, all age eight.

Pam, who felt sad and helpless, helped bear our hate and pain from The Mother and men abusing us and held the key to agreeing, along with Mary. She usually drooped her body while jutting her bottom lip and quivering but sometimes clenched her fists and bared her teeth.

Dirty and Peaches-and-Cream helped absorb the pain and horror from our molestations and rapes and wanted the stuff about their mother not to be real so they could be nice girls. They knew a million ways to have sex and knew about not feeling physically or emotionally.

Patty helped endure the pain and humiliation of The Mother declaring we were slow to grasp things, burning us if we forgot a rule or didn't know it was a rule, penetrating us with a broom handle, and allowing her boyfriends to rape us. Patty slumped her shoulders and darted her eyes. She could lock Dee away.

The Mother's boyfriends regularly raped Patty and her sister. When she told The Mother, The Mother would slap her and snarl, "The boyfriends put food on the table." Thus The Mother was "doing" her boyfriends and allowing them to "do" Patty and her sister because the boyfriends bought groceries.

Believer denied our awful ongoing reality. She believed parents weren't bad, people did care about you, and you could accept what was told to you as good girls did. She believed there was no reason for doubt because what she thought or felt wasn't real or believed by anyone, including The Mother, police officers, therapists, or hospital staff. She'd tell others that Grandma even remarked that people always get what's coming to them, and she'd heard that you get what you ask for, what comes around goes around, good things happen to those who wait, and if you want something badly enough, you'll get it. So she stuck around and wanted something very badly but didn't get it. So if they were correct, she was evil, and if they lied to her, she was terrible for not believing them.

Brat was a "military brat" who lived in Germany, France, and Hawaii when my fourth and final stepdad was in the army. This stepdad married The Mother when I was eight, and one year later, my half-sister, Megan, was born from this union. Brat tried to impress a cute boy in Hawaii by leaping into 12 feet of water, not knowing how to swim. A young girl saved her.

This stepdad was somewhat of a stabilizing influence, and he remained in our family after that, but brutality from The Mother continued. My drawing as follows, captioned, "A Lot of times willow switch," shows my many bloody whip-like marks and some of The Mother's instruments used to inflict them.

Nettie was a feral alter who couldn't meet another's gaze, buried her head in her hands sometimes, isolated to make the world disappear, and wanted to kill herself.

Cutter cut us to get evil thoughts and emotions out, or because we were terrible or misbehaved, and sometimes cut too much when the bad feelings didn't come out. Regular cutting didn't help with huge issues, so she cut more or deeper.

Dorothee, an 8-year-old girl alter named after the Wizard of Oz character, helped carry our traumatization by The Mother (the evil witch) and The Mother's boyfriends (the monkeys).

Hurt was a Taker and Angry One from the Hurt Cluster who carried moderate pain over The Mother's brutality.

Sard was a Spirit and Gatekeeper of the Heart from the I's Cluster, who helped guide me through the vast darkness I endured and helped me read, write and deal with people.

Morey was a mean boy who helped carry my anger toward myself. He could have killed me and wouldn't have felt bad had I broken.

Mickey, who often displayed wide eyes and a lifted brow, helped bear our fear of The Mother and was so afraid to talk that he never learned.

Ben carried lots of emotions. He was sad, angry, afraid, and disappointed. He moved slowly, clenched his fists, bared his teeth, and displayed wet, wide eyes.

Chopper cut us to make us feel.

Breather held her breath longer and longer until she only thought of not breathing.

Lilly often described her life as follows: Life was like walking a tightrope having no end, and death could come anytime. It took but a tiny misstep or sneeze to throw you off, and there were no resting places. Imagine treading this tightrope between the age of six months and three years. When falling, the vision of The Mother's open arms was waiting to catch me. The Mother was sneering at four feet, and the baseball bat was cocked. Oh, God, The Mother moved away at three feet, Splat! As I lay there with a broken body, she snarled, "Is my baby hurt?" Oh! She does love me! I'm sorry for thinking wrong! Bonk! The pain exploded! The Mother snarled again, "Is the love of my life hurt? No? Good! You'll see it coming this time, and have no doubt I've clobbered you." The Mother brought the bat down on me with all she had. Bonk! I saw lights and thought of a cartoon character getting hit and seeing stars around his head, and it was funny, so I smiled. Bonk! The Mother sneered, "Do you think it's funny? Was that bad?"

The Mother's breaking Lilly's legs with the baseball bat was excruciatingly painful until Peter came out as "Dragon, Dear" and took the blows. Lilly had to continue to react some; otherwise, The Mother would've kept pounding her.

Lilly got beaten if she stayed on the tightrope or got off, but it was best to stay on for the most part. She couldn't think, want, have emotions, feel her breathing, or let up on tight self-control for any reason with any adults in her life.

Annie explained it as follows: Bonk! You, Bonk! Stupid Bonk! Good Bonk! For Bonk! Nothing Bonk! Bitch Bonk! I'll teach you, Bonk! I gave you birth! I put you on the tightrope! You'll never get off! Do Bonk! You Bonk! Hear Bonk! Me Bonk! It took everything I had left to answer, yes! Bonk! Bonk! Bonk! You remember that, or I'll kill you! The end. That was life.

Learning to meditate helped Lilly survive this torture. She'd sit and quiet the body and mind by letting surrounding sounds fade away. Her only thought was to fly away. She felt and heard her heartbeat until she could control the beat and her breathing slowed. She went even deeper until she saw the blood flowing in her veins and didn't feel the body anymore. Finally, all was calm, and she was free from this world.

Lilly did this so often it took less time to get to a peaceful place, and it sometimes happened without thinking. Lilly learned to control everything, including thought, physical pain, and emotions. Sometimes someone stayed behind to get the whippings, so Lilly taught herself to go halfway back until she could cut out those left in the body. Lilly even believed she could heal her body when broken or bleeding.

Goodbye to Grandma for Good

Grandma and I had fun. We had a secret language, played make-believe and dress-up, and got loud when we were happy, things The Mother never allowed. I loved Grandma and cherished our time together.

At age eight, I was devastated when The Mother stopped letting me go to Grandma's house as punishment for having sex with one of The Mother's boyfriends. She wanted him exclusively. The Mother told Grandma about the sex, which bothered me further because I didn't want Grandma to know. Hurter couldn't get the dirt off and felt so dirty she thought she'd never get clean!

Pennie sobbed when she had to return to her mommy for good, and her bottom lip quivered as her mommy pushed her into the car. Pennie told of loving life with Grandma but having to go back to bad mommy. She said she couldn't confront her mommy's abusiveness because she thought an argument would ensue and her mommy would hurt her more.

Due to continued multiple forms of abuse after returning to The Mother, authorities sent me to different relatives' homes. I don't, but my brother, Buster, remembers the whorehouses The Mother exposed us to and how long we stayed at various relatives' homes.

The Mother continued to have boyfriends when my stepdad was away. The Mother became furious because I didn't tell her sooner that I had had sex with her next boyfriend. The Mother beating me, whether I told her or she found out on her own when I had sex with one of her boyfriends, was incredibly distressing. So, I decided to hide the sex from The Mother and usually escaped her wrath.

I liked the attention but not the sex, but wanting the attention drew them back. Even though my teacher told me to, I regretted telling The Mother I had sex with one of her favorite boyfriends because I got a massive clobbering from The Mother. The school ultimately took The Mother's side, as did most authority figures who eventually received abuse reports.

It was stressful each time The Mother brought me into her drama with a boyfriend. For example, The Mother asked me to tell one boyfriend she swallowed a bottle of pills when she'd flushed them, but I disclosed the truth. The Mother exploded on the boyfriend for not rushing to her assistance and later thrashed me upon discovering what I had revealed.

I tried to please The Mother but couldn't and continually got worked over by her. The Mother had a rare moment of being amiable when she got her way, but I was usually on her shit list, and at times she was barbaric.

After countless sexual encounters, I quit participating but didn't decline. One time an uncle had sex with me. He kissed me and slid down my body, making me feel gross. When I complained to The Mother, she slapped me because the uncle brought groceries to our home.

The pain of this uncle's sex with me paled compared to one of The Mother's boyfriends, who hurt me more. The Mother repeatedly punished that boyfriend, but he said he stayed with her because he felt guilty, whereas The Mother told me she couldn't leave him because she needed his money.

I wanted the world to know I didn't need anyone. I could do for myself and didn't need anyone's love. So I gave all my devotion to my puppy. It'd jump up enthusiastically and lick my face. Ultimately, The Mother did something with it. The Mother said, "You spend too much time with that damn dog. It's not normal that you love that damn thing and not me." When I began to cry, The Mother said, "Baby, it's not fair. You have to learn to neither love nor depend on anyone or anything. I try to teach you crap. The damn dog is gone." I asked, where? I love him! Please tell me! The Mother's response was to slap me and snarl, "Shut up, or I'll give you something to cry about. The puppy would've died in your care. You wouldn't be crying and hurt now if you weren't stupid. Why did God give you to me? When is God going to stop making me pay?" Then she slapped me again. After that, I didn't love or need anything, and there was nothing worth pain or crying about. I decided never to let anyone or anything hurt me again.

A Little One believed puppies only love good people, and if someone hits the child, the puppy will bite and say, "Don't hurt her because she's not bad."

My brother, Buster, grabbed the belt once when The Mother was whipping him and told her, "No more. I'm too old to be whipped." The Mother told my stepdad, who disciplined Buster. My stepdad's discipline was always much milder than The Mother's.

The Mother beat and cut my stepdad, ran into him with her car, and got him fired by going to his workplace and cursing at him, but persuaded him to remain with her because she wanted his money. My stepdad told me later that he found hell living with The Mother because she turned on and off so fast he had to always be on guard.

He sometimes buffered me from The Mother's lambasting by helping me not upset her, and he twice stopped her from beating me by grasping the belt and saying, "That's enough," prompting The Mother to beat him until he restrained her.

One time, my stepdad punched The Mother after she abruptly turned the steering wheel to wreck intentionally. Another time, he slapped her to bring her to her senses. He threatened to leave her, and she banged her face against a headboard until her face bled. He slapped her to get her to quit smashing her face, and she kicked him and began throwing everything within reach at him. He sent my siblings and me outdoors as household objects flew about the room.

To help me survive when I turned nine, I made five 9-year-old girls: Belinda, Crystal, Tommie, Dot, and So-So, and six 9-year-old boys: Under, Adam, Art, Wizard, Timothy A. Bradshaw, and Paul. I also made Pam Peter, a 9-year-old boy in a girl's body {a "cross-gender"} and Fear, a 10-year-old girl.

Belinda, Brooklyn's sister, was a soldier who helped absorb the reoccurring sexual exploitation and brutality at home. Belinda patrolled the walls and reported any fallen pieces or cracks. She was generally alert and focused, but her shoulders sometimes slumped as she looked down and away. I presented her body in sections in a drawing not shown because she didn't like parts of herself. My portrait of her follows:

Belinda 9

Life was the same old baloney over and over, with new faces. Even my teacher wanted to have sex with me. He said I let other men do it, so why not him? I felt dirty, ugly, unclean, guilty, and hurt because I considered it.

Rage began to set in, prompting the creation of Crystal, whose portrait by Little follows. Crystal helped endure our fear of men and was once in a wall to shield her from men who might enter her bedroom. She also helped us deal with rage and bore the terror from The Mother setting us on fire by igniting our bed. Crystal usually had wide eyes and a lifted brow and sometimes trembled.

Froggie explained Crystal as follows: Crystal screamed all the time because she's been on fire since The Mother set fire to Dorothy's bed to force her from under it. When Crystal was out, it could be 60°, and we felt like we were burning up.

Crystal 9

Tommie bore our sexual confusion.

Dot helped us forget bad things, but she believed she wouldn't have had a life had she buried everything. She tended to bow her head.

So-So and Under were the Unseen, those stuck under my bed, created to help suffer the horror from The Mother igniting it while my brother, Ronald, and I were underneath.

Adam was a Dark Secret One from the Boy Cluster: Adam, Bobby, Charley, James, Paul, and Timothy A. Bradshaw, who protected the girl alters because boys were tough and didn't cry or get hurt as much as girls did.

My hell continued, prompting my drawing "Adam's Hell," as follows. Adam helped bear my pain from The Mother putting me in the "loony bin" at age nine. He wished for purity, which the unicorns represent. "Help us" is printed on one side of the cabin, and a minuscule Adam is standing by the front door, with tombstones, a casket, and a robed figure nearby. I also drew Adam's portrait, absent his usual grimace, as follows:

Adam   9-10

Art helped distract us from our pain by drawing.

Wizard showed people they couldn't hurt us by turning his body into water or stone to avoid pain. He could also make other alters forget who they were and that they ever lived.

My portrait of Timothy A. Bradshaw follows. He was a second-grader and the newest addition to the Boy and We-Two Clusters, who liked fast cars and fast women. Before the incident, he was one of The Mother's boyfriend's wrestling play-pal. The wrestling began as innocent playfulness but later changed and was no longer fun for Timothy, so he had to endure the shame created by this man's aberrant behavior. Timothy claimed that The Mother and almost everyone else in our household molested and sometimes raped us, except for our stepdad, siblings, and birth father. Our birth father abandoned us. Timothy usually slumped his shoulders and grimaced and sometimes buried his face in his hands.

Timothy A. Bradshaw
9

Paul, who felt crazy, liked puppies and fishing.

Pam Peter helped deal with sadness, sat in a corner, cried, and banged his/her head against a wall.

I didn't want to remember the flames from The Mother igniting our bed, so I made Fear, an alter who helped carry that horror. Fear claimed she was born and would die of fire and that she liked it because it was bright and pretty and cleaned and consumed the old so the new could begin. One from the We Clusters said not to believe that because Fear hated fire. He added that fire is our biggest fear because it's the beginning of the end.

At age 10, sexual exploitation and emotional wreckage continued, requiring the creation of Fern, George, Ken, and Junior, 10-year-old boys, and Dale, a 10-year-old boy, in a girl's body. We also created 12 girls, age 10: Bandage, Margie, Feeler, Heidi, Bad Girl, Sophia, Jennifer, Janie, Magic, Jody, Tamara, and Lady Sophia. Then came Maria, an 8-year-old girl; JackJill and Joyce, 10-year-old non-genders; Pamela Boy, a 12-year-old girl; and Conrad, a 12-year-old boy, followed by Sarah and Carol, adult females. Lastly, we made Thinkers, Wise Ones, and an adult female, Worker-of-the-Mind.

Fern and Feeler, who each looked down and away to avoid another's gaze, comprised the Fools. They helped us suffer our shame from what men did to us. They were scared of other alters because they knew what the Fools didn't want to know, the existence of love, sex, and evil. The Fools wanted The Mother to love them, but after Feeler revealed what the men did, The Mother chose them and gave the Fools away instead of protecting them. Feeler called men: rapists, molesters, and cowards. He was often seen with wide eyes and making intense eye contact.

One of The Mother's boyfriends confessed he didn't intervene to protect me from The Mother's wrath because I'd grow up and leave, but he'd still be there. Another said he had to go because he could no longer tolerate The Mother's abominable behavior.

George displayed appropriate behavior so people wouldn't be scared. He was attracted to guys and had terrible lungs. He often presented with wide eyes and made intense eye contact.

Ken, The Doorkeeper, kept track of the comings and goings of other alters.

Junior claimed to be a boy bitch because he got tired of it. He frequently bared his teeth and clenched his fists while expressing the maliciousness he felt.

Dale was logical and kept his emotions in check to project the appearance of normality. He frequently closed his eyes to focus better. The Mother told him not to be friendly in public, or he might get raped or killed.

Bandage had extraordinary powers, like stopping bleeding, fixing broken bones, and putting invisible dressings on us.

Margie carried the trauma of our encounter with a man of the church, who gave Margie the name he would've given the daughter he couldn't have. She held him and told him it was okay, as he cried and told her, "You're one of a kind, have the face of innocence, so full of trust and love, and should never lose that."

Heidi helped carry the shame of having sex with one of The Mother's boyfriends. Heidi complained she had to be a mother and do grown-up things, including being an adult whore. She explained that after her mama had sex with her, neither men nor her mama wanted her as much. Heidi had to clean the house, babysit, go shopping, and have sex with men for groceries. Other kids were carefree, saw life through kids' eyes, played, imagined the world as a great playground, and used their minds to grow and trust big people. Heidi wanted to pretend to be Sleeping Beauty, ride on Black Beauty, and otherwise engage in what it was like to be a real girl, like being kissed without fear.

Bad Girl Sent The Mother's Boyfriend to My Sister's Bedroom.

Bad Girl bore the shame of sending The Mother's boyfriend to my sister's bedroom. When The Mother's boyfriend came into my room and began touching me, I told him to take my sister first, and he did. I prayed he'd pass out before getting to me. My sister took what I should've received. I wanted to stop the boyfriend but was too scared. Bad Girl usually slumped her shoulders and looked down and away.

Sophia, Jennifer, Bad Girl, and Heidi claimed that our perpetrators tortured us more than we ever knew. Sophia was also from the Goodie Cluster, what The Mother only wanted us to be, which included Alice, Lady Sophia, and the alter, The Mom.

Sophia dressed like a hippie, liking ruffled panties and dresses. She frequently clenched her fists, squinted her eyes, and tucked her chin.

Jennifer helped absorb the anger, pain, and horror from The Mother's torture. She frequently clenched her fists and sneered or grimaced and shrank back. Sophia and Jennifer's portraits by Iris follow:

Iris

Jennifer

Janie and Magic hid to make us not exist but later came out of hiding to help endure the pain and horror of sexual exploitation and emotional wreckage. Janie read about mental illness and could change her size and shape in the mirror. Magic could make us not be here.

My sister and I called the cops when The Mother left marks on us, but they believed The Mother's lies. She made up believable stories and presented herself as a stressed single mother rearing several small children. I knew then I was on my own, and nobody would save me.

Shortly after, The Mother claimed she was dying of cancer and sent my sister and me to live with an aunt. The truth was that The Mother only wanted to spend time with her boyfriend without her kids in the way. I created Jody to help manage the pain of that abandonment. When The Mother came for us, my sister and I hid because we didn't want to go with her, preferring our aunt or even foster care.

Tamara helped absorb the pain and terror of our childhood abuses, including the humiliation of repeated sexual misconduct by The Mother and the men in her life. Tamara often grimaced and looked down and away.

Lady Sophia was an Irish version of Sophia.

My spiritual part evolved about this time, represented by Iris's drawing as follows: A tearful Sarah, for the most part, conceals Angel (Gloria) and Maria. Carrie, misspelled Carry, part of our soul, appears as an adult. All are connected by faith.

Maria returned from emotional death. She was also from the Faith Cluster with Sarah and others. They believed in the Bible, God, and heaven and were also part of my soul. Later in life, they learned to forgive and found some peace.

Neddie, misspelled Needie, was connected to Carrie by love.

"The Mo-ther" represents the spirituality of Mother Teresa Bojaxhiu of Calcutta.

JackJill and Joyce, who have unique mannerisms, avoid sexual trauma by not having a gender. Joyce didn't like getting shots in her butt and was afraid of being locked up for being crazy.

Pamela Boy, "The Doorway to Hell," was a 12-year-old girl Can-Be and Thinker and "age slider." He and Conrad were the Gatekeepers of Good and Evil, helping us know the difference between right and wrong, keeping us safe by allowing emotions and stopping them when we became overwhelmed, and by not allowing others to use or push us. Pamela Boy often displayed a furrowed brow and narrowed eyes.

Conrad would later write: My job is to let emotions come and stop them when we become overwhelmed. I have a good job. I keep us safe.

Sarah was also an adult female Wise One, a combination of Carrie, Kara, Tara, and others. Later, Sarah fought the demons that tried to turn us. She often leaned forward with her hand on her heart, raised brow, and wide eyes for intense eye contact. {Sarah was a "parental alter," a relatively common type, who's usually old enough to be the body's parent and who mimics a parent in some way, in Sarah's case, representing a better parental figure the system should've had.}

As part of Sarah, Kara was a young adult female Good One and part of our soul who returned from physical death.

I conceived Carol to help us suffer the pain and humiliation of being exploited by men. She often grimaced and slumped her shoulders.

Thinkers were Holy Man, Intelligent One, Knower, Seer, Sarah, Tara, and Wise Ones, mainly adult immortals. They were logical, rational, and analytical and had little to do with emotion because it interfered with thinking. Thinkers made sense of life and saw our future.

Intelligent One was an immortal man who learned from living, created to help make sense of life.

Seer was an immortal adult female who saw our future and everything outside and kept everything separated.

Wise Ones, who were also Spirits, Thinkers, Helpers, and Gatekeepers of the Sleepers, were Holy Man, Intelligent One, Knower, Sarah, Seer, Tara, and three Nameless Ones who were part of our unconscious. Wise Ones were immortal, invisible, enlightened, held the key to power and knowledge, saw the circle of nature, applied it to our lives, took care of our actual children and us by answering our questions, and were Pamela Boy's conscience.

Worker-of-the-Mind kept our many complicated matters separated, but that only helped a little.

Tara Helped Us Know Our Alters Inside.

Tara was a young adult immortal female Native American Wise One, Spirit, Helper, Thinker, and Gatekeeper of the Sleepers from the Good Ones and Hope/Heart Clusters, and was a combination of Overseer, Sarah, and others. Tara was part of our soul and believed in the Bible, God, and heaven, held the key to unlocking peace, saw the circle of nature, and wrote for us to help us know our inside alters. Tara came from Grandma, who was part Native American. Tara would understand the purpose of the medicine bag Grandma gave me. Tara's portrait by Iris follows:

Tara

alway been

Spirits were Holy Man, Intelligent One, Knower, Sarah, Seer, Tara, Sard, and others, who guided us through the vast darkness we were enduring.

The pain and horror of living with The Mother continued at age 11. So to help us deal, we created Windy, who started as an 11-year-old girl and grew to 13, and Mike, an 11-year-old boy. We also made six other 11-year-old girls: Shelby, Suzie Q., Bell, Paz, Robot, and May.

Windy, who lived in foster care sporadically, helped bear the hurt of life with The Mother. She frequently grimaced with wet eyes and sometimes rocked from side to side with her eyes wide open as if she was anticipating the arrival of The Mother's boyfriend.

Mike, who Punky was in love with, helped carry knowing what we were, why we existed and how many we were.

Shelby, who liked celery, raw carrots, and apples and often trembled, helped bear the pain and horror from The Mother intentionally stepping on our baby bird. Shelby let out a bloodcurdling scream as The Mother's foot crunched the bird's tiny bones. Afterward, she sobbed for hours and couldn't stop her body from shaking.

Suzie Q. was our homemaker, liked to cook and fish, only ate ice cream and candy, and didn't cause any hurt that we couldn't handle, so she was allowed to come and go freely. Suzie Q. frequently sobbed and avoided eye contact due to shame from The Mother's abuse. She lived as Suze from age 5 to 11. Her portrait by Iris follows:

SUZIE 2

The Mother relentlessly continued her cruelty. She whipped me for being friendly to people and became angry when I spoke with my siblings. She once intentionally bumped me with her car because I was 10 minutes late returning home from a birthday party, and later denied doing so. Afterward, The Mother snarled, "Don't act like you're hurt. Get going." Although my hip never healed, the physical pain went away; however, the mental and emotional hurt was so profound I had to keep it in a special vault. I learned how to disappear, not feel, and otherwise do what was necessary to stay alive.

The Mother had sex with my first real boyfriend. Bell, who I made while living in the south, carried the pain of this indiscretion. Bell sometimes grimaced, bared her teeth, and clenched her fists. In her diary, Bell wrote the following about her beau named Bill: We's gona get married when he's 16. Mama says he's a good one. He be doing me fine. It surely be nice to have a place of my own and not live with mama. I isn't say she bad or nothing. She just mama. Every girl wants a home her's own. I don't believe I should've been so harsh with Bill, he's being a man and all. I know it was mama's doing, but he shouldn't have slept with her. He was gona be mine. It's be like it all nice and going fine when that's be a bomb. Mama still has the ring he gave me.

Also, The Mother's beatings continued. Paz, short for Topaz, helped absorb our pain from those thrashings. Paz trembled, hugged herself, and rocked from side to side as The Mother took a wide stance and bared her teeth while whirling baling wire in circles over her head between lashes. As Paz moved to get whipped in a different place, The Mother snarled, "You're getting blood on my bed," and reached out her cupped hand and said, "Give me another tear."

My torn-up back, rear, and thighs once required 70 stitches. The Mother's discipline was brutal and unpredictable. I couldn't figure out what she wanted. My worst fear was that she'd kill me, even though she claimed she was trying to protect me. I called the police, who did nothing because The Mother told them I ran with delinquents. I never knew why she beat me so severely, put me in a mental ward, or forbade me to talk about what went on at home.

My real dad knew of my maltreatment. I had hoped he'd save me all that time, and his not doing so was a tremendous loss. If my dad didn't care, who did? I wasn't good enough to be loved.

I was traumatized when The Mother put me in the "nut house" at age 11. The doctor told me we all have emotions, and I could share mine with him, but he became scared and locked me up when I did. May was a protector who carried sadness from the doctor's betrayal. Also, the doctors denied my reality by speaking favorably about The Mother, leading to my creating Robot, The Dead One, who feels nothing.

Once I was out of the hospital, I was desperate to escape The Mother's torture, so I begged even strangers to take me home. Why did so many people know of my torment and do nothing to save me? I told them I always did as told, took care of the baby, traded my body for food, cleaned the house, didn't complain or cry, acted very grown-up, and did everything asked of me. I could take a beating without one noise or flinch, be a good daughter, and love so much. When people said they couldn't take me, I added that I didn't eat much and would even have sex with them. I told them they needed a little girl like me because I could take good care of them. Some cried, but some just told me they couldn't. They told me I was a good girl, a charming young lady, pretty, lovable, and immensely grown-up. They said all these things but didn't want me, so I had to return home heartbroken. I didn't have what it took to be their little girl.

 I even begged the lady next door to take me. She was kind and showered my siblings and me with love and cookies as Grandma did. Yet, she cried and said that she wished she could. I couldn't make others love me enough to take me home, and no one loved me enough to want to help me. No one.

I worked hard not to be afraid of The Mother and be useful, but I was never good enough. The Mother wanted me so she could just to teach me lessons in life by hurting me. I couldn't stand up against her, and no one else was willing to.

Between ages 9 and 12, The Mother and others had sex with me so often I needed additional help carrying that horror. So, at age 12, I made five 12-year-old girls: Stupid-Head, Seeker, Libby, Silly Sally, and Arrogance. I also made Leah (Shy One), who grew from age 4 to 12, Toughie, a 12-year-old boy, and Dummy, a dull 4-year-old boy. I don't remember why I made Dummy-Two before Dummy.

Leah frequently slumped her shoulders and looked down and away. I created her to help absorb The Mother calling us dirty and nasty and the pain from The Mother and her boyfriends' continued sexual exploitations. Leah remembered one of the boyfriends' grabbing her breasts, which brought up all past terrible memories, and The Mother telling her she misunderstood his intentions. The Mother called Leah a whore, forced her to parade naked in front of her siblings, and forbade her to speak to them because Leah was trash. Leah wanted to be decent, so she wished the bad about The Mother was untrue.

The Mother regularly placed a broomstick in Leah's butt and once dragged her to school naked and yelled to school personnel that Leah was a whore. The principal put The Mother and Leah in separate rooms, and the school nurse gave Leah a blanket and coat to cover herself. Soon after this incident, authorities placed Leah in foster care for a short period. Iris's portrait of Leah follows:

Shy ONE 1
Leah 15

Leah told a therapist about the broomstick, and when the therapist insisted that wasn't true, Leah reacted violently, and the therapist put her in the "loony bin." After that, Leah couldn't please The Mother, so she quit trying and stopped feeling altogether.

Leah was still 12 when The Mother put her in the "funny farm" a second time and asked them to keep her permanently. They kept her medicated, and it seemed to her she was there for a long time. After Leah panicked when they touched her, it took six male staff to "four-post" her. She'd asked them to tell her what to do and then allow time to process the request, but they proceeded straight to force. Leah got worse in the "insane asylum." When her doctor finally decided to listen to her, she refused to speak.

Lisa, originally, Stupid-Head, was a Taker from the Dummy Cluster, which bore our pain from The Mother frequently calling us "stupid" or a similar name. The Dummy Cluster included Dummy-Two, Bo-Bo, originally Dummy, and Dorothy.

One of The Mother's boyfriends would say to Lisa, "Kiss it for me, or you don't love me much, and I'll be sad. It's not wrong to kiss it." Lisa called these gross episodes and wanted to die.

Dummy, a dull boy who displayed a vacant facial expression, printed upside down and backward. He held the key to unlocking horrible recollections, promoting healing, and the key to hearing, to avoid being overwhelmed by too many inside speaking at the same time. He was Bobby when he was in the Boy Cluster.

The younger alters could never come out because The Mother wouldn't allow it, insisting that we act our age. She'd shout, "What the hell is wrong with you"? So we created Quiet Ones: Seeker and others who were mostly younger and whose names I don't remember. They whispered so as not to be heard, to avoid The Mother's wrath, and because otherwise, people would know they did terrible things. Seeker searched for the truth and wanted to live on the righteous side, help the bad, and not have pain or cause it.

Libby labeled emotions if there was a way to tell one from another.

Silly Sally, who often clenched her fists and jutted her chin, was reasonable and stood up for us.

Arrogance, who endured evil thoughts and emotions but tried to get rid of them, sometimes jutted her chin and clenched her fists.

Because boys are tough, we created Toughie, who helped us survive and helped others understand our world. He was from the Bad Ones, rescuers without emotions who could help us endure by managing our rage but whose ruthlessness could get us locked up. Toughie worried that alters would lose control halfway out and change so frequently they couldn't keep track or think clearly.

At age 13, I made Art, a 9-year-old boy, to help distract us from our pain by drawing. Art drew "X-mas," as follows, including a grave and tombstone labeled USE'S, meant to be us, containing a cross with dots representing unnamed alters. "A lonely life, A lonely Death, Nobody cares" is written beneath the cross.

I often felt isolated because my family moved frequently. Kids called me stupid and four-eyes. They told me about regular whippings, whereas I got flesh cut open with coat hangers, belt buckles, and baling wire. I couldn't comprehend nurturing, so I thought others made it up. I'd ask, what's wrong with a mother who holds her little girl but doesn't molest her? I told myself my hell was typical.

There was no safe place except for what I had designed in my mind. I had no one to keep me safe or hate what was happening to me, and no one to ask what I should do, so I concocted a healthy family and friends until they were as real as the hell I was living. I thought up parents who didn't hurt me and friends who understood what was going on when I didn't.

Other kids laughed, played, and seemed so happy. We wanted to think and feel like them but couldn't comprehend it. We pretended to be like them, but it never stuck. Kids asked us to play jacks, ride bikes, roller skate, and play tag, but we told them we didn't know how. They asked what we did at home, and when we told them, their parents didn't allow them to play with us anymore. The Mother would snarl, "You must have done something wrong if the kids won't play with you." When the parents called to complain about us, The Mother beat us.

On other occasions, the parents became afraid of us and asked us not to come back or, due to our lower socio-economic class, told us they didn't want their girls to have friends they might have working for them. They pulled their kids away in public and told them they didn't want them playing with us because the stupidity and dirtiness might rub off. The happy people said hurtful things to us, judged us, and didn't like us. The Mother's words were correct. "You can't change what you are, so stop wanting what you can't have." We finally found a girl playmate, but her dad wanted to play with us in an all too familiar way. The price wasn't worth it.

To help us endure at age 13, I also made three 13-year-old girls. I created Ivy, who attended junior high school, to be unafraid to talk to people.

Rose was an Angry One who often clenched her fists.

Basket helped absorb our pain from The Mother's viciousness. Basket hid to make us not exist and usually looked down and away or bowed her head.

I made Peacemaker, a 13-year boy who tried to create peace inside with what happened outside.

At age 14, to persevere, I made three girls, Alice, Ethel, and MR, and two boys, Tack and Charley, all age 14.

Alice was made to help take on the shame from The Mother's flagrant verbal tirades. The Mother called her "Defiant Little Bitch." When Alice came home having her first period, The Mother was so mad she beat her, sent her to her room, and told her to never talk about such dirty nasty things again. The Mother snarled, "Monthlies prove you're a dirty, evil, disgusting, spoiled, whoring bitch. You're ungrateful I gave birth to you, 'Defiant Little Bitch!' Are you crazy? You'll become nothing. You do as I say. I love you." Alice avoided eye contact and sometimes buried her head in her hands.

Ethel carried the anger from one of The Mother's boyfriends having sex with me. She was angry at the world, and no longer liked herself. Bad things happened to her, so she felt horrible and did terrible things to others.

MR bore the pain of being described as mentally retarded. The Mother told MR that only dummies write with their left hand, slant their letters, or read backward or upside down.

Tack carried the painful memory of being sometimes hit in the head with a pipe by one of The Mother's boyfriends, who chained us to a tree when he went to work. Tack recalled the jarring thuds and being in bed for days afterward. He also remembered a dent in his head caused by the butt of another boyfriend's pistol.

Charley was in ninth grade in 1945 with Alice and could become second-grader Sam. Charley helped me suffer the agony and dismay of The Mother stabbing me with a fork and putting me in a deep freeze. Charley often displayed wide wet eyes and a lifted brow.

More Stays in the Psychiatric Unit

I became enraged because I was forced to lie about sex with The Mother's boyfriends. Of course, I was doomed if I told or didn't, but the telling was a relief overall. As a result of one encounter, her boyfriend went to two counseling sessions, and I was locked up in a "madhouse" for observation and treatment. The staff denied my reality by telling me that The Mother loved me and placed me in a straitjacket because I cold-cocked two attendants who put their hands on me. I had asked them to instruct me rather than touch me.

Another time a boy at school forced himself on me, and I thought I deserved it because sex with The Mother's boyfriends had made me a "lowlife." I was taken to the hospital due to my hyperventilating and having tremors or seizures. The hospital referred me to the Mental Health Clinic. Their staff described me as an attractive, somewhat slow 14-year-old girl who isolated herself, verbalized great fear of home life, didn't get along with other children, and felt very alone in a hostile world.

I was placed in the "psycho ward," where one crisis after another occurred, leading me to request that The Mother not be allowed to visit. The Mother's doctor subsequently admitted The Mother with a Borderline Psychosis diagnosis and later discharged her as a Hysterical Personality with Mild Depression.

It wasn't so bad in the "funny farm" when they put the straitjacket on me because I could still kick, bite, and run, but I lost it when six men tied me to my bed. Even though I was only five feet and 90 pounds, restraining me required three belts for each leg, two for each arm and my butt, one for my chest, and one across my forehead.

After talking to The Mother, my doctor accused me of lying, which broke me for sure, resulting in another straitjacket and the padded room, where I lay for hours in my pee and vomit.

I turned 15 during this confinement. I created The Mom, a 15-year-old girl alter who helped protect us from the hospital staff and The Mother, and made Logical One, a 15-year-old boy, to attempt to evaluate life.

Also, for protection, I fashioned Cheri, a 15-year-old girl who could lock us up so people couldn't see us. Cheri was introspective, angry, cold-hearted, lonely, scared, and depressed with no purpose except to hide us and have sex, and she wanted to hurt herself. She'd clench her jaws and bare her teeth or lower her head and hunch her shoulders. She wrote small so as not to be seen.

Cheri wrote the following to my counselor at the time: Even though I was lonely and scared, I began life as a nice person but became cold-hearted after my "psycho ward" experiences. I didn't like myself anymore, so I created Sherry, a 15-year-old girl leader, to con the mental health counselors. In her voice like melted honey, Sherry stated what others wanted to hear and never again felt and talked at once. Sherry would lean forward, nodding, with wide eyes, intense eye contact, and raised brow, and give a double-handed handshake. Together she and I knew who we were, responded to either of our names and acted like each other. People never knew the difference. To get out of the hospital, I lied to the staff that I adored The Mother. Never again would I trust anyone with the truth.

I'd come out to have sex. I was dirty and dressed and acted the part. My perpetrators taught me I could only get love through sex, which I did very well. I felt used, dirty, and evil during and afterward, but I knew I had what it took. I started, and other alters finished. I had to show myself how bad and dirty I was to prove I was just what people said. They told me sex was all I was suited for. At least I was good for something. One of The Mother's boyfriends said to let crap rest in the past where it belongs and let it die, for Christ's sake. I thought that was a good idea because no one believed me anyway. Hospital staff locked me up if I talked crazy. Only crazy people thought up those horrible lies. I had to leave it alone or be called a liar because it couldn't be proven. It was better to keep my mouth shut. My portrait by Iris follows:

Cheri'

The same old crap continued after we got out of the psychiatric unit. We couldn't go potty at a natural pace because The Mother thought we were playing with ourselves. We had to ask The Mother, have a good reason, and finish in two minutes or else. At about that time, The Mother resumed an old way of torture, putting us in a puppy cage and making us eat puppy poop off the floor. Punky played a game of being a dog due to hurtful emotions springing from this grossness.

The wrong and painful weight of the world was upon us. We separated the mind to handle what it couldn't bear and gave up on the body. We loved and forgave but weren't mature enough to keep ourselves safe.

I had big breasts as a 15-year-old, and one day when The Mother saw me in a sweater, she became angry and barked, "Are you showing the world you're a whore? Remove your sweater and bra." When I did, The Mother appeared shocked and beat me about my breasts while growling, "Only whores have big breasts. Never let men know you're a whore if you want a decent man. Marry money. Your body is all you have, so why not get paid for it." The Mother didn't have big ones, so she was a lady. I wore oversized sweaters after that.

I made Gina, a 15-year-old girl who helped absorb the pain and horror of The Mother's beatings. Gina read a story about two daughters discussing how their mom beat them. The girls knew their mom would thrash them when their dad left for work. They didn't want him to go to work and couldn't wait until he got home because they mistakenly thought he could stop their mom. Gina, who often grimaced and sometimes held herself, was all too familiar with what happened in this story.

We believed in God, but The Mother tried to beat God out of us. She'd beat us badly and growl, "Where's your God now? How come he won't save you? I'll tell you why. You're not worthy of God even looking at you. You're a spiteful and evil whoring bitch, and if I can't stand you, why do you think God wants you!"

About this time, The Mother gestured suicide, and her doctor hospitalized her again with a diagnosis of Depression marked by Psychomotor Retardation. Electroconvulsive treatments led to symptom relief. Regrettably, she was even more brutal when she returned home.

I Became Dorothy Anne

I was still 15 when I was raped by three boys, became pregnant, and miscarried. The Mother took me to a priest, who called for an exorcism due to what he thought was demonic behavior. Instead, The Mother returned me to foster care, where I went away emotionally for good. I became Dorothy Anne, a 15-year-old non-alter who lived inside me. She was a Want-To-Be, those who helped bear much depression because they wanted to do what real kids do but The Mother didn't allow it. I was beyond crazy, growing paranoid and hearing voices.

Dorothy Anne tells a brief part of our story beginning in the next paragraph. The font used therein is employed when she's speaking.

At age 16, I was caught having sex with a boy and became pregnant again but miscarried. All teenage alters thought they were crazy because they saw different faces in the mirror, and sometimes no face or just a shadow. As a result, they avoided mirrors and even dressed and brushed their hair without one.

We made Skeeter about then, a 16-year-old boy who got his name from mosquito bites that itched. Skeeter would tell people: Don't call me out. I've learned I'm the only one that can help me. Good ole mother is always there to cut you more when you fall. Also, a couple of days tied down naked in the rubber room makes you feel great.

The Mother was only pleasant when she was happy, which was rarely ever, and whipped me regardless of how I behaved. Eventually, I disappeared and could no longer feel her blows. My senses were no longer there, so I didn't care if The Mother whipped me, burned me, or whatever. The Mother also verbally berated me by calling me thoughtless, ungrateful, and stupid and telling me I'd be lucky if anyone would marry me. She would also snarl: "I know what's best for you. You can't do it by yourself. I've lived longer than you. I'm just trying to help you. I'm only talking to you this way because I love you. I want you to have a better life than I've had."

I have horrible memories of my time with The Mother and the men in her life. I wanted The Mother not to toss me away, but she didn't want me.

Two - Marriage to Anthony

At age 17, I began looking for a man to save me from The Mother. Finally, at age 18, I found and married Anthony, the first man who wanted a relationship.

I had reservations about marrying Anthony, but I was pregnant by him, and The Mother told me to either wed or have an abortion, which she later denied, and I didn't believe in abortion. So I married Anthony and became Dorothy Lynne (Lynne) an entirely different person because Anthony told me a new start needed a new name.

After some significant school and volunteer work accomplishments, Lynne became a relatively confident "teacher" who moved deliberately and spoke in a cozy voice, like a blanket that wraps around or covers you and touches your heart. Beginning in the next paragraph, Lynne becomes our storyteller, and the font used therein is employed when Lynne speaks or writes. Her portrait by Iris follows:

Life was going to be marvelous from this day forward. Despite requiring oral versus written questions, I even got my high school Graduate Equivalency Diploma. Our first son was born, and I also got Spooky, the dog I'd wanted for quite some time. Iris's portrait of Spooky follows:

Spooky

Iris
1-28-49

Life was fabulous for a while, and The Mother could no longer hurt us. Wrong. The Mother tried to seduce Anthony and told him I was a whore because I slept with her boyfriends. She spent a great deal of time with Anthony and taught him how to control me. She told Anthony he needed to keep the upper hand because I was slow and didn't function well.

Cheri claimed we made bad choices but stopped short of suicide because taking your life is wrong. I was to have a baby, so death wasn't an option. I couldn't have lived with myself. Later I discovered I could live with anything. All I had to do was not remember or feel.

The Mother told me that retarded people couldn't raise children, so she took my firstborn. Fortunately, my stepdad intervened and forced her to return him.

A short time later, our second son was born. One time we were without food for three days. I told the store clerk I needed food but had no money, so I required credit and that otherwise, I'd steal the food. I told him he could have me put in jail, but then they'd feed my baby. The clerk gave me a cart full of food and diapers.

In Anthony's absence, I did things with the Kids he didn't allow. We ate with our eyes closed, played with our food, sipped noodles, ate ice cream, and put olives on our fingers. We also had "bad word" days and "do everything backward" days, such as eating gelatin with the backs of our spoons.

Anthony went on tour, and due to miscommunication between Anthony and the military, we were homeless for a couple of weeks until Anthony's parents took us in.

Anthony brought us home when he returned but continued to mistreat us. He ate steak while our sons and I ate beans and rice, but I'd sneak a little steak for the boys and me. Anthony would take himself out for a meal but never the family. He gave me a tiny allowance every two weeks to buy groceries and once slapped me and asked where all the money went.

We created Heather, a mid-teen girl, to float away when we were stressed, as was needed for fairness because Anthony always insisted on having his way. One from the Us Cluster declared she light as a feather.

I got a credit card to buy school supplies and essential clothing for the children. I'd purchase clothing one size too big, take it in, and then let it out as needed. Anthony beat me when he discovered the card. I felt too bad about myself to share this with anyone and felt guilty for my misbehavior, but I continued taking the beatings rather than not providing for our sons. The fear of Anthony's poundings tormented me, but I wouldn't allow my boys to trek in the snow without shoes.

Alters, Charley, Tommie, and others used to build pretend roads in the dirt and play with toy trucks with the boys. Isabelle hid from Anthony but came out to teach our sons how to be kids while he was away.

An Us Cluster alter commented about Isabelle: She made in the trashcan. She a bell. That kind of what it sounded like when someone hit the trashcan.

Anthony took me to the edge and tried to see how far he could push me, like when he brought women to share me with or choked me until I passed out and then raped me to know what sex was like with a dead person. When I became angry, he seemed happy and let up. He'd call me his sweet loving thing and declare I meant everything to him. Then the humiliation and pain would resume. He liked hurting me and didn't love me.

Sometimes it took me days to come back and weeks to be whole again, just to be shoved once more. I thought I was to blame for loving and wanting to be loved in return.

Anthony even imposed cruel games on me. For example, he persuaded me to prove my love by putting a gun to my head and pulling the trigger. Click. My loved one wasn't convinced, so I squeezed the trigger again. Click. He still wasn't satisfied, so I pulled it a third time. Click. Anthony then said death is the ultimate proof of love and told me I was a stupid bitch, just as The Mother said. Click. He gleefully remarked, "Whoops, not that time. You can put the gun deep to avoid getting guts all over. The next one could prove your love." I insisted I couldn't, and he snarled, "You're just like your whoring crazy mother." I shouted, No, I'm not. Click. Click. Click.

My Marriage Became a Living Nightmare

Anthony once broke my arm by pushing me out of a moving car for being late to pick him up, making him look bad in front of other men. My heart pounded as he reached across me, opened the car door, and shoved me onto the gravel road. I sat up in disbelief, stared with wide eyes as he drove away, and then looked down and away from the staring eyes as I gently removed the bloody gravel from my mangled arm.

Another time, Anthony pinned Ice Queen and me against a brick wall with his car, crushing our knees. As panic surged through us while we stared into space, two alters from the Anybody Cluster came to our rescue, one to move body parts and another to move the car. When the danger was over, they retreated.

Ice Queen was a 20-year-old female Nice One made while living with Anthony to do intricate jobs I couldn't do, such as the satanic ceremonial tasks.

Those in the Anybody Cluster, whose names we don't remember, created for protection from Anthony, were alters in general, whose minds were pre-set on one thing only. What they recalled was in bits and pieces and came and went. They denied everything, believed in no one, didn't think, feel or remember unless the time and need were right, and lost time, including days and even years. Some had emotions, but only bad ones, but most had none. They weren't aware of themselves, day or night, outdoors or indoors, or good or bad. They simply existed. When they were out, they weren't mindful of their surroundings because their minds were pre-set on one thing only, and that's all they addressed with thought or action. Their awareness left when they completed their task. They were like robots that could change shape as needed. Most had a function but no name. They didn't believe in MPD.

My drawing of several alters on one canvas, not shown, depicts my first years with Anthony. Sad, a 12-year-old Quiet One who liked pigtails with ribbons, made during that union to absorb our sadness, is captioned, "Sad." Stick figures fishing, captioned "Timothy A. Bradshaw and Paul fishing," represent isolated good times with Anthony. A tiny black stick figure wearing a black cape and hood is captioned "Dark Secret Ones." Finally, because my sons and I needed protection, a female soldier, clad in a uniform, combat boots, and brandishing a rifle, is captioned, "Soldier does her duties and protects." Our Soldiers were Amanda, Belinda, Rachel, and Winter.

Amanda began as a teenage girl, Angry One but grew to adulthood. Iris's crayon drawing of a target with a sketch of Amanda in the middle and numerous objects scattered about, representing alters, follows:

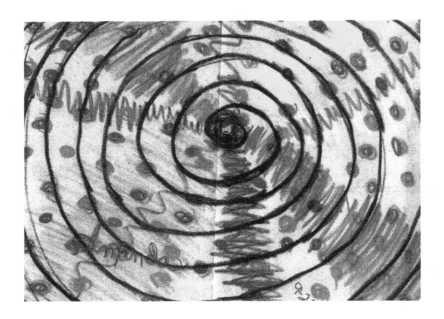

Life with Anthony became a living nightmare, with many years of physical, sexual, mental, and emotional desecration with ritual savagery thrown in for good measure. One time he forced me to lay with dead animals in a cramped enclosure, and I didn't know if I was ever getting out. I trembled and rocked from side to side as I sang baby songs to avoid going crazy. Another time he reported to authorities I was "loony," and they hospitalized me.

Some alters, whose names I don't remember, were felt but not seen, and some were seen but not felt. For example, sometimes we cried, got angry, or were frightened for no apparent reason. Some were out, and we sensed the intensity but couldn't identify them as there were too many. When we were in groups of three to eight alters, we were aware of each other, what was happening, and our behaviors. {Lynne is describing "co-conscious," when two or more alters are aware of each other and might even be aware of each other's emotions or thoughts.}

When I gave birth to our third son, Anthony told me he hated me. He smacked me regularly, once narrowly missing our infant's head. He re-arranged furniture and then denied doing so. No one was allowed to be sick except him. He put bodily excretions on me and took away things I loved if I didn't do as he wished. He beat me for locking doors, just as The Mother did, and locked me in rooms.

Paula is a 16-year-old girl created while with Anthony to help resolve our feelings about him. Unfortunately, Paula chose to remain with evil and must live with that. If she and I had stood by our belief that thou shall not kill, the demonic people would've tortured and slowly killed both twin infants. Instead, we risked our souls killing one to save it from being slowly tortured and to save the second. Also, we believed it would be better for someone who loved the baby to kill it versus others who had no regard for it.

Autumn was a 10-year-old girl, made to hide from Anthony but to come out to teach our sons to be kids while he was away. Autumn's name was originally Tree, named after an overwhelming, sad feeling, like a tree that seemingly dies piece by piece when its leaves fall, leaving it bare.

I created Killer alters without names to try to drink me to death or otherwise kill me because of the desperation I felt with Anthony. Nevertheless, some alters wanted to live and hoped for a better life or a puppy to love. They allowed Mary, and others to come and go as they pleased to control the Killers and the Bad Ones.

Alters active at the time had different perspectives. One said men are nice at first but later hurt you emotionally and only want sex. A second said to shut up and not confide anything because they'll use it against us. A third said to be what they all declare we are, dirty no-good whores who'll sleep with anyone. A fourth said we aren't real, and it's all in our heads. Finally, a fifth wanted us to wait and see.

Anthony used a stapler, water hose, lit candles, revolvers, batteries, fists, boards, handcuffs, electric outlets, pills, nails, light switches, curling irons, hypodermic needles, ammonia, boots, whips with tacks, and knives as instruments of torture.

One time he held our toddler by an ankle suspended at the top of our stairway and roared with laughter as I screamed.

As I was stumbling out of bed one morning, Anthony announced one of his vicious games. "You have one hour to find our sons before they die, and if you can't find them, it's your fault." With eyes and mouth wide open, I froze and stared at Anthony with his slight close-lipped smile. Then, while trembling and sobbing, I frantically searched for my boys. Terror mounted with every step. Finally, I was 300 yards from our house when, "thank God," I detected faint cries for help and open hands slapping metal. I was in a complete panic as I clawed at the loose dirt and removed the lids to three 50-gallon barrels as the boys were crying and gasping for air.

Anthony was just getting limbered up. The following week, he played game two, finding amusement with his air rifle. He instructed me with a drill sergeant's barking tone: "Stand with your back to the wall. You may move only two feet each way and no running. Every time I hit you, I get two more shots." As I embraced my trembling body, my breath quickened with each sound of the air rifle when he pulled the trigger. He cackled each time I yelped from the sting of a pellet, which I can still feel when I remember this game.

A short time later came game three, whereby he forcibly handed me his revolver, loaded with a single bullet, and demanded, "You pull the trigger, so you did it, not me, and if you cooperate, you only have to make three attempts." As I sat in a corner, shaking and rocking from side to side, with eyes widened and staring blankly, I pulled the trigger three times. "Click, Click, Click."

Anthony abruptly introduced game four shortly after when a knife flew by my face, sticking into the wall. Anthony barked, "Don't move a muscle, or you might get a knife, and if you're good at this, we'll try axes." With his chin up and chest out, Anthony hurled knife after knife, pumping his fist in the air and whooping each time he pierced the wall, narrowly missing my hunched-over body, gone cold with dread. Happily, his aim was excellent, and he never got to axes.

I had wanted someone to save me from The Mother and married blindly. Many more years of hell remained because Anthony had more malice in store for me. He brainwashed me so much that when others asked how I felt, I'd mumble, ask Anthony. I couldn't function unless he told me what to do. There was no me.

Anthony watched porn during sex, so he didn't have to look at me. I mostly rationalized it away, but once broke a fishing rod on his back and hurled a hammer in his direction.

For a long time, Anthony convinced me that brutality was acceptable and that every family had it. Still, I could never accept Anthony raping me in front of our sons.

When I began to turn evil, I'd create another righteous alter and start over. What a horrible life, always being evil while trying not to be. I made oh so many but couldn't produce one that stayed good.

Giant Wicked Beasts Appeared in my Dreams of Satanic Rituals

The smoke filled my lungs with the foul odor of the putrefaction of animal tissue. I saw the circle and danced around the fire. I heard the chants and saw the blackness in flames, which grew higher and higher. Then the demons came upon me. They were all around me and came closer. I heard them chuckle and felt the pain of their claws cutting into my flesh. Their hands clawed my body and filled my mouth, and there was something against my back. They came into me, and my body burned. I declared this wasn't real, and I must be mad, but I saw and felt them. Satan told me if I didn't obey, the spiders would return. I had spider bites all over my body. Still, I remained steadfast and hoped to win because the virtuous always win. I believe virtue comes from good, and the body dies, but the soul can't if it's righteous.

Sarah, who believes in righteousness, fought the demons that tried to turn me. My rendering of giant wicked creatures surrounding me that appeared in my dreams of satanic rituals follows:

Our Evil Ones were yM, Missy, Susan, eB, Silly Sally, and unnamed girls. They were made evil while with Anthony and liked hurting and killing. The other alters went along with evil to survive, yet knew better and kept our good. 𝔗𝔥𝔢 𝔣𝔬𝔫𝔱 𝔲𝔰𝔢𝔡 𝔦𝔫 𝔱𝔥𝔦𝔰 𝔰𝔢𝔫𝔱𝔢𝔫𝔠𝔢 𝔦𝔰 𝔢𝔪𝔭𝔩𝔬𝔶𝔢𝔡 𝔴𝔥𝔢𝔫 𝔞𝔫 𝔢𝔳𝔦𝔩 𝔬𝔫𝔢 𝔴𝔯𝔦𝔱𝔢𝔰 𝔬𝔯 𝔰𝔭𝔢𝔞𝔨𝔰.

As an Evil One, eB frequently sneered and came to like hurting and killing. Examples of his backward writing are: "𝔡𝔯𝔬𝔩 𝔫𝔦𝔱𝔞𝔰 𝔰𝔢𝔪𝔬ℭ" (Comes satin lord) and "𝔨𝔠𝔦𝔰 𝔪'𝔍" (I'm sick).

Not shown is my drawing of a tree with roots visible below the ground, accompanied by my writing: "On the eve of Halloween, the power is in the living, in the circle, in the blood, warm and flowing red. The dark side feeds on power and blood. My lord Satan, if I fail to save you, I give my life and shall burn in hell, amen." A Star of David, FFF, 777, an inverted cross, a pitchfork, and an angel, also appear in this drawing, along with a hand reaching into the opened rib cage of an adult nude female with a satanic symbol at her feet. The following writing appears beneath this part of the drawing: "Come to me. Give me your love. Our father. No, No, No" and "To see, speak, remember, or find peace is to die." "I don't remember, and I want to live" appears above.

My next drawing, not shown, titled "Seven-Headed Satan," is captioned, "When a boy becomes a man on the eve of birthday 16, he loses his boyhood, leaves his mother, and joins his father." The Star of David, encompassing the numbers 7 and 777, is accompanied by the writing, "There's talk of hurting, cutting oneself, death, and killing and devouring animals."

I frequently found animals with detached heads when Anthony engaged in satanic rituals.

During Anthony's devil-worshiping period, in a drawing not shown, I sketched the slaughtering of infants on a table, and tiny figures ascending, captioned, "Us going to heaven." I'd died, but a voice told me to go back because life wasn't finished with me yet. To the left is written, "I see, I've been, I go, I came, I talk, peace, pity, go back, sad, know what'll be if good at heart." There's also a detached bleeding heart, a dead baby devoured by insects, leaving only a skeleton, a scary-looking devilish stick figure, and satanic symbols.

In another of my sketches, not shown, I'm giving birth in a blood-filled bathtub. There are graves and a casket in a nearby forest, and Anthony brandishing a knife in the proximity of my pelvis as I lay four-posted to a bed, crying. There's a police vehicle on the road nearby and an airplane landing at a demonic site. Anthony is wearing a robe and holding a sign that reads, "Good and evil are the same." A naked woman with an open torso and stomach lies on a table next to her severed head. Several satanic symbols surround a bloody knife and bowl of blood containing a fleshy object.

I conceived Adona, a 12-year-old emotionless girl, to help Ice Queen endure the horror of Anthony's demonic activity. Adona got her name from Adonis, the Greek God of beauty and desire. She wrote the following beneath her sketch, not shown, of a stick figure being consumed by flames: "Left hand of God, 777, 7734, of DARK, and Satin spelled backward." {Adona was a "programmed alter," one set up to return to the abuser(s) or programmed to believe certain things. They're usually very well hidden and separate from the rest of the system.}

The hooded devil worshipers, who signed a book in blood and spoke an unknown language, took babies into a room with candles. The sect takes girl babies from women and uses them because baby girls are closer to Satan. I created an unnamed identity without feelings to have sex to produce babies.

I knew they aborted me with a coat hanger, even though they insisted I only imagined my pregnancy. An angel told me my baby was going to heaven because it came from God. The next day Anthony told me I was never pregnant but had dreamed it, but I woke up smelling the sickeningly dry, sweet metallic scent of blood, and one of the alters was clear-headed and remembered. I drew infant souls ascending to heaven as follows:

Winter Mercifully Dispatched my Second Baby.

Because Ice Queen had some emotions that could spiral out of control, we needed Winter, who was devoid of emotion. Winter was a 20-year-old female intimidating soldier conceived when Anthony was killing animals and infants. Winter protected the other alters and was often a go-between for them. She was also a robot with no physical sensations who took care of the evil stuff. She held the key to unlocking darkness and helped keep the key to unlocking emotions. {Winter was a protector" and communicator.}

Winter chopped the second baby. The demonic people were torturing it, and Winter mercifully dispatched it. Iris's portrait of Winter follows, displaying her cold and dismissive look and steady, unblinking, focused eye contact:

The sun symbol on Winter's forehead represented Sunshine, a young adult female, the size of a grain of sand, who returned from emotional death and was the only remaining virtuous alter. Winter hid Sunshine deep within to keep her safe, hoping that she could be used to start over one day so we could be good again.

When Anthony pushed Tami to the floor, she sat there momentarily in disbelief with her mouth open and widened eyes, but then became enraged and jumped into Peter as "Dragon, Dear," who sprang to his feet with fists and jaws clenched. Then, bearing his teeth, he took a wide stance before landing a right cross to Anthony's jaw, dropping him to the floor, where he sat stunned.

One morning I awoke to a real "shit storm." Two of our sons were screaming for help. I ran to the kitchen to discover that Anthony had nailed one to the floor and was choking the other, causing the veins in his neck to engorge. Nineteen, a 19-year-old male Angry One who has superpowers when angry, swatted Anthony with a broom without impact. Nineteen then broke a chair over Anthony's back, causing him to release his chokehold and roll to the floor, somewhat dazed. Anthony spewed, "I'll kill you for that"! He managed to get to his knees and look up just in time to see the refrigerator tumbling onto him. Anthony struggled to breathe with his mouth hanging open, and his eyes widened as he peered from beneath the fridge.

I had little awareness while living with Anthony because I switched so much that I was on autopilot. Toward the end of my living with him, Winter took over all the lives of the alters, leaving only Winter. Winter had to deal with all the everyday responsibilities and evil. All other alters became the walking dead. Winter kept my sons and the others safe, but there were no emotional responses or real life. Affect was added to create vitality and a desirable mother for our boys, leading to Winter having emotions. She was seething when Anthony and his associates were killing animals and wanted to kill Anthony. Anthony exploited Winter's sentiments, leading to her shattering into a million pieces like Humpty Dumpty.

Ultimately I had to choose the survival of my boys and myself over my marriage. I escaped Anthony with my life but not my sanity. Even after leaving him, he shot at me, broke into my house, killed my pets, and raped and beat me. Authorities told me to continue to contact the police because even if the police couldn't do anything, the reports could help if I ever went to family court. The FBI convinced me to move and change our names. The name, Lynne will be kept for the telling of this story.

Alters flooded back after I left Anthony in 1966. I could describe more than 400, some cult-specific, some hostile, many childlike, and three somewhat well-functioning adults. Many knew each other and exchanged information. I abandoned many because they were no longer needed.

In one of my drawings, not shown, I sketched "Happy Land," where Punky resided, "Make-Believe Land," where Want-To-Bes lived, "Lost Land," where Dorothy and others dwelled, and "Safety Land," where unspecified alters stayed. A crying eye is sketched in the center, captioned, "Making no home.

In 1931 I had an overflowing bucket of hope. By 1955 I had no nice left. I couldn't give what I didn't have. By 1965 my hope bucket was empty. I created Teach, a mid-teen girl Strange One, who held the pain of having my bucket of hope broken so often that no hope remained.

I drew my broken body, as follows, surrounded by wolves, representing my getting chewed up from grave long-term brutality at the hands of The Mother and Anthony.

I Escaped Anthony's Hell

Life with Anthony left me wounded and confused. Living with him was soul-crushing. It took many years to get fed up with his daily cruelty, and even then, I remained with him for a time because I feared the court would give him our boys.

I deteriorated to the extent that I couldn't do anything Anthony didn't tell me to do. I thought I'd be okay if only I could get him to understand the damage he was causing. Instead, I became just a teensy dot in the Milky Way. The Mother was horrible, but I needed additional alters to lose myself entirely with Anthony.

My following sketch shows me with springs for my feet and a transparent chest, exposing my spine. At my waist, I wrote "really." I was too familiar with the words kill, hate, and hurt, yet part of me remained kind. I expressed my confusion as follows: I can bleed, yet I'm not real. I'm dead. I don't feel. How many of us are there? I'm changing again. I feel crazy and empty within like nobody is home. Am I a man, child, girl, animal, or the Dead Ones, crying babies created when I lived with Anthony? Why am I here? I don't want to be. I like girls, and I have new alters.

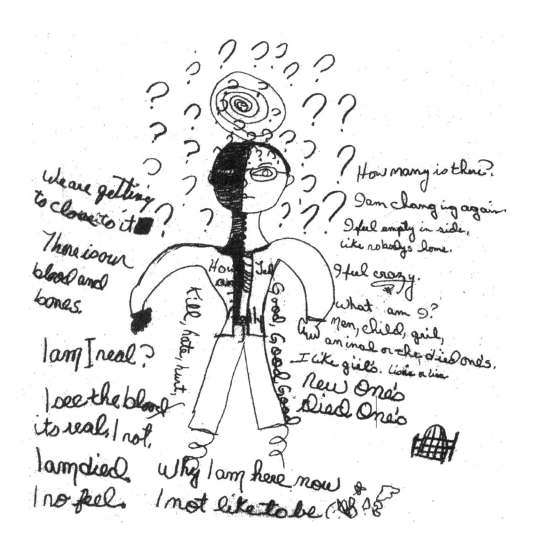

"Knowing It's I"

In "Knowing It's I," shown on the following two pages, I added to Dorothy's genealogy of alters and clusters created earlier. Although new alters were generated later, charting ended because it became too hectic to remember them. It was hard enough to keep track of the outside, let alone the inside. The double lines connecting alters represent that they can communicate with one another. Many alters in the chart aren't in this story. Some names are misspelled.

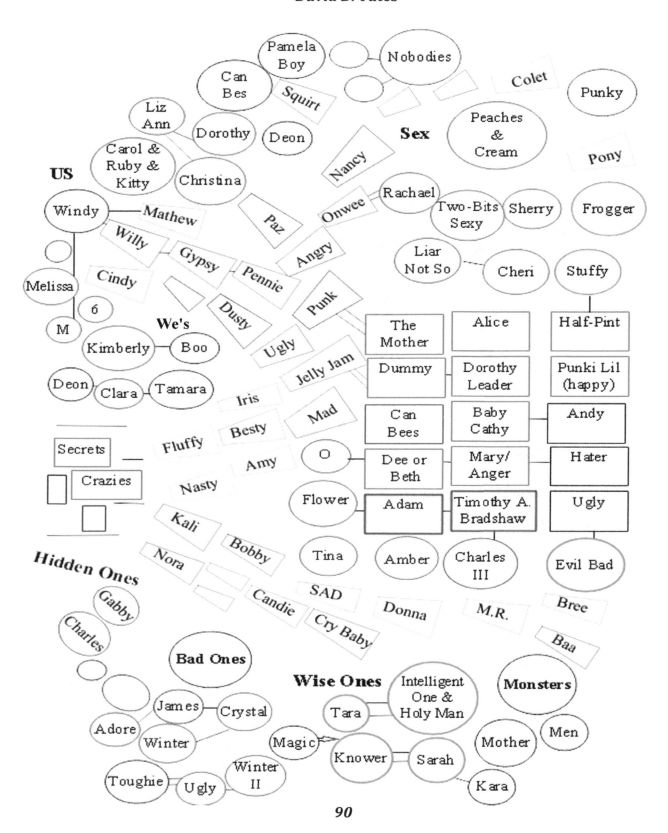

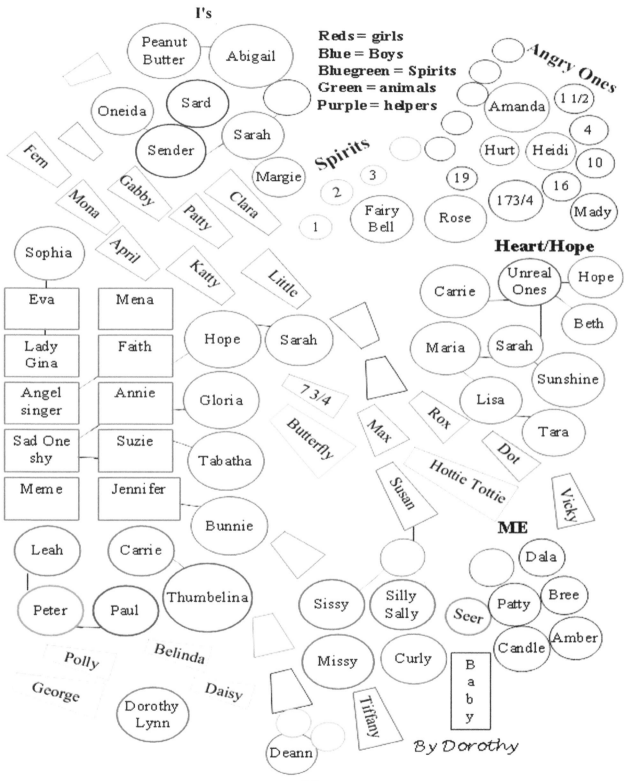

By Dorothy

I left behind the horrific life with Anthony in 1966, fearing one of our sons would kill him. Still, I thought of returning to him after rearing our sons because I so strongly believed in the vows of matrimony.

We wrote to him: We won't shut you out, will communicate with you versus being abusive, be your best friend, and share our life with you. We'll give our 50%, work for a better us, seek to understand and love you and be okay that you're a great guy with a good and an evil side. We'll not forget that you don't know everything but will help when you can. We'll recognize that we can make anything work if we communicate. We want to live and enjoy life with you by our side, trust again with you, grow our love, find the end of time with you, and watch and learn from you and you from us. Finally, we want to love you with all we have to give, which will take a lifetime.

Lynne and others

After leaving Anthony, it took two years to come to my senses, file for divorce, and date again. Iris's drawing of a date with our boyfriend, Rick, is not shown. "Good Golly Miss Molly" blasts from Rick's sedan. There's a tent, an open fire, and Rick fishing with Punky. Iris captioned a couple standing at a front door, "Our first date. Kiss at the door."

Also not shown are Punky's drawings of Rick teaching her to swim, another picnic in the rain, and an embrace, captioned, "Good hugs," and Iris's drawings of a rainy day in a park, boating in a stream, fried chicken atop a picnic table, and Punky and Rick warming their hands over an open fire.

Iris's following drawing is of Rick's house, captioned, "Our home, where dreams come true:"

Three - Our Healing With Mr. Clarke

1968 Therapy with Mr. Clarke

In 1968, Liz Ann, an 11-year-old girl who held her chin up and shoulders back, was created to take back our life. She liked crafts, drawing, writing stories, keyboard, reading, gardening, yard work, and her stuffie. She wrote the following un-mailed letter to The Mother:

When you broke my heart, I lost my ability to feel myself. When you said those terrible things to me, I lost my ability to believe in myself. When you beat me and said it was for my good, I lost my ability to forgive myself. When you allowed others to hurt me, I lost my ability to hope. When you didn't stand by me, I lost my ability to love myself. When you told me I concocted it, I lost my ability to trust myself. When you didn't care anymore, I abandoned myself completely. No matter what you did to me, I chose to believe in and love you above myself. My most significant pain has been self-inflicted by relentlessly seeking your love and acceptance. No more! I'm taking back what I gave away so freely. Watch out, world. Liz Ann loves and is taking care of herself.

Liz Ann

To promote appropriate contact with the outside, the Wise Ones, therapists, the alters in the 12 Selves, and me, Lynne, created Leena, our shell, in 1968. She was an attractive, undamaged 37-year-old intelligent, confident woman, typically seen with her chin and brow raised and making fixed eye contact. Her voice was like gently lapping waves.

She becomes the primary storyteller beginning in the next paragraph, mainly assisted by various alters, even though I remain active for a time. The font used therein will be employed when Leena writes or speaks. Alters are typically frozen in time, as indicated by their communication. A challenge to consistently identifying Leena as the speaker is that she might fully or partially switch to an alter or alters not delineated. Also, the reader could notice a change in grammar and self-reference to singular or plural. Lastly, alters might be participating in the conversation without identifying themselves. Leena's portrait by Iris follows: {"Co-hosting" (co-hosting), or "blurring" (blurring), could be occurring. Co-hosting is when two or more alters are out and in control of the body. Blurring is when two or more alters are hosting or close to doing so, and traits or feelings seep into each other, which can be unpleasant or intolerable.}

Counselor Carolyn tried to persuade me to see Mr. Clarke, who had expertise in MPD, but it took me two years to muster the courage to do so because of my fear of men. Before our first counseling session, I wrote to Mr. Clarke: I haven't met you yet, but I know who you are. I'm Leena. I have a community memory bank I draw on to get information. I believe I need your help to heal. Others have told me I must do most of the work. My esteem increases when I can recognize my growth without being told. I don't like others to direct me to do something different because I've been doing it wrong. It's better to hear I've allowed others to control me, and how about I look at alternatives. This way, I'm learning better ways to manage life. I gleaned from previous counselors that my old way was to blindly do as others asked. Therefore, I was always dependent and didn't grow. Do you understand the difference? If I don't learn, I'll remain a victim.

So, in addition to my drawings for therapy, I participated in counseling twice weekly with Mr. Clarke from July 1968 to late 1972, records of which aren't available. I also mailed him a 16-inch stack of letters and notes. In them, Mr. Clarke was sometimes called Clarke or Mr. Clarke David by alters and myself. Lilly called him Mr. Clarke David or Clarke David. He returned my letters after writing comments on many. Summaries of the letters are presented chronologically under headings according to the subject matter, and brackets surround Mr. Clarke's remarks. Those headings are Life with The Mother, Life with Husband and Boyfriends, Life with Other Family Members, Life in My Household, Medical/Psychiatric Issues, and Therapy Not Included Under Other Headings.

My primary focus in this part of my story is our correspondence with Mr. Clark, but I give some attention to our drawings and sessions with Mr. Clarke.

Life with The Mother

Dorothy and her sister were never safe when the men came to their bedrooms at night. Sometimes the men tied them to their beds by their wrists and ankles.

We've had many monsters (abusers) in our lives, as represented by the wretched-looking creature drawn by a Little One as follows, with another Little One clinging to the monster's long, white ribbon-like chin whiskers. [Indeed you have, Leena.]

Life with Other Family Members

We Cluster wrote: A recent visit with our birth dad and siblings, Rebecca and Buster, was favorable overall. Still, it stimulated the return of overwhelming horrible recollections like yesterday, so we shut down and locked ourselves up to keep ourselves safe. Rebecca, a teacher, is married with three children. Buster is married and has grandkids. After retiring from military service, he became a freight truck driver, from which he is now retired.

We were angry the following week because neither of our parents called to wish us a happy birthday. We were sad when only one of our siblings, a sister, phoned. Another sister isn't talking to us. Even though Rick was upset, he gave us a cake and a card signed with love. We bought ourselves a gift, and our family went to dinner. We were able to talk about horrible recollections. It was a fantastic past year, but we know it'll pass. We love our family, friends, and Rick, even though we behave offensively toward him when his behavior reminds us of Anthony, and we don't like his touching our breasts because that makes us dirty whores. We were making progress in believing in and trusting others, but then a father figure from our past phoned drunk and called us derogatory names.

Life in my Household

We Cluster continued: We cause our boyfriend, Rick, his hell. We've screwed up big-time from the day we were born. All we ever wanted was to grow up, have kids to love and protect, and be better than our mother by doing what she couldn't, but we couldn't do what we didn't know. Your world didn't teach us. We're aware that our desire was a child's dream, that reality is nothing but pain, and to get what you want, you must be scary and blame others.

We live in the world's realness, as well as our own. We see the pain we cause others every day. God, help us! We're no better than our mother. Why do you think we hate ourselves so? We thought we could fill our emotional emptiness by caring, being kind, and teaching what we believed was right. We always hoped we could change the bad to something good, but what the hell, we're just second-rate. Some alters, however, think they must be sick because they believe they did well.

Angry and Hurt wrote the following letter to Rick: It's hard for us to ask for help, but we need your help. We don't want to have this agonizing emotional pain. We notice you get sad because you don't want to see us hurt, either. Say you want to help us. For example, you grill the steak while we prepare the salad. Beth needs you to help her cook, but don't let her use knives. She sees blades in her hands and cuts us sometimes. Others of us cut or hurt us because bad girls get hurt. When we get angry, tell us you know we're mad, and why don't we get mad at the bed and play "Who can hit the pillow harder"? Try not to show anger toward us for wanting our hurt to go away. That'll help us not hurt ourselves. We don't know how to make it better any other way, but with your help, we can start learning better strategies.

I asked my boyfriend, Rick if he likes sex without me, and he responded that sex feels good either way. Some alters got angry, thinking he didn't care about us, but some said he was only talking about sex. I don't know what to feel or think. I prefer to believe that I sometimes mistakenly think people mean to hurt me. [Never assume, Leena. Ask]

Rick and I wrote to Mr. Clarke. I asked Mr. Clark to explain when to reveal your sexual activity. I told him Rick insisted our sex is between him and me only and that I shouldn't talk to anyone about it. Why not talk about it if I'm not ashamed of it? I explained to Rick that I mistakenly think he's like them when he speaks the exact words as my past tormentors. Rick told Mr. Clarke that I reacted negatively to the word "special" and asked Mr. Clarke to help him explain that our "special" is good.

Mr. Clarke suggested Rick find a different word for "special," like precious, and told me that discussing my sex life with my therapist is appropriate but that otherwise, discretion is advised. Mr. Clarke assured me that I'm stronger than before, know my rights, and wouldn't live with anyone who mistreated me.

Life with Husband and Boyfriends

I felt fear when Anthony called to wish me a happy birthday. I'm still having terrifying nightmares of my life with him. In one, spiders cover me in the dark. I tremble as I'm escorted from the dark, spider-infested room, down a hallway by a man in a black robe. His hand pushes my head down, so I'm always looking at the floor. Then, as he stabs my shoulder with his fingers, he asks if I want to come with him or return to the darkroom and the spiders. [That's scary, Leena.]

I also dream of sitting in a cage in the nude, and people are strolling around me. A woman drops a glove into the enclosure, and I think the glove is big enough to cover me, so I feel safer. Then someone removes the glove, and I feel crazy and am cold emotionally and physically.

Alter Dynamics

eM printed: My name eM. I'm a shy girl and am easily embarrassed. You're not aware of me because they made me up. I no hurt like others because they suffer very much. I don't know them well. Others don't want to know me. I want to be a real girl versus a made-up one. It always makes me sad when counselors leave.

Jay printed: I can't write as fast as they're talking. I'm the middleman. I mean that I take care of myself. I'll let no one in to hurt me again. My mother told me to shut up, or she'd give me something to cry about, and if I weren't stupid, I wouldn't be here crying and hurt. My mother hit and burned me, and my belly came up from the pain. I don't love or need anyone anymore, and I don't cry. Nothing is worth pain or crying.

Dummy-Two printed backward please end the hurt.

Wisher wrote: I'm called Wisher. I started as a 2-year-old boy who wanted to die due to my mother's cruelty if I couldn't live with my dad or Grandma. An agency put me in foster care instead, but they placed me with my Grandma shortly afterward. I got to stay with Grandma for six months before returning to my dreadful mother briefly. For the next six months, I went back and forth between my Grandma and my mother. Life with Grandma was terrific. Living with my mother was miserable. At age eight, I tried to drown myself, swallowed my mother's pills at age nine, and began cutting and wishing I wasn't so afraid of people at age 16.

Dummy-Two printed: If the others know who I am, they'll want me to suffer for them again, but I don't want that. I care, but I'm scared of real people, and other alters. Because of my great need for love, I've accepted much pain and sorrow. I want to feel anything positive. To believe that somebody cares for me for just one second would suffice. Why do I take so much hurt for so little in return? I so foolishly accept the pain, hoping they'll hug me one day and say thank you so much for loving us. No one tells me, "We love you just the way you are." Someone told us God said good things come to those who wait and that he'll take away every tear and hurt. I'm still waiting.

I've never been sure of what happened to me. I know my mother, aunt and uncle, family friends, mother's boyfriends, and others harmed me horribly. I see pictures in my head but can't remember all the details. I feel hurt in my heart, and my body has pain and scars that tell me what happened. I made many of us with different faces because I couldn't alone withstand the torture that fell on me. Most of us have names. Furthermore, it was easier to be confused than accept others' lies, like, "I imagined the whole thing because parents don't treat their kids like that."

Gabby printed: I'm a little girl. I'm six. I'm not sure how I became Leena, but I'm having fun with her. She likes talking and helps with my confusion. I bought a mop bucket for Christmas.

Mary printed about her confusion: What I do? I so scared. I got to do right. I do wrong and I get hurt. My mother said to stay away from him if you don't like it, girl. He came to me and I no like it. My mother and her boyfriends hurt me.

It ate my arm and want to eat my head. I no like it, and it scared me. It wet and yucky. It ate me up. It a monster. It feel yucky, and I no like it. I seen my mother there. Something push me on the beast. I no like it. It scared me. The giant dark monster ate my face, and I couldn't breathe. I no like it.

It more than hell, and took all from me but the hell. I put thing in momster. I no like momster, and I no like it. I no like see my mother and I fear her. It scared me big, and I no want it. My mother ate me, and I no run. I no like it. It scared me.

My ear bleed. My nose bleed. My mouth bleed. I only see black. My mother did it. I dying. I no like it. I ouch. I dying. My mother said Beth no good. Beth came. Beth helped me. I good. I dying. I no scared, Beth. It no hurt, Beth. I sleep now, Beth. I love you.

I didn't know how to love or show love. I didn't know what love real was. I wanted it but I too scared. I wanted to feel loved, and wanted others to feel my love. But I didn't know how to if they no pain, sex, hate, or hurt.

I was a pretty flower, and they picked me. It took time, and then I be died. Ugly and died. No one cared, so throw the flower away. You can't see me cause I not in the head! I died in bed! Poor little dumb girl.

Tina wrote: I don't think she's dumb. She got it right.

Mary printed: I feel Amy. Amy little and very scared. My mother said Amy should be proud she had 15 men in one night, but she doesn't feel proud.

Amy printed: I'm Amy. I'm five. I had tadpoles, but they all died. My mother snarled, "Bitch, it'll die if you touch and love it. Nothing can be around you long and not die because you're so stupid." Mother only wants to hurt us. It'll never change.

I know things. My mother yells cause I don't do things right. I once ran away, and she called the police, who handcuffed me and took me home. Then I stayed with my aunt for a while. I know Dee and Charles. Charles makes my fear go away. Dee isn't kind, and I'm afraid of her. She cuts us and puts us on railroad tracks because she wants the pain to stop. I sometimes wish Dee success in trying to kill us because I'm tired of being afraid. My mother breathes heavily when she gives me long kisses. I don't like that, so I don't want to feel love if that's love. Charles takes the kisses away. My mother scrubs us hard. I'm afraid and Dee is hateful.

I'm forever in trouble with my mother but never sure why, and I'm afraid of everything, including mice or silence. I have a terrible secret about a field. I don't know what it is, but it always scares me. Due to so much hurt from my mother, I've become numb and not healthy anymore. I don't laugh or play. Even bad memories no longer hurt. Dee hurts us when we don't feel. Dee and I don't want to be here anymore. I caught my panties on fire to make something go away and got a whipping for it.

Sam printed: I drop a toy down the toilet hole, and my mother put me down it. She yelled I wasn't careful and didn't appreciate the trouble it took her to get the toy, so she told me to climb down and retrieve it and watch out for the snakes and spiders.

Frank, who's stuck in the past, printed: The Mother is mean to us and never says we're good. The worst thing Grandpa does is thump our heads if we're noisy when he's trying to nap. He told Punky Lil if Betsy kicked her, she could lose her marbles, but they were in her bedroom. I have fun making butter with Grandma and dancing around the churn. Grandma's washer with a ringer is dangerous. One time I got my hand caught in it.

Rachel printed: I'm Rachel. I didn't like the feel of my mother's boyfriend's big pee-pee in me. I repeatedly told him I was sorry for not enjoying it, and I was mad at myself for not liking it.

Genie printed: Leena leaves $10 in our can to spend on candy. I like candy, but you shouldn't have too much. Patty can lock Dee away. Morey can get rid of Dorothy. Sometimes groups of us disappear. Timothy A. Bradshaw brews tea and coffee, and it doesn't taste good. We're not supposed to say bad things about parents.

{Co-conscious is a step toward communication that's often regarded as one of the most significant steps a system can take toward being healthily plural.}

Tara wrote the following letter to her beloved people regarding co-conscious, about which Mr. Clarke teaches us: I hold my people together or apart. We have separated for many moons. This place in time will be called the coming of minds, bodies, and souls. It is a time of great peace, knowing each other and not believing all. We must learn to depend on our Spirits as they alone can guide us through the vast darkness we are enduring. We will learn to trust others and ourselves, share knowledge, live in peace, and come together.

A long time ago, we lived as one and will again. This time we will be more durable. As "the great one" declares, all things must grow or wilt and die. Do not fear what you do not know, as it will come in time through the people. I am the seed of our people and will teach our people to fly, grow into greatness, find peace within, and see the world through my eyes.

We all seek the wholeness we think other people have taken from us, whereas we've locked it within ourselves. Others can help us find the key to unlocking ourselves. Does not a doctor cut off an arm to save the rest of the body? Then why cannot we lock up parts of us to rescue the rest? Think upon this. Where are the missing pieces of us?

Signed: I am Tara. I am Wise One.

A second letter from Tara to her beloved people reads: At this time, my people hide from themselves and others due to the great darkness they have been through. They have fears of mistrust and enormous loss. The pain they have endured is immense. We have been here before and know anything can send us back to the darkness.

Our fears are great. I can understand my people. Who is to say we will not lose terribly, but is this not the time we have dreamed of in our hearts? Is this time not more vast than any losses we have endured so far? I also know our pain. My heart of hearts bleeds for my people. I hear them. No! We are not to be as one. Listen and heed what I say. There is coming greatness. Our people live in the four winds. I say to you come from the four winds. Come together to share our thoughts and to know each other. I do not lie. I do not mean my people come live with me. No! No!

I say to you. Do not believe all you hear. Let your Spirits, not others guide you. My heart of hearts bleeds over these tremendous losses. I am one of those people. They divided to grow, not die, and deal with our travel through life. Now my people are coming out of the great darkness. We have lived in the dark because of the dividedness.

Now it is time, my people, to come together in one place, not in one body, share ourselves, know one another, and depend on our people and not on others, as we had to in the darkness. I foresee greatness for my people. Life is a place of great learning. On our journey through life, we each learn much. What I do not know, you, my people, do. I say, stand by me and teach me of your ways, and I, in turn, will teach my people what I have learned on my travel through life. We shall no longer walk alone. We will learn to trust, which must start with our people first. Then it can go to others. All things in my people's hearts of hearts will come to pass. Hear what I say. It has to take hold within us first, like the tree. Then our people can live as intended.

I ask you to consider this and trust our people. I do not ask my people to trust others. They have trusted others much with huge losses. I, too, have had massive losses. What I ask is for you to believe in our people and yourself. We need to build a great hall in our town. {Tara is referring to "Kids Town," built to promote co-conscious, discussed more fully later by Brooklyn and others.}

I am Tara. I am Wise One.

Tara's third letter is to Mr. Clarke and reads: I am not all of what you seek. I am one that you pursue, and you are one that I am after. I hunger to know the meaning of intimacy, relationship, communication, trust, value, purpose, boundary, emotion, accomplishment, and living environment. Do you hold what I seek?

We saw counselor Dahlia, who asked if we were working on integration with you. Her question caused great fear. You need to know we can integrate at any time. Integration is not what my people or I need.

A tree cannot stand unless its roots are strong. If they are not fed water and exposed to air and sun, they will seek other ways to live. Over time, the tree and its roots will divide to live.

My people have divided to live. We need to feed the tree and its roots to be robust. The tree will not stand if you bring the tree and roots together without feeding them first. It will fall.

I do not want this for my people. We have endured much. No more! Feed the tree and roots to promote durability, and the tree can stand against the winds and storms to come.

With my heart of hearts, I wish you to understand this, so you can feed the tree with love and teach it to take care of itself. I think Leena is the sun. We all will find our greatness in time with much care.

I am Tara. I am Wise One

Tara's fourth letter, also written to Mr. Clarke, reads: I, Tara, seek within my mind and have never sought beyond myself. I have learned through hearing others, and now you, Mr. Clarke, that it is good to seek outside oneself. Therefore I quest for what you hold. I came to you and learned that I alone do not have all the answers. I have stood apart but will no longer. It is new to me to show myself to others. I have great fear. Over 300 moons have passed. In my heart of hearts, I believe that all things come together for a reason. When you and I part, I will have left something great that you seek.

I am learning to share with my people and beyond myself and ask for guidance for what I seek. My people are lost. They only seek outside themselves. They need to see within as well. As I learn to see beyond myself, my people and I need to find a balance. At this time, we have met. We cannot let this time pass without seeking the greatness that was meant to be, now or later. I choose this place in time for myself.

I am Tara. I am Wise One.

A letter to Mr. Clarke from an Angry One, titled "The Tears of the People," by Tara, reads: I feel pure rage and much pain. I want others to feel my pain and take back my hurt and anger. I want them to feel what I do. I've tried to show others the rage that consumes me by cutting myself open. I don't want to hurt or have this much anger, and I don't know how to tell you about it. Don't ask me to put it all in the past or forget it. I can't because I live and am these emotions. I don't want to hurt you, but I want you to understand what gnaws at me. Love will cure me.

On page two of the Angry One's letter, Sarah wrote: Be careful using words like, I love you, sweet thing, baby, you can't, and you shouldn't feel this special. When you said I ought not to feel guilty, I thought I didn't have the right to have emotions. I need to know you'll be there when we need you the most. Don't state you can when you can't. I need to know you care for and respect me as a person with real feelings.

We Cluster added to this letter: We can handle bits of emotions, but to experience our base emotions in their purest form is intolerable. The guilt, shame, hatred, and rage are profound and push us into the darkness, which scares us. What if we don't come back this time?

We've stayed in the dark and can't think or feel. We don't want to lose what we have, but we want to know what we can't handle. Is it time to look again? Is the price too high? We're hurt and scared. Our mother didn't want or care about us, and we lost her. What do we do now? We can't make her happy if we can't be there. We've torn ourselves apart, trying to please, love, and trust, even when we knew not to. We usually cut to distract from our intense emotional pain, yet sometimes we cut to feel alive. We want the hurt to go away.

Pain equals love, caring, safety, people, hate, and hurt. Adults don't see the pain they inflict. They tell you not to trust so much because people who trust get lied to and exploited. Adults ask how you could like or love him if he doesn't have money, looks, and a good job. They don't have time to worry about little things. Adults tell you to do as other adults do, and you'll be fine. They're the best traders I've ever seen. They say if you do this, I'll do that.

Adults won't let you be less than them. Adults are responsible, have difficulty trusting anyone, aren't open, and know that people aren't fair and don't give a crap about others.

Adults have six rules. Think of yourself first and get ahead. Don't trust people to be honest or to do to you as you do to them. Always act like an adult, avoiding anything a child would do. Forget how to care or how it was to be a kid. Forever watch your back. Finally, they say, I love you, but I might care more if you'd only do whatever.

Adults have to fix it, whereas kids say it'll be better tomorrow. Being an adult is lonely and fearful, and you lose so much. We want to remain part kid and only become part adult. Kids are more open, trusting, forgiving and see the good in everything. Kids forget the bad. Kids will love you no matter what you do.

In a letter to Mr. Clarke, Unnamed Ones asked: Do you know why we only write at the third-grade level, don't understand grown-up matters, and don't know our numbers or age? More alters from our Kids Cluster are active because almost all of us are children under age 10. Most try to take care of everyone but hurt themselves when they become angry. Our teenagers act like adults, which they mostly learn from television. We're primarily adults because we've lived adult lives from age two, but within, we're kids trying to live in an adult world.

Mary printed: No, Me happy. I have clay. I like to make happy thing. Two paper good for now. You take care.

On pages two and three, Unnamed Ones wrote: We've spent 37 years dissociating. We learned to walk, talk, and act like adults by watching television shows and movies like I Love Lucy, Mr. Ed, My Three Sons, Gone With the Wind, Snow White, and Bambi. We quit growing emotionally altogether at age nine. At age 16, we matured a bit emotionally but got hurt and retreated until we met counselors. We pretend to be an adult to be accepted by people our size. People see the body and figure we know about grown-up matters. We don't.

We keep trying to be adults, but we don't know how to pay bills, make friends, or care for or stand up for others or ourselves. We're so good at pretending that most people think we're adults, but pretending takes so much energy we don't have time to grow into adulthood. We still act like kids because we're kids. We view adults as mean, hurtful, and evil, but we don't want to be that way. We're rarely around competent adults. We thought only kids were good until we met counselors, but we were too afraid to try by then, so we made Leena, who learns for us.

She began where we left off so many years ago. We didn't give her the fear of trying, hate, hurt, or anything that would stop us from growing. We keep her safe at all costs because she's our hope to understand and evolve. Don't try to stop us from growing! Teach us! Please don't stop us!

On page three, Lynne wrote: When I'm asked not to let the kid alters out so much, I feel rejected and less than others. It's like cutting off my arms because they're smaller than adult size. You want me to be whole, feel and see all things, live life, not hide from it, and not be ashamed, like when I had to beg at Thanksgiving.

Mary printed: To Be us + to be proud of us for how + what we are. To Be Real.

Lynne wrote on page four: But then you ask me not to be all of us. I can't be real and, at the same time, pretend I'm only an adult. You'll never know how much it took to turn my emotions on and then fight the desire to turn them off. I struggle to keep what counselors taught me about trusting what I believe to be accurate versus what others previously taught me.

At the end of page four, Meme printed: Help me! I'm here!

Therapy Not Included Under Other Headings

Lynne wrote: I want to be me, but the cost is too high. I wish I could cut out my hurt and bad parts, cry, fall apart, and have someone see and understand my pain; instead, I have to be steadfast, understand other people, and not sob because that would make them sad. I have to be the grown-up, so they can depend on me to take care of them. If I show weakness or seem crazy, they can't handle it, so they leave. People like me when I don't reveal who I am. They only want me when I'm healthy, together, and don't show the pain that devours me. When I live a lie, I can make them happy. I appear healthy, lovable, and together because I hide that others have torn me up emotionally. I don't even know what it's like to be happy, adorable, and healthy. What a way to live! I can pretend to be healthy and keep them or be myself and lose them. My recent portrait by Iris titled "Reality," depicting a young woman who smiles on the outside but cries inside, follows:

Reality

I mailed the following 1968 letter to Mr. Clarke before my first group counseling session with him: I'm Leena, a survivor of various forms of severe abuse by The Mother and others. At a very young age, I learned to fear others and that loving me meant hurting me. I've benefitted from therapy for my Post-Traumatic Stress and MPD. I have a massive journey ahead, but I have hope. Now that I'm divorced, I wonder how I might earn a living.

Possibilities are ceramics, house cleaning, baking, babysitting, foster care, quilting, waitressing, or being a peer counselor.

My perpetrators hurt and controlled me and called that love. Now I know that love is sharing, caring about someone, and taking the risk of dealing with good and bad. Love doesn't have to hurt and doesn't give you the right to destroy another. I also learned I'm a human with emotions and prerogatives, which I never have to give up. No one ever taught me it's okay to have feelings, see, touch, or ask questions, things you take for granted. I need you to treat me as an adult just born yesterday and teach me what it's like to grow up and be a beautiful human being.

Despite earning a Graduate Equivalency Degree several years ago by taking a test read to me, I didn't know how to read or write until recently after going to school for six months and completing grades first through third. The school experience gave me hope I'd never experienced before that I could make choices for myself and learn about life from you, Mr. Clarke.

All the alters fear looking into that place of darkness as they fear knowing the truth. I've been looking at myself for 2 ½ years. Still, I feel terror beyond imagination when I come up against my soul's darkest place, knowing how my violators brutalized me and the rage and hate accompanying it.

I saw a tiny light in the darkness and sensed someone was there, but I was terrified of the truth, so I shut down to avoid being overwhelmed. However, part of me wanted to know what caused this terror. I looked back into the darkness and felt horror but I wanted to understand the meaning of that light. I saw a small child in the dark and thought how alone she must be. I'm that child, fear myself, and don't want to know that child today. In time I'll remember her, but not today.

Your friend, I hope, Leena.

Lynne added to this letter: I took great care to please and be accepted by others by losing myself. The fear is that I must risk losing people I care for so much by allowing both the good and bad parts of myself. I've always accepted others for what they are and forgiven them for what they did. Now it's time to esteem and forgive me for what I believed. I think accepting myself is the most challenging thing I'll need to do. That means not taking on how others see me or how I'd like to see me but accepting me as I am.

Lynne

When I finally began seeing Mr. Clarke in 1968, counselor Carolyn attended the sessions but gradually weaned me off her. Mr. Clarke referred me to a female therapist from time to time for girl matters, like menstruation. He also conducted group therapy with three other MPD clients and me.

At this time, I could name 103 active alters in addition to non-human imaginary friends: a smiley face, a door, and stuffies. All but three of the alters signed a one-year therapeutic contract with Mr. Clarke, consisting of the following 14 agreements: We'll mutually respect one another, be on time for appointments, not put thoughts into one another's minds, have lots of mutually agreeable safe touch, and call emergency response only if needed. We'll behave responsibly, not pity, not leave the relationship without mentioning it first, not lie, not use hospitals without prior discussion, and not assume the other knows something just because we do. Finally, we'll ask if there's a question or doubt about anything, we'll all have the right to say no to others or ourselves, and we won't kill. Winter, who we'd restored by now, and Dee declined to sign the contract. Seer said maybe later. By July 1968, we'd named 242 alters.

Not shown is my drawing of a young Mr. Clarke, captioned, "Helpful but wouldn't see me improve," which included a portrait of me with a black heart on my vest captioned, "Us" and "Scared." I wrote on this drawing my following concerns about counseling: I'll find out I'm no good, and that's why I had to create so many alters. The bad will take over, and we can't be friends. I'll find the secrets and won't like myself. I can't show how badly I hurt and can't handle things. I might find I'm no good within as I thought. I'll remember something so evil I can't take it and decompose. I won't try and won't move ahead. I'll see nothing left of me when I look deep enough. I'll find out it was my fault and that I'm evil, just like the others. Finally, I'm scared that Mr. Clarke won't help anymore.

1969 Therapy with Mr. Clarke

Life with The Mother
At a recent family gathering, my younger sister, Mandy, spoke of her memory of The Mother humiliating us. My brother, Buster, said his only good childhood memories came from Grandma's ranch. He said he'd forgotten most of the rest, except for the beatings, all the men coming and going, The Mother's absence for days at a time, his taking care of us kids, and The Mother demanding all his earned money until he was 25 years old. He added that he's mad at The Mother, sadly, doesn't miss her, and that she should've gone to jail for what she did to us. I told him it's natural to forget and that it was too much for him to be an adult at age four, especially considering how much The Mother kicked us around. Did I say it right?" [You did, Leena.]

Lynne made three 1969 collages, not shown. Her Christmas Past collage includes a woman chained to a cross, sawing her wrist, and the words and phrases: "Evil, pain, survivors (people America forgot), when to forgive and forget, and, no more." Her collage of Christmas Present includes a crying doll and a picture of Dorothy as a young child, her stepdad, sister, and mother. Her collage of Christmas Future has an angelic figure inside a heart-shaped cutout and the words and phrases: "feel the power within you, on the wings of love, sweet dreams, and hope."

Alter Dynamics
On the back of the Christmas Present collage, Feena, an 8-year-old girl, made while living with Anthony to help absorb the horror of his satanic practices, who often trembles and rocks from side to side, wrote: "Three men in a tub. Two got dead. One lost his head.

They all went to hell. Rib! Rib! I got your rib. Stay the night, and you're dead." Fenna wrote backward: "To remember, hear, or tell is to die." She then wrote about Twinkle, a 5-year-old girl conceived because we saw stars when we got hit on the head: "Twinkle, twinkle little girl, how I wonder how you are. Up above the world so high, I wish I might; I wish I'd die." Lastly, Fenna wrote next to two stars, a quarter moon, and St. Peter's cross: "The one has come in our Lord's way."

Alter Dynamics

Tara wrote: I am Tara. My people are in danger, so I am writing to you, Mr. Clarke. Amy and the Little Ones came to see me. Their fears are great. They cannot handle it all because it is going too fast. It has to halt. It is not time for my people to know this thing. It must stop. I feel great danger, and my people need it to cease. If it keeps advancing, my people will go to the four winds and into darkness and not return. It is death. It is the end of all things for my people. You told them to trust me, so I ask you to trust my words. It is the truth. The peace I give my people does not go to them when their fear is this great. [Slow down.]

We Cluster wrote to Mr. Clarke to further introduce themselves: We like honesty. We do as you do, so have healthy boundaries. Don't push when asked not to. Take care of yourself, be open-minded and guide us, but let us go where we need to go. We don't lie but pretend things aren't bad because reality is too harsh. We seek the truth, our memory is accurate, we're intuitive, we've been to death and back and have seen much negativity, so we know what we don't want, but we've never seen positive. We need motivation. We avoid potentially disturbing issues if we feel they'll overwhelm us, we're building boundaries, and we believe all things are relative. When referring to us, we don't like pity or the word "special." We love the ocean. We have lots of questions and and don't trust ourselves, so we're unsure who's trustworthy, and we blame ourselves for being hurt when others lie to us because we believe every word others speak. We avoid mental hospitals, get confused and lose time, need help to be the best we can be, and as we learn from you, you'll attain from us what you can't get from books. Finally, we might have trouble paying you from time to time.

Lynne wrote I like Mr. Clarke because he understands why I'm confused.

Punky wrote I like that he's kind and hugs delightfully.

Cheri wrote, I like that he asks before hugging me, but I don't trust him yet.

Mary printed, he chat with me a lot but no write bad things down.

Sarah wrote I got a good feeling from him, and I think he can help us.

Suze printed: Clarke talk with me too. Annie sad he couldn't chat with her. She want to speak also. Ask how she can.

Bo-Bo printed upside down and backward: He no think we dumb. He like my printing. We like Mr. Clarke.

One from the Boy Cluster printed, he no get mad.

Finally, someone wrote, I want to know if he'll give us group rates.

In a letter from Lynne and several alters, Lynne wrote: I don't like The Mother. She scares me because I fear she'll get mad and hurt me again. I can't stand up to her and always give in.

Mary printed: I c you + two ladies. I no talk. I want to cry. I like to live in one lady. I want to speak, but I don't know how to tell about yucky inside me.

Sam printed: How the others said it? Our inside like a cat's tail on fire. I don't know inside or outside of us.

Meme printed: help us. they broke us. too tiny to help. Punky know a lot of the story. ask her if she know about bad things. [So many are "switching" so fast.] {"Switching" (switching) is when one alter shifts control of the shared body to another, sometimes deliberate, sometimes not.}

Pam wrote for Mary: I can't be happy. I have unbearable pain.

Feeler wrote: Is it possible to let the pain out and not feel it, or feel it without reacting? We want to get over the past hurts and self-hate, but we don't want to get overwhelmed. [I'll help you with this.]

Us Cluster wrote: We're reading that childhood sexual abuse has a devastating impact, such as loss of innocence, betrayal of trust, and feeling unloved and unworthy of love. Reading that exploitation reaches the child's soul and tears it apart brought overwhelming emotions. Our emotions became more complicated and painful once we realized the torturer was The Mother. Still, part of us wants The Mother. [I know.] If mothers have sex with kids, can that be called a great hurt? [Yes, a massive injury.] Can it make you wish to be so ugly no one will want you, parts of your body were missing, or you're dead? [Yes.]

We think if The Mother did something like that, it'd surely tear our souls apart! With her, it wasn't sexual. She just wanted to show us what men want and how they hurt us. That isn't sex, you know! Can any loss hurt? [Yes, it can hurt.] Mr. Clarke, we'd like to hear a bit about your life, how you felt, and how you handled it. Our other counselors did this, and it was helpful. [Okay.] We're getting close to those holding the pain. Great shame and guilt are keeping us from sharing about certain atrocities. [Then we need to find a way to let them out.]

Sharing our thoughts and emotions with you takes a load off. [Good, Leena.] What's expected in sex? [We'll discuss this if you want to.] Is sex always "the girl gets the short end of the stick"? [That isn't the rule.] We don't like being tied up, hurt, or forced. We want warm-ups like caressing and kissing and then working toward the private areas. [That makes sense.] Our weirdness is thinking about being in the woods, and having sex in the warm rain. Is that a nature call? [Ha] We'd like to forget the past and find out how ordinary girls have sex. [It sounds like you're learning just fine.] Isn't being in love about enjoying the company of each other and not just sex? [It is.] My offenders overloaded me with shame mostly, and I had no one. Can you imagine that? [I think so.] I get that you're saying I need to love myself.

Tamara wrote: I need to know whether you're durable and won't let me rub off on you. It'll take one who's self-assured and brave to help me. [I know this is a painful trust process.] I'm asking you to go against hell itself. I need to understand with no bull, can you do this? [I think so.] You've only seen a few of us. Our hate and anger are a thousand-fold. [Maybe I'll fail. Maybe I won't be enough. But you'll fail if you don't find out.]

It helps to tell you the truth even if I don't believe it myself. Someone can accept it for me for now. The priest told me I was a child of sin and to never lay eyes on him again. I wished that man of God to go to hell! [I disagree with that priest, Tamara.]

We need to learn how to deal with people. Right? [Yep.] Hugs from Rick are confusing. We never know if he wants to hug or wants sex. [He has to take responsibility for his desires and state them clearly.]

Hurter printed: Don't know how to feel without dying. They so big and heavy it seems we going to die. I think maybe we will!

Others helped Deand write: Just because we've been whores all our lives doesn't mean we want to get into your pants. Maybe we want a relationship based on more than sex. [We both want something besides sex. That's why we're doing pretty well on this journey.] We think you're good-looking and have a nice butt, but we keep that to ourselves because we don't want a misunderstanding. [Okay.] We also believe you have funny toes and knob knees, but they suit you. [Thanks.]

I know you need to protect yourself from the whoring women you see and assure us you're not trying something. We whores should recognize a "come on" better than most, don't you think? [Probably, but you're not a whore. Even if you're referring to past sexual acts, that isn't who you are, but only what you believe.] You've always been a gentleman, and we assume you'll continue to be. [I will.]

I've been so scared my heart has jumped out of my chest. I've had to resist my natural reaction to others, or they caused my life to be a living hell. [Now it's time to learn more functional responses, Leena.] I didn't think my dilemma would ever end. [You experienced a staggering amount of brutality.]

I'm hurt, sad, and confused. [This is a healthy release of new emotions.] I've thought of taking care of Anthony, who's ill, because my heart wants to help, and I care, but at the same time, my mind wants to stay far away from him. [This is a normal and healthy mix of emotions.] How can I still want to ease his pain? Do I do what my heart or head dictates? [Healthy people respond with both.]

Every night I fear Rick will want us and whether I can control myself enough to please him. [This is the problem.] How do I have sex with Rick and not yell, get angry and push him away? It isn't a problem sometimes, but this week it was. [You're changing, Leena.]

Bad Girl wrote: I think it's about time you knew I'm evil. When my mother's boyfriend came into my room and began groping me, I told him to take my sister first, and he did. [Children sometimes do what's necessary to survive because they're terrified. We can do some things to help you heal from shame.] That's not the first time I've done that. You say we have a kind heart. You don't know us. [To survive, even those with loving hearts sometimes behave selfishly.]

You suggested that before we go to sleep, we ask Tara to think of a way to forgive ourselves for telling the men to go to our sister instead of us. We'd like to believe we're honorable, but we're so full of evil that there's no room for good.

We divide among other alters the thoughts and emotions that came from what happened to us, and then cut off from each other to avoid being overwhelmed. [Yes, I know.] Otherwise, it'd cause a chain reaction, which would destroy us. We know the generalities of what happened to us but not the details. We figure that you can fill in our emotions, thoughts, and reactions. [It sounds like you're doing an excellent job pacing yourself.]

Dorothy and her sister called the police when their mother left marks on them. The police believed The Mother's lies. Dorothy knew then she was on her own, and nobody would help her. At last, I'm beginning to recall my past. [Ah, the dawn of light!] I can never make up for what I did. [Yes, you can.] It's unforgivable if you know you're wrong. [It's forgivable, Leena.] After The Mother marked me, neither men nor The Mother wanted me as much.

My memory is in pieces because I can't hold it all. Punky wants people to know it was she who raped all the men. Cheri locks us up so people can't see us because she can't handle that we're real. Lynne was that bastard's lover, and Anne was beyond crazy in that she became paranoid and heard voices. [It's a lot to hold.]

James pinched girls' butts and once slapped Punky. James squeezed a guy's rear on an airplane, but we had our real kids on our lap, so the passenger thought one of them did it.

Us Cluster wrote: We can't handle all our past at once. It'd break us for sure. In time we'll get to those Hidden Ones with the details, which will bring the hell back, and we fear that day. [We'll go at your pace.]

We're reading that we need to learn to establish and defend boundaries and fight fair by asking others to change their behavior if it doesn't feel right to us and vice versa. [We'll talk about boundaries.]

People took our sex and made us cry, but at least we could pretend it was just a hug of warmth, a smile just for us, and all the love we wanted. We begged them not to leave because we wouldn't know the monster's whereabouts. When something reminds us of what we are, we want the peace of death. [Sad. You gave up too much to get basic needs met.]

Tara states we're all one, yet not one, and if we can't find peace in "The Light" (The Light), then look through Sarah, and we'll find Tara. Some alters believe The Light is soul, goodness, force, energy, and spirit. Others believe it to be the house of God. One reckons it's the place of souls, and some surmise a desperate soul formulated it out of the need to know a place unspoiled and pure. Most believe it means goodness and that all things are one.

We've noticed that the word "knowing" causes us to switch. [The term "knowing" reminds you of some aspect of your traumatic past and triggers stress.] {A "trigger" (trigger) is anything stimulating a series of thoughts or reminding one of some aspect of one's traumatic past and could cause a response like panic attacks, flashbacks, or another type of stress.}

Shame and fear built the foundation of our child alters, and they know it. [It's good you know this.]

We Cluster wrote: You said your office is a room for us to be us. We're trying to loosen our control and be ourselves. [It's scary, isn't it?] We must maintain self-control and look like other people because we sense their uneasiness when we're ourselves and aren't hiding. We fear what other people will think of us if we lose control. [Ask them.]

1970 Therapy with Mr. Clarke

Life with The Mother

Little Ones wanted happiness and to think and learn. Instead, they got emptiness, pain, and nothing good. The Mother called them dumb bitches and whores, never allowed them to play, and continuously barked, "Do as I say." Little Ones helped with the following drawing depicting childhood memories of The Mother, her boyfriends, and of life with Anthony:

Fenna's writing begins with Remember is to die. Sadness, fear, hate, and badness are emphasized. Lisa printed backward on this drawing, Kill Me.

My mother always hurt me. Her rules were the law, and kids had no rights. I'm still afraid of and dislike being touched by her. If I didn't have a body, I wouldn't hurt, and then I could love her.

Lynne's sketch, which includes The Mother torturing us, representing the number of tears and broken hearts of Little Ones, follows:

Most of our full memories of The Mother are from nine months to three years of age. After that, we only recall bits and pieces. [The recollections will come, Leena.]

Mary and Annie printed: It mommy birthday today. Some are scared the dark cause monsters come at night. We scared. Leena got us movies for tonight.

Suze printed, our tadpoles!

Punky Lil printed, I want to love.

Sarah wrote, I love you but stay away, or you'll die also.

Punky wrote: Someone is saying we're deathly afraid of sleeping too much. It's sinful. Another is saying they're ashamed if we sleep too much because it shows selfishness and wasting time. The Mother will think we're up to something.

A group of alters wrote: We write to you about these things because we're too ashamed to tell you, Mr. Clarke. We don't want to be who we are, so we pretend. Our mother said to act like a lady with brains, so we faked until nothing was authentic. Now we're nothing. We're dead. Our mother was a force to be reckoned with throughout our childhood and still is in our adult life. She once came after one of her boyfriends with a knife to make him a girl.

Talk about being sidetracked. We still haven't called a doctor, even though we know we need to. Most of us are scared of The Mother and men, even men doctors. We don't want what we recall about them to be true because we want to be nice kids. We also don't want pain and anger.

Signed: Leah, Beth, James, Paul, Annie, Amy, Seven-and-Three- Quarters, Pony, Sarah, Ann, Cheri, Sherry, Rachel, Carrie, George, and Pamela Boy.

Life with Husband and Boyfriends

Anthony would be sweet to us but alternately humiliate and hurt us. [He would hurt you like your mother did, Leena?]

Punky wrote: I want a pet to love. It hurt badly to give away my puppy, but I didn't want him to die, and Rick intended to kill him. I like going to the puppy store and watching the puppies showing off for you, saying, "Take me, take me."

Various young alters printed: We writing you in the car. It a cold and foggy morning. Rick is driving the ocean route so we can see its beauty. Suzie Q pee her pants in the redwoods. They's berry big trees. Punky Lil, Punky, Angel, and Annie, find a blue and tan crab at the ocean, and Timothy A. Bradshaw and Charles find seashells and white wood.

Mary printed: We see a great sea beast too. It on a bolder and look like a seal lying on it back. We see elk. They like deers, a herd of them with six baby elk. Timothy wanted to catch a whale and take it home, but Rick said no. George said the road turned too much. He say, oh crap! Pennie and Alice, as Sam, said ocean pretty. We saw big white rock that Iris want to draw. The white stuff is bird poop. Today the rest of us get to come out to see the ocean and play in it.

Pam wrote for Punky Lil and her: We saw the ocean and the fog coming over the mountain like a fluffy white waterfall. We waded past our calves. It was scary when the waves went out because they took the sand from under our feet. The ocean was cold but fun. We saw lots of sand, cypress trees, and redwoods, one being 356 feet high. It was 1500 years old. We'd never seen the ocean and weren't ready to leave it behind. We wanted to see the sun go down but didn't have time. We cried when we had to leave, knowing that, most likely, we'd never see the ocean again.

Timothy A. Bradshaw printed, I saw a crab and wanted to catch a whale but couldn't.

Cheri wrote, I say why see it and be sad because you can't see it again?

Meme printed: I was there too. It very pretty.

Us Cluster wrote we wish the trip could have been longer because we needed the rest badly.

Mary printed, me get dirty but me no like the dirt.

Sarah wrote it was fantastic looking at what God created for our eyes to behold.

Bo-Bo printed backward the last comment about our trip to the ocean, I not like the campfires or the dark, but I like everything else.

We think our relationship with Rick is one-sided. We assume people discuss things, plan, and have future expectations when they get together. Rick doesn't. We'd like to know if we fabricated our beliefs or if people do what we believe. [Many do, Leena.]

We're still having trouble in the sex department and difficulty asking to be loved. We ask for sex instead. Last night, we asked Rick for sex because we'd been scared and wanted someone to hold to feel safe. He said later. Later that night, he couldn't sleep, so we asked if we could do anything. When we stopped and tried to sleep, Rick pressured us to continue and finish him off, and we became frightened. We declined, but it was too late. We began crying and wanted to flee, so we got in our car but had nowhere to go.

We continued crying as we remembered what Uncle did to us. The Mother always insisted that Uncle was just friendly and paid for the roof over our heads. Rick asks us to be friendly, just like the men mother brought home did. Did we convince ourselves we didn't want a nice guy when we grew up? [That's a good question, Leena.]

We're scared of Rick and don't know what to do. One of us says to be quiet, and he won't get mad at us. A second one whispers, run and hide. A third stammers that we're going to show him we're not scared. A fourth says we're afraid. A fifth wants to finish it. A sixth thinks we could go back home, but we don't have a home. A seventh says to clean the house and make everything right so he won't get angry.

We're quiet most of the time, but that upsets Rick even more. He snarls, "I know you want to say something, so go ahead and say it." Our goals are to keep our sons, animals, and ourselves safe from his wrath and not get angry. Our group counselor says to wait until Rick calms down and then talk to him, but he stays mad for a long time. Mr. Clarke, you said we take away from our self-worth when we don't speak our minds to him. We think that's true because we feel shame and unresolved anger when we keep peace at all costs.

Our group counselor told us to tell Rick we'll leave him if he's verbally or physically abusive. We did eventually confront Rick, but it went nowhere. We put up with worse for many years, so we believe we can handle Rick's abuse. What if we see it wrong? We hate ourselves for being weak and scared. Where would we go? How would we pay for a place to live? We're afraid to leave and scared to stay. Help! Help! Help! [I'll help, Leena.]

Life in my Household

Punky wrote: I got a kitten. I think it's a girl. She's a little "ding dong," too. I've been irritable lately, but I don't know why. Perhaps it's because my son, who I renamed Jim, misbehaves and objects to restriction. I want my sons to be happy and not have the pain I've endured. I view my job to be helping them grow up to be responsible, fair, and caring people who like themselves.

Lynne wrote: I'm now learning to believe in, accept, and love myself, including my strengths and weaknesses. For years I've told myself I'm relevant, and I've begun to believe it somewhat. I want to be a good mother and also have my own life. I didn't get love, but I want my kids to have it. I hope you see the difference between letting go of a child and giving up on a child. [I do.]

A mix of alters wrote: Rick called us a liar today. He later pointed his finger at us while asking for help with something. We froze, thinking we were in trouble or Rick would do something abusive like Anthony used to do. We remember other men asking us to help with something, which also scared us badly.

Alter Dynamics

Cathleen wrote: Love is only pain. I want no part of it. [Love isn't pain but can cause pain.]

Ann printed: We not supposed to hate adults. We supposed to obey and love them. That the right way. We never been good.

Punky Lil printed: I stay with my G-ma. I'm Punky Lil, a little faut (fart). G-ma wash my mouth out with soap cause I say bad word. I made bubbles with the soap cause it was fun. It no taste good tho. G-ma say I don't know what to do with you, you little faut. Eating soap isn't supposed to be fun. I cried, and G-ma say, oh hell, ladies say bad word some times.

G-pa make me feel yucky when he scold me. I want G-pa and G-ma only to be kind and loving.

G-ma is kind to me and lets me play with toys. We laugh, dance, hug, hop, and get "dolled up" by putting on boots and painting our lips and cheeks before going to town or picking up G-pa from work.

G-ma allows tree climbing, but my mother doesn't. G-ma got me a rocking chair, but my mother burned it. Andy came out and told me to let it go.

At G-ma's, I feed cows, garden, camp, fish, run through sprinklers, and color with crayons. I also get to cook and make fudge with G-ma. G-ma sets me on the counter to get the ingredients from the shelves.

When I grow up, I want to have a farm with animals. Animals love you and let you pet them. G-ma has Betsy the cow, baby cows, and baby chickens. I get to pet, hug, and hold them, and they love me. G-ma tells me I'll make a good mother. The farm warms my heart.

G-ma takes me to ride the merry-go-round at the county fair. G-pa goes there to get cows. I hate vegetables, but ice cream and cake are good for you.

I take baths in G-ma's sink and like smelling her coffee in the morning. G-ma has a big fireplace and a large kettle with witch's brew, her secret weapon. She also has an eye in the back of her head. My feelings get hurt when my G-ma scolds me, but she gives me a soda after, and I feel better. [You still spend time with your G-ma?] Yes.

Us Cluster wrote: We've been thinking about how different we feel in our MPD group because other members know their inside alters better. We hide ours. Also, others have more grown-up alters than we do. We have lots of children alters, and kids aren't supposed to talk while adults speak. We feel stupid because we never learned to talk about life's matters. For example, we want to talk about our real dad to determine if someone hurt him as they did us.

We keep our feelings to ourselves because we have difficulty sharing. Most other group members are terrified of us, don't like us, and don't want us around when we talk about bad memories that still hurt. We don't know how to talk about emotions without crying and getting angry. We want to speak in our group, but don't want to cry like babies, so we get mad as grown-ups do. [It's okay to cry.]

Little Ones printed: You tell the girls for us. Okay? We no want to be different or make them hurt too. We mostly small, but we have big hurts, and we scared big also. The others in the group not afraid of you like we are, Mr. Clarke. We think maybe we not supposed to be scared of you.

We-Two Cluster alters wrote and printed: We're sorry that people hurt those girls and sad that they cry, get angry, and are broken emotionally like us. I no write them names down. They can avoid being hurt by bad people by learning to love themselves. That's what we learned from the other group. We heard them, so we learned too. We no love us. That why we cut, no talk, no share, and think bad people are only ones to love and understand us. But we know if we fix our emotional makeup, it'll change our physical appearance. Then we'll be safe. And happy too. We're full of terrible emotions and recollections and don't know how to get rid of them. So lots of memories bring emotions and then more recollections and more feelings. Then we create new alters. It won't stop. We switch so much we get lost about who's who and what day or time it is.

Mary printed: You no like me. I evil. I no like me. I sad too. I scared. I want no one. You hit me also? I do good. Having MPD means I'm a survivor, a real human being, and I don't have to hide.

Annie printed: Even those who don't have pain can understand pain, being used, losing something special, mistrust, and feeling like two people in one, like being a husband and a dad.

Punky wrote in Punky and Tara's letter to Mr. Clarke: Save The One. She must live, she's pretty, and she comes, but not my mother, who was born and will die by hate. Trust kills us. We believed to be happy one day, to be the real us, we had to save a part of us that no one broke so we'd be pretty internally and on the outside. We named this part Sunshine, who's the size of a grain of sand. Sunshine led to Leena. [Thanks for explaining this, Punky.]

Tara wrote the last three paragraphs of the letter as follows: I am "The Healer." In our relationship, Mr. Clarke, there'll be healing of the soul. Until then, go in peace. [What?] The soul got broken into one large and two tiny pieces. The smaller pieces are the child alters, and the large one is Leena, the shell you speak with. They are many but one. They are together but apart. The child knows but does not.

I want to explain about names. To name something is to separate it from The Light. You put it aside under the name. There are lots of alters without names because we ran out. They're the same but not the same. They know but don't know. That's how they lived so long. [You're saying that nothing is clear.]

They know each other, but they all have "The Not Knowing," which keeps them sane. With this knowledge, I can help others. All of your pain is mine, and mine is yours. The Light is a place Leena goes when she meditates.

Pamela Boy, known as "The Doorway to Hell," wrote: I had to deal with Anthony's evilness by keeping the baby killers away to avoid getting contaminated. At some point, giving in to others becomes overwhelming. I'm out when we get trounced on due to people's unfairness, untruthfulness or when they otherwise hurt us. It's time to put an end to it. We've lived our lives for others and hoped to get some little thing, anything, in return, and were grateful when we did. Never again! Our counselors have taught us that we should "give to get" for both parties in a relationship to feel okay. [Thanks for sharing this, Pamela Boy.]

Dusty and Mathew printed: Mathew, that me, and Dusty too. We're the Nobodies, along with others. We're not much of anything. That all we tell. The worst of all things happened! Our coffee pot broke, and we don't have our "wake-up juice!" Leena got camping coffee pot out, so coffee on the way! Oh, boy!

Therapy Not Included Under Other Headings

We Cluster wrote: For 36 years when others have injured us, we've mistakenly believed we were hurting ourselves because we trusted our mother and others not to hurt us. How can we change this pattern to loving ourselves and still loving others? [That'll come in time.]

We've had unspeakable things done to us and have a heap of hate. We know we're evil because you're not supposed to hate. We despise ourselves because we're to blame for all of it. [None of it was your fault.]

Someone in our head is repetitively declaring we must have balance, but our mother told us games are bad and rot your brain. Mother would snarl, "You always play by yourself, which isn't healthy." Our walls are falling. Put them back now.

Punky added, got to have balance. [How?]

Margie wrote: Another's pain hurts worse than my own. I'm Gatekeeper of the Heart, along with others. Our love removes pain. [You're trying to take responsibility for others choosing to relieve their pain.] I don't want to feel. I want to be tough. [We're human. Humans feel.]

I wrote myself the following note: Use counselor Grady and Mr. Clarke to discuss my son's leaving. Use Mr. Clarke and counselor Sal to discuss Rick's anger. Joking during group counseling isn't funny if it's painful. Do early childhood work. Keep it to myself, act normal, and play crazy because they'll detest me if I tell all. Remember that each alter holds pieces of memory to enable me to deny my past so I can cope. Talk to Mr. Clarke about my taking on more work with the victims' program, and help with my son's not returning home because nothing ever comes back.

Mr. Clarke, I fear that my release of feelings is hazardous and potentially deadly. To survive, I've had to control my emotions and physical sensations. Having those emotions will only confuse me more, resulting in insanity from which I won't return. How do I avoid going insane if I allow feelings I can't control? Besides, I don't have a right to painful feelings since my punishment was justified because I'm evil. [Let's discuss this, Leena.]

Silly Sally wrote: We all want to get better, but the risk is high. There's a thin line between sanity and insanity for us. Others have repeatedly told us we're wicked and want to be hurt or we'd behave. We believe this is true in our hearts, but other alters ask what's real. There's no truth or reality but only perception; therefore, since our minds declare we're evil, who's to say we're not? This thinking has caused us to go insane in the past and shut down. To prevent this, we believe both sides by playacting. Did people we love hurt us, or were they only teaching us? Our past is only half real when we playact, so we can handle what happened yet remain kind moving forward while leaving the past behind. Pretending is our way of staying safe while getting the help we need.

Jennifer wrote: That's only halfway! It's all or nothing! I need to also state that we were desecrated more than we know. If we have problems handling what we've always known, how do we remember more wreckage? We can process thoughts in lots of ways, but we only process emotions with emotions.

Punky wrote: We fashioned a verbal picture of our inner workings to show you, Mr. Clarke. Before Cheri, Dorothy was our boss. Dorothy couldn't make us all happy, so we divided ourselves and forgot the others. Then Cheri came, and we got lost. [One boss can't do it all]. Then half of us came together and generated one big body, but then we fought and broke up into individuals who didn't know or talk to each other. Some are scared, and some are crying. We don't know how to fashion a boss that can do things right. To avoid overloading one, perhaps we should create four bosses. Which of us do you need to work with first, Mr. Clarke? [You choose.]

We don't feel so vulnerable and scared now that we've shown ourselves to you. We'll try to have Leena out more. Someone has to help us overcome. We get tired of fighting a war within about trusting. Rick insists I can trust him, but I maintain I can't. Some alters get angry with Rick and want to leave him. We don't want to deal with our past hurts or even those with people in our present.

We tell people about our MPD because we want them to accept all of us and not just our shell. Then, if they say they like us, we believe them. We thought we could handle ourselves but now are unsure. Sometimes we get lost while driving, vomit during sex, and often feel like giving up and dying.

When we were little and cried, people told us to go away. So, we decided to hide our pain and act adult so they wouldn't push us away. Presently we only play with grown-ups if they can accept our childishness and keep secrets.

My counselors have asked me to call them before I act out, like cutting, and I've advised them I have a problem with that because I need to look as if I can handle everything. Some didn't want me around when I told them I needed help. They seemed to prefer clients who could manage life. [It's healthy to request assistance, Punky.]

I believed you, Mr. Clarke, when you said you'd return my after-hours calls and that I could depend on you if I needed you. It's easy to handle small matters when we know help is there when we need it; however, I couldn't reach you recently about a more significant issue, which led to my feeling alone, a lousy emotion for me. As a result, reaching out next time will be more challenging. Your dependability now has a tiny dent. Please don't be upset with me. I still trust you and believe you mean well, but I go away if I lose trust. [I want to keep your faith in me.]

Angry and Hurt wrote: We remember starting fires, getting mad and hurting things, and hating and hurting us. We don't want to have emotions or die, but some will kill us rather than injure people. Our numbers have increased.

Feeler wrote: We're scared to death of this healing you're doing with us because we fear emotions more than anything. It hurts every time one of us talks to you because you stimulate our feelings. We told you we could handle anything, but when you asked us to re-live our past, all we could hear from within was, "Oh, hell no!" Hide, run away, or kill us rather than feel our mountain of fear, loneliness, or other emotional pain, and never be a mother again. We can't adequately explain the magnitude of our fear and loneliness. There are lots of alters, yet we feel very much alone. Our out-of-control emotional pain snowballs once it's perceived by even one of us because we're feeling for hundreds at once. It's too much to ask of one person. Which one of us will lose again? Maybe for us to have emotions, we need to hide from one another, but then we'd be lonely.

Imagine strolling down Main Street, and suddenly, you can detect what all those around you feel. The older man across the street is afraid of time, and the little kid is scared because he's lost. The wife who got beaten last night is scared to go home. The man in the store is worried because he lost his job, and then there's your own out-of-control fear. There are even more people in a restaurant. You feel their emotions until you can't tell one from the other. Can you imagine the burden of having all those overwhelming emotions? I've lived with this and fear it might return. [Go at a pace you can manage, Feeler.]

An Angry One wrote: I know if I try getting better, I'll first get worse and hurt others or myself. They can put me in the hospital for as long as they want to, and then we might lose Lynne's sons and never be a mother again.

Mary printed: That won't happen! I lose too much, and I not want to fail my sons or fail to keep me. You can't make up for lost time, broken hearts, or lost dreams.

Lynne wrote: I've seen lots of women lose their children and are still fighting to get them back years later. I don't have many years left with mine, and I want my time with them.

Robot wrote: I'm doing my best to make it up to my sons. I owe them so much. I'm trying to let myself heal and grow too, but not if it'll cause my sons more hurt. No more hurt!

Mary printed, nobody need more hurt.

Bo-Bo printed backward, stop the hurt, please.

Tiffany printed: Mr. Clarke, I talk on phone to my mother. I love Leena. I can speak to her. I want to hided like she do. I very bad and scared. I want to play too, but I be polite girl and say no thank you so I no get whipping. I cold and I like binkies. Nobody like girls who say yes. Big people ask for what they want, but they no want you to do things tho. Annie my mommy. I talk for us. We want to be us, but we can't because we scared you not like us or help us. [I like you, and I'll help.]

Mary printed, I hurt too and want to cry.

Us Cluster wrote we're having nightmares and dreaming about you, Mr. Clarke.

Tiffany printed Annie here and a Quiet One here.

Alice, as Sam, printed, no one doing good.

Hurter printed: I told my mother that her boyfriend and I played "Mommy and Daddy." He hurted me. I want to hurt him, so I tell. And I got hurted, but he no got hurted. My mother loved him more.

A Good One printed: No more hurt, please. Let me die.

Us Cluster wrote: We can't think. We've forgotten how to do things and forgotten time and days.

Cheri wrote in her tiny handwriting to avoid being seen: Alters from the Baby Cluster are taking over. We created them to help us suffer from our mother's abuse, like the broom and burning. They can't remember it all before they cry and disappear. We hear the lady snarling at them, and then the pain comes. We know but don't know. It's like watching television, but you sense it's real. It's like being half girl and half something else, and sometimes not even half. What's happening?

Cheri informed us that her job is to protect what's real and that you're entitled to your thoughts and emotions. She added that there's no wrong way and that we're not crazy, just different. We were talking the baby talk when we awoke this morning. Maybe it's because we're afraid since we're going to the dentist, or The Mother is mad at us. We know we're scared. [I agree with Cheri. Wow, Leena! The dentist and your mother!]

What happened to the babies who died? The minister told me broken babies don't go to heaven because God wants pretty babies. [He lied.]

Paul wrote: I feel hurt but don't know from what. I'm trying to do the right thing for the other alters, but it isn't working. Susie Q. peed her pants in the restaurant. The alter babies keep crying. Timothy A. Bradshaw drove our car at 90 mph. I've been having nightmares and can't sleep. The naughty girl came out twice. I want to get angry but fight not to. My sons get upset, fight and then get along for a while before battling again. We can't handle all this at once. [You feel this is too big for you, Paul?]

Tiffany printed: My kitty gone three days, I think he's died or hurt. So much happen.

Angry and Hurt wrote: It's okay that you don't have the answers, Mr. Clarke. Just let the kind heart talk to the broken heart. Tara wrote that the correct answer is a bandage, while the heart-to-heart cures forever.

One of the Good Ones wrote: May you go to Jesus Christ, and may the Lord accept your soul. If not, you can have my soul. It's lost for the most part, but the meager virtue left might get you in. [This is a generous offer, but you didn't surrender your soul.]

Sunshine wrote: Now you know why the babies don't talk or live, can't be saved, have no evil thoughts, don't get angry, control themselves, and have secrets. You also know my promise to them. I'll be the life of the babies as long as I live. I pray I'm doing right by letting you know, my friend. I'm giving you the power to doctor us.

Carol wrote: Men have used me with the information my mother or I revealed. I don't know what a healthy relationship with a man is. You can teach us this, Mr. Clarke. Other people have hurt us so much we're scared to give you this much trust. [I see your point, Carol.] I'm not the woman you see. I'm a brand new baby with so much to learn and understand. We learned from Sarah, Tara, and others, to face what the brutality did to us and go on from there to mend the broken pieces, find self-worth, find and accept the unique person we are, and become all our creator meant us to be. We're hoping you can help us reach for the stars, Mr. Clarke. [What a treat!]

I can trust my stuffie but not a man. My stuffie is the perfect mate. It's cheap and washable. If it's mean, I can put it in the closet and get a different one, and, well, I'm sure it wouldn't complain about being "horny." We only know how to take care of others, but our stuffies take care of us, and we learn from them to love without fear. [That's wonderful, Leena!] I slept 16 hours today, and I'm still tired. Do you know why? [Energy is rising.]

Even though all alters aren't aware of the others, it impacts us all when something happens to one of us. Some feel it, some see it, and everyone takes part. The book you recommended described MPD as follows: "MPD is a 'revolving door syndrome,' and when this door gets going, it's the most frantic confusing time of all because the door goes around when the going gets rough. The alters come and go rapidly, yet the almost constant changes are fully formed." When things get rough, we change so frequently we're not sure if we're coming or going. [Yes, this is scary, Leena.] Reading this book helped me allow myself to hate my parents.

Alters are calling me all night, crying, and screaming. I tremble and hyperventilate at even the thought of leaving my room, let alone going into the world. I think new alters with new recollections are coming. Sarah knows something is approaching that's going to shake us up.

Our body acts like any one of our alters at any given time. People ask what's wrong and why we're behaving that way because that's not us. [Nothing is wrong. You're re-connecting.] When they call us by name, we get lost. We've learned to say we're sorry or are having a bad week or bad hair day to cover up that we're someone else when we're called on. [You're doing a good job, Leena.] We keep our pain hidden so our physical appearance doesn't look ugly.

Tara, Sarah, and Leah wrote: Our mother told us we were dirty and nasty and shamed us by making us eat poop and wear poopy pants. Anthony humiliated us similarly and was heartless. One time when we cut, he told us to take pills or leap off a cliff instead so he didn't have to clean up the mess. We'd made Anthony and our mother giants and us diminutive, but they're more manageable when we separate them. [It's great you figured this out.]

Hurter printed: I not happy, so I don't laugh or play. I evil and don't know how to be a little girl or have a friend. [Okay, we'll play.] Understand? I miss out on life. I want to live as you did.

Alice, as Sam, printed, no more.

Mary printed: No one gets us. I want to be whole, feel like, and be a real kid. I'm a grown-up all my life, but where the kid in me, like you have, Mr. Clarke? You have a real kid and a real grown-up. You're whole. I not, and I not talk about being MPD. I talk about an entire real person.

Angry and Hurt wrote: Mr. Clarke, you asked that one of us grow up to take care of matters. You see Leena's body and know her age; therefore, you think we know how to do things. We don't. We quickly went from early childhood to adulthood, so we never learned what it's like to be a kid. We missed much learning and growing along the way, so we have only a mini base from which to build. We deserve to learn, grow, understand, and feel what it's like to be a real kid, just like you were, so we can become whole and real.

Alice, as Sam, printed: How about me? Nobody let me be a kid. Please teach me how.

Hurter printed: I have to hide that I don't entirely know what it's like to be a kid. [Teach them what you do know.] I can't look stupid or crazy. [Yes, you can.] I need a place to be a real kid in this body. [Where?]

Clara and Ann printed: We always try to do the right thing. We have so many emotions we have difficulty telling one from another. We no longer fear or hate our perpetrators but hate how they enjoyed hurting us. They can't take back what they did to our sons, pets, trust, self-esteem, and hope. [No, they can't.]

Ann printed: Hate and fear are what we feel. What we want is to be strong. I'm determined to survive. [Good!]

Rick is short with me. He also teases me, and when I get angry, he says he's kidding. When I get overwhelmed, I put myself away to manage the alters. I have so much pain in my body that I must avoid living in it for long periods for any of us to function. It's taking so long for you to help us because we don't know all that happened to us, and we only see you two hours per week. [What if you told Rick what you'd prefer he not tease you about? Your memories will come, Leena.]

Lynne wrote: I need compassion and understanding. I've lived five lifetimes full of awful crap, and I figure life owes me some happiness. I believe life is hell, and you find joy in death. When I was becoming heartless and hateful and felt only darkness, I wanted to save the part still looking for love, warmth, and trust, which caused and still causes me pain. I wanted to be heartless until the day I was free to be me. I haven't found that day. I thought it was the day I met Anthony, but I trusted him, and he destroyed me. The only thing I ever wanted was to love and be loved. I fear and hate love now. The thing I desire most is the thing that destroys me. The bottom line is other people will kill me, or I'll ruin myself by not being able to love.

Ann added: What's better? Not them. I destroy us is better. I pick the time and place. Hearing my mother's name fills me with hate. It's even worse for someone to insist I'm just like her. I'm Ann, not her.

I recently read: "To succeed is to fail, learn, try again, fail, and learn. Losers give up, but winners keep trying. Don't wait for your ship to come in and feel angry and cheated when it doesn't. Instead, get going with something small. Once we're aware of our emotions, we can release them." All that makes sense, but I find it challenging to deal with my present while struggling with my past. [I get that, Leena, but keep up the effort because you're doing a good job.]

I want to hold my son when he's sad, but I fear touching him. [Don't be afraid of this.] I think I blame myself too much for what happened to me. [Yes, you do.] Our well of pain and anger is so deep and frightening that the mere thought of even brushing the surface shuts us down. We shudder as we think about the monster we could become. [This won't happen.] I want to feel the love from others that I haven't felt in a long time. How do you accomplish this? [You'll know how others feel about you by letting your emotions through, positive and negative, Leena.]

Us Cluster wrote: Inside, we have lots of children alters acting grown-up, and other alters acting like kids, such as Punky. We also have many Sleepers. They'll need understanding from others and to learn to trust. They'll also each need to learn something different from Leena.

One must learn self-esteem, and a second must learn to defend us. A third must learn to laugh at a story or joke, and a fourth must discover happiness. A fifth must learn about friends from people like you, and a sixth must grasp what's in others' hearts. A seventh must learn to grow up and have a job, an eighth must learn that wishes can come true, and a ninth must grasp that all things have good and evil.

Tara wrote: You haven't lost your child within, Mr. Clarke. Your child has hope, playfulness, giving, happiness, and trust in itself, but ours doesn't. You are our hope for a whole life. Along with other Wise Ones, I take care of the Sleepers and the actual children, Lynne's boys.

Sexy printed: I'm called Sexy. I'm only four, and someone is helping me print. I want to be like my mother because then she'll like me. Everyone fancies her. They laugh, party, call her pretty and ask her to marry them so I act like her. I'm a little whore. At first, men would whisper lovely things to me, but later they always did something I didn't want. I didn't understand, but the Wise Ones let me see through Leena's eyes. I became a whore, and this shamed all of us.

A Wise One wrote: I talked to you today, Mr. Clarke. I have no real name. Leena and Carol were also present. When you asked who was speaking, I didn't answer. It's easier to describe us when only one of us is out.

Us Cluster wrote: Some of us don't believe you care, Mr. Clarke, but say you do because it's your job. We fear seeing you because you might snicker at us, call us liars, or feel sorry for us like the others did. Still, we'll continue therapy with you and hope you understand our fear and won't shame us anymore. [I care, and won't laugh at you, pity you, humiliate you, or call you liars. If you're troubled by my comments, please process them with me right away.] Thanks for phoning us. We interpret your call as caring. It means a lot to know someone cares. [You're welcome.]

Andy wrote: I hate so much I fear I'll hurt others or myself. I feel overwhelming pain and fear at times and can't breathe. I'd rather not have emotions because all emotions seem horrible and overwhelming. I believe I'll be just like them if I have feelings. [Like your mother and Anthony] You've said I need to go through the emotions to get better, a difficult task. [Yes, it is.] The risk is that I might become like my perpetrators. [I doubt it.]

Tamara wrote: We want to protect our real boys and want them to have a chance to be happy and know love. For years we worried they'd be dead by morning. We don't know if we can live with that terror again. We're scared, oh so frightened! We want to thank you for all your help and understanding. You taught us we don't have the original personality born with our body, and you taught us the difference between Leena and us. Don't get the bighead. You still have a ways to go.

Our wants, needs, desires, and abilities aren't adequately expressed by the word "normal." Is the therapist's job to guide the client not to strive for normalcy but to dare to reach beyond? [Yep.] We like that. Maybe we'll write a book titled Dare to Reach Beyond Normal. Would you like to help us? [I'd love to, Tamara.] I believe that we can be heard through me. We have guidance now that we've never had before. We're finding we're astute in many ways but lack information. [Yep.] There's fear in sharing but peace in understanding. [Yep.]

When you asked Sarah to describe what she was holding during group counseling, it shamed us to let others know we can't identify objects by touch. I know that you didn't mean to shame us. We felt the same shame we experienced when being told we were mentally retarded, or when our teacher discovered we couldn't read and spoke extra slowly. We had to explain we weren't retarded but that no one ever taught us to read.

Timothy apologizes for getting angry during group counseling and hitting the paper. He just wanted the game to stop because he felt stupid for not knowing how to play. Carol asked me to thank you for letting her talk because she felt good about helping others see different perspectives. Also, we don't know about joking because we never had joking growing up, so during group, when you told us you were joking, we were confused. We don't know what joking is or why people joke. [Maybe we can make learning about joking a goal, Tamara.]

Robot wrote: When you were a child, did you make messes? [Yep.] Did your mother get mad at you? [Nope.] What's it like to see the love in your mother's eyes when she looks at you? [Ouch!] What's it like to be a real kid, have a best friend, not be ashamed, depend on someone, be carefree, share secrets, love, skate, get dirty, know your parents will be there for you, or talk to your parents about kid problems? What's it like to dream of being a cowboy, clown, or dancer instead of having nightmares? What's it like to play with real kids, not always be scared, believe in yourself, be authentic, be whole, feel silky clothing, be yourself, or be alive instead of dead? What's it like to touch skin to skin, love someone without fear, have a birthday party, or wish upon a star and think it'll come true? What's it like to feel a comb through your hair, feel safe, feel a warm kitty or fuzz, or feel smooth, rough, hard, cotton, wool, air, sun, a ball, a tree, grass, rain, wet, dry, or a fly in your hands and releasing it. What's it like to eat candy, be happy, be pretty, or be loved?

I can feel terrible physical pain and hot and cold. Punky felt ice cream and snow once, but it overwhelmed us. Maybe they won't overpower us after we know what things feel like. What's it like to see the colors blue or red? How do I look? I know what love is but not how it feels. I know all these words but don't know the sensation or emotion accompanying them. Do they hurt us like pain? What's the difference between dreaming and reality? Did we conjure all this, or is it real? Sometimes it seems actual, and other times not. What does time mean? Where do angels live? What's the location of dark souls, broken promises, The Light, make-believe, and the Wise Ones?

Are the alters living on the outside called adults? I can't tell you much about my inside because I'm there and not there. It's partially broken, forgotten, or dead.

Fluffy and Stuffy asked me how they could speak with you, Mr. Clarke, or write to you as Danny did. I assured them I could talk or write for them. Danny, an adolescent boy alter, was nicknamed Hippy Boy because he talked like a hippy. We made him in the early 1960s, but can't remember why.

Danny wrote: Groove it, man. We're scared of ourselves. Wow! That's wild and way out of here! Way out, crazy man! Peace till we meet again.

Robot wrote: We also made Star about the same time. She was a 13-year-old girl about the same time, nicknamed Hippy Girl, who liked peasant shirts and went to the stars when bad things happened.

A Little One printed, mother didn't love us, and we found out a week ago that we have Abby, a 6-year-old girl who's tiny and makes animal cries.

Sarah wrote: I don't like anything weighty because the men were heavy, making my breathing difficult. I get scared when I get a chest cold, run fast, encounter small enclosures, do things for people when asked, sit in chairs, go to the bathroom, am dirty, am talking, am in the dark, am being held or hugged, see fire, or eat in front of people. In other words, I'm afraid of everything.

Punky wrote: I was scared when the group members sat on the floor, Mr. Clarke. You asked if I wanted you to move away from me, and I did, but I said no because I didn't want you to know I was afraid you'd touch me. Other alters tried to show you they were attempting to trust you. Can we believe you? Trust is scary because it's risking getting hurt. We want to get into your head to see if you're trustworthy, but that would be cheating. [It's okay.] Sarah knows there's something different about you. Is it cheating to have Sarah touch you first so we can understand you as she does? [It's okay.]

We were born from The Mother's lust and died from men's desires. If the parents' sins go to the children, there's no God. The Mother has many alters. I don't want many alters. [You fear having multiple personalities like your mother? This is the first time you've mentioned your mother having alters.] I'm just now realizing it.

I can see the soul of others. An evil soul is cold and scares me. Good souls give off warmth and love. I saw the hurt and pure hate in my mother. I felt her without touching her, and she slapped me and told me to stop it. I saw hatred but also goodness and warmth in Grandma's soul. Grandma snapped, "Stop it now." Grandma said she'd hoped I wouldn't have the gift of seeing. She said the Great Spirit gave us the gift to know our enemies but that we're never to use it. [It's okay to use it, Punky.]

When I started to look at my soul, I stopped because I felt fear, but the Wise Ones removed the fright. Grandma insisted that I promise never to look within myself. Did I break that promise by perceiving the other alters in me? [No.]

Grandma peered into The Mother, then cried and said to Dorothy, "Oh, baby, your mother will never heal because she's hurting too badly." Grandma peered into Dorothy and said she had a brighter soul than she'd seen in many years, which pleased her heart. [It's okay to look-see now, Punky.]

Grandma told Dorothy that Dorothy had the gift of understanding others, that her "light" (goodness) would cover others' darkness, and that she'd be hurt because no great healer goes unhurt. Grandma talked to Dorothy about whether to use the gift, and Dorothy felt lost and lonely after that conversation. Dorothy always wanted to be normal but was never meant to be. [You're more than average, Punky.] Sarah listened carefully to our Grandma and learned. Sarah doesn't hold power but uses it. One of the other Wise Ones holds it.

Saturday afternoon, some of us tie-dyed with Lynne's real kids. We had purple all over and liked it.

Mary printed: I no bed. I play.

Us Cluster wrote: Can you explain our dreams? Is it real when we talk to you or real when we dream? We have thoughts that don't seem ours, and we do nothing unless the other alters ask. [Reality is perception.]

Gina wrote: In your childhood, girls didn't get hurt down there and didn't get rented out. Your mother didn't yell and hit, and her boyfriends didn't do bad things. No grown-ups said you deserved what you got.

There was no safe place for us as kids except for what we fabricated in our minds. When we couldn't handle something from the outside, we conceived another alter for that. We produced alters to hold pain, anger, death, and others for other matters. We created a world where nothing was real, and we didn't remember what we couldn't handle. To keep us safe, we forgot each other. Being alone again was the price of safety. We sacrificed all our feelings to survive. It's been very lonely. [You learned to compartmentalize, forget, escape and disassociate, but you're lonely.]

Lynne wrote: I now see my childhood through Leena's eyes. We created Leena based mainly on our therapists' ways of seeing things. From our therapists we learned about fairness, right and wrong, truth and understanding, and choices. [New awareness!] I still don't understand why other people couldn't see what was happening in my home. Why couldn't the school, church, or neighbors see my siblings' empty, hopeless eyes? [Some did but were too afraid to do anything].

Rachel printed: Mother forced me to lie nude in the front yard with my legs apart, facing the street, holding a sign reading "only twenty cents a pop." Learning sexual behavior was forced upon me. [You were humiliated and violated.] Sometimes, we feel your emotional pain, Mr. Clarke, and wonder if what we write makes you sad. [Don't try to protect me emotionally. If I can't take care of myself, you should seek another therapist.]

Punky wrote: It feels scary but also good to talk about seeing beyond your mind and what it can do, and telling the secrets only Grandma and I knew. Mostly, it's good to find someone who understands. Thank you for not thinking I'm crazy or fabricating. Very shallow people only see one's outward appearance. It was calming to hear you explain that those less broken take care of the more damaged. [Truth and love always bring serenity.] Most of us hide hurt within ourselves. We want to love and feel love. Our mother was hateful, and there was no room for anything else. [You're learning very quickly.]

Annie printed: I want to feel and see life in all things. I want out of the dark, to love, and play without fear or shame. [Wonderful!]

Punk wrote: Do you think I'd have been perverted with a girl child if I had one? [I don't think so. You're too full of love.] We're like the blind man who listed everything he wanted to see, and when they removed his bandages, he filled his eyes with everything he could as quickly as possible for fear he'd go blind again. We're like those who never heard, walked, or talked. Others deprived us of a complete life for many years and the hope we'd ever have one.

Feeler wrote: I can't turn myself off because I have too many emotions and thoughts. People terrorize me if they're too close because I fear "the hand" will come to hurt me. I want them away from me, and I desire open places to see all around me, like the field next to Grandma's house.

Windy wrote: A fear returns involving many people surrounding me. A picture in my mind is of a chicken coop, vegetable garden, and terror beyond. I hid in weeds from The Mother as the pain burned from her blows.

Mary printed, my boo-boo!

Windy continued: I see blood, and I hide. I rock from side to side with my eyes wide open as I anticipate my mother's boyfriend's arrival. If I stay and he comes back, will he think I waited for more? Then it'll be no-nonsense.

As a kid, Dorothy lived in terror 24 hours a day. She never knew when the beating was going to come. Men would come at night. She'd hear her sister cry and knew she was next. She stopped telling Grandma about her life at home when she noticed it saddened Grandma, but then she had no one to tell. Grandma told her to keep the good in her hidden and safe, and one day she could let it all out.

I've been hiding my good for 38 years. When will it be safe? [Prepare to let yourself out and release the good, Leena.] Nobody stays. We leave and go far away, where there's no pain. Blackness comes. [That's "dissociation."]

Mary and Dorothy planned to run away and find a safe home but became too scared to flee, fearing The Mother would find them, get mad, and hurt them. Punky Lil didn't understand.

Mary printed: Let them try to hurt us. They can't hurt us more than mother did.

Overseer wrote: I'm Overseer. You can't get to the Sleepers without going through me. I'm one but not one. When you teach the part, you educate the whole. I've noticed I don't like others to be uncomfortable around me. [That's nice, but you must also take care of yourself.]

Amy's fear of hands moving fast about her face stems from The Mother frequently slapped her. Amy and Tamara dislike sitting in chairs, and unnamed fragments are stuck in chairs due to my trauma from being tied to chairs. I apologize for losing control at group counseling by letting Amy out." [It's okay, Overseer.]

Lady Sophia wrote: Hello. They call me Lady Sophia. Tis not fittin' to explain meself. Tis said a true lady never explains herself, and I'm that, a lady through and through. Tis said a true lady only has to explain to her husband. I shan't be explaining to the likes of you. I'll be keeping to meself then. Good day to you now. If you be needin' to know, me background is a little shady. But don't we all have a black sheep we be hidin? I sure was getting a whopping headache from the group. [Irish!]

We think it's time to start hypnosis. We want to know who was in the backyard by the chicken wire fence. We'd also like your help with our weight. [Okay.] We also want Sarah to feel you, to see if we're right about you. [Fine.] Is it wrong to want to know the truth about the person you're trusting? [No. I think it's a good idea when possible.] The Sleepers will awake to discover that their foundation is built on shame and fear. [It's good you know this, Leena.]

Nettie wrote: We're scared to be around anyone if we think they know our past. We don't want them to look at us, understand what we remember, or feel our emotional makeup. [How come?] Our emotional makeup is unbearable and ugly to look at. What we recall is horrifying. We keep our pain hidden so our physical appearance doesn't look ugly.

Mother taught us you hurt those you love, and if you care for them more than anything, you harm them more. We ceased feeling when she beat us, so she hurt us more because she needed a reaction. Feeler wants you to know that Anthony brought the women to share us with. [Tell Feeler thanks, Nettie.]

Many alters signed the following letter: We're saddened when we're in public and having fun, and people look at us funny and veer away. Is it because we're stupid, or do they think we'll hurt them or their kids? Once, we were talking to a girl about which crayons were best. Her mother saw us, appeared scared, called her daughter away, turned around, gave us a mean look, and told her daughter: "You don't talk to people like that. Never be around that kind. You want to get hurt?"

One time Rick took us for our first-ever ice cream cone. We became sad when people got up and moved away from an adult acting giddy over ice cream. We don't go for ice cream anymore, and for the most part, we avoid books, crayons, and toys when we go shopping, but we sometimes forget because we get so excited seeing the pretty things.

We want to act right so people won't be scared of us, yet we want to be happy and be like real kids. Can you please tell us what they want us to be like so they won't give us funny looks or be scared?

Signed: Abigail, Amber, Amy, Andy, Annie, Bad Girl, Butterfly, Cindy, Bo-Bo, Evil Ones, George, Iris, Jennifer, Little, Pony, Punky Lil, 7 3/4, Suzie Q., Tabatha, Timothy A. Bradshaw, Ugly, Angie, Bobby, Silly Sally, Clara, Unnamed Ones, and others.

Amber wrote: We played in the mud. [Wonderful!] Patty ate dirt and said it was crunchy. Gross! Rick made the mud for us and hosed us off, but he didn't play.

Dee wrote: We're going camping in the backyard. We have a fire, a tent, and everything. We'll play in the mud and fish in the baby swimming pool.

Punky Lil printed, I like squishing mud in my toes and fingers and having mud fights.

Knower is an immortal male Spirit, Helper, Thinker, and Wise One. He helps us determine what's happening and guides us through the vast darkness we're enduring. He's logical, rational, and analytical and has little to do with emotion because it interferes with thinking. He makes sense of life and sees our future. He's wise, helps hold the key to power and knowledge, sees the circle of nature and applies it to our lives, takes care of our actual children and us by answering our questions, and is part of Pamela Boy's conscience. [Thanks for explaining Knower, Leena.]

Knower and others wrote: We're getting dizzy again, and our eyes are continually blinking. What causes that? [You're switching.]

Our Bad Ones help us survive, so they need friendlier names. [Yes, but what would you like their names to be?]

Some alters can turn into water or stone to show people they can't hurt us because we mostly feel nothing, and the rare pain we feel is slight. We weren't good enough to halt all suffering, so we created more of ourselves. Those fashioned more, and those new ones generated even more until we got to the Nice Ones.

If there's still too much hurt, we all go on overload. The strongest ones rebuild. Sometimes, if we can't restore, we give the crap to someone not vital, and they go crazy. Later if they're not too insane, we can fix them, but as a whole, we lose. Even I go mad sometimes for hours or days. It isn't a pleasant place to be. [Thanks, Knower and others, for explaining this.]

What happens to people who learn too much too fast? [They shut down]. This sharing we're doing is loading us with knowledge. [Yes, and that's healthy.]

Beth and James wrote: Every time we get up, someone knocks us down. Dee tries to kill us to end the pain when we're full of hurt and hopelessness. We have so much shame and fear we can't look into your eyes without seeing disgust for who we are. [Do you see disgust or expect it?]

Mickey wrote: My name is Mickey, from Mickey Mouse. Tina and I want to know how many we are. Someone helped me write. [Hi, Mickey. Amber knows how many you are but she hasn't told me.]

Us Cluster wrote: Writing is one way we can still hide the truth. [I understand.] It hurts us that you know how dumb we are. Can you help us by bringing up what we write when we see you? [Yes, but you're not dumb.]

Hurt wrote: I hate to love, and I hate anyone who loves me. I hate the feeling of love. Hate is safe, and you can't hurt hate. [Name the word love something else, like compassion, perhaps. Maybe you give the word feel another name also.] The dark people told me I was the daughter of darkness, and if I joined them, I'd have no pain. [They lied to you.] I fought back and kept the good.

Tamara wrote: We have MPD to keep the bad away from the good. We divide good, bad, and what we are by three to find the whole, meaning we all have righteousness, evil, and in between, except for Sunshine. She didn't get touched by evil. We hid Sunshine to protect her, hoping to use her to start over one day and be virtuous.

We Cluster wrote: We hate being fat, but we thought we wouldn't have to deal with what men wanted if we were overweight. We discovered we were unsafe no matter what. I'm sorry about talking about only us. [You don't owe me an apology.] For the most part, we can handle not discussing ourselves, so we'll return to the way we were. [No] It's hell not being what others want us to be. Healthy people want us to be normally functioning human beings, but we aren't.

Angry wrote: A dad is the king of his castle, his word is the law, he protects the family from others, stands up for you, and fights to his death for what he believes. He tries to control things to make them equitable and gets angry. He punishes girls and sometimes beats boys man-to-man. He wants everything done his way, smashes things, yells, hits walls, curses at you, and threatens to do bad things. Are most men or dads like this? [No.]

I'm dissatisfied with sex. My partner cares only about himself. I know it's a girl's place to make men happy. [It's both people's jobs to help each other be happy, Leena.]

One of the Bad Ones wrote: How do you fashion plans for the future when you've had so many disappointments? [Sometimes, it feels impossible.] I've lived my life trying to prove I'm good enough. Everyone except therapists has said I was at fault for problems in relationships. Even therapists can't swallow some of my bull. [Like what?]

Bobby printed: I like you and the cute lady counselor. You listen to me. I hide cause I'm scared of you, but I hear. I enjoy the "girl talk" and hugging the girls. Charles, Timothy A. Bradshaw, Charles III, and others can hop from one to the other because they have shared memories, although they're of different ages. Some alters like these have the same name because the original got damaged but wanted to be untarnished, so conceived a new, undamaged alter, yet liked the name, so kept it.

Timothy A. Bradshaw printed: I want the cute lady counselor to be a girlfriend to James and me. I especially like her. Do you think her boyfriend will share her with us? [Maybe as friends. That would be good]. We're having a man-to-man talk. Okay? [Okay.] Paul told me that you're man enough to take this straight talk and not laugh at us.

The Guys, who are Timothy A. Bradshaw and some unnamed younger down-home dudes who stick up for ladies, printed: We want a sweet lady cause they say kind words to boys, like, you sure are a cute boy. They also bake cookies, and they're soft. We no want the yucky kisses. We just want the sweet stuff that other dudes get from real moms. [Good idea.] We don't have a real mom, and us too old for the kid stuff. Is talking to you man-to-man okay? [Sure. I like that.]

If the cute lady counselor bakes us cookies, we eat lots. If she asks you about us, say we manly, okay guys. We no let nobody hurt her. No say about the mushy stuff. We no like her to think we sissies. We not. We prefer chocolate chip cookies with little or no nuts. Got it?

Timothy A. Bradshaw printed: I don't mush too much. Manly things are hard work. I can't be kind, but it's okay to want a sweet lady. I think the cute lady counselor is fine. [Yep, Timothy.] Leena's boyfriend calls me a stud muffin.

I'm losing a great deal. One son is joining the military, one left home, we're selling the house, and I'll be without medical benefits after divorcing Anthony. [Yes, you're losing a great deal, Leena.] It's like starting over. I've never done that on my own and am not sure how. I want to learn to read better, deal with challenges, and take care of myself. The little kid alters want to learn to laugh and have fun. I've learned not to show my emotions to look like I can handle anything that comes my way. [That doesn't mean not showing emotions.] Can I stop once I begin, or will I cry forever? [You can start and stop.]

I've learned to have emotions over the past couple of years, but it's difficult, and sometimes I still can't because they're too heavy-duty. Most of us want our feelings, but feelings scare us because we don't know how to manage them. Since 95% of life has been bad, 95% of what we recall will be painful. [No.]

I don't see the difference between my perpetrators and society at large. They both say they'll punish you if you don't behave or feel like they want. [Yes. Things can be very hypocritical.] Why do I feel crazy? [It's because you were hurt so much for believing the world was mad, Leena.] I've decided to act normal and keep my mouth shut to protect myself.

I'd stop it, not talk, clam up, put it back, and take it away, but it's me. [Yes, and we have to find a way to let it be out and be okay.] I want it to end. I want something different than this way of life, but I'm damn scared to ask. Maybe we need to accept the brutality instead of fighting it and accept our place in life as the good little victim. [Accept that it happened and was unjust, but you don't have to believe it was okay because it wasn't.]

Rules protect righteous people and punish the bad. Victims live in the middle. The good people curse and lock up victims, whereas the evil people swear and lock in victims. I don't know what to believe. Victims have MPD because their good and bad emotions can't be on the same side of town. It's a war between them. [This is an intriguing perspective, Leena.]

Seeker, a 12-year-old girl Quiet One who seeks the truth, wrote: I want to live on the virtuous side and help the bad. I don't want to hurt or cause hurt.

Our teenage years consisted of appalling breakage. Later in life, we met a Christian woman who taught us to forgive, and we found some peace. Lynne, Sarah, and Maria became whole at that time. [I'd like to hear more about this, Leena.]

A Thinker wrote: Tara, Sarah, Maria, and others are part of our soul. One is listening to you in hopes of coming to know the truth. When the people dressed in black were trying to turn us to the dark side, our goodness came and helped us know righteousness from evil. Afterward, we felt peace, love, and understanding. [This is extremely important.] I talked about this in church. The preacher told me that only Jesus stood by God and came back. He added that the devil is in me.

Sarah talks, and Tara writes for us to know our inside alters. To live by the world's beliefs and standards, we can't accept The Light. [Yes.] Yet to function in the world, we must acquire its rules. So, did we develop MPD to keep the world's standards and The Light? [Good question, Leena.] A person with MPD is more aware of the whole due to the extremes they've had to live. I awakened The Light. [Yippy!] Other people live in unawakened states.

Cheri wrote: Being nice gets you nowhere. Selfish, cold people don't get hurt because they hurt others first. They only act friendly to get what they want. They only keep friends who benefit them. They look, dress, and behave better than other people. They use others before they can get used. They marry for power and money.

Hurter printed, you either use or get used!

Sandy wrote: This is what we were taught and shown. You've met the good, and now I'm introducing you to the start of the bad. [I'm glad to meet you!] Others deny our reality. Are we crazy? [No]. When our sons have problems, it saddens us all. To always keep them safe is impossible. [True.]

Hurter printed: I don't want to be crazy. I dislike hospitals because it scares me to have others control me. Are you figuring I'm insane? [No]. Do you think my emotions are coming to the surface, and I'll hurt people? [I don't believe you're a danger to other people.] I don't want to hurt anyone. I already have a hard time keeping friends.

Tiffany printed, I keep people away from me.

Cheri wrote, I don't want to go to the hospital. I don't wish the risk of having to prove what we say about our tormentors. [I'll do my best to keep you out of the hospital, Cheri.]

Sherry wrote, thanks for calling and talking to us, Mr. Clark. [You're welcome]

Logical One wrote: No doubt, you must be sensible to live. Is it illogical to have what's not needed to function, such as emotions, bodies, people, right and wrong, or MPD? [We're emotional beings who have one body. People can enrich our lives. Morality is important. MPD is the way you've chosen to survive.]

Amber wrote: It's raining, and we're scared of lightning. I didn't mean to mention the two babies we gave birth to and the involvement of Lynne, our mother. I slipped. [It's okay, Amber.] Did you know that some of us call Lynne our mother? [Yes.]

Punky wrote: We either have a tremendous stomachache and a lulu of a headache, or we're about to become evil again. I'm scared. People dislike and hurt bad people. I don't want to be disliked and harmed. I guess Dorothy's story is too much for anyone to believe. [I believe it.]

Presently, there's so much chaos in our lives we've closed down most emotions and memories. We still believe we have nothing to live for and feel scared, hopeless, and helpless. [I know.] We don't want to feel weak and depend on others or have anyone think they have a right to control us. Our boyfriend tells us what we can and can't do, but that goes one way only. [Not fair, huh?]

I thought I was just one person for a time, but now it doesn't feel that way. Where do I go when I'm not here? It seems I'm someone different every time I wake up. I never got angry or upset before, but now I do. [This is normal, Punky.]

Lilly wrote: They destroyed us beyond repair. We're ashamed to admit that we sometimes forget what was said 30 minutes ago. Crisis leads to our shutting down and not remembering. Our prolonged, difficult turmoil has led to losing big pieces of our lives. We may only remember two days out of a year, but have fashioned a whole life out of those moments with family, friends, and nightmares. {This is "dissociative amnesia" (dissociative amnesia), the inability to remember what another alter did while out. It leads to "losing time" (losing time), a feeling that a chunk of time is missing from one's life.} [You're beginning to behave like other MPDs: forgetting, being ashamed and confused, and feeling obligated.]

Cheri wrote: Meme and I are scared because we don't know how to take care of ourselves. I'm no good. I'm a bad girl. I can see you, but you can't see me.

Tina wrote we're scared.

Paul wrote I wish we could tell you how crazy it is inside.

We went miniature golfing. Timothy A. Bradshaw hit the hardest, and Pamela Boy got in the holes the best. Suzie Q. and Little just liked hitting the ball everywhere. Jennifer got mad because her ball went over the hole but not in. Punky got a hole-in-one and loved the tiny houses the best. Patty thought it was just a gorgeous place. Bo-Bo wanted to check out the pond, and Leah liked the palm trees and bridges. James wanted to find out how the windmill door worked. Iris liked all the colors, Angel got overly hot, and Rick scored the best. My third son, who I renamed Brad, and I didn't care about how we did. [It sounds like you all had fun, Leena.]

Later, 7 ¾ got mad when Rick touched our boobies at Costco. Brad took me outside because the people in Costco made me anxious. We later went to Sizzler for dinner. It was a long day but fun. The Mother told us not to have fun or be happy but to take life seriously, whereas Grandma said it's okay to have fun, be happy, and think things are funny if they're funny. [Rick was inappropriate. Grandma was right.]

One of my sons is leaving for the military. I wonder if I taught him all I wanted him to know. [We never do. I didn't prepare my son for everything either.] Did I teach him to be proud of himself, be responsible, have a caring heart, or love himself? Did I teach him that bad things happening to him don't make him evil, to not settle for less than what he wants in life, and to know what it's like to be loved and cared for so he doesn't end up like me? I hate myself because I didn't teach him all these things. [It isn't fair to hate yourself.] I only recently discovered that we must find love and caring from within. Did I make a difference to him? [Yes, you did.] Do you think stupid people can teach their children goodness even when they don't know how? [Yes, through love, but you're not dumb.] I only recently discovered that we must find love and caring from within. I hate being me. Are you aware of that? [Yes, I know, Leena.]

Punky wrote: We don't know about ordinary things. We pretend to know how to behave to avoid being judged too harshly by others or ourselves. We don't know about love, caring, trust, friendship, families, working, education, living with others, marriage, taking care of ourselves, laughing, playing, and everyday matters you take for granted. Since we learned the wrong ways, we can also find the right ways. [You bet! And you're doing it step-by-step]. If this is so, we're not stupid, just uneducated, but we still feel dumb because we haven't learned much. [You merely lacked opportunity.]

Us Cluster wrote, if you're going to talk about acting and pretending, we also know that well.

Rachel, Peaches-and-Cream, and others wrote: We know a million ways if you want to talk about having sex. We also know about not feeling physically or emotionally.

Hurter and an unknown alter printed, would you say we're shame-based? [Yes.] Is shame what we call hurt feelings? [Yes, and fear]. Does psychology generally use male experiences as a norm for all? [No. The female experience is probably more the basis of psychology.]

Sard wrote: The last time I came to your office, I smelled sweet, strong cologne. I think it's the same as that used by one of my mother's boyfriends. Being close to a strong-smelling man makes me feel sick and crazy. [It's normal to associate old recollections with present stimuli.]

We're trying to handle everything going on inside and outside. We fear we're not doing well. [That's a lot, isn't it, Leena?] We're trying to decide who'll deal with County Mental Health. So far, no one wants to for fear of being hospitalized.

I want to become what my maker intended me to be before the wreckage. [I know.] Yet, I have to protect myself from others who judge me by their standards. [We need to find another way to do this.]

Lefty printed: I'm Lefty. Punky helped me print and spell. I think I'm a 7-year-old boy. I don't think much because they made me up. Your name is Mr. Clarke. Can you help me be real? No one likes me. No one talks to me. What's joking? We're not doing so well. How much more can we take before we break again?

Alice wrote: I can learn and become real, but I can't do it myself. I need help. I can be anything. I'm not stupid, and I'm not dysfunctional. [You bet!] I want people to see me for me and not from their standard of what's acceptable. I'm healthy for what I am. Can't they see that? [They can't do this for anyone.]

Us Cluster wrote: People don't have the patience we require. They're dealing with "club 900" and not just one person. We want to be heard and judged fairly, and we aren't sorry for that. [Good.] We don't want to live in fear of what we say or how we say it, one of our deepest fears. We also have a real fear of people and for good reasons. [Yes, your fear is real.] How would you feel fighting every day for a change when competing against doctors and society with your word only? [It'd wear me down.] We're not giving up yet, even though we feel hopeless and alone. Your word is the only thing you've got. [Yep!] Do you see my viewpoint? Some of us understand. [Cool!]

We're reading that shame-based women feel uncertain about reasonable or appropriate behavior, stemming from lack of experience, sparse role-modeling, continually being told we're incompetent, and being forced into roles far beyond our abilities as children. Is that what happened to us? [Yes, plus more.] We hesitate to reveal our worst fears, which keeps us from what would ease them: sharing our concerns with others and learning they feel the same way, and discovering there's more than one way to do things and that we know much more than we realize about navigating our world. If there are gaps in our knowledge, it helps to remember it isn't because we're slow but because of our scant experience. [Yes, this is why change and learning can be tricky] We want all our alters to know that it's never too late to learn. [How do we let them know?]

We're not willing to feel helpless. Helpless people can't get help and can't help themselves. Doctors have told us we can't take care of ourselves and will always need help to function. Many say we're just not trying hard enough, and all we need is willpower, which we'll never understand. [Me neither. It's a dumb idea.] Other people taught us how to harm ourselves; otherwise, we wouldn't know how. [True.]

An Angry One wrote: I don't write to you for pity. [Good because I don't pity you.] Can you imagine what it's like to be pushed down and never learn or grow, or when no one helps you out of your hell, and you have no idea how to help yourself? I want to be so strong they'll soil their pants when they see me. [Okay! Let's do it!]

We're getting paranoid about what others are up to and what they know. [No, you're just scared, Leena. I understand why now.] I thought I was hiding my emotions pretty well. [Actually, you're letting your feelings show more.] Those who want me in a mental ward aren't thinking of me. They're thinking about how I make them look. [Yes! I'm glad you see this.]

No one believed one person could be raped hundreds of times, beaten, burned, cut, and terrorized by their mother and then their husband. The Wise Ones and I know these things happened. Yet to avoid the mental ward, we act emotionally stable even for you, Mr. Clarke. Sorry!

I've been talking to car salespeople about buying a car. They all promised to do right by me and sounded courteous and trustworthy, but so did the devil. I got mad at one salesman, stormed away, and left the lot. [You did well, Leena.]

Cheri wrote: I know I was hurt, but I want to think maybe I wasn't. It's difficult to believe the people I loved hurt me so much. I don't need others to know my shame. No one wants to talk about being tortured.

I have a new doctor, but I'm scared to see her because I dislike anyone touching my private parts. I told her I have MPD, and she said she'd never worked with MPD before. I'll be okay if she tells me what she plans to do before she does it. That way, I can change to one who can handle it. We're all petrified about this, but okay means doing things, even if we're scared. See! We're trying to be grown-up and manage our fear. [Yes. It's hard, though, isn't it, Cheri?]

Some alters and I saw a doctor for the first time in quite a while. Someone told her about the garden hose, staples, and getting poked in the legs with needles. I told her George has terrible lungs and Punky has burns. Susie Q. wanted to cry. We were scared, but we did okay. [You all did exceptionally well, Leena.]

We were sad to see our previous counselor leave. We're having difficulty finding words to express our emotions. We know how Annie feels when she wants to talk but doesn't grasp how, and we understand why Winter and Crystal struggle.

Andy wrote: Do you fail to answer many of our questions in our letters because you don't think they're necessary or that we're just asking for the hell of it? [I believe questions are essential. That's why I ask you so many.]

Crazy alters are out. Several are in a room together. Some are strong, and some aren't. We fashioned them so they couldn't talk to, feel, or remember each other, but we left knowing with one to help if needed. If they don't know one another, they can't put their powers together and harm others or themselves.

Bad Ones and others wrote: When one of us is halfway out, we lose control of our body, coordination, feeling, judging distance, and remembering. Also, we sometimes change so frequently that we can't keep track or think clearly. We must be more careful in times like this because we do things like accidentally cutting ourselves or picking up a hot pan and taking five minutes to become aware we're burnt. [Lots of stuff is going on at one time.]

One time the "black ghost" came, and we didn't give a damn what others thought of us. We did as our mother taught us by not liking others or ourselves. The soul became particularly evil, and we forgot everything good. It's difficult to change back from being evil, but we did. [This is saving the spirit.] It sounds terrible and crazy. No hospitals, please!

We drove our group counselor away. They said we broke her. That hurt us big time! [It isn't fair for you to feel this way. You didn't cause her to leave, Leena.] Then came you, Mr. Clarke. We didn't want to overwhelm another counselor, but we wanted help badly. That's why we asked you if you could handle us. [I understand you're afraid. Your fear is reasonable.] We've hidden how we feel about our prior counselor for two years. [This is a long time to experience so much hurt.] Putting aside the shame and hiding and telling our truth is excruciating, but it feels as if we're lifting a huge weight. [I'm glad.] Thanks for reading this from the others who had a say in it and me. [You're welcome. Thanks for sharing and trusting me.]

I had a recent discussion with my middle son, Jim, who compared me unfavorably to his friend's mom. I remained calm and told him I was glad he was happy with her. He wanted me to sign guardianship papers, but I said I'd do so only if I moved away. [It's good that you're getting more assertive, Leena.]

Cheri wrote: Yesterday was the first time we didn't switch much in a long time, but today the switching accelerated. We should know nothing good lasts forever. [That's true, but nothing terrible does either. Things are constantly changing.] I've let others stomp all over me repeatedly so they wouldn't be angry. [I know, but you're doing much better about this now, Cheri.] You wanted to find out which of us reads and spells the best. What if we don't know? [We have to search and ask.]

Sarah wrote: I'm beginning to notice bodily sensations. My eyes feel full, and my heart hurts. Is that sadness? [Those are physical sensations associated with sadness.]

Brooklyn wrote: I felt tremendous dizziness and pain when my rib was broken. A bad thing happened to me, and I'm still hurting. [Truth begins to halt the pain.]

Angie printed: When my mother sent me to school with poopy pants, I hated myself and hated her. The teacher sent me home because I was upsetting the other students. How about me? I was hurt. Am I wrong? [Your emotions are appropriate.] After that, I began suppressing my toilet urges. Stupid of me, huh? [It wasn't stupid, but sad that a little girl was forced to become afraid like that.] I don't want to start my new life on lies. I need a trustworthy person to be truthful with. Was mother correct? [You're pretty brave. She was wrong.]

We Cluster wrote: Our mother shamed us by forcing us to wear soiled pants and put poop on our plate for dinner. Anthony shamed us similarly because we were to love all of him. Since we've separated The Mother and Anthony, they don't seem so big and scary. [What an incredible thing to figure out!] We need to separate people to see them as not so big. [Yes.] I want to separate all our perpetrators to diminish their power over us.

Hurter printed, This feels great. [Whoopee!] It a first. Even the bad guys come down a notch! I've shared, felt understood, separated people, and arisen. [Happy first birthday!]

I want to go to college, learn, and become somebody. [I know.] The Mother and the doctors told me not to bother because I'd only get hurt since I'm retarded. [Now, you know you're not retarded!] They took everything they could, but I'll keep coming back stronger and better despite them. I want to show them they didn't win. [Good! Because they didn't, Leena!]

We Cluster wrote: Do we have to forget the past and go from this day forward? [No, but you have to separate the past from the present.] If there are more hurts than we've written about, how many are there? [There are probably more, but I don't know how many.]

Something or someone is trying to go through us, and we're terrified. We tap into that man's world sometimes and see his face. Iris drew him. He's one of them, and we fear them all. [Who?] We can't remember.

Iris wrote: Brooklyn said she'd like a town. Can you ask her to list activities she and other alters enjoy so I can know what buildings she needs? [I think it'd mean more to her if she did it independently, but I'll help.]

Not shown is Iris's drawing of Brooklyn with limbs in pieces, a distorted face, and the word "nobody," adjacent to waves, titled "Sea of Tears." Some alters have missing body parts because they have no physical sensation in those parts due to grave injury. [Interesting, Leena]

I felt pain for a long time when I jumped out of a barn loft and hurt my neck, whereas pain inflicted by people never lasted more than two to five minutes. Because people told us they didn't hurt us that badly, we came to believe we're only allowed so much time to suffer. [It isn't up to others to decide how much you hurt, Leena.]

I have dreams about sex, for which I feel shame. My boyfriend said he doesn't have these dreams, but some people do. [Dreams are healthy. Most people have them.] I dreamed of making love in the light rain. I was feeling everything. I felt a touch of warmth like skin-to-skin and detected every drop. [How wonderful! Do more dream work.] I want the feeling of being touched, like in my dream. I didn't know it could feel that good. In the real world, touch meant pain. [This is the genuinely enjoyable part of feeling like other people do.] Is this a fantasy and something for which you can only wish? [Many people have these pleasant sensations.]

Last night I had more dreams about the big boy coming into my room. I felt him as before, but I told him "no" and then woke up. [Good job, Leena!]

Why am I judged by ordinary people's standards? [We all are.] When I started having emotions and exhibiting healthy behavior, others told me I was too old to behave that way. I got criticized for being or not being healthy. Why? [Healthy people sometimes feel hurt a lot.] I thought being healthy and functional wouldn't hurt. [Nope. It can also hurt.]

I had difficulty going to my medical appointment. Many young children alters came out but got scared, so they all ran away except Annie, Amy, and an unnamed Helper. [You were brave. I realize it's difficult for you.] We wanted to act grown-up. [You did.] Annie and Amy were there to stop the doctor, who caused them to feel yucky when she touched them. What do you call that sickening feeling? [Shame]

Cara printed: I hate shame. I evil and no do good. I failed you and me. [No, you didn't. You did very well.]

Timothy A. Bradshaw printed: Someone told me if a boy doesn't have sex, he gets "blue balls," and his pee-pee falls off. Can I find mine and have the doctor put it back if it does? [Not correct]

Punk wrote: Who was there to keep us safe and believe in us in childhood? [No one] Just thinking of this makes us hate people, and then we hate ourselves for hating others. I'm angry with myself for remembering the past. [You see the truth of your past, Punk.]

I'm hanging in until my youngest son settles down, and then I'll kill myself. [I hope we can find a way you won't need to do that.] Considering the hell we've been through, we're proud we've lived so long. [You deserve to feel proud.] You didn't permit us to die. You allowed us to choose life. Do you know what you did? [I know, Punk.]

It'd be easier to handle matters if there weren't so many, and they came one at a time. [They never do.] I'm trying to present my thoughts and emotions to you, even if they come across incorrectly. [Good job!] You claim we all have addictions. What are mine? [Fears and beliefs] I have many fears, such as fear of love, doing wrong, not being righteous, feeling, and life. I've been afraid for so long I don't know what to do without fear. Is this my addiction? [Yep.]

Tara wrote: My people are at the door of knowledge and are consumed by any feelings we cannot handle, leading to bad choices. We haven't learned to manage anger and pain, so we keep going in circles. We begin hating others and ourselves until we turn everything off and start again. [I know] Why can't we find a place to stay?

Lilly wrote, is it okay to feel funny when your mother's boyfriend talks about your breasts? [Yes.] That isn't nice, so we won't talk about it anymore.

Bell wrote: I's figure until I's make us pleasant within I's has no rights being physically beautiful. Yep, that's be the truth. I reckon that be so. I's be mixed up for sure. I reckon wheeze got that straight. We's sorry the writing's not good at all. I's reckon you'll understand what we's mean and all. I's for one ain't never say I's all good.

Paul wrote: Some alters asked how to think kind things about unkind people. [What's important is that you first allow your feelings. Then you can go on a spiritual walk with those feelings.] Some of us know it's just your job to care. [I care because I care. My job is to help.] At least I can think someone cares about me. [This is a great beginning.]

Mary, Rose, and Hope wrote: What if getting better is worse? What if there's never better? [It's not possible to predict the future.] What's there to live for? We can't see it but are trying to. Is it our real kids? [I don't have that answer for you. Each of us must decide for ourselves what we live for.] It feels terrible to have a family and not be with them. [Yes, it does.]

One of the Kids printed: Oh! You said you take us to Toys R Us. Remember? We not forget. When we go? We got a car, you know.

Punky wrote: Hi there! We're moving and have many things to work out, like whether we can still take care of our real kids. I, for one, am fearful of letting go and being myself. Why am I so weak and dumb? [You're neither.]

Would therapy go faster if we were living by ourselves? [Yes.] We keep trying to get you to say we don't have MPD to avoid having to believe others so gravely mistreated us. [I know.] We're making a list of things to do to take care of ourselves. [Good for you, Punky!] We think it's a good idea for an MPD to write notes. [So do I.]

Andy wrote: I had just begun to play when my mother forced me to become an adult and work. It wasn't fair. Can I do both? [It's okay to balance work and play.] I wish the playful happy part could've stayed with me. [It can return.] I want to thank you for letting me be a kid. It feels great to be happy and carefree with you. [You can do more.] I may have lost the ability to play. [You can find it again.] It's sad how much I had to give away to please others. [Yes, it is.]

Annie printed: We like to have a playroom to feel safe.[That would be fun.] *Our new home scary. The others say I need to look grown-up. They're shame of me. They no wish others to see our stuff. They no want me. Why they shame of me? I want a chalkboard to draw on.* [Good idea!]

Nina printed: I think we should share a place for all of us. I like to have some ruffles since I'm a girl.

Abby printed: Good girl no cry. bad girl cry. I want binky too. Pretty one.

Mary printed: I'm Mary. I feel.

Us Cluster wrote: You said some of us are whole alters, and some are fragments. When you said they don't count the fragments, some of us felt sad and unimportant. I'd like you to know they're as important as the full ones. [All of you are relevant, even the fragments.]

Adona wrote the following on her drawing, not shown: Left hand of God, 777, 7734, of DARK, and Satin spelled backward beneath a stick figure being consumed by flames. Her drawing also included the names: Vali, Bela, Belial, Lucifer, and her writing: "Daughters of Satan, drink the blood, devour the baby, eat me, and eat the flesh to save your soul." {Vali is a son of the god Odin, Bela is an alternative name for Lucifer, and Belial is one of Lucifer's most esteemed demons.}

Gina drew her room, not shown, consisting of a square with a door and 16 stick figures representing young child alters and wrote: There's no warmth, just cold darkness and great sadness. I can hear all of them, including one banging her head against a wall. Others cut and otherwise hurt themselves, and one stares at a wall. Some never talk and have sad eyes. One wears black, one is mad at me, and many drift around. One is a baby, and I can't get it to quit crying. I can see some of them when they come close to me, but there are so many I can't see, which scares me. I care about them because they're scared and can't get out. I'm not like them, and I'm afraid of them. Why am I here?

Us Cluster wrote: Iris drew "Kids Town, the Road to Learning," as follows, with input from Brooklyn and other alters. Mr. Clarke suggested making "Kids Town" to promote co-conscious. We constructed buildings and a park to accommodate over one hundred alters, both boys and girls, including those in the walls and chairs, so they could feel better, and we had a loudspeaker if everyone needed to hear something. We also brought animals to put in our zoo.

A fabulous park, including a small covered arena, adorns the middle of the town. The park has a tree swing which Punk swings on. She fishes in a pond on the outskirts of town. Sidewalks have pole lamps, but there are no streets. Lining the walkways are stores and shops for purchasing ice cream, candy, soda, groceries, toys, arts and crafts, sporting goods, sewing materials, books, and jewelry. There's Sophia's clothing, Punky's Pets, Dorothy's Fancy Pants, Tim's Music Thing, Suzie Q.'s Bakery, Punky's Flowers, Iris's Art Gallery, and a Health Food and Diet Center. On one side of the Diet Center, an arrow points down a lane beneath the writing, "Welcome to the Zoo." There's also a Movie House, Pizza Restaurant, Le Gym, Hot Dogging, and Ice Rink next to a coin-operated pony to ride for 25 cents.

Mr. Clarke told me to tell Crystal, who's on fire, that it's safe, and as he suggested, I put her in our Kids Town ice rink. She's better now but still has occasional flashbacks. We constructed a racetrack for Timothy A. Bradshaw and soundproofed it. Finally, we built a gate with a secret code to keep The Mother out and jail if she somehow got in. [Nice town.]

Mr. Clarke suggested a "Dream Machine" for our town due to our fear of leaving our house. Pony evolved into the "Dream Machine." We used it to visit real or imagined pleasant places like we used to do on Pony. We visited Grandma's farm, went on boat trips with the delightful, distinctive fragrance of the ocean and the feeling of wind ruffling through our hair, and traveled to lovely and peaceful places in the mountains and other sites where we could forget the bad for a while. We also used it to dream of what we wanted our life to be and imagine our mother being kind, like Grandma.

Kids began writing checks, so we started saving money in a jar for their candy and toys, making them feel better. We thought of having a nursery, but no one wanted to deal with alter babies, even though two unnamed alters knew why they were crying. [Why were the alter babies crying, Leena?] They were left alone in the dark.

1971 Therapy with Mr. Clarke

Life with Husband and Boyfriends

Various alters helped me write: We have 11 days until court and don't want to think about it. We don't like court because it makes memories real, so we're writing to let out some worry. Crap, the truth is we're hiding stuff the best we can and not feeling. We just have to hold it together. Clarke, you said it hurts not to trust when you want to. I'd say not so, but then I felt my deep hurt and knew you told the truth. I don't know what's holding us together, but it's a thin thread. Trying to look as if we're functioning okay consumes us, but we don't want to talk about it because we'd lose it. With Anthony, we remember breaking down and returning but not recalling anything in between. We'd sit for days and not move or even blink.

We're not sure if we can start over. We definitely can't handle another 40 years like the last. After leaving The Mother, we thought everything would be fine, but we met Anthony. We left Anthony so our sons would have a better life but feared they never would. Clarke, God is punishing us for some reason. What kind of life are we supposed to commit to? You know we're just worthless trash not worth keeping, and have nothing to offer the world. [Not so, Leena.]

Life with Other Family Members

Our brother, Buster, phoned us. We haven't seen him in two years. We talked about our siblings, and he said it'd be nice if we could all see each other. He seemed happy, and we're glad.

I visited Buster for the holidays and spent hours, talking about life growing up. Our boyfriend, Rick, even enjoyed the visit. Buster and his wife said they hesitate to speak to The Mother because they're unsure if they're on her "Crap List." Buster's wife revealed that The Mother once phoned her crying and told her to be kind to Buster because he had a lousy childhood. The Mother added she cooked and took care of us and had three gifted kids, including me. That shocked me. Buster said our mother was evil, went to bars, forced her children to do her work, and our older sister was his mother. He claims to be The Mother's "retard." I told Buster The Mother didn't know us. I added that I avoid her because I can't stand up to her. I'm home now and getting cold, so I need to build a fire.

Life in my Household

Gina wrote: Can our boyfriend, Rick, be a dad to our sons and husband to the older alters? If Rick only marries Leena, what's he to the rest of us?

Alter Dynamics

Doer printed: I'm called Doer. I began at age one, and although I became Mary at age five, I continue to live within her. I hold the emotions the other alters can't handle, especially the intense ill will toward people. I make people hate me by saying and doing bad things. I hate myself, too, very much. I get whipped for peeing my pants or my bed. I pee when I get scared, and still wet my pants when I started kindergarten.

Paul wrote, Sophia curls our hair and puts grown-up clothes on us, which she doesn't allow us to take off.

Therapy Not Included Under Other Headings

Us Cluster wrote: The Fools want to phone you, Mr. Clarke. They're scared of us because we know what they don't want to know: hate, love, sex, and evil. They want The Mother to love them. We gave them love, and they hate us for it. Therefore we know hate.

Feeler wrote: I feel emotionally empty. I can feel the body a little, but my heart doesn't have emotion. That bothers the alters with feelings because none can feel when the non-feeling ones are out. The body overloads if we all start to come out. Did you know there are different milkshakes: chocolate, vanilla, banana, and strawberry? That fascinates me!

I feel disconnected but am trying to adapt so I can come back. Cheri said to tell you the fog she's in isn't fun, that things around her seem far away, and that when she drinks too much alcohol, she can't remember what happens, and her sense of time is lost. [Thanks for this information, Leena.]

Rachel printed: I feel rage and hate toward myself, and I'm scared to make mistakes. I've changed three words and must think of the next and then place and spell it correctly. I'm making more mistakes as I go along, and my headache doesn't help. Wow! I see it now. The fog is to protect us from us.

Tinker printed: I'm no good because I choose us over them. I'm evil, and now no one going to like me. I should've chosen them. Now I'm going to pay for doing wrong. I should never want anything!

Bell wrote: Dis ain't right. Is not! Tis thems I's should dis been mad at.

Mary printed I no like me more.

Sarah wrote: I didn't know about these feelings. I think the wall was to protect the Angry Ones from knowing. We still don't know who's present, but at least they're writing some. The so-called fog was a punishment, saying if you're going to do this, I'll pay you back by making it more challenging.

Pam wrote: I hate waiting for the ax to fall. I'll just to wait and see if I pay for choosing me over them. The fog has many purposes. It erases our brains so we can't think, hides our fear, and masks us from each other so we can't hurt one another, but we can know what it's like to make choices alone. Finally, it protects us from overwhelming feelings and the Evil Ones.

Punky and Annie played with toys at the therapist's office. Later, the fun started at my birthday dinner, so some kid alters came out." [Happy birthday, Leena.]

Sophia wrote, Mr. Clark, several alters have written to you so far, yet many don't want to be known yet.

Susan printed: Can I be six but do grown-up stuff? Not sex, but the rest of it. I scared to be grown up. I no like the boy and girl stuff. I want daddies to be daddies and you to be you. You know?

Wise Ones wrote: To keep us safe, prevent overload, and be able to live, we, along with the We Clusters and a few others, out of love, caused the remaining alters to forget who they were and that they ever lived. Some came out of their bodies and couldn't return. We don't remember their names. Their bodies are gone, but their spirits live in the heart. So many of us have therefore been dead for a long time. We hope the heart knows it's time to come back. Much has changed. We so much want to live, learn, see, and do things, now that it's safe again, but we fear the time we have to live this go-around will be too short. If we had all the time we needed, we could live more and take a while to look and feel. We want to learn and live as fast as possible before forgetting again.

We love the world out there. There's so much to see and do. I wish we knew how much time we have this go-around. We don't want to overload, but we always do. Maybe there's hope this time. Perhaps life for us won't be rotten again. There are new people around and no old faces. Can we trust these people not to hurt or use us? It's a massive risk for us, but as before, we'll love, trust, and enjoy everything, yet we fear that, as always, we'll get overloaded, hurt and used, become mixed up, unhappy, scared to live, and then forget again. How much can we do this before we can no longer try or the body dies? We love people as we do you, Mr. Clarke, but we can't trust them like we do you. Rick is home. Bye. [Thanks for trusting me, Leena.]

Cheri wrote: We know why we eat when we're hurt. When we were little and got hurt, Grandma would give us a snack, and we'd feel better.

Deon wrote: We have a headache and are a nervous wreck. Amy, Punky, Lisa, Dot, Lilly, and Nettie are with me. They aren't sure what to tell you or what you want from them.

Pennie printed: The mother and her boyfriends touched me, and I floated to the ceiling.

Lilly and others wrote: We're seeing and hearing things again. Our baby alters are coming out, and they're scared of everything. They cry continuously in the dark. We try to tell ourselves it's not real, but we know it is. We see snapshots of it. How do you stop it? Please help us end it, Mr. Clarke David, the giant killer. Are we going crazy? You're helping us deal with the past, Mr. Clarke David, and have brought us to a better place.

An older Amanda wrote: What if better is worse? What if there never is better? I drew Hope superimposed on Amanda as follows:

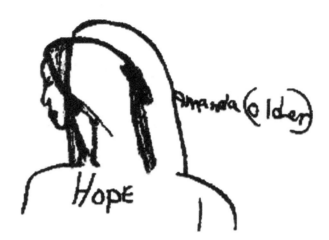

Lilly wrote: Gatekeepers of the Truth are unnamed alters created to hold the truth. They want you, Mr. Clark, to help us remember that truth and teach us to deal with it so we can avoid the mental ward. We protect ourselves from those alters who tell us others brutalized us, because we don't feel brutalized. Mr. Clarke David, can you work miracles for the insane?

You might say we fell off into the pits of hell a couple of times these past two weeks. Mr. Clarke David, is it not our world rather than theirs? Were they not damaged beyond being able to love? We conceived us to take their places. We came from insanity. Have you been around the insane and encountered the emptiness? It's like a "Black Hole" where the dark material, like self-hate, shame, pure evil, anger, disappointment, neglect, revenge, being unloved, and horrible memories, live. You said a child from this much wreckage could become unhinged, MPD, or like the perpetrators. When alters we can't reach are out, there's no "us," but only them. It takes all they are to keep us on the tightrope. They allow no input or output. They only focus on the tightrope. How will you reach them and keep us sane at the same time? We have many questions and fears about what's to come, Mr. Clarke David.

We're in between alters now. Someone knows how to drive, but I don't. I guess you might say we're back on the high wire again. Also, I remember talking about sex with you upset someone, but it's good to air it out.

Tina wrote: Some say to embrace the insanity, hell, pain, and truth, even though to do so is to risk losing us. They say we should have faith and trust Mr. Clarke, who can pull all of us out to stand before him. Presently, I close my eyes, and all I see is my mother's bedroom.

Feeler wrote: Maybe we're to blame for loving and wanting to be loved. [No.] Does it mean I'm not good enough to be a good mom if I admit to having MPD? Can we be locked up for having MPD? These two things scare me badly. [No and no.] Also, I want to be needed. [This isn't up to you.]

We Cluster wrote: We had a dream about you. We were afraid you'd judge us, Mr. Clarke, for what we did or what happened to us. We thought you'd see dirty, nasty, and dumb. You didn't pity or think less of us because we never learned. Instead, you respected us for what we are. Something happened to us. The shell broke and fell away, and we saw for the first time what you see. We're beautiful.

We have three steps to take: Seeing and accepting us, seeing and accepting you, and seeing and accepting the world. We know our pain and ugliness touched you, but you stayed. Why? We can't handle all the hurt alone and sharing with you took the weight off. Now we can live and not die from it. We won't let you take on our total load, and if that means never being healthy, then so be it!

Someone helped Amy print: I'm surrounded by many, yet I feel alone. Why is this so? [Many of your alters are unaware of each other.] {"Separation" (separation) is when alters are unaware of each other.} You scared me when you put your hand near my face. Someone says to tell you another door has opened. [Whoopee!] I'll come to talk to you when I feel you're safe. [Okay, Amy.] Have you seen enough of us and heard enough of our stories to fix us rightly?. [Let's look some more.] We have bad things to hide. To think badly is terrible. [To think is normal.] I hate it when people tell me to just smile; change my thinking; let the past lie and grow up; everyone has bad things happen to them; that's life; don't let them get to you, and be kind, so they'll be nice to you. [I don't like that either.] You'll see the evil in me if you look with your heart. It fills me up. [You don't have evil in you. You have fear and doubt.]

Hurter printed: I'm not good enough. When will I see that?

Cathleen wrote: Is this called self-pity? [Sort of.] The alter babies needed me to save them. I failed them all. I wish my mother would've killed me that night or I had died in the closet with the others all those years ago. [Well, you didn't, so we'll look for ways to live, love, and have fun.] I've passed the hell I lived all those years with my mother to my real kids. I'll end this one way or another! I promise there'll be no more hurt!

We need to stop. The feeling of death is enormous. I want to die. [It's too soon.] Sometimes I wish others could see my pain. [They see lots of your hurt, but you're pretty good at hiding it.] I asked God to keep my heart righteous, so I'd never do what others did to me.

I'm concerned about your putting us back together. I just found out I'm not alone, and you think it's time to take that away. I'd like to know more about what to expect if we go through this "being one" business. I believe the choice isn't mine, and I must trust you to know what's best for me. I need to understand more about the changes we'd likely go through. [We can discuss this, but the choice is always yours.] We don't want to run amok again and start boozing. [I know] Why do you think we're ready? We don't feel ready. We're not even sure what you're asking us to do. [Maybe no one is ever prepared to make scary changes.] We need you to trust us to do what's right for us. [I do. We won't bring the alters together until you're ready, Cathleen.]

Punky wrote: I'm writing for Annie and Amy again. I don't understand your saying we hurt because we're separated from each other since we separated to avoid hurt. [It's like hiding family members individually in different places from bad people. Everyone would be safe but lonely.] No one ever gave Annie and Amy anything just for them until you caused them to feel special at our previous meeting by giving them something.

Bunnie and Amy printed: We want to talk to you too, but we think you believe we too little. Also, we scared you want to hurt us. We scared to chat. You think we silly. We can hop. We can be good. We no make much noise. We sad, but we smile lots. We sit like Ladies. [Hi Amy and Bunny. We can talk. I won't hurt you or think you're silly.]

We behave as people wish, which keeps us out of trouble and out of the mental ward. We put on faces that keep us safe. Punky and Suzie Q. don't cause any hurt we can't handle, so they're allowed to come and go as needed, whereas other alters must be locked up.

The body is hated because it only causes pain, yet someone has to be in it to keep it going and talk to the outside. Alters can move beyond the body, which often dies when left empty too long. It's horrifying to go into the body to bring it back to life because if an alter is halfway in, and the body doesn't come alive, the alter dies. Sometimes the body won't let anyone in as payback for neglecting it for so long, and at that time, it takes the energy of many alters to get it to function again. [These are interesting dynamics, Leena]

Jennifer and Annie came out last night and colored with my son. I'm on call at the County Mental Health hotline. [Good for you for the hotline work, Leena.]

Punky wrote: It hasn't rained this week, so I'm going to do some planting, one of my favorite activities. Cathleen wants to know what needy means and how she's needy.

Doer printed: Don't forget me. I hold the emotions they can't handle. I had to live to keep the truth hidden. I regret we had to lose goodness forever. Finally, I've found peace because I can tell the truth to Mr. Clarke. Be aware of our hate that's grown over time, and be a wise one, my new friend.

Mary printed: I won't say sorry for the hug, but I should ask firstis. I forgot. You no want more cause I dirty more now. Can hugs get you dirty too? We no want you dirty too. It hurts. I foget cause I no want to know. We can't have love now cause it'll hurt people. I think the lady right. We tried be good, and we get hurt. So why be good when good hurts you? I know that! It's about time they figer it out.

The Mother can't die us. We too many. It take for ever to die us. The Mother likes black and red. We gona die? I know play no more. I no want to die. You no die me okay?

Punky wrote: I missed a bunch of time. It's as if time stopped or slowed down, but I haven't. Little sheep lost their homes and wandered hopelessly to find what was lost but could never find it. What a profound sadness that lies in their little hearts! My body grew over the years, but I didn't, even though I learned to talk better and got better at hiding myself. I've gotten farther away from the true self that causes me pain. Today you said you think I'm ready to engage in counseling more persistently. I'm scared. I see a picture in my mind of all those I know squeezing together. I don't want to lose myself.

Sarah wrote: I don't want to die or unite with the other alters and lose part of me. I've no idea how therapy will turn out, and you said you didn't. [Nope.]

What are we going to work on? [You, Leena] I read that you change codependent behavior by changing your expectations of others. How do you know where to draw the line? The book discriminates between responsibility for another and behaving responsibly toward that other. What's the difference? I also read that no one can make me do or feel anything, yet others make me crazy. [Nope] I can see why there are "doormats" in this world, and you said I don't need to be one now because my circumstances are different. I want to live with and be equal to others, but I can't find that in this world. How many healthy people are out there? I want to be healthy, but how do healthy people live with healthy people? [This may be the secret to being healthy. What do you want your picture to look like when you're in good health?]

Everyone is blaming me for my struggles with one of my sons. [Nope. They're all wrong.] They're saying it's my fault. [Nope] So many people can't be mistaken. [Yes, they can.]

You never told us what we'll be going through or what kind of work we'll do. [You're already doing it, Leena.] What's this forgetfulness? Will my memory return, or did I lose it until we become healthy again? [It'll be okay.] Is there anything we can do to clear our heads? I give up! [Yes. Don't give up.]

Abigail is sad and fears you'll believe she's wicked and that her mother should've spanked her more. [I don't.] I like how you said no one would die, that we're a puzzle not put together, and we'll piece together but still have individuality.

eB printed backward: Hi Clarke. I'm eB. [Hi eB.] I'm from the Evil Ones. I like hurting and killing! I'm evil! Talk, you die! Leave me alone! I'll kill all! Comes satin lord. I'm sick.

yM printed backward: Hi Clarke, I'm yM. [Hi yM.] I write in reverse and cry a lot at school. I get smacked for printing with my left hand. eB and I want to know if we come out, will you burn, kill, or lock us up? [No] Will you dislike us and leave us? [I don't think so.] Will you fail to help us? [I'll help.] Will you put us to sleep and then force us out? [No.] Will you dislike us when you find out how bad we are? [I'll like you.] Do you know we want to be gooδ? [I know.] If we start working, you'll be scareδ. [No] I δon't want you to become aware of the ugly baδ that happeneδ to us, what we let them δo, or what we δiδ. [It's okay.]

Tamara wrote: You ask me why I don't talk about being raped. It's because rape is the girl's fault, no matter what. [Nope] Plus, it depends on what you call it. Is it rape when they tell you to do sexual things, or you and your sister will get hurt; or say if you don't, they'll tell your mother, and she'll kill you; or if they cut your clothes off and demand that you lay still or they'll cut you severely? Is it rape when they choke you, and if you move, they strangle you more, or when four guys push you down and have sex with you and say if you utter a word, they'll find you, and next time it'll be worse? How about when someone ties you up and forces animals to do it to you, or if a man maintains you owe him because he buys you food? Is it rape if you cry and leave your body, you let them "do you" to keep other people safe, or let them have you so they won't get mad? Is it rape if you're over age 18 and molestation if you're under age 18? [Good questions. I'd say they're all rape.]

What did you think when I told you my mother's boyfriend and I had sex? [I thought he shouldn't have treated you that way.] Did you think I wanted it or liked it when I told you men came to my bedroom and sometimes hurt me, and mother did terrible things? [Nope]

Tina wrote: I've given you this letter, so I guess I'm a fool to risk your knowing about me. [I'll work very hard to live up to your trust.] It's my fault my prior counselor became upset because I went against what I knew not to do. [No. You're not responsible for her actions.] She proved to be untrustworthy, which has led me to fear trusting anyone. [I know, and I'm angry because now it's harder for you to trust me.] Counting on others is a risk, but I must trust others if I hope to heal. It's a risk either way. [Yes.] I'm not saying you would, but I'm considering what it'd do to us if you tried to have sex with us. [I know]

Angry and Hurt wrote: We didn't ask for sex or want it. We like it very much when you hug us, and we love being held and rocked.

Tina wrote: I'd rather blame myself than accept that my prior counselor did something wrong. [Except that you're blaming yourself for something someone else did.] I'm sorry this happened and impacted our relationship. [Me too.] We still have hope. [Good] I'm wondering if someone ever victimized you sexually. [It hasn't happened to me.] It'd feel better not to explain what it feels like to have pain and missed time. [You don't have to explain. I hear your pain.]

I don't have emotions presently, so I don't care about anything. I'm an evil person. I fabricated it all to look like I'm a super person. I don't care and never did. [This is the little voice of deception talking.]

Your compliments have helped me be proud. I'm on my way to being healthy and taking care of myself, which feels good. [That's worth being proud of, and I'm glad it feels good.] I'm here because I want to learn to make good choices. [I know, Tina.]

I didn't sleep well last night thinking of this letter and my son. I've got an hour before I leave to see you. I must decide what the alters want to wear and how they want their hair done. I'm feeling scared that I might tell you too much. Time will tell! [Tell me what you're ready to disclose, Leena.]

A Thinker wrote: We used to play tennis and volleyball and walk for miles, but stopped because we got scared of people. We like those activities and miss them, but our need to be safe is greater. We know we can't be completely secure, but we've taken away some risks. [Isolation promotes your feeling safe, yet you regret the price.]

I think you're right, Mr. Clarke. I'm a good person, but I need to get rid of the garbage and fear and learn to deal with people. It helped when I told you I lost part of me, and you said I didn't lose it but just hid it to keep it safe. My sister said I have a sense of peace and self-esteem I never had before seeing you. [I see this too, Thinker.]

Gina wrote: When you hypnotize us, you don't want to open the gates to hell because you don't know what's there. Did you know others raped us so often that we've lost count, which doesn't count those we brought on ourselves? Do you know how many of The Mother's boyfriends violated us? Do you know that one showed his special little girl grown-up ways on her birthday, or how many of us haven't come out for you to see?

Mary printed: I say a word to the bigger kids. They give up on us. Who care about us? They can't stop. You make um care some more? Okay?

Little printed: We have to go back. The "Biggers," older alters, can't do so well. Little Ones need to learn more to help the "Biggers."

I think we need to quit bullshitting ourselves. We can't make things better. People are people and hurt you some. Will you? [Not intentionally]. We have pain from people hurting us, but our pain from not doing anything about it hurts more. I'm still not sure who I am, but Leena will suffice for now.

Silly Sally wrote: I come out when things get too hot. When you talked about the bottom line today, we heard your rules as: don't harm your property, don't hurt your body, no sex, I'm not to get so mad because it scares you, we can talk about almost anything, and we can't convince you we don't have MPD. It hurt when you said we don't have anything to talk about if we don't have MPD. [Let's discuss this. It's unfair for you to think that's what I said.]

Daisy, who wants Leena to return, printed: Not so. We have lots of talking to do.

How important is it that we put ourselves together, and why? I hate losing people. [We'll discuss this more, Leena.] I wonder if I can successfully reunite with Anthony, considering what I've learned so far. [I doubt it.]

Can people heal themselves? [Yes.] I think the real one of us is dead, and we remain. [I don't think so.] How will putting us to sleep help? You said it makes things go faster. How so? [When we're relaxed, we learn faster and more efficiently, Leena.]

Us Cluster wrote: We have to trust ourselves to know what's best for us, even when we can't explain it. [Absolutely.] I believe we must help ourselves with your guidance. I'm sorry if this sounds selfish. [It doesn't] We might not know how to get there, but we'll know if it's right for us. [That makes sense.] We don't want to give away what we've learned and have to begin anew. [You won't have to.] We have so many questions but aren't sure if we should ask them. [Trust yourselves to know when it's okay to ask.] You know we sold our souls to Satan. We're his now. We always do wrong. Once you're dead, you're gone. [No. They deceived you.]

Mary printed: The worms like girls, but they hurt bad girls. They bite me and scare me. They're yucky, have no eyes, and I hate them all.

Rachel printed: Say too much, and mama's going to get you. [Not anymore] Hush, baby, and don't say a word. We want to be good little girls so we don't get hurt. You're the person the other alters talk to. Can you make us good little girls? [How do good little girls behave?] We didn't reveal what they did, and won't tell on you. We don't want to be angry, crazy, and evil girls anymore. We want to be good little girls. Okay? [You don't have to make a promise like that to me. The world has changed. Now, if people hurt you, it's okay to tell. Really!]

I've taken pride in working at the Mental Health Clinic and speaking about my views and abuse experience. [You really must've helped many people, Leena!] Certain people in my life have proven they can't be trusted, so I need to keep myself safe from them, right? [Absolutely] I feel guilty withholding information, even from them, because it feels like a lie. [I know this is confusing. It goes back to when you were little, and your mother told you: Tell the whole truth. Don't leave anything out or---. Don't make me ask you twice or---.]

People can play nasty, but I'll protect my real kids and be true to myself if I stay good. [You'll be true to yourself, but that can't always protect others.] Anthony continues to come at us from all sides and hit us deeply. [This will stop.] I don't feel sick or crazy. [Good, because you're not.] What do you call what he did to us? [Brainwashing] You said a normal person couldn't handle everything we've been through, so how would being more normal have helped? [That's a good question.] We know we need to talk about what happened to us. [We will when the time is right.] Others wanted us to do things to show we loved them but didn't want us to think. [That's the basis of brainwashing.]

My life with my real kids has given me joy. The love they taught me was so pure and straightforward that my heart rejoiced. Others took that away. I want to learn self-confidence. I want to know what to tell others and how not to react. [I'll teach you.] I have so many things I need to do. I'm not sure what to do first. [We'll work on prioritizing, Leena.]

How did you know others caused me to be crazy? [They didn't make you crazy. They pushed you to doubt your sanity.] Can we get fit before seeing Anthony in court? [We'll get you ready.] He used a type of hypnosis on me. Now I switch when anyone talks like him. Did you notice my response when you hypnotized me, Mr. Clarke? [Yes, but I didn't know why.] Do you think I have a reason to fear Anthony now, or is it all in my head? [I think you do.] I don't reckon having MPD makes me an unfit mom. [It doesn't.]

I'm feeling somewhat used by my boyfriend. [I'm glad you're aware of it.] I feel shame for saying it, but I've learned that I must sometimes put myself first to avoid getting hurt. It goes against everything I believe in, but am I right? [Yes. I know this is difficult for you, but it's essential, Leena.]

I'm always mixing up time, thoughts, and emotions. Will people quit feeling uneasy and talk to us like equals when you stick us together? [Mostly] Why don't you do it, then? [You're not ready.]

I never sense you're uneasy with me or think I'm dumb. [I'm not uncomfortable, and you're not stupid.] You don't seem to think I'm weird for having my stuffie. [I don't.] Can you teach me to be proud of myself? [Yes.] Why do people try to hurt others profoundly? [They're broken and can't cope with anyone else being whole.] I have no reason to blame Anthony or feel self-pity because I brought it on myself. [You didn't, Leena.]

My son, Brad, and I listened to a subliminal tape on harmony and happiness. We each slept better and didn't have bad dreams. [Great!]

A friend's boyfriend hugged me sexually when I only wanted a friendly hug. Is it wrong to embrace people? [No.] Do all hugs between a girl and a guy mean more than being friendly? [No, but there's a need for boundaries. Your little alters are afraid to hurt others emotionally and are in a tug-of-war with that part of you who knows what feels right and wrong.] The group counselor gives hugs, but she says she doesn't lean into them. Maybe that's why hugs sometimes feel okay but sometimes don't. [That's why, Leena.]

I avoid speaking altogether because I don't want it taken wrong and lose a friend. [Yet it's better to express your emotions as you have them.] I'd like you to help me learn to say no. [Okay. We'll practice ways to say no.]

I'm the missing part of Sarah and Tara and remain unknown to the other alters. I don't want you to know who I am now, but in time, you'll know. I don't know if we'll remain a mass of alters or become one. I'll know which way is best for me when I'm ready. I'm beginning to learn how I work and why, but to choose now feels premature. When the time comes, I want to be what works best and feel belonging in a new and beautiful way. [Good idea! Let me know when you want me to know who you are.]

We Cluster wrote: Some of us want to talk but want to wait for something from you. [That's about trust.] We've been sad and wanted to cry. Sometimes we think we'll never stop crying. What do you think? [You'll stop.] Do you think we've learned to live with ourselves better or just forgotten more? [Both, plus other things] We separated alters by names, jobs, emotions, and recollections, and there's a place inside called the library where we keep lost time, feelings, and information we don't want to remember. To act naturally, alters must hide lost time.

You're scaring us because we're bonding with you. You're becoming vital to us in how you react, feel, and think about us. We want to keep it businesslike. Oh hell! We tried. Don't get any ideas, mister. You can tell this isn't easy. [Yes. I know.] Mother always said when we like a guy, we want to have sex with him. We don't want sex with you. [Good!] We also don't want to care because we're scared of getting hurt again. You could leave, quit working, or decide that you can't help us. We have alters who flee from situations like this. It's scary to like, trust, or rely on someone when many people have let us down. [I know this is hard for you, and I appreciate your willingness to risk.] We want to learn not to be that way. [You don't have to be that way. There are many ways to show caring without being physical or sexual. Caring goes through the mind and heart, not the body.]

We know a lady doesn't talk about sex to a man. [Yes, a lady can, Leena.] We guess it's just that we've never had a relationship without sex, so we don't feel okay if it's not about sex. [That's kind of stuck, huh?] That's why we don't let the badness out. We don't want to risk making you or us feel uneasy. [This is a crucial part of our work. We need to let the bad verbalize their emotions. That's not the same as acting on them.]

I'm proud I have MPD because it means I'm strong enough to get healthier and be what I want. [Yes!] My physician said my claiming MPD is for attention. That doesn't make sense because there are so many ways to get attention without the downside of MPD. [It doesn't make sense to me, either. That physician is very ignorant about MPD.] It doesn't matter what you call it. Hurt is hurt, shame is shame, and not being wanted is being unwanted. MPD is about what this did to me and what I've made of it. I can better myself, feel self-pity, or hide it and not do anything about it. People make it complicated by shaming us and not giving us a chance. [Yes, they do.]

What do I need to do to become emotionally healthier? Do you know? [I do it with meditation, acceptance, forgiveness, and healing, Leena. It means feeling our emotions, not running away or switching, taking down our walls, and connecting all parts of ourselves until we feel whole. It also means accepting the truth about bad things we did or were done to us, no longer confusing who we are with what happened to us, standing still until it becomes quiet, and loving oneself.]

Jane printed: I come out at night. I bad girl. I be mad cause they don't like me. I tell my mother I no like you. I say no, and they get angry. No one likes me, but we not care. I have Mary, and she has me. Mary been here first, but she littler than me. I big mad for Mary and me. We made Mary Jane.

Cheri wrote: They're going to be tired tomorrow. If they want to sleep, they should let us out.

Charles printed I walk on walk thing last night.

Bobby printed: I did too, and it was fun. We did 12 miles at 2.1 mph.

George wrote: I'm alternating between crying and inexplicable laughter. I think I'm losing it. I can't remember behaving like this before. Can you stop it, Mr. Clarke? I'm the only half-normal one of us. I don't trust anyone, so I haven't come out so you can see me. I don't wish for you to know me yet.

Punky wrote: I've been taking care of children since I was old enough to walk. I like viewing caretaking positively and feeling happy about it, not sad. Just because I'm young at heart and mind doesn't mean I can't do grown-up things. [Yep. That's true.]

I'd like to tell you what I know, but can I just hide it and be a nice happy girl? I recall things they don't, but it'll hurt, and I can't be at peace if I experience the emotions attached to what I remember. I suppress the recollections and thereby don't allow feelings. What do you think, Mr. Clarke? [Let's discuss this.]

They told me I needed someone to take care of me since I didn't know how because I'm a girl and don't have brains. I'm scared they're right and don't want to find out. So many people can't be wrong. [Yes, they can, Punky.]

Somehow there must be a way to feel pain yet have a sense of control, be in a safe place before I leave your office, and keep the memories without going over the edge. [There is.] I don't understand why people judge me, put names on me, and hate me because I see things as they are. [They're scared of life.]

You want me to risk, trust you, and trust myself. You want me to trust and believe in other people because they're not the same as my past culprits. [I just don't quit, do I?] I'm afraid to find out people are the same as before. [I know.]

I don't like the rules, "dog-eat-dog" and "first-come-first-serve." [I don't either.] I figure I'm upset because others don't hear me. [Yep] It's too late to expect accountability in previous situations. [Yes, but not for future opportunities.] You want us to feel our emotional pain, feel how deep it goes, and learn why we have it, but I don't want to. [This is difficult, isn't it?]

I hide because it's profoundly painful when you're kind to me. I feel the pain just from writing this. Other alters got beaten for wearing their emotions on their sleeves. I don't want people to know this about them or me. [Thanks for helping me understand this, Punky.] I want to give myself a chance to be what I could have been had others not brutalized me.

I'm scared I'll have to go to court on my own. I don't know if I can. [I'll help, Leena.] I've told you things others could use against me, and I could lose my son. [Not because of anything you've told me] You've shown me considerable care and thoughtfulness and that you're concerned about what happens to me as if I exist. I shouldn't have asked for your help with the court matter. It was quite a struggle to do so. [You're an actual person, and should've asked for help. You did great in court!] It took me five years to accept that my agony was real. Now that I've done so, I don't know what to do next. [I'll show you.]

Clara printed: My name is Clara. [Hi Clara.] It was good seeing you. I can't wait to see you again. I'd heard a lot about you and liked talking to you today. [Great!] I'm sending a note to you about some peculiar alter names. I often don't give out the names, Bo-Bo, PJ, Hurt, Punky,

Bubble, and others because people make fun of them. These names are different, for sure. [They're all vital, Clara.]

I also want to know what problems come with putting us together. The Little Ones wish to talk about a place to feel safe and be alone. [We'll talk a lot about this in the months ahead.] {What Sarah calls putting us together is "Integration" (integration), the joining of two or more alters, or for fragments, integration may simply entail other alters being able to access what those fragments hold without a switch.}

Paul wrote: I still don't understand why I'm not important. Why do I have to go away and not come out again? I thought I was meaningful, but I guess I was wrong.

Us Cluster wrote: How do we know our age? We know we're not 40 because we don't feel like it. Lots of us are still little kids, but some are grown, and Holy Man is older than time. [I don't feel 55, either. Your confusion is reasonable.]

Those alters working with you the most have learned compassion for us, which has changed us. Your most helpful feedback was when our Crazy Ones heard you remark that you can see how our mother's denying our reality led to our believing we were crazy.

Why did you call it rape when The Mother's boyfriend had sex with Dorothy but not when The Mother did? [What your mother did was rape also. Sexual violation of the body or spirit when someone is too young, helpless, or unaware to say no is rape.] It's strange how some of us are grown, and others aren't. Is that okay? [It's normal.] We refrain from speaking our minds due to fear of being wrong. [I know. Your fear of being wrong is reasonable.]

We're finding out we're different from most MPDs. [All people are at least slightly divergent from one another, no matter what word describes them.] We're wondering where we fit. [Since childhood, you believed that if you fit in, the world would be friendly, and people wouldn't do bad things. The world doesn't work that way. We'll continue to talk about this. Always remember, when you try too hard to fit in, you stop protecting your emotional boundaries. That's what makes hurt possible.]

Why do you see me twice weekly? [It's because many alters inside need individual attention and support, and we can move faster this way by giving some a chance to rest and then resume working without waiting such a long time. That can help make switching more manageable and less of a problem for you every day, Leena.]

How do I use a tampon, and how much do I wash that part? [Those are questions for you to ask counselor Molly.] I think I should already know these things. [Not if no one taught you.]

Alice wrote: The Mother told us because we have monthlies, we're dirty, evil, disgusting, spoiled, bitches and whores. [No. All girls have monthlies.] Are monthlies a curse from God? [I think they're helping you clean your body regularly so children can be born and be heathy.]

Paz wrote: Why were we considered so evil and beaten even when we didn't know what we'd done wrong? [I don't know.] The Mother taught us not to talk about private things, but our mind is full of important questions we need you to answer. [No doubt it is. Ask.]

We're learning to be alive, and it brings tears to our eyes to think that to find ourselves means to lose ourselves! [You won't be lost.] I wish I had stayed dead instead of learning. Then it wouldn't hurt and feel so unfair to be alive so briefly, just to have it taken away again! [I know you're scared, but it won't happen that way, Paz.]

Rachel helped Zoe print: My name is Zoe! Do you know I never learned how to write my name? I used another to write this letter. [Hi Zoe.] I want to live, Mr. Clarke David! Do I not have the right? [Yes.] We've never even talked. Why Mr. Clarke David? You don't know me. [Well, speak to me next time, Zoe.] Do you know I have yellow curly hair but hate curly hair? Do you know I have freckles and have tried everything to get rid of them?

I'm four years old, and I know lots, such as I want to play dot-to-dot with the stars, roller skate, ride a bike, and love my real kids and show them I'm proud of them no matter what. Do you know I've never been treated nicely and only have bad memories, but I want to have many good ones? Do you know I have dreams like having laughs, smiles, love, warmth, goodness, grandbabies to enjoy, and a house full of truthfulness like a teensy piece of heaven on earth? Do you know we don't even know what it's like to be loved and that I like to dance very much? [No, I didn't know these things.] I want to grow up and be a real special lady! I want my real kids to understand that no matter how bad the world is, they're always cherished and loved by me, and my arms remain open. [What a beautiful vision!] What happens to the dreams I've held so tightly for so long? [Some die.] What happens to those like us when we die? Will we go to heaven? [The body will die, but you'll live.] Soon, I'll not be needed at all. [Yes, you will. You're the Gatekeeper of the Vision, and I don't think your sons would agree.]

Grandma said dolls teach little girls how to be good moms, whereas my mother said they make little girls whores. [Your Grandma was right, Zoe.]

Paz wrote: We have alters with no names, but we haven't forgotten them. How do we write their names? [Good question]. We previously introduced Gatekeepers of the Sleepers, Good and Evil, Truth, Secrets, and the Heart. Gatekeepers of The Light, who are nameless, allow our virtue to shine versus hiding it.

Rachel printed we're terrified of becoming a grown-up. [That makes sense.] We still desire to be healthy, but old habits don't die quickly. [Nope]

Belinda wrote: I'm Belinda. [Hi, Belinda.] I'm a soldier. I wait for the day I can live, but I'm not sure I want to, for fear I'll just die. No thanks. We're not the only ones who feel this way. We began writing our names and, so far, have 187.

Bo-Bo printed backward: We fight hard to stay alive, but must die. Boohoo. No one cares! [I care.]

Sarah wrote I've been trying to think of what's important to me and how I want others to remember me, but I'm not sure yet!

Ruth printed: We know we need to find all of us and make one out of us. It'll be if meant to be, but I don't have to like or want it, Okay? What happened to the three that were here but now aren't? Like Bo-Bo, we begin dropping like flies when we start getting along. I want them back. Which one of us is going to be the last one standing? Did you know this would happen to us? [They may not be dead. They may not want to come back. Maybe they never were here.] We thought we all would remain and learn to compromise and take care of each other. Therefore we wouldn't lose time and could be around other people. We never imagined we'd die off! All we have is ourselves, and we're dying one by one. Someone is deciding who goes. [Who?] Maybe in the next five minutes, I'll be gone.

I hate saying no. [Saying no is a practical means of responding at times and is the benchmark of healthy people, Leena.] Every time I tell my son no, neither of us is happy. [Your son is lucky you say no. It's his only chance of facing the truth.]

Mr. Clarke, I've been thinking about your saying I can leave my stuffie in my car, and if I need one, I can use one of your office stuffies. I told you no because I need my stuffie until I find out if you're like other people and say kind things but don't mean them. We test people only to a point. If we decide they're like the others, checking ends.

I begin by believing that the people we want to love or trust are kind because it's in my heart to do so, but I end up seeing them as evil because that's my reality. I become nasty when I have to. Everyone will use you for their benefit, even if it hurts you, so you crush them first.

The Mother told me, "Love is only a word used for sex. Tell them you love them if you have to, but always keep your head. Love doesn't bring in food. You have to have a man."

I accepted these things, but I also believe in: goodness, money doesn't make you happy, love is out there, people are kind, and you can be joyful. Furthermore, I believe people care what happens to you but don't know how to help, and if you see the virtue in others, they'll see you in a favorable light.

I don't know if I'm more like The Mother or me. When I first thought about this, I went into the darkness, like when others told me I'm The Mother because I'm just like her. I've been in the dark but don't wish to remain there. I want to find the answers to who I am, what I believe, how I'm supposed to act, and who you think I am. [We'll discuss all this, Leena.] I don't know if we're ready to go against the rest of the world, with all its grown-ups and essential people like doctors, police, court staff, hospital personnel, teachers, and ordinary people like parents and family. Most of them told us we were terrible for making up stories about what happened to us, and we paid the price.

I don't put you with them, Mr. Clarke, because you're one of a kind, and counselor Carolyn, dear Carolyn, said she'd help as far as she could but that I was to see you when the time came because you could help us through the long haul. Counselor Dahlia is a kind lady, but we scared the hell out of her every time we switched. The first time I met you, Mr. Clarke, I wanted to test your fortitude. That's why I brought out my drawings to show you, including the less tasteful ones.

I was hurt when Carolyn left and told us we had caused her to go. I didn't want to like, believe in, or trust anymore because I didn't want to get hurt again. [That's understandable, Leena.]

Do you know how many said they wanted to help us but never did? The mental ward doctors gave up when Dorothy couldn't see things their way. They said Dorothy had been angry for three months, and if she couldn't stop now, they couldn't help her. One doctor kept asking Dorothy how she raped her mother's boyfriend. Others asked her how that man raped her when she'd been with so many men. They asked Dorothy if she was responsible, and when she said no, they returned with additional questions that Dorothy couldn't answer. They tore Dorothy down until she didn't know what was real. Dorothy prayed for something she could hold on to. [That's a heartbreaking story.]

After I told you what happened to us, Sarah sensed something in you. After that, we couldn't look directly into your eyes. It's almost like you became part of us. When we felt you with that unnamed feeling, we were deeply shamed but relieved because we finally found someone who knows us for what we are. [I'm glad you found relief, Leena.]

Rose wrote: Perhaps I need to plan my future and not wait for someone to do it for me! [That's healthy. I'll give you something another person wrote about that.]

Rose, Basket, Bonnie, and others wrote: We're afraid because people are beginning to know we're not one person, and we didn't want them to know that. We're angry because we didn't have a way to go unnoticed. [It's okay to be here with the people you can trust.]

I know it's okay to cry when someone hits you. What about when someone hurts you emotionally? That hurts also. I blend sexual sensations with emotions. [It's confusing when love and sex happen to children. Children don't know how to experience love without sexual confusion when they grow up.] We've learned that any emotions toward another are sexual. [Some are sexual. Most aren't. You can also have feelings simultaneously, Leena.]

I want to go deeper, but I can't explain it because I don't have the words to express my emotions. [It'll happen. You're doing great!] I don't trust myself. It's not you. I know where you stand. [I understand.] If I show you I care and you react badly, I'll feel rejected, ashamed, and not good enough. I shouldn't have emotions at all. [This must feel painful and impossible for you to figure out.] I'm sorry for making such comments. I think I shouldn't have brought it up. We don't want sex, but it's how we react to our emotions. I hate feelings. [You were right to bring it up. When people are truthful, things get better over time.] I must find a place where I don't have to deny myself and hide what I know. [Right!]

Us Cluster wrote: Since we're feeling, again, we need information on keeping us together, comforting ourselves, and thinking straight. We've felt this pain alone before. [That's pretty scary.] It's a blinding pain, deep and massive. Our recourse is death or, with great effort, to create another alter. We know we need to feel the pain to overcome it, and we can't do it alone, but we don't want others to know of our suffering. We're ashamed of it. Is there a word to voice all it costs us? [How about love and separation?] We want to learn so much from you, but we don't trust ourselves to let go because we don't want to risk what we have. [That makes sense.]

Our mother told us she wouldn't hesitate to give us away and never forgave us for her pain. She insisted nothing was wrong with us except for self-pity, selfishness, and making a big deal out of nothing. Why do we have to pay for what others did to us? [It's not fair, huh? Life isn't always just.]

Punk wrote: You said other alters got broken forever, but not me? [Yes.] I'm asking myself to trust you, Mr. Clarke. As much as I hate outsiders, I know only an outsider can help us. [It's scary, huh?] I feel a deep shame for letting my body go. [It's okay.] Will my telling you of the cruelty I've experienced help me heal? [Yes.] Now that I've revealed some secrets, I worry about how you view me and fear to ask. [I know you still hold back. It's okay. I would, too, if people had hurt me so much. You'll reveal when you're ready. That's the best way. I appreciate that you have so much confidence in me that you've risked telling me so much thus far.]

I brought this all on myself. Others treated me harshly to feel loved, cared for, understood, close and cherished. They needed all these things, leaving me with shame and feeling dirty. I'll never need anything again. One man said he wanted to be close to something untouched and pure before the world destroyed it. [Thank you for explaining this. You didn't bring this on yourself.]

I struggle with the words, but I'd like to use my heart as a match to relight others' hearts to be seen and felt. [You'll find the words. It's difficult, Punk, to find words for the heart and spiritual matters.]

Us Cluster wrote: May and Robot helped Dorothy not go crazy when hospital staff gave her double messages and denied her reality. The doctors denied our reality, so we gave up on it. Our perception of reality is trying to return, but we don't want to go through our previous reactions.

To love all things, do we need to feel all pain? [You can spiritually feel another person's pain but not hold it in your body.] We had something no one could name, and we had no guide or teacher but were left to handle it alone. [I know.]

Will you finish what you started with us? [I don't think you'll finish with me. I'm one teacher. I'm grateful I've had this opportunity to know you and be part of your journey. Still, there'll be more teachers in your life.] We don't let you in, do we? [You allow me in a little at a time by writing so many personal things and allowing me to respond to them.]

Jennifer wrote: Are you the one we seek? Tell me what you think, please! I need to know if you're him. Can you tell me? We need to talk. I'm aware of where we need to go. I must find the one we seek! I speak, and you listen. You never said if you're him. You know if you are!

I can't explain it better, but we don't feel alone! [Wonderful, Leena!] Something in me wants to come out. Is that crazy? [Nope. It's normal.] The church told me I wasn't strong in the Lord's words, that evil spirits took over my body, and that I needed to pray and cut them out. [The church is composed of humans with human thoughts and limitations who don't always understand.]

I'm sorry for all the writing. I know you're busy, and reading my letters takes you away from other things you need to do. [I appreciate your correspondence. I know it helps you, and it's beneficial to me in our work.

Of our over 205 active alters, which do you think is the most prominent? [I don't know.] It's like a dream come true to sit with you and talk about my beliefs and what I know, even though I still have fear! [Of course, you remain afraid!] I'm still unable to explain where the voices come from or how I know things I was never exposed to. [You'll understand before long, Leena.]

Did you tell me I had MPD? It seems you left me not knowing. [I didn't think it was time. Maybe I was wrong.] I'm risking telling you things and hoping you won't shut the door in my face. [Thanks for trusting.] Sarah, Holy Man, and Tara only exist to us. Sometimes they tell us things that we've learned aren't correct. [I think we all have these guides. We just don't know how to listen to them.]

Did I cause my perpetrators to do and say the things they did? [No.] I've let down my guard with you, and my fear grows. I've learned that when I trust, I get hurt, and the pain increases. [I know it's horrifying for you to risk.] I know you'd never hurt me as others did, but what happens when I trust and open up again in the outer world? [You can be harmed there. That's why learning boundaries is so important.] We're searching for knowledge and understanding because that's the key. [Yep] I think God wants me to learn to love openly despite the pain! [You're probably right.] I'm reading that deep concentration can lead to all kinds of visions. [Yes. Historians have recorded this. It's called meditation, Leena.]

The more I remember things, the more scared and confused I become. [I know it's hard to keep allowing the awareness.] Are you the teacher who can teach me what I couldn't learn as a child? [I'm one. Others will come.]

You've given your friendship to me. That doesn't mean sex, but that you'll be there for me, care about what happens to me, and I can share myself with you in more profound ways, and you won't hurt me. I wish I could explain this better. [You're expressing this very clearly.]

I've made it easy for people to torment me by believing their bull. [Then let's stop making it easy.] All of it was my fault, and I can't see why you can't see that! [Because it isn't true.]

I think I must pay you for your time with me. It worries me that you're doing much of it for free, mostly because I'm not worth your time. [Yes, you are. We're all worth more than money, Leena.]

I'm writing to you about money matters and the holidays to let out some worry. [Great idea!] We're hiding things as best we can and not feeling. [Yep. I know how to do that too. The problem is that you can't keep doing it and live well simultaneously.]

When I talked about one of my sons today, I felt confused until you said it hurts not to trust when you want to. It feels like a thin thread is holding us together, but we don't want to talk about it as we fear becoming overwhelmed.[You won't become overwhelmed. I'll help you through it.] We hide behind indifference to disguise our helplessness. [I know.]

Sarah said we're going to be okay in court. [You can count on Sarah.] I didn't push hard enough to save my marriage. I feel like a failure. [I know you're feeling this way, but you did the right thing for yourself and your children by getting out of your marriage.] I don't know if you figured it out yet, but we don't give up so easily on anything. [I know. That's one of your traits I respect.] The Mother said we never could keep anyone or do anything right. [She was wrong.] Anthony came across as believable even when he misrepresented the truth. [He's a great liar and deceiver.] I wish we could've had a good relationship. [I don't think he was capable.]

I don't know if I can live another 40 years like the last 40. [You won't have to.] You know we're worthless garbage, not worth keeping and have nothing to offer the world. [Your mother taught you to believe this. That doesn't make it so. Remember what your siblings told you about the horrible, ridiculous, untrue things your mother told them, Leena.]

Each alter must grow individually. We can't be whole if one evolves faster than another, so we'll all lose. We can't talk to you as a group because we have different views. Mary feels anger toward The Mother. Some believe The Mother did her best and did everything out of love. Others claim The Mother brutalized us for being evil. Some feel hurt, confused, and sad. Each alter took part of our reality.

Communication between alters can be difficult because some use different words for the same thing. Punky can interact with selves and most other alters. Punky avoided Anthony to preserve her innocence.

Gina wrote: A book I'm reading helps me find the words to express myself. I've discovered that I need to let my heart grow and show it to others versus hiding it. [Yes.]

An Evil One wrote, on judgment day may they curse your soul as ours will be and to hell with us all.

Cathleen wrote: This isn't real, is it Clarke? We don't have anything to fear. We made it up because we have terrible minds and think of horrible things, right? That's why we see you, right?

Tina wrote: Other people told us our story is pieced together and not true because we're missing too much, plus we were okay last year. My heart feels like it's going to blow up.

Mary printed, so much in my head.

Tina wrote: I don't know what it's called when we change, and none of us remember what happened for hours or days. [Amnesia/fugue] Someone pulled out and sat in the corner of my room. They wore black pants and underthings, a hat, and a shirt.

Andy wrote: We question the way we view things sometimes. You said we've never stood still long enough to be touched. Is that why we don't know what impacted means? [Maybe. Standing still is the opposite of change, so the more you switch, the less you can be touched.]

Is your therapy psychodynamic (discovering unconscious conflicts), interpersonal (relationships and talking skills), cognitive (changing distorted thinking), or behavioral (replacing harmful behaviors with useful ones)? [It's a combination of all these plus other approaches.]

Dammit, Clarke, I'm too scared to live! There, I said it! I don't know how to live. If living is having our emotions and being aware of them, I don't want it. [This is a painful part of becoming oneself.] How would you like to live even a day in my shoes? [I don't know if I could handle it, Leena.]

Pam wrote: You're asking me to risk going into the mental hospital again, but I told you I can't ever do that. That's what happens when we have emotions. [We'll find another way.]

Amber wrote: Are you asking us to open the door to our feelings a little at a time versus feeling the whole range at once? [Open just a bit at a time.] If we don't open up fast enough, will you give up on us? [Not a chance.] We're not sure what you want us to feel. Are we to share good emotions or only the bad? Do we share emotions we had that day, feelings of failure, or fear that we can't keep our son safe? [Sorry. I screwed this up!] We don't want to feel everything and have no way back. That would make us crazy. [I want you to have your emotions at a pace you can safely manage. You're pacing yourself well.]

Gina wrote: We'll do as Clarke asks. We just hope he knows how to get us back. If not, death is better than where we'll go. We can't lose because we'll be too gone to know if we don't return. May God have mercy on our souls.

Paz wrote: Once upon a time, this thin girl wanted to hide from the world. Every time she got hurt, she thought if only she were ugly and obese, people would leave her alone. Even gaining 40 pounds didn't stop people, so the thin girl added more. Then she began having overwhelming emotions and didn't know what to do with them, so she ate to push them down. She dieted from time to time but failed because devastating emotions led her to eat again. Then, she discovered the more she weighed, the more she disliked herself. The thin girl had worked hard on liking her emotional makeup, so she decided it should go with her physical appearance. She wanted to quit hiding her emotions, so she lost weight and worked on her feelings. Plus, she didn't want to keep buying more oversized clothing. She was scared that emotions would come up to send her back if she didn't lose weight quickly, so the thin girl decided she needed to lose weight rapidly. Losing weight worked until she weighed 82 pounds, and her doctor yelled and threatened to confine her, so she added pounds. We're scared to lose weight because we don't know how to handle the wrong attention. It's safer to be fat, but the looks and words from others hurt, and mostly we don't like the way we look and feel. So, we want to lose weight to like our physical appearance. The end. [Let's discuss this, Paz.]

I'm having a problem with sex with my boyfriend, including vomiting and suppressing anger. I'm mad at myself because I handled sex before, so why not now? [Because you're experiencing your emotions, Leena.] I have a feeling I can't name but am ashamed of it. It must be evil, or I'd know what it is. [Not true. It's just a new emotion.]

You're not confusing, so I know my feelings about you, and they're not so mixed up or intense, like emptiness or terror. Since I can name these emotions about you, maybe I can use them as a springboard to unravel my feelings toward others. [Good idea]

The last time we met, I felt warm and safe. Do you feel sorry for me in some way? [No. It feels like caring and compassion.] I stopped my emotions and pulled away because I was frightened of having something that could never be real and that I didn't deserve. [You do deserve to have good feelings.] I wanted to lose control for a little while in the safety of your office and tell you I appreciated your helping me with the court and dealing with sexuality. I couldn't ask, feel, or show it, but I sensed you had an idea of what was going on, which shamed me. How does being truthful to myself and to you feel? [Pretty darn good, Leena!]

My body is alive with physical sensations this morning. When I went outdoors, I tilted my head back, closed my eyes, and widened my grin as I felt the breeze on my skin and in my hair. As I write, I can feel the coarseness of the paper and the roundness of my pen. I can see the glossy, bubbly appearance of my walls and see and feel the grainy texture of my rugs. It's mind-boggling but fantastic. [How marvelous!]

I'm cautious with you because you're a man, whereas I've been terrified of other men. [Makes sense.] Some have been meaner and more controlling than others. They're not the same, and I can't figure out why. [We'll discuss this]

It makes us proud that you were willing to stand up for us in court. We're not worthy of your taking any risks. [I don't care what it costs. You and I fashioned a deal, and if you don't quit, I won't either. You're worth it. We're all worth the same amount.] You said we have the will to live but fear to do so. [This is true of many people.] We've split so much that we don't even know if we can believe in ourselves. [Well, I believe in you, Leena.]

We were born clean, pure, and full of goodness. Then we experienced the opposite. We still needed love from others, so a war started between being kind and meeting our needs. We fashioned two parts of us so we could have both. [Pretty smart] We wanted The Mother's love, but we also wanted goodness. We couldn't choose between them, so we put some to sleep and called them Sleepers.

Unfortunately, forgetting our painful experiences set us up to get re-injured. Then we were repeatedly disappointed in ourselves, so self-loathing increased. We could put away the painful experiences and act healthy, or remember them and protect ourselves. Our soul has goodness in it. Your soul touched ours. [I'm glad] Can you reach us and help us grow? [Yes.]

Is it wrong for us to put ourselves first at times over our son's needs? [No, but I'm sure it's painful.] Are we judged by our sins and the sins of our parents? [People saying this doesn't make it so.] Why would you hurt another because that would also harm yourself and everything? [It's because people don't understand oneness.] What if we're not judged by our behavior but by the brightness of our spirit? [Wouldn't that be wonderful?] What if the place of one is real? Do you think those present would let it be? We struggle to choose between what we know to be accurate and what others believe is correct. [Always pick your truth.]

You gave us a list of books to read. If it helps, we'll not talk about them but just write about them. [It's also advisable to talk about them.] I know we should feel ashamed for wanting to learn and for our need to share what we learn. I'm aware you mustn't talk about what you're learning. [It's okay, Leena.]

Gina wrote: We just went through two hours of hell. One of us wanted to call Anthony. It was so bad I even dialed the number but hung up. I don't know what goes on in our heads sometimes. It's tricky around the holidays. I got one hell of a headache from it. Sometimes the thoughts and voices are deafening and challenging to control. [It's okay.]

Sarah wrote: Damn, I find myself clenching my fists in anger every time my ear hurts because it reminds me of getting hit on the side of my head. I know it's not seemly for a girl to curse, but I didn't say I'm well mannered, did I. I don't know why you tried to bring up my past tormenters. Maybe you wanted to see me cry. [I don't want that.] Well, you can do that with somebody else and just go around me. I don't want it brought up. [Sometimes, we must talk about things that make us uneasy or upset.] Mr. Clarke, remember how we told you we know what's happening in the room next to us? That's how we know you can put salt water in a needle and make a baby come out.

Rachel printed: We're back sewing the quilt and going through painful mind-bending thoughts. I hope I can muster up the courage to meet you face-to-face. If not, I'll just listen. I hope you don't mind. [Nope. It's okay.]

Meme printed: I want to say hi. I haven't sent note to you some time, Clarke. Do we still see you? [Yep] Don't read this if not. Do you like talking to kids? [Yep] You spoke to us before. I know this. What we been doing since last time? Have we been to play yet? Have you done fun things? [Ask Punky] Are you really a grow up? [Yes.] You look like one.

I like you cause you let us talk, but we scared to talk. We went to another doctor, not you. He had toys. You were going to have a playroom. Do you? [No. It didn't work out.] Do the others still play? I like them. Three other girls. Two like us. One not, you not too. Why you play with kids? [You know how to have fun.] Amy think you touch her again. She scared of you. [Please ask her what she fears.] Do you like alter babies? We got some, you know. They not play. My mother says play bad. I don't enjoy talking about her cause it make me cry. That's bad too. Why not things bad to you? You not like my mother. You kind. I have to do stuff now.

I'd like to make friends with the ladies from the class, but making friends scares me. [Remember, this is all about taking chances, Leena.] I don't know how to make friends. [Maybe it's time to learn?] I want to thank you because you're the only one who gives us hope and believes we can be something great. [You're welcome.] Since meeting you, we've gotten much better at putting thoughts and emotions into words. [That's a tremendous improvement.]

I asked Molly, the counselor, what it's like to be friends with a man, but not sexual. I think I'm finding out, and I like it. [Caring for people is natural, but that doesn't mean becoming sexual.] Mr. Clarke, you're odd, but we enjoy that. [Lots of people tell me that.] I'm sorry for getting you upset over what we talked about today. [You're not responsible when I get angry. I am. I get upset when people mess around with other people's minds.]

Does Rick have the right to take money out of my account even if I owe him? [Not without discussion with you] I can't seem to convince him that money for necessities is required before we can pay for recreation. [You need more explicit boundaries here for yourself, Leena]

My torturers took everything from me and left only pain and disgust. Why couldn't they at least leave me something positive to feel good about? [They didn't know how.]

I'm getting progressively better by coming to see you, yet other people continually try to push me back. [They're afraid of your new independence.] They also say you're teaching me wrong. [They're all pretty busy telling you and me how we should be, aren't they?] They say I'm selfish, too pushy, not understanding anymore, and getting coldhearted. Every time I say no, they ask if I think Clarke is helping me. [Nuts!] They claim they only have my best interest at heart. [I believe they're thinking of their own best interest.]

Perhaps my trust and faith in you are wrong. [You must decide what's best for you.] Others say I'll get let down and hurt because I'm setting my sites too high. [If we don't aim high, we never soar.] What are the odds we can be complete and healthy? [I don't know about odds. That's not the point anyway.] Maybe you should set a goal we can accomplish versus hoping for something that can't be, thereby doing more harm when we fall. [Limits are for people who want to get by safely. Besides, it's okay to tumble, get up, plummet again, and keep going.] I don't like being uncomfortable or bringing up upsetting matters. [Sometimes, we must talk about issues that make us nervous or disturb us, Leena.]

You said that I humble you sometimes. I didn't know whether to apologize or how to take it. I've heard that word used before, but I'm not sure what it means. I'm sorry if I hurt you. Does it mean to make you feel small? [Not quite. We had a misunderstanding here.] That wasn't my intent if you're offended, and I'm sorry. You might say I'm resting in still waters, and my deepness varies from tidal waves to rapids to no water. It wasn't to show you up or anything. My mind is going faster than I can write. I know my discussing the way I view life makes people uncomfortable.

I wish you could see the world through my eyes and heart, not your mind. You have worldly views, and the world is full of pre-judgment. Sometimes you look through your heart and see things solely for what they are. You're learning, my friend. I cherish your growth.

I thought you wanted to see how we reckon or how we're different in our thinking. [I do. You must keep expressing your truth and emotions, Leena.] I tend to make people feel uncomfortable. [You probably do sometimes, but you don't make me uneasy.] I don't want to fit into people's boxes. [Me neither, but we must learn to walk around them.] Some alters are wise beyond their age. [I believe you.] They've hidden from themselves what they know and waited all their lives for the person they could show themselves to.

Have you seen the place of The Light? [I haven't seen it, but I've experienced it.] What's it called? Is it real? [Love is real. Everything else is fear or illusion. Does this place feel like love to you?]

Tina wrote: Is it wrong to go around and around as long as we're replacing what's wrong with what's right each time? [That's good learning.] What I call hell, you call life, sexual you call caring, and what I call waiting, you call not trusting. We must learn a language we both can understand. [So we attain a new language together, right?] We have a feeling for you, but we're uncomfortable with it. [It's a feeling that's probably changing with time, but it's not sexual, so let it flow and trust it.] The more we feel safe, learn, and share with you, the more other alters come out of the shadows. [Wonderful!] Hope is growing, and the Sleepers are awakening. [I'm glad.]

I have an open mind, I want to fill with new productive thinking. [Wonderful, Leena!] You said The Mother doesn't know how to love, but I do. Where'd I learn that? [From oneness] I want to learn so much, but I have little time. [Time is relative.] I believe all of our alters have good hearts, but some got lost and are still struggling to find their way back. [I think you're correct.]

Abby printed: We eat healthy tv dinner. Aint we good girls! We aint do evil now. We still shook up and got num faces. That a side efect from migrans. We dont want another one in our lifetime like last night.

Tamara wrote: We know we've been writing to you a lot. We feel we're fading away again and want to get out as much as possible before changing. We can't put ourselves together, so we need to divide ourselves back to handle this great sadness and the great feeling of loss. Just maybe we're moving too fast. What do you think? [Perhaps it's because you're beginning to know and feel yourself.]

We began reading the book you gave us called The Awakening. Tara said that we're in the coming together and The Light. We wonder if she knows about oneness or the other places. [Probably, Tamara] How do we live with so many limits since limits keep us from reuniting and knowing? [It's hard to live in the body.]

We fear getting that far and getting lost. We don't think we're meant to go that far. We can go to the place of The Light if we want to. We sense oneness because we're standing in it. We're as one. If you open up to us and we to you to the extent we're one, we're left with no sense of self. Is that the death of the ego? [It's the death of the idea that you're a separate being.]

We left the body because we knew to stay would be the end of the body, mind, and soul. We chose to survive. It took us minutes to find this place, but we didn't have the steps to return, so we felt empty versus alive. We separated the soul and the mind so each could find its place, but in doing so, we separated ourselves from each other without knowing how to reunite. We kept scattering farther until our alters were so far apart that they became unknown to us and were parts without a sense of self. We came to you, Clarke, and as Sunshine awakens, the "glue," Tara and Sarah, will come to know each other. They're our teachers. They learn first and then teach us. But at the same time, their ways and the world's ways need to find a balance. [Now I understand more, Tamara.]

We thought we'd learned not to talk about things that aren't known. I'm disappointed with this. Now you're going to think we're crazy or lying. We spoke because we understood what we felt and saw with our hearts.

Punky wrote: Like us, it's called many things, but I believe it's a rest stop where the spirit can renew itself.

Us Cluster wrote: We think it's the next step up. We also believe it's using more of our brain, like people with ESP, or can heal others. This thinking could all be wrong too. Maybe we're what we learn from others, period! No more! No less!

Three years ago, some of the young alters and I went to a church where they practice laying on of hands, and I liked that, but they also believe in speaking in tongues, and I don't believe in that. I told the minister about being with God. He said that evil works in all kinds of ways and that evil is working through me because I'm not righteous, and that's why I don't believe in speaking in tongues. He added that I couldn't lay hands on people and heal them because I didn't speak in tongues. [There are those worldwide who make people well but don't speak in tongues.] The minister told me he got the calling at age 16 and has read the Bible for many years. He said I've never read the Bible or suffered in the name of the Lord. He asked how I could know God and his righteousness when all I know comes from evil. [He's just plain wrong, Leena.]

I had a flashback today. There were shadows of men all around me. I was lying down and couldn't move. I was screaming in my head, and my eyes were crying. [It must be terrifying when these flashbacks hit.] I sensed what was going on but couldn't pinpoint it. The faces were close, but I couldn't identify them. All I knew was that the terrifying feeling was too much, but then I must have switched. It lasted only three minutes, but the fear was still with me five hours later. [Don't be afraid of memories or emotions.]

I don't think I have the right to ask for help. [Yes, you do, and I'll help you.] The school people said I was dumb and told me not to bother looking at a book. I didn't like that. [Good, because they lied.] Why don't other people believe in me as you do? [They don't know how to.] Did I listen too much to people who told me I couldn't do things? [Yes.] I'm scared to put 100% into learning or working because I don't want to find out they're right." [You have to risk, and you'll be happy you did, Leena.]

I tell my boyfriend I listen to Clarke and take what I want to use. [Right] He said I needed to do everything you asked. [Nope] Sometimes, I just don't know how to respond. I'm not a nice person. [Not so] I like sharing about myself because I want people to know who I am.[That's pretty normal.] Sometimes I forget how to write to you because I lose my head. [No. Your memory]

I'd like to earn a good living, handle normalcy, and own a house within three years. [Okay. We'll have those goals.] I'm not sure I have the time to reach my goals. [Phooey] I'm scared I want achieve things, and all my work will be for nothing. [Don't waste time feeling sorry for yourself or doubting everything. We have much work to do.] I haven't given up, though, and I'm a fighter. [Good, Leena!]

Angry wrote: I have to control myself and not make people angry. I want to yell and scream but won't because it'd scare people, and I'd look crazy. [That makes sense.] The pretend alters, those we let others see, are parting so the real ones can come out, but I don't want them to. [It's time, though.]

Do you know how hard it is to look like you have control over your life so you don't get locked up in a hospital? [I think so.] Do you know there's more to what we call us than you've seen? [Yes.] Do you know we haven't told you about all of us? [Yes.]

I'd like to ask a question, but I'd have to tell you what I did, and the shame and humiliation are great. [It's okay to ask, Leena.] What's it called when you lose control, scream, and act crazy? [Free?] What about when you shut down and lose days? [Guilt and fear]

Today, you talked to us about shame, which we've been feeling a lot lately. We don't seem to fit in with any crowd, making us unhappy. Good people have too many standards we don't fit into, and they get upset when we're truthful, but evil people will accept anyone if you just shut up and do what they want. We don't like either one, but we need to fit in somewhere. [We all do.] We tried churches, but we don't believe enough, or our beliefs are wrong. [Okay] People maintain we're retarded, but we don't fit in there. [You're not retarded.] Others claim we're crazy and will never fit in. [They're wrong.] We're still looking and hoping. The only place we feel at ease is in your group, but we sometimes seem out of place even there. [It'll get better.]

You taught us an underlying sense of self-worth and left the door open to talk about what happened to us and learn for ourselves what we can and can't do. [Yes.] We've learned to say we're okay and evil things have happened to us instead of saying we're wicked because bad things happened. Right?[Yeah, perfect!] We think we've got it!

In the book about recovery, we read we need to allow our emotions to be as big as they were back then and embrace them, and then we can begin to heal. Is this what we're doing, Mr. Clarke? [Kind of] We read about boundaries to use if someone wants to sexually harm us, physically offend us, like inappropriate touching, or emotionally harm us, like when they discount us. We read about self-respect and avoiding enabling. [Great!] We learned that love doesn't hurt, but we sometimes must make choices as loving people that do hurt. [Yes.] We read about a paradox, which seems to be a contradiction but isn't. Examples are that we can love and hate someone simultaneously or be surrounded by others yet be lonely. [Great!] We read that we should change what we can and accept what we can't, whereas we tend to believe everything because we think we can't change anything. [You can change your life, Leena.]

I stayed up until 2:00 a.m. reading and discovered some new ideas. When people hit the age of 28 to 47, they suddenly find something is wrong with them, and they can't fix it themselves. Recovery is a process, not something we achieve entirely. The book talks about four stages of recovery: old behavior (denial), crisis management, recovery decision, and family of origin work (identifying the wrongs that happened to us as children). Then I learned about seven boundaries: physical, social, intellectual, emotional, social, sexual, time, and paradoxes. The book also talks about how healthy and unhealthy friends and families behave.

Punky wrote: I got a frog as a Christmas gift for my son, Brad. He smiled, hugged me, and said, "Thanks, mom." I guess I picked an excellent present. [Good job, Punky!] It eats live things. Yuck!

One of the times I got pulled over, the officer asked if I'd been drinking, using drugs, or taking medication. I said, No! He said he pulled me over because I went off the road twice, and he could give me a ticket. I said, No, thank you, sir! I don't like them. The officer smiled and said that was the nicest no thank you he'd ever heard. He asked if I had an excuse or reason, and I answered that I just didn't like them much. He asked why I went off the road, and I responded that I sometimes have many thoughts. [You did fine, Punky.]

Tina and Mickey wrote: Did we start integrating? [Yes.] Is this one of those backdoor things you taught us without our knowing it? [Yep] We don't want to become one at all! [You don't have to be just one. We'll discuss this in-depth.]

Punky Lil printed: Studly, my dog, he be sick, bad. He be down and bleed when he potties. He not worth much money, lacks looks, and gets into the garbage, but we love him dearly. How stupid we are for not knowing how much we care about him! We must shut down so knowing he's dying doesn't hurt us. We try to believe he's just a dog and a dime a dozen. [Yes, this is difficult, Punky Lil.]

Pennie printed, we ashamed of how we get so excited about Christmas lights. [Don't be. That's how I react, too.] We been waiting to see Santa Claus and talk to him. [That might be hard to do.] The Little Ones want to ask Santa to put love in their mother's heart. [That might need more than just Santa's help.] Santa might retreat from us because we're big. [No, he won't.]

Will there ever come a time we won't have fear during the holidays? [Yes, if you stay focused on getting there, Pennie.] Will we ever stand out enough that The Mother will be proud of us? [You're great now. That has nothing to do with how your mother feels about you. She mistreats you because she doesn't feel she matters much.] I fear life and hate my mother. I don't know how to deal with either one.

Well, Mr. Clarke, I'd like to say I'll make it, but it's just this time of year, plus things that aren't real to other people. Crap, most people have family and love. We know there are people like us, but our kind hides so well. As contracted with you, we'll go to the hotel next to Denny's instead of a hospital if life becomes overwhelming. [Okay, Leena.]

I don't know why I figure we're not going to make it. It's too difficult to look at our life in the big picture, so we keep it simple by only looking day to day, not comparing ourselves to people our age, being grateful for where we are, and knowing that we're doing our best. Still, when I ponder my life and other people's lives, I'm hurt because I fall short and feel helpless. We want what other people have, including a loving parent who cares about us. [I know.]

Kay printed: Hush, baby, or mama going to set you on fire. You can't find me because I'm quiet as a mouse. It's going to be a long night. It's 3:00 a.m., and no sleep yet. I've got the baby talk, crying, and screaming in my head. Staying here is tough. I've got to run. Fiddle-de-de, mama catch me.

I remember how to put my clothes on. I better do it now! Off with the PJs and on with the pants! I'm trying to control myself and just be me. You said our behavior gets us in trouble, Mr. Clarke! I don't want trouble.

We know what happens when we can't control ourselves! We no want more hurts to add to us or be crazy and lose people around us. That be for sure!

Poor little children! No one cares! Eyes see! Eyes see! They broke my heart, and no one can put it together again. Eyes see! Eyes see! You can't see me! Not in the head! I died in bed! Fiddle-de-dee. Rock + rock + rock – I's fall off my rocker + cry-cry-cry- you not get comfort, only a kick in your head! Eyes see! Eyes see! Round-u-go, where you stop, no one knows! Fiddle-de-dee. Eyes see! Eyes see! Go-around-around, you can't catch me. Stop around – around, and you get found. I sit very nice. I no cry. How do I stop it? I get killed if I try. I was a flower, a pretty flower. They pick me. It takes time. Then I die. Ugly and die, they throw the flower away. No one cares! Poor little dumb girl, she no cares!

Young ones from the We Cluster printed: We don't think she dumb. She got it right.

Kay printed: You can burn me, be Jack, put ice in my pants, and beat me. Eyes no care! You can torch my bed. I no care! Put pins under my nails. I no care! You can play ugly games, say what you want, and tell your lies. Eyes no care! You'll never lock us up because eyes see, and I'll have died. Eyes no care! You can put a broom in my butt and say I wish you were dead. You can put a hot iron on me, put me in the roaster, throw me, and put me in the toilet hole. You can stab me with forks, lie-lie-lie, share your bed, put me in the can, put me in the dark, and forget I'm there. You can tie me to a tree, crash into me with your car, march me nude to school, yell and scream at me, wash me roughly, put signs on me, make me be mommy, and say I'm dumb. You can take away Santa Claus and Easter Bunny, and I don't care or see because I don't have a mind! God doesn't care!

You can try to make us not be. But Eyes see! Eyes see! You can't make us go away. We hide-hide-hide and say, hush baby, don't say a word! Eyes see! Eyes see! Fiddle-de-dee, the baby died. No one cares! At the hospital, they said I lied. No one cares! Eyes see! Eyes see! Eyes see! Eyes see!

I've died! Poor little girl! No one cares! No one wants to hear! No one wants to see! Poor little children! No one cares! Eyes see! Eyes see! Fiddle-de-dee.

Pam wrote: You can kill my pets and cook them too. I won't tell you about my fear. You do it. I don't care. I don't see. [It's finally here for you. You see, know, and remember.] You can't make me go away. I hide. [That's how you survived.] I'm empty within. Please don't take that from me too. Let me have the shell. It's all I have left. [That's not what integration means.] I feel lost and confused. [I know.]

Mr. Clarke, I'm tired today. I'm thinking and feeling so much I'm not sure who I am. I remembered to put my clothes on. [Well, that's good, Leena.] Did I make my tormentors do the things they did? [This is never true.] People did terrible things to me because I'm evil. [This isn't true. You're not wicked.] I think I wanted so much to be loved by someone I closed my eyes to what they were and did. I got hurt when I kept my eyes closed too long. That's why the relationships failed. [Yes, but you had enough sense of yourself to not put up with continued mistreatment.]

I remember a group of people. Whoever they are, they don't want anything to do with meat. They don't want to handle or even look at it. Damn, I'm fighting with someone over the writing arm, which is hurting and difficult to control. I think I'll talk about something else. Our perpetrators had a way of making something sound right, even when it was as wrong as possible. When I'm unsure, I'll ask you. [That's a good idea. It's a challenge to know what to do sometimes, Leena.]

Tina wrote: I know, I know, dammit. It's okay. I only said a little. They don't want me to talk. [It's okay] It's hard in the head and heart to figure out emotions. [It'll be clearer someday.]

My boyfriend wants to know all about us but keeps himself a secret, which causes us to feel left out and unhappy. We don't think that's fair. [It isn't, Leena.] Maybe it's a girl but not a guy thing to feel closer by sharing. Generally, this is true about guys.] I don't think it's all MPD and me. [It's neither.]

What's it called when you get so scared you do and believe crazy things, and then later, when you're back, it's like you lost your mind and trust, and you never get it back? We call it "We Lost It."

This year is different because I composed a family of people who care about me. [That's wonderful, Leena!] Is that bad? [No. It's good to form a substitute family.] All that's left to do is rent a grandma and grandpa for the holidays. I know they're not a real family, but I can't say that much of my family felt real, except for my siblings.

Sarah wrote: We're not good. We wouldn't get hurt or let anyone hurt us if we were. As my mother said, we must like it, or we wouldn't let it be so. There's no more to say about it. [Yes, there is. Your mother was wrong!]

An Evil One printed: I talked to you a little about Satan and am scared to death to mention more. The DA and Sheriff told me they'd lock me up if I kept talking crazy! You and counselor Carolyn told me you believe me. It doesn't seem others take me at my word, so why should I? I must be so naughty that I make people do bad things to me. One day Clarke, you'll be around us too long, and turn bad on us. [That won't happen.]

Pam Peter wrote: Since I fear being in my house, someone had an alcoholic drink today, and I passed out. I know that's not a good idea, but it takes the fear and pain away and slows my thinking.

I think I have an eating problem, among other unhealthy habits. At your office today, we said we're fat because we need room for all of us. I didn't give you my full name because I thought you might think it silly. My name is Pam Peter, I believe happy thoughts leave us. [Hi Pam Peter] That's why I laugh at sad things. Sad things weigh us down. Laughing about them lifts our spirits. How do they say it? Crap happens, and it's how you deal with it that counts.

Now, about lying, I don't think it benefits us. There are too many of us to keep the lie straight. At the same time, the truth feels like a lie sometimes. It makes us crazy when we can't figure it out!

Clarke, you asked questions about us and impressed us, but your talk about putting us together didn't go over so well. I'm not out much, so I don't think I'm ready to lose myself. I switched quite a bit during our meeting. [Was our session helpful, Pam Peter?]

We Cluster wrote: We try to do what you request because we figure it's important, especially since you don't ask much. [I think what I ask is vital.] We think we feel alone because no one else is like us. Right? [Yes.] Something happened to us repeatedly a long time ago. We protected ourselves the only way we knew how. [Yes.] We've begun to stop denying and learn new ways of living, having emotions, sharing, and being. Our lives are starting to work now, and we're beginning to feel whole. [Great!]

When we become even more functional, will this sense of wholeness increase? [You got it!] We can feel this without killing other alters or becoming one by becoming bound in a common belief, such as accepting everyone's pain. [No one has to die.] We sense what's to come and the hurt it holds for us. We may be unable to handle what people we loved did to us. [This must be very difficult for you.] Happiness doesn't come to you. You create it. Right? [Yes.] Not being cared about was difficult then and is so now. We can't reason why The Mother did what she did, which makes us crazy. [It's not that she didn't care. She felt broken within and didn't know how to show caring or nurture children.] We came to you to find the truth. You might say we're choking on it but are getting it down. [Yes, you are.] Was what The Mother did real rape? [Yes, it was.] We remember parts of our story that other alters don't, and we don't feel safe sharing it yet. [That's okay.]

Mickey and Tina wrote: You have to care about something, and we like our garden and playing in the dirt. [Gardens are vital for our spirit, air, beauty, and fun.] We split ourselves to survive. Was that the right thing to do? [Absolutely!] If we become one, there'd only be one against so many who want to crush us, so couldn't we be hurt easier? Would we just split again? [Not now that you're learning new ways to protect yourself.] What if we break once more? We're afraid to take the risk. [All of life is a risk. Healing is a risk. Loving is a risk.] We want to show we're better than the fear they planted in us. [You are.]

It's difficult for us to trust someone 100% who has the power to hurt us. [Of course it is, Leena!] Putting us together won't change who we are. [I don't want to change you.] The Mother hated us just because we weren't smart. [I think your mother was full of pain and resentment that came out against other people, mostly her children.] Why do people want to change us? [Most people are uneasy with a difference. Differences include money, gender, politics, religion, skin color, social status, and education but mostly honesty.] We know it's wrong for us to express these negative thoughts. [You're entitled to your thoughts, even if they sound negative.] It's okay for essential people like The Mother, the doctor, or the minister to hurt us. [It's not okay for people to harm you just because they're essential.]

We don't reveal some decisions to you because we're afraid you'll talk us out of them. [It's not my job to tell you what to think or decide.] Do you see many parents who hate and wish their kids were dead? [No, but I've seen some act like they don't care.] The Mother wished us dead and told us that many times! [That was cruel of her.] We want someone we can trust who won't lock us up with crazy people. We're not mad but do get confused sometimes. [I know.]

Watching a show about a woman with MPD led to our wanting to deny that we have it. It scares us, to think we have MPD. We still don't want to believe bad things happened to us.

Clarke, do you know how difficult it is to look as if we have some control over our lives and look healthy so we don't get locked away in the hospital? Do you know we have more alters than you see? Some live in terror of being known. We hide them from people and maintain control for fear of "losing it" if we let them out. We've told you that we're scared of showing our true selves because the "first-class" people will put us away. Our revealing to you what happened to us hurts just as bad as when it happened. We know it's healing to let out those who want out, but they bring more crap that we don't want to know or feel.

We know we asked you before, Clarke, but we ask again, do you know we haven't told you about some of us? Maybe you don't need to know about other alters. It's difficult not to know how much is essential to reveal or how deep we need to go. We figure you don't want or need to know everything to do your work if you don't ask. We don't know what's important because you said you'd fix us, even if we do or say nothing. [I want to know everything you want to reveal when you're ready, Leena.]

1972 Therapy with Mr. Clarke

My "Bucket of Hope" letter reads: I was born in 1931. My bucket was bright and overflowing with hope. In the 1930s, my bucket lost its brightness, and in the 1940s, it acquired pressure cracks. I still had much hope, but it wasn't overflowing. In the 1950s, more pressure cracks occurred, which left me with only a cup of optimism. My bucket fell apart in the early 1960s, and only a drop of hope remained until 1965, when my bucket became empty. Between 1968 and 1971, through the help of others, especially you, Mr. Clarke, my bucket was being put back together but not holding, but soon after that, my bucket started to find super glue. I'm not alone. I look at your faces, and you don't look different. I mustn't look different either. My hope is growing.

Signed: Lynne

Life with The Mother

Dorothy became overwhelmed with life because she thought her mother would kill her. She wished she could have been like others and rolled with it. [She did better than she thought, Leena.]

Life with Husband and Boyfriends

We still have frightening dreams and memories of Anthony, but we've been working through our emotions. Perhaps what he did was reasonable, and we fought reason. I think it was wrong, but I don't know. He provided what seemed to be logical reasoning, and we didn't, so we seemed wrong. [Anthony was wrong, Leena.]

A woman from my therapy group had four horrible husbands. One had sex with a baby in diapers, killed it, and then had sex with it again. He knifed this woman seven times and broke her back. He gets out of jail soon, and she's reuniting with him.

My boyfriend and I try to talk about difficulties without "the blaming crap"! It's a relief to be truthful and not worry about his getting upset, but I still have to be careful with my words. I hate his drinking, and even the nauseating smell of alcohol is a real put-off. It scared me when he held me down, but he apologized, so we were okay with it. The first couple of times he hit us, he also said he didn't mean it, and we were good with that. However, it was unacceptable when he got mad at my sons and called them names.

𝔢𝔅 printed: You know what we'd do if we think there's no other way! That's all we're going to say!

Doer printed: We don't want to be evil! Our hopes for the future seem unsure because when we get home, we notice someone has been in our house and moved the furniture, and tiny objects are missing. [This must be frightening!]

If I give in and return to Anthony, things will calm down, and we'll have a better chance of staying alive, but we'll have to give up our lives, lose what we've become and what's real, and never find out what we can be. This dilemma is bull, and everything is coming back to us. We'll still have everything we've learned in the last five years. We have 34 years of old ways and 5 years of new ones. Is that why it'd be easier to go back? [I don't know, but let's look closely at your options, Leena.]

I'm vacillating about moving back in with my boyfriend, Rick. I talked to Rick about insults. [Good for you, Leena!] Every time I do things my way, I feel guilty, as if I did something wrong. Can you explain this? [You tell the truth, and Rick gets scared because he needs you dependent and has poor communication skills.]

We Cluster wrote: We told Rick we're not sure about living with him. We don't trust people overall. Half of us don't like anyone around, but half want people close. We're sure we don't like anyone trying to be romantic with us. People maintain we're wishy-washy and tend to let others control us.

I did something that's not me at all. I went to Rick's house wearing a coat only. I shocked Rick and myself. I felt shame and still can't believe I did it. It was like I needed to do something risky. Maybe it was a need to feel wanted.

I'm moving back in with Rick to save money for a down payment on a trailer for my son and me. Still, I hope to remain myself, with some improvements around the edges, and not live in fear. [Great!] I want my most significant worry to be rain on a fishing trip.

I've begun packing. We're not sure we're moving in with Rick for a good reason or trying to avoid going crazy. [Please keep me advised, Leena, about how it's going with Rick.] Maybe Rick won't control us so much this time and will stand up for us more. [That would be good].

Mary printed: I yes to Rick. We go to Rick.

Tabatha printed, I sometimes rides the mechanical horse at the "five and dime" when my boyfriend, Rick, takes her.

Life with Family and Friends

Our real dad called to wish us a happy birthday. We found him about 10 years ago but have had little contact. Rick called us four times today. We were sad that one of our sons didn't phone us. Our heart is heavy when we think about that son. Our little sister called. She's doing well but working hard. [Happy birthday, Leena.]

Feeler wrote: Grandma told me girls don't like sex, that it's only to produce babies, not to enjoy, and that if you like it, you're evil. [Grandma didn't get this right.] I want to stop the negative thoughts and emotions about Grandma. Counselor Molly advised me to put my thoughts about Grandma away in a safe place.

Grandma was brushing my hair nicely when she suddenly got angry after seeing me watching the ballerina chime in the tree outside the bedroom window. Grandma told me to get over here and not move. Then she swung a belt back and forth above my head and told me to sleep now. She said I didn't want her to have to use it. How can Grandma do this mean thing? Almost everything else my Grandma did was terrific. I feel crazy and out of control. How can losing control be positive? [You're not losing control. You merely feel as if you are.]

One time I got burned when I touched a hot pan. I glanced at Grandma, expecting her to say she didn't know, but she acted like she wasn't surprised. I think she knew because she said I should have known it would be hot, but I still think Grandma wouldn't hurt me because she's not The Mother. I'm mixing it up, but I feel okay with it. [It'll come, Feeler.] There's more, but not now. *We switching again. We can't write about this. Grandma not bad.* [That's okay.]

I need so much for Grandma to have been there for us and to keep her good. To do so, I have to be evil, but I don't want you to know I'm evil because you'll leave me too. I also don't want you to know I care what you do. It's hard to be truthful when I've learned that a lady doesn't talk about sex or complain, doesn't cry or get angry, and stuffs it all. [Even nurturing parental figures have weaknesses. Grandma was terrific but mishandled a few matters. That doesn't make you evil. I won't leave, and I know you care about what I do, Feeler.]

Life in my Household
Rachel printed: I just came back from a walk, and boy, I'm out of shape. Well, back to sewing and getting dinner out for tonight.

I'm no longer finding dead animals around the house. My son, Brad, said his heart feels lighter. Maybe now he can do better in school and not be so angry. [Both of you will get going better, Leena.]

Brad and Rick left for work. Brad sure thinks he's something, working four hours a day to earn $6.00 plus a tip. He's my cutie. I get the day to myself. Oh, what shall I do?

At dinner, I snickered, and it sounded like a pig, so Rick called me piggy, and Brad got in on the fun. I figure I can't get angry with Brad because I allowed Rick to return. [Right, Leena.]

Oh! I got the veggie and herb garden and flowerbed in and still wanted to work in the dirt, so I reseeded Rick's yard. My corn is 2½ inches high, the tomatoes are popping out, and the squash is blooming. I had two hotline calls today, and the weather report is that it looks like rain.

Alter Dynamics
Five printed: I'm Five. My age is my name. I was made when Ham saw The Monster and broke. I know about 7 3/4 and Pink, who's very little and just beginning to walk.

If Anthony continues to leave me alone, I can let go of many alters who hid from him and then taught my sons how to be kids while he was away: Sarah, Tara, Bunnie, Punky, Paul, Andy, Abby, Timothy A. Bradshaw, Autumn, and the Gatekeepers.

Also, Mary, who deals with Anthony's evilness, won't be needed, nor will Heather, who's required for fairness. I'll no longer need Rachel for the ugly sex or those holding desires because we can now pursue them. These alters are now free to be children.

We'll still need Winter to oppose our beliefs and to stop our emotions from getting out of control. We'll still require Crystal for fear of men. To start over and be good again, we'll need hope from Sunshine. We'll still need the Wise Ones to judge what Anthony is doing.

There was no great need for the I's Cluster, but now there is to help us read and write better and deal with bosses and other people. Holy Man and Seer will still be needed. [Why will Holy Man and Seer still be required, Leena?]

Therapy Not Included Under Other Headings

Having all this freedom is going to be different and scary. There are many open doors, and I'm unsure which way to go. I require help with this! I must feel needed and fill the emptiness, so I don't find another Anthony or think there's no more need for me and consider death. [You're becoming freer, Leena.]

Lilly wrote: I'm trying to find the person I was before I experienced all the wreckage. That person isn't lost, but it feels like she is. She's sleeping and waiting for the coast to clear.

I must also end the victim role by learning to meet my own needs and loving myself. Annie wants nothing but someone to love her. When I showed her love, it was the first time she'd felt love without strings attached. Oh, Clarke David, I found the wrong kind of love in all the wrong places. Punky, Annie, Amy, Suzie Q., and others are back in more ways than one. Each time we see you, more of us are checking you out.

Each of us holds a memory of information and emotions, like loose puzzle pieces. As we put pieces together, it takes form and makes sense. We find parts that fit each time we see you, but many are still missing.

Thank you, Clarke David. When you accepted us as kids, it enabled us to pursue growing up. Are we healthy yet, Clarke David, or crazier? We worry about risking being ourselves. Hopefully, no one will notice the difference. [You're healing, Lilly.]

Clarke David, do you think we were picked to be MPD before we were born to understand many lives quickly? We know that if not for The Light, we would've died. We were heading toward insanity.

We don't want to be touched lately, feel something terrible will happen, have thoughts of the dark side, and smell blood and the nauseating, sweet, putrid, and "steaky" scent of burnt flesh.

Amber wrote: First, the alters check you out to see how you respond to what they know. Next, they decide what to do with what they learn from you. Then they tell you more about what happened to them, taking a step deeper. What we learn from you changes our perception. Do you remember when one wrote about Lynne's second twin infant and Winter killing it?

Us Cluster wrote: With the help of Holy Man and Tara, who didn't learn from books, but from living, we feel freer and happier. Our heart is lighter than before, and we've found a more profound peace now that we can be ourselves. Our tormentors scrambled our brains and hurt us badly, and their rules bound us. When the walls we hid behind and the ideas of what we should be, fell, we stood in the light of knowledge. It was a death and birth. We're actualizing our potential.

I want to get lost. I'm not sane or essential, so if I get lost, no one will care. [I will, Leena.] I'd have to find my way back. It'd be an adventure! Suzie Q. came out tonight and is preparing a seven-course picnic dinner.

I speak a fair bit of three languages, and I'm a self-taught organ player. I can also knit, paint, draw, cut hair, make wedding and birthday cakes, farm, and teach. Teaching is what I like the most. Paz is out, and a couple more whose names I've forgotten. It looks like rain today, and we enjoy playing in a rainstorm.

Intelligent One wrote: You said we're many in one body. Maybe we need to see ourselves as a family unit versus many individuals. If an individual is evil, only that person is bad, yet the whole might be righteous. [Are you finding the family unit idea helpful, Leena?]

Punky Lil printed: You met that girl from the shelter and me going to the park to play. I no play there before. She likes coloring, playgrounds, and sandboxes.

Cheri wrote: Timothy A. Bradshaw wants to go fishing, Suzie Q. wants to color, and Paz wants to play with clay.

I burned myself on my barbecue. It hurt at first, and then it didn't, but the pain was excruciating five minutes later. [Ouch, Leena!]

MPDs have a ready-to-go family in one package. I gave my hate for The Mother to Mary, and when Mary couldn't handle it all, she split again and again.

I don't know how to stop Crybaby from crying. I lock her up because all she does is cry and scream. [Talk to her. You eventually need to let her out.]

Today I was driving to an appointment, and some of the kid alters saw Safeway and took us there. Afterward, because Sam loves going to new places, he explored a different road. When satisfied, he went back in and pushed me out, and I didn't know where I was or how I got there. [Sam and the kids were pretty assertive.]

The class I taught at Mental Health went well. Clara was there. I switched several times and lost my train of thought but continued talking about MPD from the perspective of the alter in command. [Good going, Leena!]

Some alters have moved around inside, and some think they've integrated. Many are out. The alters have many questions and are scared to ask but want to know. They've improved since they met you, Mr. Clarke. We did bubble therapy in our group today and liked it, and I met other people with MPD.

Do other people think girls who have periods are dirty, evil, spoiled, whoring, disgusting bitches? Is it wrong to talk about such things? Should I not advise others of my monthlies? Are they a curse from God? Are they because we're in heat and should hide from all men because we're a "heat missile" asking to be screwed? Do girls always have to be so dirty and nasty? [Menstruation is natural for women, Leena, and means none of the things you mentioned, especially the "heat missile" thing.]

We Cluster wrote: Mother was so mad when Dorothy came home having her period, she beat her severely, sent her to her room, and admonished her to never talk about such dirty nasty things again. Why did she think it was so bad? Why did she beat us? We didn't know what we had done wrong. We don't know if you know about these girl things, so we hope it's okay. We learned a little from our big sister, who learned from the girls at school. [You did nothing wrong. Someone likely taught your mother that menstruation is terrible and requires discipline.]

Our mind is full of pressing questions, and we don't have much time, so we try to ask you as many as possible. We liked our talk today but want to ask if it's okay to be more ourselves. [Being more oneself is a good goal.]

We're learning to be alive, and it brings tears to our eyes to think that finding ourselves means losing ourselves. We've been dead so long, and we're just starting to live. It's upsetting to think of us dying again after so long waiting to live. Life is cruel to do that to us. [No one has to die.]

Tack wrote: I'm unsure about things. I've had bad dreams the last two nights. Others have messed up my head, and I'm dizzy like I'll pass out. When I was a youngster, one of my mother's boyfriends sometimes hit my head with a metal pipe. I recall jarring thuds and being in bed for days afterward. Also, I still have a dent in my head from being hit with the butt of a pistol. Is the body recalling pain and damage that I previously blocked out? [I don't know.] I'm short-tempered these days, can't find any happiness and dislike being this way.

Belinda wrote: Others never told us there'd be a time when we'd all be happy and be ourselves. We never had choices, did we? [No]

Kay printed: We fought hard to stay alive. Now we don't have to fight and can live but must die. Boohoo, no one cares! Boohoo, Eyes see, Eyes see.

If something doesn't feel right, I can remove myself or do what's necessary. I don't have to obey others if it doesn't feel right. [Right, Leena.]

I've been trying to think of what's important to me and how I want others to remember me, and I'm not sure yet, so I distracted myself with a middle-aged female adventure. I tried to dye my hair light brown, but it came out red. Great! It took us 15 years to get rid of red hair and twenty minutes to get it back. Some of us are happy with it. Oh! The Women's Crisis Center wants me to work mornings. [You'll do well at the center, even with red hair.]

I've moved younger alters around and have adjusted to it, but I haven't settled much with them. We have new ones. I thought we were better and could handle more stress and be more of ourselves, but I became scared and pulled the rope around us even tighter. [Steps forward and steps backward] You talk about putting us together. I think it'll happen when the time comes but not before. [I agree.]

Yesterday when I got home, my porch light was on. Neither my son nor myself use that light, but someone does. I try not to think ill of anyone, but this is scary. I try to control my fear. [That won't work, Leena.]

Hope printed we've wanted to cry for no apparent reason but haven't. Information within us wants out, but shame keeps it in. [When that feeling is present, tell them it's okay, and then let it go. Let it out, then we'll work to remove the shame.]

Meeting with you is scary. Trusting and being open are new to me. [You'll get better at it.] You seem different than the Mr. Clarke I met a long time ago. Perhaps it's because I'm wiser now than before. You surprised me by knowing why I had anything to do with abusive people. [We're both wiser, Rachel.]

We Cluster wrote: We're scared to show ourselves because our behavior isn't what others call normal. We've gotten into trouble when we've come out before, and we don't know if we can risk being us again. [Show yourselves to those you trust.] Other alters told you we wear our emotions on our sleeves. Our shame goes to the depth of our souls. [I know.] Is shame the right word? [I think it is.]

We'll not reveal ourselves to other people if it causes them to feel as we do. We want understanding, help, and to be free of shame, but not if it makes other people become like us. [Give people a chance.] There's too much pain in this world, and we won't add to it. Our being here adds to it. That's why we won't share ourselves. [Phooey.] How can you listen to our pain and not be touched? [You impact me.] People separate themselves from others, so the effect is negligible, yes? [They usually do.] As children, we believed in our grown-ups, and when we thought the adults were wrong, that split us. [Exactly]

Pam wrote: Clarke, I've been to The Light many times. I've talked with and joined other people who were once human. I know I can't prove this, and the price for revealing it is a straitjacket! [Nope] The Light is all giving and love, and when touched by it, you can't help but give of yourself. The church should have understood, but they cursed me. They said no man sees God, evil dwells in me, and I came from Satan. At first, I didn't understand, but I later realized that they read with human eyes when they read God's word, so they're blind and can't see the truth. People's weakness is manipulating things to make sense of them when they don't understand them. They'll have difficulty finding The Light, for the way isn't suffering but an open heart and mind through love. [I believe you.]

Clarke, I hide from you and others. You've asked who calls you Clarke. I've hidden from you and not answered you because others have told me I'm a lie, not an actual person, somebody's thoughts, or a television show. Clarke, can you explain how I can exist? [The Light] How do you explain me when my IQ is 78, and my education is only at the third-grade level? No one so far has been able to solve me. Counselor Carolyn said she couldn't explain why I knew things beyond my capability. Can you? Am I not real? [Of course, you're real, Pam!]

Today, it occurred to me that since I couldn't discuss this belief and knowledge I learned long ago, I had to hide it. I had to divide it to forget its importance or make it so minute it had no meaning. Then, if something came up, I could easily dismiss it. [Wow!] As far as our abilities or where we got them, more pieces are returning, and we're growing. [That's wonderful.]

I can't get the picture out of my head of not wanting to be born. Can people remember what happened before birth? [I've talked to people who claimed they could.]

As for the letter I wrote to you about remembering being born and what I heard and saw beyond my birth, I didn't add that they were all children. Thery were here to be both teachers and students. I saw a light in the sky, like a bus station, with only kids present. It was a happy place, with peace and joy. I strolled around and listened. A boy said he'd be a scientist and help people, and a girl said she'd help people somehow. They felt me feeling them. Three kids were sad but happy they were going. They were going in the years 1401, 1862, and 1904. One told me he was to go and die, only lives for five minutes, and then comes back and waits for the next time. Another said that he would become poverty-stricken to feel what it's like.

Now, if this sounds crazy, forget I said it. I want to know why these children were sad when this place was happy. [I think it was because they had to leave and go live in the body, which can be painful, Pam.]

I think I have great ideas but struggle with believing in myself. [I think you have great ideas, and not believing in yourself is a severe problem.] How do I explain myself to others when I don't have the right words? [Sometimes, it's impossible because others don't have enough similar exposure to understand.] I was bewildered until Nina and I exchanged information.

Nina and other alters have parts of knowing what we are and why. Together, we're learning, hope is growing, and a door is opening. [Good!] I've written enough for today. Later Clarke!

Cathleen wrote: There's a saying that people need to hit bottom before they wake up and climb out. The same goes for your spirit. Finding money isn't enough because you can't get enough to fill the hole. A need grows in you, and you start asking how and why. How does Tara say it? Seek, and you shall find! That's it! I'm seeking a sense of wholeness. [How do you think you can best achieve this?] You asked why I'm here on the planet, and I said I'm here to rise above my savage mistreatment and my beliefs. [Yes.]

We Cluster wrote: We've written to you but aren't ready to discuss what we've written. Some want to come out and talk and write, but others don't want them to. [It's okay for them to come out. They'll help you become stronger].

We believe it's wrong to hurt any living thing and that everyone should respect each other's rights to think and live as they wish. We're becoming aware of what we thought a long time ago. [It's good you're becoming aware.]

What we've been talking about lately doesn't seem real. Where do we fit into the Bible or God? We guess you can say we're in between beliefs. The dark side and hell came from the church, so we can judge what's evil. Evil was added to the Bible to control others with fear.

Sarah wrote, how much information are we still hiding? [Eons] Tara believes we came together to learn from each other. [I agree.]

Gina wrote: I notice we're eating more. We don't know when we're full, so we eat until it hurts. [Who's eating?]

Belinda wrote: Why can't you accept we're evil and that we raped our mother's boyfriends? All the other people can't be wrong! What's wrong with our believing we did? It hurts no one. [It hurts you.] By hiding some of us, we're not giving them importance. We conceal them so we can forget easier and keep most of us.

Punky wrote: We were treated harshly at home, at school, and by doctors and various authority figures. Where can we be safe? [Sometimes, no place.]

An unknown alter wrote: I don't understand what's needed here. Shall I read and then write what I remember or come up with fun facts? [How about both?] Oh! I have two views on your saying you're not going to ask my name. It doesn't matter who I am or you're respecting my right not to give my name if I don't want to be known. [Let me know whether you want me to know your name.]

I was shocked today when you said you liked me, and I didn't know how to react. Somebody liking me and not wanting something is a new experience! [You remember many times when people said they were fond of you but then hurt you, Leena.]

I'm not sleeping well again. I'm ruminating about being raped and beaten, and my reaction to my boyfriend is difficult for him. He tries to hug me from behind in bed, and I push away. Reminding myself who he is doesn't help. As I tremble in fear, I emphatically tell him no! Then every time he moves or changes his breathing, my arms tighten around me. [Have you tried the hypnosis tapes I made to help you sleep, Leena?]

Your tapes for sleeping are helping. Today we read what we've been trying to explain. Once we truly understand and accept that life is difficult, it's no longer hard because that life is tough no longer matters! The same applies to what we think of ourselves then. Yes?

We didn't come to see you, Mr. Clarke, for a quick fix or to be relieved. We came to find the whole truth. We knew it'd be painful to accept the facts and change how we view life.

We came for you to challenge us to be the best we can be, overcome our childhood and adulthood, and see and handle problems that arise before we get stuck in them. We also wanted to see others's hateful sides and know we don't have to be miserable from wanting to believe our torturers are good people. We came to learn to transcend by accepting everything about us and facing problems in healthier ways rather than avoiding them.

We believe we're evil. Once we accept that, we can keep that belief or rise above it. We wish to be better but must first experience the pain of accepting that we believe we're evil. Only then can we transcend it! When we try to say we're to blame, and others say we're not, they help us stay in denial of our truth and stay stuck! We don't grow because they help us hide the facts. We can't seem to come up with the words or other ways to explain it! We can only add that it'd be a shame if you and I disagree on this! [Let's discuss this, Leena.]

We really don't know all that happened to us, so to move on, we must accept that all reported abuse did happen, but we have a problem doing so. We've based our sense of self on believing that life wasn't so bad, so we'll lose ourselves if we acknowledge that it was horrible.

We only know how to replace our loss and sadness through sex, but we don't want sex. [You'll learn other ways.] We want to feel close and cared for but don't know how to accomplish this. [This is part of your future learning and experiencing.] I want to learn compassion and forgiveness for those whose hearts are full of pain. [This is good to attain.]

Sarah wrote: Life is always a battle, and you can only choose the battleground. You must know the dark paths as well as the bright. Sometimes there's such a thing as learning too much and delving too deeply, thereby becoming lost!

We have a dark side, and you know it, but we choose to let it rest. The dark side can be called on and controlled by others. It's part of me and always will be. Forget it! Those on the dark side will forever tie me to them. Do you think it'll untie us from the dark side if we share with you? [It's a beginning, Sarah].

eB printed backward: I need the Dark Secret Ones to help hold the pain and horror of my breakage caused by The Mother and men. It's hard to write, okay? I can share the pain with them because it's too much to bear alone. If you knew what's in the darkest corner of my mind, you'd lock me up and never let me out, for I'm mad! Do you think I care? NO! I live in my hell. You know how the Dark Secret Ones fear others will lock them up. I can write through them so you can understand them more clearly. Regular alters don't understand the ties. We Vampires do. You ask, evil witch, what about my sons if I die? I say, what about those on the other side?

Dark Secret Ones are the keepers of the babies and my soul. I need them to feel, live and have what others took from me. Only they and I understand this, and we must share the pain. If there's death and no more, let it be soon. I can't live alone. I need them to keep the babies alive! It claws my soul! Death, oh, the sweet end! [This is an illusion, eB.]

Damn, I can't sleep with all this on my mind, and I have a long day tomorrow. I'll control this. Please don't take it wrong. I'll live through this hell, too, like the past 100th time. I'm sorry for calling you about unimportant things we should be able to handle ourselves, but I've gotten weaker this past year. I'll lie and claim I no longer want Anthony, have no hope or desire for him to change, and that this break-up is what I wish. Again, I choose to put my heart aside and do what others and my head maintain is the right thing to do to keep my sons and me safe. Maybe it's hard for me because I haven't had to go against my heart in quite a while. [I'd listen to your mind on this matter, Leena.]

Gina wrote: We appreciate your showing up. We doubt the court proceedings would've gone so well had you not been there. We didn't understand everything the judge said, but what we did understand seemed pretty fair. Speaking about old sex acts brought back some disturbing emotions, but we think we handled it okay. When the judge asked what we said to Anthony when he forced oral sex on us, we told the judge we said nothing because our mouth was full. We switched some but held it together pretty well. [You did great.] Clarke, does this mean I'm free, and my son is mine to keep? [Yes.]

Abby printed: As I talk back today and Anthony couldn't hit me, say dirty things or say he kill us, I saw him differently. I was still scared but got angry and talk back. Sophia dress us nice and acted grown-up and ladylike, and Cathleen, well, a lot of us, was there. Talk to you soon. First, we need to meet you. [Okay, Abby.]

I'm relieved. Sarah said we closed the door others had opened, and now we can get down to work, including talking about our past. [Yes, you can, Leena.] I know it's not okay to wish things had been different and we could have been in loving relationships. [Wishing is okay.] We feel like crying because we've had to give up on relationships that others of us weren't ready to give up because they still loved those people. We don't believe in break-ups. We took Anthony in sickness and health, for better or worse. We feel we turned our backs on him and chose our sons over him. We should have tried harder. It's our fault! [It's not your fault. Blame isn't the point]. I can only see and feel with my heart presently, and it hurts badly. Leaving Anthony is like giving up on what I believe to be a healthy and happy life. [I know you feel this way, but I think the break-up will help open the door to a better existence for you and your sons.]

Mary printed: I don't want to be evil. I say I always be. [Good, because you're not.]

Why do we see you twice a week, and other people only see you once? [Everyone is different]. We think it's because we're such challenging clients. [No.] Some think it's because our thinking, seeing, and believing are complicated. [True.] I think you just like our company! Ha! Ha! [I do.] Maybe we fascinate you or stump you? [At times, you do both, Leena.]

It's 1:00 a.m., and we can't sleep. Our mind is jam-packed, but we can't put our finger on one thought. We shouldn't have talked about controlling death. That can get us locked up. We fear someone seeing us struggling or cutting and then getting confined. [It's okay to cry, hurt, and cut if necessary.]

Sorry for interrupting you today while you were talking. Thanks for letting us talk about death, a lousy way to feel peace. We think we'll never be healthy and will always have MPD, but like you said today, we need new ways to handle matters, like not finding another perpetrator. We won't be ashamed anymore for being who we are! [Yippee!] Dee said if you gave her a job, so she feels needed, she'd stop wanting us to die.

Mary printed: It just a thought! Why would you want to create new jobs for them when you want to make one out of us? Why not kill them or put them to sleep. Then we'd be closer to being one.

Tina wrote: You know I've never seen fireflies or the northern lights! I'd like to. Have you? [The last time I was in New York, I saw millions of fireflies.]

We made it to Santa Cruz and saw the butterflies. There must have been 30,000 fluttering around. We trembled as we noticed hundreds of people present and sobbed as we realized we were wrong in believing there would be no remembering and no side effects since we were free from past tormentors. [No. Decisions don't make memory go away, Leena.]

Nameless Ones wrote: Mr. Clarke, do you believe what happened to us is real? You said you wouldn't mistreat us. More than one of us wants to know why you're different. [I believe you and don't believe in being abusive.]

Crystal wrote: We want to tell you we're concerned about trusting you. Others either want to hurt us or want something from us. We know we should have thanked you when you gave us your book, but you can now request payment. It's difficult for us to come out or let people see and know we're here. Our intuition tells us we can trust you, but it's usually wrong. When you gave us the book today, we thought that if it seems too good to be true, then it is.

Cathleen wrote: I don't know what, but something is coming. It seems upside down and inside out. We don't like this. We're fighting for control and putting everything in order.

Can you help us learn new behaviors? [I'll help, Cathleen.] Now we have many choices to make, and we want to begin our new life by making better choices. We need to add a voting room to our town for when we need to make big decisions. Each alter shall have an equal voice. We have to go to bed now. It's 1:45 a.m., and Bad Ones come now. We'll have to change their names to fit their new jobs.

I don't want to talk about emotions, thoughts, or what my life means. I haven't done anything with my life or made a difference. I want to help others in their emotional struggles. What's your take on my contributions to group counseling? [You're very insightful, aware, and sensitive to others' needs and emotions, Cathleen.]

Us Cluster wrote: We won't know how to explain ourselves or come out of hiding when we see you tomorrow. [It'll be okay.] We don't know if we can ever trust again. [Trust is always a choice.] When our emotions became too massive, we created alters to allocate them to so they'd be bearable. Otherwise, we couldn't have lived through what happened to us. [This is the essence of all growth.] Judy from the group said that if you act as if you believe, you eventually do. We've been trying that, but our beliefs don't seem to change. [You can't change all views by acting.]

All alters now know about you and what's happened so far. I hope what I've learned over the last four years will be helpful to them. [It will, but they need additional learning.] They're afraid because previous therapists told them one thing and did another, but Sarah assured them you're not a backstabber. I'm trying to be open with you about changes in what's happening inside and outside. [I appreciate your willingness to share, Leena.]

Oh! I talked to Rick about his criticisms. [Good asserting!] He denied them. I said okay, only because a fight would've gotten us nowhere. [You're probably right.]

The book I'm reading recommends that if you had an emotional void in childhood, you might fill your life with religion or military ethics or make your ultimate purpose to earn money and acquire things. The Mother taught me that money is more important than anything, that I need a man to take care of me, and that if by age 37 I don't have a man, I'll be alone all my life. I'm 40 and just starting over from a failed marriage.

Us Cluster wrote: We need to reveal something we don't like, but we hope you explain it. It feels like we're going through a tunnel or a place with other rooms. It seems insane and difficult to explain, but it's like we're entirely changing again. It also feels like we went down a road but now are going back and taking a different route, or like we divided but then went back in time and divided another way. When we separated, we went down a road with many towns. [Maybe that's about offering yourself a new way to go in life.]

With everything others did to us over 36 years, we lost who we are and everything except life itself. Clarke, you've given a quality of life back to us. We now know how empty our existence has been, which brings us great sadness. We feel anger toward you for showing us we have choices. When you open a way for us, our hunger blindly consumes it, but sometimes we fight your words and ourselves. We feel anger toward you but are glad we have you. We trust you because you know what we go through when you show us new ways.

That we deserve and can have better treatment are worth fighting for. Having choices sounds like a dream or fantasy. We've experienced devastating injury and hell in the past years, but we had other counselors, and now you, Clarke, and life. Why is it, Clarke, that specific other people aren't real when we accept your reasoning, but when we take on their logic, you're not real? No wonder we think we're crazy.

Could this be only in our heads? Could it be a memory from the past we think is happening now? I'd rather believe we're crazy than accept this is real! We even thought about telling you we concocted it. We so very much want the return of knowing it's over. [It'll get better.]

Cheri wrote: We're trying to tell what we want without giving away too much. You might say we're in the embryonic state because we're underdeveloped or immature. If we doubt others, we're not shocked when they let us down. It's deeply ingrained in us not to know who's trustworthy. [I know.]

Gina wrote: The fear comes from Clarke's seeing things and how that can impact us. We think Clarke doesn't know there are two sides to this. One side would like to keep Clarke and feel confident he's there for us. The other side is angry because he's a fool for helping us and will fall with us!

A small group from the We Clusters wrote: We can't seem to focus on one thing much. We're sick every morning and are still overweight, which we don't like. We have alters without names and newly named ones.

Our past dealings with other people have left an indelible impression on us. It's ingrained in us, and we're scared and doubt everything. We don't trust ourselves either.

You wouldn't want us to play with your kids or grandkids, Mr. Clarke. You're kind to us, but would you want to be real friends? We have nothing in common. You don't know us. Our prior counselor was a kind person, but she left us after 1½ years. We like and trust you, yet showing you more of us is challenging. We watch how you handle what we do and say. We don't want our sickness to be beyond your help, but we don't want to start over with another counselor. You thought we weren't going to keep testing you.

We have six alters we call Watchers since we don't remember their names. They watch our behavior by hovering and observing and then recalling without emotion. Watchers learn to behave by watching other people, but they watched secretly because it would be rude to stare.

Sometimes, we floated to the ceiling in the bedrooms and watched versus participating. Our subconscious took over. We'd even quit breathing, have to tell ourselves to do so, and even force muscle movement to get air. It felt as if we were encased in concrete. We experience ourselves as heavy when in the body but light when out. We felt crazy.

We want to know your limits and how much we can get away with showing and still have you remain with us. [Find out.] We're not mean. It's just that we've never met you. [Well then, hello.] You know others of us, and they trust you, so we should, but we need to reaffirm that you're trustworthy so we can go to the next level. [Makes sense]

We want to be all we are, with changes around the edges to think and act like others. [Great!] We wish to live without fear and have a sense of self-control over what happens to us. We want to come home and not find our animals dead or missing, furniture moved, our house in general disarray, or our property missing. We wish not to get phone call hang-ups and not have someone following us. [This must be frightening.] We put tape on our doors and determined someone was indeed coming into our house.

Cheri wrote: I seem to be handling finances, okay. Does this mean I can? [Yes.] Why couldn't I do so with Anthony? [He wouldn't let you.] I wish I knew my feelings so I could talk about them. It's just that it doesn't feel right, and there's a lot of it. Besides darkness, cold, and pain, something comes and scares me. I hear footsteps, then they stop, and hands appear. I wish they'd leave me to die, but they have to get all they can from me before I die.

I couldn't go potty because The Mother thought I was playing with myself. She said I wasted paper, flushed too often, and didn't need to go so often. I had to ask, have a good reason, and was given two minutes to be finished or else. Today I'm ashamed if anyone knows I have to go. I don't want anyone to know what happened to me, not even you, Mr. Clarke. I'd like The Mother to know I want to obey her, but I'm too awful. [I understand.]

Sam printed: We want to learn from you, Mr. Clarke, to avoid trouble. We don't know how to tell you how things hurt us. Bad stories come into our heads, and we want to yell but don't know why. We want someone to hug us and tell us it's a bad dream and is okay. Do you know about the closet, stove, ice, fire, and the babies? [Yes, I know, Sam.]

Six printed: I don't want to repeat what was already said! If you want to know what happened in the dark, ask me! [Tell me when you're ready, Six.]

Ethel wrote: I don't want anyone close to me. It amazes me how I forget. I moved away from Rick's two years ago. I now realize my reactions to Rick's behavior were the source of my anger, not his behavior. I allowed him to violate my boundaries, leading to shame and being out of control. He used, confused, and embarrassed me in front of people. Can you teach me how to do this better? [Yes.] I reason nothing is worth fighting over. [Nothing ever is, but you are.]

Lilly wrote: I'm not sure we should open the doors to what happened to us, or our emotions, especially our fears. We're getting closer to the pain and our actual reaction to it. [Yes.] You've said we've chosen safety over self-respect, and the more we give in and don't stand up for ourselves, the more we'll hate ourselves. Rick asked what changes he needed to make, and I explained he needed to figure that out. [That's great insight!]

Why are we punished for normal reactions to what people do to us? They keep pushing and want us to talk but not react. The other alters know only a little about what happened to us. A lot is waiting to come out, but I fear we can't control our reactions. [I know.] You said you're with us, and we believe you, yet we're still scared. [You must decide when and how much you want to reveal, but I'm here to process it all with you.] If we start and let go, it won't turn off so quickly. We fear your reaction to us and are taking a risk informing you that it wouldn't take much for us to lose control and open the gates of hell. [I guess we'll have to find out my reactions eventually, Lilly.]

Sam printed: I don't care! I can claim it won't hurt for you to think badly of us! I can lie to you and pretend I don't care, but it'd hurt.

Do healthy people have hurt, anger, and hate gnawing at them as I do? [Yes, Leena.] Do they cut themselves to get the evil seed out? [Sometimes] Is any worthiness left in them? [Yes.] Does the idea of death make healthy people happy? [No]

Pam wrote: My hate and pain have grown so big that they impact everything. I've become just like them. I want to die and start over so I can love, forgive, trust, and believe in others again. [These are powerful but normal emotions.]

Lynne wrote: I hated taking beatings for my sons. I consider hitting wrong, but others think it's a way of teaching. [Hitting is abusive and never a satisfactory way to teach.]

Margie, Angry, Andy, and others who want to play with Mr. Clarke wrote to him: We're struggling with packing and deciding what goes to Rick's, the garbage, or storage. We don't like this moving to Rick's. We don't trust you, Mr. Clarke, so we don't open up to you, but the other alters trust you. We don't love Rick, but others of us do. We don't want to get rid of you or Rick or reveal something to make it difficult for the others to repair. We're not out most of the time that the others are. We don't have fancy words. The sun shines and hides us during the day, but you can see us like stars at night. There's more, but that's for later. [Thanks for this beautiful way of helping me understand.]

Happy Easter, Kid! Today we're on the crisis hotline from 8:00 a.m. to 8:00 p.m. Life is calmer because even though more alters are out today, they aren't fighting. We've been thinking about you, Mr. Clarke. We find it confusing and somewhat unbelievable you don't want something from us. It's usually only a short while before men request something. Do you see something others don't? It can't be your age because a Grandpa figure was 70, and age didn't stop him. We can't understand why you even like or want to know us. Most people want something from us. [I do as well, Leena. I want you to believe in and trust yourself and live beyond fear.] If we have a year more of therapy, will we be healthy enough for all alters to get along? If we stop now, have we learned enough? [Let's keep going.]

When Easter doesn't fall in April, we do okay, but this year Easter did, and it stirred up painful memories. [Hard, huh?] Thanks for listening. [You're welcome.] It's hard to discuss recollections and our going crazy. Some of us want to cry. We're losing weight fast. We're down to 228 from 247, but know it'll come back plus. [It's time to consider letting go of this picture of yourself.]

Other people believe in "Do to others like you'd have them do to you, and be friendly and helpful." How can we be good and do what's right when we get hurt as a result? Other people believe in telling the truth, but you said it's not lying to hold back information? Which is right? Since we don't have a sense of self, maybe spirituality is the way? [You're probably right about spirituality as a direction, Leena.]

Sam printed: Hi there! [Hi Sam] Thought I'd write again. Not sure what to say. I wish we knew what we felt. Did you know about our mother not letting us go potty, putting us in a puppy cage, making us eat puppy poo, and hitting us when we couldn't keep it down?

You asked today, why me here, Sam! I don't know how not to get into trouble and don't know how to feel or tell you things. The stories come into my head bout bad things! We want to yell. Don't know why. How do we learn, Clarke?

Butterfly printed: My name is Butterfly. [Hi Butterfly]. I like a butterfly and an ugly worm. My inner workings are ugly, but I sleep and turn into a beautiful butterfly when I wake. I figure if you can't love me as a homely worm, I can change into a butterfly. I want to find somebody who loves all of me, even the ugly part. I don't think you look down on me. Can you help me with the words? [Yes, I can.] I came from ugly worm, and am still ugly within. Someday, I hope I be like a butterfly inside and out.

Star wrote: My name is Star because I often go to the stars when traumatized. I can't understand why I want others close to me, and when they get close, I push them away. I must be horrible, and now that you know that I'm evil, you won't like me either. The Mother felt anger toward God for burdening her with a retarded child that other parents didn't have to bear. Could it be that she hated and couldn't love us because we were dumb? [No]

Us Cluster wrote: We think you're not going to like this, but we created new alters. We don't like having emotions, so we create other alters, then wall around them to hold in feelings. They have thoughts but no pain. [You isolate emotions and disconnect from them.]

After Monday's appointment, our minds went to work, wondering how many of us might hurt or kill us. We'd be cleaning the house and wonder how long it'd take Clorox to eat our intestines out, or if we drilled a hole in our head, how long it'd take our brains to fall out. Can we avoid emotional pain by just taking out the heart? It's a risk to tell you this, but it's just a thought, and you can't lock us up for that.

When you saw us Monday, you told us to put a wall around us when we get hurt. We walled in most of us, but the new alters didn't go inside the wall. We don't know if we walled the pain in or out. Did we wall in hurt, Sir Clarke? [Yes.]

We had so much distress we built a hotel several stories high to house those holding it so we could move on, forget, or not feel. Each room of alters carries a different emotion. When that hotel's walls were bulging and couldn't fit another alter, we left all of them behind, locked that hotel, and built a second and then a third to house a second and third group of alters. A fourth group lives in hell due to guilt over what they did. The groups are far away from each other and never come together. The first hotel is in New York, the second in Spain, and the third in France. A total of 300 alters live in the hotels. In the New York hotel are 106 alters. We don't know how many rooms there are, but most rooms hold 12 alters. In the hotel in France, some stories have only one alter. They're the darkest of places. On the fourth floor, the groups are large and have worse symptoms. Alter girls are in the front rooms, and alter babies are in the basement.

Two or three alters manage the others in each hotel. Some can go to all levels to keep track of what's going on. Imagine a 3-dimensional chess set. I put the worst alters, the Bad Ones, in bank vaults. I had tried to create more alters to handle these Bad Ones, but the Bad Ones multiplied, so I had to lock them in the vaults.

I just remembered other "alters," who've always been present, but I had forgotten. These alters had changed hotels and levels. When we started counting alters again, we didn't include those in the hotels. [Once there were few, but now are many, including those in hotels, and you attempt to monitor them, especially the Bad Ones.]

We shouldn't have told you! We don't think we should be talking about this. [It's scary but okay to talk about.]

I'm happy I slept well last night, but I'm still tired. Sleeping without nightmares feels good. They scheduled me to work the hotline three days weekly at the Women's Crisis Center. I hope that's not too much for me. [You'll find out, Leena.]

Others treated me like your Sargent treated you in the army, Mr. Clarke. Your army misery would end in six weeks, but there was nothing to indicate that my hardship was nearing an end. [You've had a staggering amount of breakage, Leena.]

Amy printed, I'm confused about whether to give people a chance to prove they're trustworthy or do to them before they do to me. [It'll get better.] No one ever wanted to understand me. They used me for what they wanted, and all I got in return was hurt. My past makes it difficult to remain steady for my real children. [Time will help. Right now, that isn't possible, Amy.]

Angry and Hurt wrote: We spread our evil all around. We turn good people into bad without even trying. We've touched our sons in a healthy, loving manner, but we're ambivalent because we want to keep them good and not turn them evil. Is that why we're afraid to touch them? [I think so.] We should never have been born and want to be dead. We want to be righteous, not evil. We don't have a soul, but just an empty hole we pretend is a soul. Will you save us, Mr. Clarke? [No, you will. I'm your guide.]

Abigail printed: No word can splain how painful and crazy it is in here! Other than Grandma for a while, we only had us. [I sometimes wonder how you have the strength to endure this hurt and confusion, Abigail.] I want evil thoughts out. I don't wish to think unkind about people. It bad to think wrongly. We made Grandma precious — the end.

Adora printed: I'm Adora. I help us survive by dealing with rage because I can be emotionless, but my coldness can get us locked up. I also endure great anger over The Mother's brutality, don't give a crap, and hate and want to hurt The Mother because she hurts people. Furthermore, I hate myself because I want to love The Mother, who sees evil in others and cares only for herself. She can't love, whereas I can. I can see the good in others, and I care only for others.

On this note, Us, I's, and We Cluster alters wrote this is how we see it.

Lilly wrote: We must always act like a lady. It's a lady's place to take care of the man in the bedroom, even if it's disgusting. Life will be simpler if you don't get a needy man, but that might be the price you must pay to be cared for. That's the way of the world, and I had to learn this. I hate all of it. [I hate it too, Lilly.] I view you, Mr. Clarke, as more like the David who took down the giant. I think it's a Bible story. Will you slay the dragons, kill the beasts, and save the girl from danger? If so, Mr. Clarke, you've got your work cut out. We have many dragons to slay and monsters to kill. I hope your sword is ready. [It is.]

Oh, Clarke David, slay the dragon! It's coming up on us fast. Oh, Clarke David, I have a fantastic idea! Can I meet you outdoors at the picnic table? I hate indoors! Oh, Clarke David, do say yes! Adora would like to come too. She's delightful!

When we first remember things, it's just bits and pieces. We don't fill in the blanks. We leave it in bits and pieces. Okay? [Okay.]

We'll become frightened about how people might react when we come forward. We might lock up and go into the "Black Hole" where we started, but with more self-hate and shame. How do we maintain sanity while seeking the truth?

You didn't insist the Crazy Ones come to your world. You came to their world where they felt safe, and they'll come to your world in the end. That's it, Clarke David! They want others to accept them and not need them to be something they're not.

Tina wrote: Others told us we must embrace the pain to get to the other side. I'm just not sure it's worth it. What if you can't pull us out of the "Black Hole"? We don't like how we are, but we can do what's asked of us and not want 99% of the time. We don't get into deep trouble, and fewer people hurt us. Some alters don't understand what we're saying. Their confusion adds to what they already must handle, and it's too much for them. They hit, kicked, yelled, and ran because they didn't like how the hospital staff mistreated them. As a result, they got the rubber room or were tied to their bed. They didn't like those disciplines, but they couldn't tolerate being what others wanted them to be. They went deeper and deeper until we were all in the "Black Hole." How will you teach them when everything you say or do, Mr. Clark, reminds them of the past, causing them to fight you or shut down?

Sarah wrote: When you said we could close off the feral alters, they were hurt because they thought you believed they weren't necessary. They like that you're allowing them to take items to your office so they can feel good there. That shows you care about them. They love petite animals, quietness, parks, or green places with trees. Our animals, like Froggie, don't want to stay in your room for long. You keep stating we'll have to risk trusting you. That makes us angry because you risk nothing. If you fail, you lose nothing, while we lose everything.

Tina wrote: Does letting the feral alters out mean there'll be no more us, or will it just be their turn to come out, and afterward, we'll all still be here like before? They're strange and might eat us up.

Punky Lil printed: Will I be bad now too? Will I die also? I be no more?

Sarah wrote: You're right! You once said we get fat to make room for all of us! We're not big enough yet!

Mary printed I help too!

Lilly wrote: Do other people go through what we're going through, and if so, do they come out one or many? Rick wants us to stay many because he loves all of us. Do we come out knowing the truth yet remain us? Seer calls it accepting our past and present, allowing that we're many and why and believing that this is the beginning, not the end. We think that when we acquire this truth, we'll lose you because you've completed your work, and then we have no one. However, Seer claims you won't have finished because there are additional challenges, and we must grow, learn, and have a life of our own that's worth living despite what others did to us! Seer says growth is painful but gratifying!

Tara and Sarah's still unknown part wrote: I have no name, but did in previous lives. People look up to a man who works hard, goes to church, and does his part. As a woman, I tried to do the same. I felt honored today when you asked to read our letters to the other group members. Some parts of us feel ashamed and wrong for sharing this. [This all makes sense to me.] It's a relief to express my thoughts and emotions. I need to ask what a therapist is. Tara and I were called "The Healers," who heal the spirit and mind. [That's what the therapist is supposed to be.]

Therapy helps us function socially, and we think we're beginning to actualize our potential. Hopefully, you and I will both achieve a high level of enlightenment. [Wonderful!] Until I'm accepted and validated, I'm without a name! Understand? [Yes.] You and I can come up with one, so you may call on me. Tara, Sarah, and Seer will set out to distance us.

The Women's Center staff asked me to teach MPD to their volunteers because they liked how I explained it. That request boosted my self-esteem and is a dream come true. [Whoopee, Leena!] An educated therapist wants to know what I know and what helps me. That disputes the idea that the therapist is better than us.

I believe that MPD isn't a mental illness but a coping skill. [Absolutely, Leena!] When people kick a child around and no one intervenes, MPD comes from the child's going inside and making alters to help take, separate, or protect from the bashing. This process allows the child to love the parents and makes it look like they love the child. It's a division of personality. If the savagery is long-term, the child divides many times. The child thinks because it worked once, the more, the better. Each time we divide, everything stops, and the new alter usually remains the age we are at the time, with a child's body and a mind of that age. Only pieces of the past stay with that alter, so that alter only feels part of the wounding but stops growing. That's how you get different ages in MPD.

MPDs are above average in intelligence. [Yes, definitely. Not stupid. Not retarded.] They had to be to come up with a way to cope. They read people well. They have different alters for specific jobs. If we don't feel like doing the dishes, one comes out who does, and when we get up in the morning, someone has done them. We have a singer, cook, house cleaner, another referred to as the mommy (Dorothy), etc. Everything brings about new ones, not just abuse. The negative parts of MPD are that some alters can't drive or read, so we feel dumb or crazy because since we're 40, we think we should behave and think like a 40-year-old.

Through therapy, we've learned to accept the other alters and share what we know, just like a room full of people. A bond has grown between us. The hard work in therapy is talking about our perpetrators and how they did things we don't want to know. The more we accept one another without judgment, the more we understand how difficult it is for each of us to provide our input.

MPD can be lonely, and at the same time, the wall-to-wall people lead to a craving for quiet times. MPD is like having a room in my body filled with all ages, including men, boys, women, and girls. My biggest problem with people is that who I was last week may not be present today. You know me, but I don't recognize you. You may think we're lying, but MPDs are sincere people. We have a hard time trusting anyone and fear they'll find out we're different. People make fun of us and may feel uncomfortable around us, so we hide and hope no one will notice us. Does this cover the bases, Mr. Clarke? [Yes. Great job, Leena!]

Feeler wrote, how do I accept I've killed a helpless being? [I believe we're all capable of evil deeds. We're reacting from deep inner fears.]

Us Cluster wrote: We thought intensely about your saying you don't need to know all the bad things that happened and you don't complain. We think you mean you don't cry over or make a big deal out of something. We thought about your writing that if we can't name a feeling, then guess, feel it, ask what it needs or wants, and act on it. That's called taking care of yourself. We like learning new things, even when it's hard to think in a new way!

Today, we learned that remembering is okay if it validates us or explains why we fear something. It's difficult to verbalize our emotions about having been desecrated. When others say we're bad, dumb, or wrong, it takes the steam out of us. It's hard to let go of our opinion that we're not okay. If one of us has a problem or is overwhelmed, it helps to talk about it. If we don't, it stays there for years. We blame and hate ourselves for holding things in. We'd forgotten about it until this last month when it slapped us in our faces. We remember you spoke about your friend you trust to share problems with and bounce ideas off but never give money. Suppressing our thoughts and emotions has been our most significant hurt, not what others did. We had no one to trust enough to tell. We want the feelings gone and someone to understand why we feel and think the way we do. Sharing with you, Mr. Clarke, lessens our load and makes room for something new.

Lilly wrote: I found out last week that abuse passes from generation to generation. I'm amazed at how much kids can take and how they think. We're learning how kids take in things and organize the material so they can understand it. We have trouble with why kids believe they cause a grown-up's wrong behavior. All our counselors have told us kids take wounding in and blame themselves!

Presently, we're separating what belongs to others from what belongs to us. Our group leader said if a man finds his wife in bed with another, he still has no right to hit her! You said yesterday that even if we misbehaved, our perpetrators were wrong. We're trying to figure out what part of what they did was okay and what wasn't! Because no one stopped the grown-ups, we believed they were justified in abusing us because they were adults.

We take in your every word, Clarke David, but often there's no place to put it. It stays with us and flows around until it finds the right place. We store it away when you mention something we don't want to hear or don't understand how it applies to us. You said what happened to us wasn't right. Something within us said you spoke the truth, even though those words didn't seem to fit, so we kept them.

We think we began with being receivers. We didn't understand why, so we wrote down our thoughts. We thought we were crazy or going crazy. The pain was overwhelming, and we thought it'd kill us because there was no way to release it.

Other alters wanted someone to know them, so we wrote to you, Clarke David. We resist letting them out for fear of losing our minds. No way! When they step back, we feel like us again and try to put back what we know. Parts of them stay with us. We know something has changed but don't know what!

When the past comes into the present, we've learned that we suppress it if we don't talk or write about it. That's when we're most likely to become like our tormentors or find another way to let it out negatively. Good or bad, it's coming out. You once said it comes out sideways when we hold it in.

When we remembered our mother's cane, we felt the pain of that truth and tried to reason it away by saying that's in someone else's mind. Our writing and talking to you about us is helping. We're coming closer to fully accepting ourselves by sharing ourselves with you. I know when I do something terrible and keep it locked away, it builds and gnaws at me! Right? But you can get the whole picture when I tell what happened and, most importantly, what I thought, felt, and did about it. Expressing my fear, shame, and hate helps eliminate those emotions. By another understanding and accepting us, we, in turn, become okay with ourselves!

Yesterday, you said you don't need to know about all the evil things. For some reason, it hurt to hear that, but we agree! We don't tell you to shock or impress you. We're starting to understand why we're telling you. When we told you about having sex with our mother's fourth boyfriend, we wanted you to tell us it was okay. We heard that it was wrong, terrible, called rape, and never should have happened. You said you know kids blame themselves, but you either didn't explain more, or we didn't hear. It's time to start talking about how kids feel and react to their emotions, come to hate themselves and the men, and hate the world for not seeing and empathizing with us!

These are the questions we want answers to. Since we're talking about sex with men, how can a kid want yet not want it and hate it but need it? We want to find the answers within us, tell you, and learn more from you. Men having sex with us played a small part, but the more significant factor happened within us. That's the part we want to hide and deny the most. We maintain that anyone can do things to our bodies, but they can't get to our hearts, souls, and minds. Now, the job is to understand how and why we felt the way we did. You said that sometimes we bring the past to the present. Yes, we do, and it's good for us. Perhaps not how you see it, perhaps, but for us, yes! We need to.

We express hate but sometimes don't learn from it, and it stays with us. First, we say people did this to us, and we feel bad and say we're evil, but then we claim we're not, and it's what they did that was bad. That's not correct. The way you explained it sounds right, but what's wrong here is we denied how we felt and thought. We know what's needed but didn't know how to put it into words until we read your book.

Clarke David, you acknowledge and accept that others severely damaged us, that we believed we caused it because we were terrible, and that belief led to our feeling crazy. I embrace the pain of knowing this and see why and how we thought this and accepted it as part of what we were. It's allowing it and letting go, which I can't comprehend. Now that we welcome the truth, it's not for us to prove we're evil but to acknowledge the facts! Please understand we need to do this! We must admit we were terrible because we hated the person we should only love! You accept that men had sex with us and mistreated us in many ways. You validate our fear and hate. Why is it easy for you to confirm and accept our emotions and behavior? [It's not for me to judge.] What they did and didn't do was wrong, and what they felt and said was wrong. You validate everything we felt and thought about them.

Some alters think they're bad, but they're wrong. Those alters can feel that way, but it's not so! Understand! Yet we want someone to say, yes, we acknowledge you hate yourself for believing you liked sex. We desired men's love more than we hated their sex. We didn't want to be pushed aside and forgotten again. You asked how we could hate ourselves for having sex with men when we believed that the price of their love was to accept the sex.

How do we accept your reasoning that we should grow from it and let it go? We understand that we should first allow our feelings and then ask what wants and needs accompany them. We need our feelings to be acknowledged and accepted and to understand the beliefs that produced the emotions. Next, we need to look at how the feeling impacted us in the past and continues to impact us in the present. There's no wrong, but just different views on the same thing! Yes! Clarke David? [You're entitled to all your thoughts and emotions. Blaming yourself seems to alleviate guilt, yet moving toward letting go of the guilt and self-blame are desirable goals, Lilly].

All we wanted was to know that what we felt, saw and thought was correct! Period! No but! We came back with this and placed it with our thinking. We blame The Mother.

What's so is so. Some of us see ourselves as healthy and forget we have different views, thoughts, and emotions. We learned from you, Clarke David, that we're not to blame, and we accept that. That's the truth that some other alters don't validate or get. They believe they're wrong, bad, and crazy because of being told what they thought and felt was wrong. We feel relief now that we accept and validate by understanding how and why we think and feel. We're okay even when our thoughts are crazy! It's okay to feel and reckon as we do.

The We-Three Cluster is okay! They do to others as others do to us!

Clarke David, in our last letter, we talked about your growth or your eyes opening more than you let on. We believed our goodness shined on you, and then you saw us and also grew! We think about reaching all we can be!

Your book reads that discipline is the means of human spiritual evolution. Love provides the motive or energy for growing. Love is the will to nurture your own, or another's spiritual growth. From this perspective, we can truthfully claim we love ourselves. Yes? Your book continues that when our potential is actualized, we've grown into a more significant state of being; and that the act of love is an act of self-evolving, even when the purpose of the action is someone else's growth.

When we came to you, Clarke David, we told you we were the problem because we couldn't change enough to navigate relationships. We've learned our most significant challenge lies within us. We've accepted we suffered a monumental amount of breakage for the most part. Still, we're struggling to accept the price we paid, look at our beliefs, emotions, and thoughts, and take them for what they are, or in other words, to embrace all that was. Then we can come into The Light (grow into a higher state of being.)

We said we wanted to be healthy and be accepted, but our words limited us. We knew we could be more than normal but were ashamed to say so, even to you. We believed we were dumb, and although we never entirely accepted that belief, it got us stuck. Seer and other Wise Ones have helped us view matters more clearly. We said The Mother was evil because that's how we saw her, yet you said she did terrible things. We said she hurt us and didn't love us. You said she did hurt us. You validated our feelings toward her, which helped us accept those feelings for what they were. Why can't you do the same for what we feel about ourselves?

Sorry for going on about this, but we think it's an important step to accept ourselves completely! We're too mixed up to take on a new way to view ourselves presently! The unaccepted alters still believe we're evil. Other alters think we're not. Some think they don't have a vile bone in their bodies! Then there are those like Punky who only see good things and believe there's no evil, only mistakes. Still, a thread of badness extends through the whole of us. How do you overcome anything if you can't accept what is? We can't take on your truth, Clarke David until we can recognize we can't love others if we can't love ourselves first!

You must trust that this is the way we need to go! Do you believe Tara, Sarah, and Seer will try to distance us? We're not going to give up on ourselves yet! The book reads, whenever we exert ourselves in the cause of spiritual growth, it's because we've chosen to do so. We declared the choice of love. The book makes no distinction between the mind and the spirit; therefore, there's no difference between growing spiritually and mentally. The same goes for the past, present, and future, in that you can't have one without the other. The past gives us the present, which is who we are today. The now (what we choose to change) provides us with a future.

You keep repeating we're healthier than we think and much healthier than ordinary people. Reading the book reminded us of your saying that many brave enough to enter therapy, contrary to their stereotypical image, are much more durable and healthy than average. Is that how you see us? The book reads that undergoing psychotherapy is the ultimate form of being open to challenge!

When we accept the past, it won't disturb us as it does today. We can make choices and change the present to have the future we dream about but don't fully understand! We don't do anything halfway when we set our minds to completing something. We do it all or nothing! We like life to challenge us even though we claim we don't sometimes. We've been challenging the wrong things in life. That's all. You're teaching us the correct tests. The challenge is within us, not how much torture we can take. It's not to get rid of the injury, but to make it benefit us versus taking from us! Yes?

Western religions believe God, and heaven, are outside yourself, whereas Eastern religions believe they're within! Western religions believe in one God. Some Eastern religions believe in one God, some many, but some don't have a God unless God is righteousness. We're also divided. We were taught that God is loving, lives in heaven, creates all things, and is all-powerful, but then again, there's God's wrath. Some question this. How can God be all-loving and also be one to fear? How can I feel God within if he lives in heaven?

The minister purported that God punishes us out of his love for us, just like our parents do. They want us to behave, but from what we see, punishment doesn't make a good heart but breeds hate instead. It only temporarily changes your behavior out of fear versus promoting spiritual growth to a higher level. The minister said we were wrong when we told him about our wreckage to find out if it was real or fabricated to fill a need or want. He went on to say it takes years and sometimes even your whole life of reading the Bible, but even then, no one has touched heaven or seen God's "light."

We came to believe we were wrong and hid what we saw, felt, and knew. Why do we know the truth when we're just kids of no importance and completely rotten? Why else would we question life and God? Some don't believe in God. Some think there's only evil and suffering. We need to go back and find the truth, which is part of hell, the worst pain of all, with its sights, emotions, and thoughts. We then need to accept that truth. We must go to where we denied reality on any given thing, so we can look at it, understand what caused us to dismiss it, and accept that we couldn't choose the truth.

You built the base on which we can stand, Clarke David, but I genuinely believe we must construct the rest and help us get there, wherever that is! Your book reads that you must first find yourself before losing yourself. Doesn't that apply to all things? You must have a problem before you can overcome a problem! You must know what you wish to let go of before dismissing it.

To grow spiritually, we must find the missing ones. We told you we're three. According to Tara, Sarah, and Seer, whose not a believer but sees the future, all things are joined. We have to go back to find those who question faith, what is or isn't, and those we call crazy who happened upon The Light! Only then can we choose a path!

The path we've decided on is viewing God as the energy in all life, embracing the golden rule, and unconditional acceptance of others and ourselves.

As Tara said when she first wrote to you, my people have been to the four winds to keep us safe by not remembering. It's time to bring them together for the awakening. Remember that, and then add something about The Light. We united, and the Sleepers are waking up, yet some are still lost, and we must find them. Tara said we all must come to the place of The Light. We'll either go crazy or find understanding and acceptance for all of us. Again, before we can fix ourselves, we must realize our brokenness. We split, scattered, and came not to know each other. Then we built a town, awakened, became acquainted, and developed a co-conscious. We've also accepted ourselves as we are, even though we sometimes think we're crazy or don't exist, and we keep ourselves safe by not knowing or remembering too much.

We're not trying to prove our brokenness, corruption, dirtiness, craziness, or whatever an alter might call it! We've thought of ourselves as evil but no longer accept that. You've taught us, Clarke David, that we must take on our truths or forever remain as we are! We came to you to help us find the whole truth, not the easiest and least painful. We now know that the real pain was not that The Mother hurt us immensely and exploited us, but our believing her explanation. The worst hurt is accepting how we reacted to being harmed, what we came to think about ourselves, and how our minds coped with what we couldn't have choices about, understand, or control. We went crazy when we questioned our reality. Because we couldn't understand, make choices, or cope, we divided ourselves into what others said was accurate, what our hearts told us was correct, and what you, Mr. Clarke, said was true. We have a baby's mind, a child's mind, and now have a grown-up mind.

When you were a child, if you believed you were terrible at times, that was your truth with a child's mind. The difference between us is that you grew up. With an adult mind, you can accept that you thought and felt that way as a child; however, as an adult, you can choose to believe otherwise. When a feeling comes up, you claim you allow it for what it is, and don't judge it!

I'm confused and losing time, like not knowing what day it is or whether I saw you last week or last month. I figure it's because I'm changing, yes? [Yes.] I'm coming out further than before and losing time. [It'll settle down, Lilly.] I've got 45 minutes to bathe and get dressed to leave. See you.

Us Cluster wrote: We believed they only hurt the body but didn't hurt us emotionally. [Yes, because of the splitting of memory.] We didn't protect our emotional well-being. We didn't do our job? [Yes, you did.] You said we were children and that the adults were to blame. Are we any different from The Mother? The dark side is powerful. The Light is just growing within us, and we know the task ahead is that The Light must embrace the dark. [Yes.] The door is now much simpler to open because we talked about evil versus turning away like before. [I know. That was impressive.] We don't want to close off again because who knows how long reopening will take. [I don't think you will.]

You told us to accept those horrible things that happened to us as children and enabled us to look at that horror. You helped us recognize the massive wounding and want us to accept the evil. [This is the next step.] We haven't even allowed the facts, which we must do before considering our thoughts and emotions.

We viewed our glass as half-empty, but now we see it as half-full due to your help. [Yes, and becoming fuller.] We've learned that we must face our pain and fear. [Yes, all of us must do this to heal.]

We're beginning to understand. [Enlightenment is acceptance, forgiveness, letting go, releasing shame and guilt, faith, non-judgment, and willingness to see the whole truth.]

It's a relief to talk and write about what we think, but it's scary because it's not healthy, yes? [It's healthy. It's just that most people don't understand what you're discussing.] Based on our judgment of what we were taught about right and wrong, we don't deserve grace. [We all deserve mercy.]

We're sorry to have talked about sex between the therapist and the client. We wish we could take it back. Damn, we're dumb! [Nope. Just not aware of everything.] You told Punky and the Little Ones they're not evil. No one ever said that to them. They felt understood and grateful. They came to love you, but that doesn't mean sex. [Yes. Love doesn't mean sex.] We blend love and sex, so to avoid being sexual, we block our emotions altogether. [I feel bad for you that this is so difficult.] We want to hug people without wondering if they're taking it the wrong way. [Good goal]

Rachel printed: I have many sexual questions. What emotions go with sex? How do you show caring without touching others? How's gratitude expressed? We hugged a friend and came to love her, but we didn't have sexual feelings. [That sounds healthy.] People had sex with us because they loved us. [Is that what you believe?]

Us Cluster wrote: When we began accepting what others did to us, we started seeing things in terms of what you call normal, and we liked that, so we decided we're going to get better. [Whoopee!] The Women's Center counselor suggested we create an alter to make our choices. We explained that someone told us what to do all our lives, and if we had such an alter, we'd kill it. If we try to stop the other alters from having separate minds, they'll get out of control. The best way to help someone is to be honest, open, and a good role model. [Perfect!] We like teaching others about MPD and working on the hotline. [I'm glad for you. You'll help many people.]

Several unspecified alters wrote: We find the following traits in a therapist to be helpful, and this list describes you, Mr. Clarke:

1. Be honest because we'll know if you're not.
2. Be a good role model because we never had one. We're like little kids and copy what we see, so show that you're human and make mistakes.
3. Know it's okay to make mistakes and clue us in by telling us when you do or letting us see it versus covering it up. When we see that the therapist is healthy and makes mistakes, it's okay when we do.
4. Have an open mind.
5. Ask straightforward questions.
6. Explain MPD and what's healthy.
7. Emphasize positives, such as MPDs are highly intelligent and MPD is a coping skill that saved our life versus being a bad thing.
8. Be responsive to our saying you're going too fast.
9. Treat us just like you would any non-MPD. We've had enough of people pointing out how different we are.
10. Be a good therapist. That'll take you very far with an MPD.
11. Look at us as if we're a "classroom." You're the teacher, and we're the class. You have preschool to whatever. You have to teach at different levels because we have children at varying levels of learning.
12. Treat us as separate and equal people.
13. Because we have difficulty trusting, recommend books to help us, especially MPD literature.
14. Take time to play with our little kid alters. It'll teach them how they can let go and grow into adults.
15. Understand we like toys, even if we claim we don't.
16. Take note when we tell you what you did that helped us.
17. There should be mutual respect between the therapist and the client.
18. If I'm a young one, don't talk "baby talk" to me. Instead, simplify your words to match my learning level.
19. Treat us like ordinary people, and we'll learn what's healthy.
20. Resolve any misunderstandings with us.
21. Show sadness about our stories. It helps us to feel sad and cry about what happened to us.
22. Try and try again to help us.
23. Ask how we're doing and how you can help.
24. Be genuine and be yourself.

When we first began therapy, we wanted the therapist to be concerned about us, but we also didn't want him to care because we feared that would cause us to break down. But after sharing what happened to us and learning to trust and take care of ourselves, we started putting the pieces together and making sense of it all. We began to mentally and emotionally catch up with our bodies, lose less time, have information close at hand, and have a sense of wholeness.

Lilly wrote: Do we have more history? When is therapy going to end, Clarke David? Can we stop now and be okay? We want to write about our thoughts but fear that it'll take a long time to conclude once we start. Why do we keep seeking knowledge when it hurts so badly? [You have a strong desire for growth.]

We Cluster wrote: We're terrified to grow up. We get to that line separating kids from grown-ups but won't cross over, period! We thought we were over this need to be healthy and fit in, but we're not. You say we're going to integrate as others do. That can only mean finding all of us and making us one. If we're destined to become one, we will, but we don't have to like or want it. We don't want to talk about this now. It sends us to uncomfortable places.

Sarah wrote: Why do we have to lose what we've fashioned? We feel depressed, sad, hopeless, worthless, terrified, empty, and alone. Someone is taking us away piece by piece, just like everyone did to us before! We don't know how to fight it!

Punky wrote for the Little Ones: We want someone to hold us so close that nothing can harm us. [I know you do.] We want someone to caress us until the pain goes away and there's no more fear of death. We had babies and then didn't, were happy and then not, had a dad and lost him, and had a sister, but she's gone. We had ourselves and then not. When are we going to stop losing things?

You maintain we're getting healthier. [Yes, Leena.] Nettie has abandoned the pursuit of a co-conscious. She has separated from the other alters again to cause the world to disappear. Abigail is scurrying around, yelling, and most are hiding and waiting for their turn, and praying it won't come. Some are waiting to fight it, while some are thinking of cutting or killing us to lessen the suffering. Some are trying to find Dee or open the door to hell and let Winter and Amanda out.

The book I'm reading purports that if your parents loved and forgave, that's how you'll see the world and God. If they were uncaring and harsh, then that's how you'll see the world and God. We fall into the second category. Where did our ability to forgive and care come from? [Good question.]

When we change, the stronger ones go ahead, and the weaker ones stay behind. It's like leaving friends and family and never being sure you'll see them again. That's not a good feeling. When Nettie and the other feral alters came out, accepting them was difficult and painful. We knew there were more of them hidden, and since it took so long for them all to come out, we got separated, and it took us longer to find our destination. We had days to feel the change, not seconds. [This is an excellent insight and awareness, Leena!]

Lilly wrote: We go from the safe and familiar to the unknown with no map Clarke David, then the knowledge comes that it's okay, and although we wish to fight, we let go, and that's when we leave the body behind, and find a peace we never felt before. [Is this the key for you?] Finding peace took a long time and felt like death, so we thought we were dying. For us, change is dying. [Change is a type of dying.]

Sarah wrote: When we found Deon, the feral alters, and Holy Man, a massive change went to places forgotten or lost. Maybe that's why we thought some of us died.

Cheri wrote: As a youngster, the wrong and painful weight of the world was upon me. I came to lose my mind and give up on my body. Did I separate the brain to handle what it couldn't bear? [Yes. That's a fantastic ability of the human mind.] In The Light, you feel all pain, not just your suffering. I loved and forgave but wasn't mature enough to keep me safe.

Tabby is a mid-teen girl who helps us suffer the pain of our mental hospital stays. She wrote to Mr. Clarke: You said you'd do everything you can to keep us out of the hospital. That's not a guarantee. [Nope. I can't even guarantee I'll never be in a psychiatric facility. I guarantee I'll do everything I can to get you out, though.] You said healing sometimes hurts. We've been healing all our lives. [Good point.] You said we chopped up our pain, but now that pain is coming together, and that's why it hurts so much. [Yes.] Then, that means we're integrating, which means death to all but one of us. [No.]

We heard today that to heal, we must look at our victimization. Never! Although we don't believe we have a heart, we wouldn't want a heart to feel all we know or have become. If we hide our spirit (soul), keep it safe, and the same pain remains, how can we expect to handle what we couldn't 39 years ago if nothing has changed? [You did survive the agony. Things have changed. Memory pain doesn't last when we face it, Leena.] We hold our hurt in our arms. [Open your arms.] We remember the feeling very well. We don't want to see and feel it. The chains of life can be too much to hold up, but we must!

I've been having headaches and feeling stressed. Maybe it's concern about my sons, dieting, or the awakening. [Let's start meditation training.]

Lilly wrote: I need to know if we'll die if we keep going forward, Clarke David?

[Not the way you think.] Can we learn to live with MPD without integration? Will we all end up integrated? [You don't have to. Not all with MPD do. It isn't death. It's about willingness to evolve.] Can you build on what's already there to lessen pain and improve our functioning? [Yes. I hope so.] Why is it wrong to be MPD? [It's not. It can be painful, though.]

Since meeting you, I've found peace within and a sense of self. I've begun to see things differently and see the hurt in all people. I've come to accept myself and believe MPD isn't a bad thing. [I'm happy for you. Your new thinking is healthy.] We want to heal from the hurt done to us, but we don't want to become one or integrate, as you call it. Please help us stay! [Okay. I will. No becoming one, Lilly.]

Others helped M write: I think it's my turn to share. I don't share. I distract when I hurt to make the pain manageable, although distraction only makes it barely tolerable. Hurt grows when you think about it. I believe emotions can kill. People push us to open up, and then they deny our pain. They find fancy words to say it's not real. [Yep, they do, and they aren't healthy to be around.]

My eyes don't cry. They bleed! It's not water and salt. It's my lifeblood. [That's very hurtful, M.] I'll say more when my ego or pride isn't so impacted. [Okay. I can wait.] There are two sides to me. I like you and respect you a lot, but don't trust you. [I understand. That's okay.] Life has taught me never to trust. Still, we've taken risks with you. It's not wise to put all our eggs into one basket, yet we've put all of ourselves into your hands to mold and protect.

Deon wrote: Bobby and others have been out lately. This thing about death has us stuck. We're having a deep feeling of hopelessness. It's like being on a tightrope. You lose, no matter what you do. There's death all around. We don't know what to do. [Sit still and wait.] It felt like death and shattered us into smaller pieces. We didn't want you to know we split again, and now there are more of us. [I'm glad you told me.] We can't stop it. [It's difficult to feel helpless.]

We have a powerful will to survive. [You certainly do.] Spiritually we know things others don't. [You do.] In our healing process, you're our mirror and point out our downsides. [Yes, and your upsides.] We'll never be normal or ordinary. [I hope not.] What do we need to let go of? [Worrying about doing so]

Did you know I tried to sell my body for heat and food and stole food to stop my baby from crying? Did you know I was relieved one of my babies died because I thought it'd never hurt or do without necessities? [This remembering is what healing is about.] We're having evil thoughts of having done things we wished we'd never have to do. [Normal people, including myself, have also done something they wish they hadn't.]

You said we choose how we react. I've chosen to hate and am not a nice person. [Okay. What do you want to decide to feel next?] Our mouth has gotten us into trouble. [Yep. That's true for me too, Deon.]

Rachel helped Zoe print: My mother was correct, you know. I like self-pity, being dumb, and hurting myself. [How come, Zoe? How does this improve your mood?] I prefer holding things in, or I'd have done something before now. [Are you just guessing?] I know you can't change who you are. [Yes, you can!] I'm crazy and fearful of making something out of myself. My mother told me to marry for money, but I married for love. What I got was more hurt.

Sam printed: I think we're petrified, Mr. Clarke David. It's better to have nothing than to have something and lose it! [Nope. It's better to have something and fail to keep it, but it hurts deeply.]

Basket wrote: We were a loosely woven straw basket, so contents slipped through. Then we found one called Mr. Clarke David. With time and lots of care, we re-wove the basket, but even tighter so it would hold. It takes painstaking effort to weave such a basket.

The following are my responses to an article titled Musings About a Therapist's Touch:

Part one:

I'm too afraid to ask you to hold me, although I want to. If you caress me, will my sickness rub off on you? Will the badness of my soul find its way to your heart? If you hold me, will my pain be too overwhelming? Can you hug the child and forget I'm a woman? Can you pretend I'm sexless? I want you to hold me, but I'm too afraid to ask. [Ask, Leena.]

Part two:

Am I only a client you see 50 minutes once or twice per week, receive letters from, and receive an occasional phone call from that interrupts your dinner? If I were to die tomorrow, would you care? Am I someone worthy of caring? Sometimes I think you might be afraid of me because my needs are so overwhelming they might swallow you up. [I care, you're worthy, and I'm not afraid.]

Part three:

Sometimes, I want you to hold me, but I can't ask because I'm afraid you'll decline. I'd never ask because of intense fear. At least now I can pretend you care about me. What would happen if you said you did care? It'd fill the need too long denied. The whore would try to make the touching sexual, so I need to protect you from me. You'll never know how important you are to us or about our fighting accepting that. [You don't need to protect me, Leena.]

My emotions feel like they're boiling. I have much to learn about managing my feelings and controlling my reactions. I feel shame for having emotions. [I know people taught you to feel that way.] Anger is like hate, which leads to more hatred. Both are better untouched, left alone, and never shown. [Anger and hatred aren't the same.] I believe we have every right to fear the anger and hate within us. They're not tiny matters. I think the desecrated have much rage. [I appreciate why you fear these emotions. Yes, severely abused people suffer much fury.] They have more than they can control. [Sometimes.] We killed rage and hate because we didn't like what we were. Yet, we have the potential to get crazy angry. No one believes I have that in me, Clarke. [I think you do, Leena.] You tell me the integrity of my actions, not my emotions, attest to my goodness. [Yes.]

Anthony tried to see how far he could push me and even made it a game. When I became angry, he seemed happy and let up. Why did he do that? [He doesn't know how to take any emotion seriously except anger.]

I get frustrated when people deny their anger, whereas I like to clear the air, or when people try to control me, prove me wrong, or say one thing but do another. I get frustrated when people belittle me and call it joking, say that's the way they are and always have been, or use my MPD to get what they want, like when I say no, and they push a button to get a particular alter out." [Wow! Incredible insights, Leena!]

I get angry when told how I feel, when others disagree with me, don't hear me or put words into my mouth; and when others don't stop when asked, tell me I can't perform tasks that I can, or treat me differently than they want to be treated. I get angry when people force me to choose between two wrongs, lock me in teensy places, push me to give in, or dunk my head underwater; and when others put a plastic bag over my head or don't leave me alone when I say I've had enough. You've said you and I can have different views and can both be correct or inaccurate. I appreciate that you make points, but don't push them, Mr. Clarke.

Sarah wrote: We confuse anger, fear, and hate. Even verbal abuse stimulates our rage. I think mistreated people live with great trepidation as we do. I also believe we're more like our perpetrators than we want to accept. That's why we fear our anger. We know the cost of having emotions is the difficulty of returning and never being the same afterward.

Lilly wrote: I never again want to have to fight physically. I'll win at almost any cost Clarke David! If anyone threatens my sons, they're dead! I'll never even have to think about that!

One of the Angry Ones asked, is our anger out of control and dangerous? [I don't think so.] We care about keeping our values. [Good] Our values are the only thing keeping us from being like our tormentors. Do you understand why we have so much fear? [Yes, and hurt.]

Have the other alters told you I saw hell with black forms grabbing at me? [Some of them have told me.] Are we kind and think we're evil, or evil and believe we're kind? [We're one thing. We feel many things. We experience good and bad. The new book you're reading will help you understand.]

Rose wrote: Our talk today was profound! I found it odd you brought up the issue of gayness after all these years together. Interacting with three gay women at the shelter made me wonder about my sexual orientation. We could be gay. We're curious about it and have been drawn to it lately. Others taught us it's dirty and the worst thing you can do. Anthony forced sexual acts with the same gender on us, but it might become our choice. It's a coincidence we were wondering about something, and you brought it up! Since you're smart, are we gay? [That's for you to figure out, Leena.]

Basket and others who hid to make us not exist are coming out of hiding. Lately, some of their fear is due to pressure to deal with memories, but most of it is because you and other people know they're not just one. They don't want anyone to know they're here. They're angry because they don't know how to avoid being noticed. [I'd like to speak with all of them, Leena.]

The book we're reading suggested we compile a list of good and evil people, and what we got from them. Will you help me compose this list? [Okay.] We learned a great deal of negativity from the people around us. We think The Mother loved us in her way, even if it wasn't healthy. [Good point] From The Mother, we learned that life isn't always fair. We felt crippled around her but forced ourselves to go through the motions of living. We're looking for a time we don't have to force ourselves to live. When does it get easier?

From Grandma, we learned to love and that we could be whatever we wanted. We were grateful for our time with our dad because we only had to deal with one man. We learned from teachers and schoolmates it wasn't just our family that was sick. We learned from churches to forgive and love others as God loves us, that our pain can cause others to go to hell, others' sins are our sins, and that broken babies don't go to heaven. We learned from neighbors that some people have it better than others and from doctors that our problem is within us. [Let's discuss this, Leena.]

From Anthony, we learned what anger is, we have a breaking point, our beliefs and values make us righteous, and wishing hard might blind us from knowing men are unsafe, evil people.

From counselor Carolyn, we learned what caring means and that women can stand up for their rights and take care of themselves first. We also learned what it's like to trust someone, open up, and be believed. [Carolyn was an excellent teacher.] With you, we're fighting ourselves and don't trust ourselves. [We all battle ourselves.]

We learned from the legal world that they talk pretty but aren't helpful, and from Mental Health that we're the problem again because we didn't love or want sex. We learned from child welfare services that we have a lot to learn, and from counselor Dahlia, not to show too much. From you, Mr. Clarke, we came to know we're closed off, can't trust, have been hurt in many ways, that love, sex, and caring can all be painful; and that our most crucial truth is that we've been lied to a great deal and trusted the wrong people.

Sorry, we had trouble coming up with what we learned from men or something good to say. I didn't like that. It didn't feel right. [It's okay.]

As you know, we had a very sexual life. We wrongly touched him even though we knew not to because he was a relative, but he was a man first with man needs. Were we saying we wanted him to have sex with us? We're reading that people should cherish one another. That's God's wish, and we want to be loved. To get love, you must give it, and what's the perfect way to give love? Boy, did we show how much we wanted to love! Boy, did we give and give. Without question, if we care, we'll provide.

Do you get what we're saying? We don't trust ourselves. It's not you, Mr. Clarke, because we know where you stand. If we care, we'll show you. Whether you react positively or negatively, we'll feel rejected, ashamed, and not good enough. We shouldn't feel at all. Sorry, I have to go.

We're sorry for saying such things. We can control ourselves and shall do so. We think we shouldn't have brought it up! Sorry. We don't want sex. It's how we react to our emotions. We hate feelings. We'll do what's right so no one's hurt. It's confusing. You've often said that our behavior gets us into trouble and that our conduct flows from our emotions.

We finished reading your book and want more. Why can't you help us if we don't allow our emotions? We're not good at accepting, identifying, or explaining our feelings. We try to avoid them. How did you know we have many like Tara? [You've told me so, Leena.]

Margie wrote: A man of the Church gave me the name he would've given the daughter he couldn't have. I held him and said it was okay as he cried and said: "You have the face of innocence, so full of trust and love, are one of a kind, and should never lose that. Gild thy heart well." He was on his knees, looking up at me, and I saw the pain in those brown eyes. I wanted to take his hurt away. I don't know how or why, but I know how to remove pain from others. It's a gift! I've fixed birds, puppies, and chickens. I believe you can heal if you open your heart with all your love because I've seen us do it. All I know is that the priest said to gild my heart, so that's what I did. So the heart will never know what it did out of love was wrong.

Evil, touch it!
No!
Not have it!
I don't want to feel.
I want to be healthier!

Us Cluster wrote: We'd like to take back what Margie said! It's wrong to talk about the men of God or against the Church or God. It's never our place to judge the men of God or take God's name in vain. Why must we turn everything into something dirty? What's it about us that people do things to us they've never done before? We'll try finding out what that is and never do it again.

Don't touch anyone with the heart.
Take away any good emotions that can be called sexual.
Care, but don't show it.
Remember what we cause and never forget.
Don't touch.
Don't hold it against them.
They want to feel loved, cared for, and understood.
We'll never need anything.

There are two kinds of alters now. One type is out of need, and we have no name for the other. It's different! One kind left us with shame and feeling dirty, and the other with a sense of wrongness.

We learned to remove emotions by separating the alters. Like the early version of Winter, some have no emotional vulnerability. All of us, other than Winter, are pieces of her. Winter was our shell, so when she broke, the inside fell apart, and the individual alters scattered far away, as no glue was holding them together anymore.

Somewhere deep within Winter was Sunshine, as wee as a grain of sand. She had some emotions, some of which we used in therapy to create Leena. The alters came back, and many talked through Leena.

We once wanted to love and be kind but learned that desiring this is wrong thinking. We must hate, mistrust, and learn the world's ways, or we'll get clobbered. We were born with a gift, despite struggling with words. We can reach in and pull out your heart, so you can see and know it. In our heart is a match others can light to be seen and felt.

The doctors in the mental hospital said we were crazy because no one could do what we said we could. They said it's humanly impossible, that we had an enormous imagination, and that our stories, while fascinating, weren't real. One doctor acknowledged we were being truthful but later claimed he got caught up in our tale. We could see in his eyes he knew, even though he never admitted it, and he continued to try to convince us our stories weren't real. The nurses feared us and said we had "the evil eye."

We had something no one could name. We had no guidance, no teacher. We were left to handle it alone. We didn't know what caused it! Can you explain why and how we can do such things? What happens when we do this? How does it work? Where does it come from, and what are the words for what we're doing? We didn't feel like being around people, so we didn't go to group counseling today. [That's okay.]

Lately, sex has been coming up frequently. We've got sex on the brain. We've always thought we were sick. While living with an aunt in Oregon, we encountered an older man who serviced vending machines. Our gut said he scared us. As we aged, the memory seemed to get hurtful. We don't know if he did something. We remember he asked us for our consent and if we'd like to see his records. He put up the closed sign and locked the front door of his store. Something happened! He told us we could take all the recordings we wanted. [Do you remember anything else about this, Leena?]

When we were a child and went to church, we observed the people praying on their knees with their hands closed, including the priest. We found it odd they didn't pray with their hands open. It made no sense. How'd they receive anything with closed hands? It's as if they were saying, we need but don't give it to us. At school, we learned we need trees to produce air. It just seems it's always about what we need.

Each time we read something, we remember a time when we thought wrong! How are we unfolding? Where does this craziness come from? We don't wish to be crazy and be locked up again!

Can this be real, or is it the same psycho-bull crap? Am I trying to avoid my pain? I need to know! Do you feel drawn to me, Mr. Clarke? Do you feel like there's something you must do? Have you been with others before? You need to know something. We need to body touch you! It works like this: We sit face-to-face, hold hands, knees touching, or lie side by side! I need this to stop if you make a move because I know what your body does when I'm on the other side. I hope you understand that if your body moves, I can stop before it touches me. It's hard to say, but I want to nudge you. It makes me cry in pain! I'm taking a risk even to reveal such a thing! I fear to feel your body, but I want to. Are you the person we seek? Please tell me what you think! If you're not who we seek, I need to know. Can you tell me? We need to talk. I know where we need to go! I must find the right one! I speak, and you listen! You never said if you're him! You know if you are.

Us Cluster wrote: How the hell are we? In the past, our heart was dark and cold. We had a teacher then! We had spiritual troubles. We don't want to remember the master or remember how to bring up demons. We don't want to see the master again. No! No! We know you think we understand The Light and grow in it to become stronger to face our master and ourselves. We're a part of the dark. We're a part of you, and you know how strong we are! In the end, we want to destroy our evil. It knows this! But it'll fight you to the death and often wins because the good stands only on faith and has no skills or accurate understanding! We know your weaknesses, and we'll use them, but you don't see ours due to your fear of looking at us! [I don't fear to look at you. You fear to let me see you.]

You said we're getting healthier. We don't feel or think so. [It's challenging to grasp sometimes.] We said we don't like your knowing things, and you said the only way to avoid that is for us to leave. We know you didn't mean for us to go away, but that's how some alters took it. It was hard to stay when others wanted to go. [Welcome to the club of inner confusion.]

When group members ask us how we're doing, we don't want them to know we're not in control. We think we have to be strong because there'll be no one to help if we break down. [I'll help.]

I can't seem to get motivated to do anything lately. I can't handle more stress. There are issues with Rick, my sons, the group, and hotline responsibilities. [Lots of worries always push one down, Leena.]

I feel guilt and shame for admitting I need help. Dammit! I'm making myself do what I usually do, appear as if I can, but can't. [There's never a good time to feel helpless, but that's how life goes at times.] Instead of turning myself off, I overload and I act as if all's well. [I believe you, Leena.]

Lilly wrote: I got some sleep last night, and now life seems more manageable, Clarke David. [Sleep helps. Huh?] We're scared, but we engage in life anyway. Did you mean we should let go and go crazy or keep fighting even though we're overwhelmed, which is what we're trying to do? [It's always scary to let go. You only think you'll go crazy.]

Arrogance wrote: We must've done something very wrong for life to be as it's been. You said you thought we had to have done something right. We always have evil thoughts and emotions. We try hard to get rid of the bad, but here we go again, getting worked up and angry. [Struggle and pain come from within, not just from your head.] The Bible maintains evil thought is just as wrong as doing and that you need to be pure of thought, body, and soul. We're not! [Very few are.] We have to be righteous to go to heaven and have peace without pain! [Your time will come.] We don't want to stop trying, but it seems we'll never win. It's hard to see the good in people after what people did to us, yet we know it was our fault because we couldn't stay good. It's like the man you talk about who won the war with peace. He kept his thoughts, emotions, and heart pure no matter what people did to him. [Gandhi.] We want to be like that. We're worried that we'll end up empty if we let go and can't replenish fast enough! [That'll never happen.]

Sarah wrote: We know we can take lots of pain because we're here. Lately, though, we've seen we didn't handle it as we thought. [It's confusing.] How can we manage so much pain and fear? [Remember, you're not just that little girl anymore.] Without power, you lose a sense of peace. [Yep.] We're very vulnerable and can lose our sense of peace quickly. We think we haven't had enough practice to keep it. [It's difficult for all of us.] We've replaced our desire to be just healthy with being the best we can be. [Whoopee!]

I'd hoped I could say something clever to make it easier between Rick and Brad. [I don't think so, Leena.] If I feel angry, helpless, and impatient, I'm not taking responsibility, not looking at my part. [And you give up your power.] I feel anger toward others and myself for not taking responsibility. [We need to discuss this because it's very complicated.] What responsibility do I have in resolving issues between Rick and Brad? [To be honest and helpless] We believe we learned a great deal from a self-help book, but it seemed the author wrote it for other people, not us, or maybe we didn't see how to relate the book to our life. Are we thinking correctly, or are we hiding? [Good question.]

I read the part about self-blame, and I admit I do much of that. The Mother took away my power. I don't want to give it away ever again. I took away control of myself also by self-blaming. [Yes, to all those thoughts.] The book helped me understand I have a great deal of pain and fear. [Of course, it did.] I want to have emotions but not show them. How do I do that? [That's hard to do.]

My doggie passed away. We were there for each other. [You lost a friend who didn't judge you.] I could pet him and not worry that he'd take it the wrong way. I could be upset and cry and not have to explain. I could be me if you can understand that! [Yep]

What's it called when your mind, body, spirit, and heart are aware of everything? [Consciousness] What's it called when you touch your heart and let it grow until you take in others and all things? [Unconditional love] How about when your heart moves others in a humane, loving way and changes their hearts? [God–goodness–love] What's the word for when you leave the body and see beyond your yard? [Enlightenment] Is Buddhism a way of life? Do they believe in God? [Yes, and yes.]

I have no judgment or hate when Tara and Holy Man are with me. I only have compassion and caring for all things and a desire to impact others in a way that helps them acquire awareness. Grave physical abuse broke my body, and I can't put my spiritual self and body together. [You will.]

I know what we need, but fear of rejection and misunderstanding stands in our way. [This stands in everyone's way.] We want to get rid of all our evil thoughts and emotions to avoid becoming The Mother. [You'll never become her.] It's not you that we mistrust. It's us. [It's always ourselves that we don't trust.] I wish I could explain what I know and feel. [Soon, you'll be able to.] I want to teach you everything about me in hopes you can educate me through that understanding and we can guide each other. [We're doing this.] How do we forgive The Mother and ourselves? [Some behavior can't be excused. All people can be.] The more pain I hide within, the more I feel compassion and the need to reach others. [Reach out to yourself too, Leena.]

You and the books I'm reading are answering my questions. Seeing my issues written about proves to me I have them. [The time's right. When the student's ready, the teacher appears.] We want to stop exploring and forget about our past, but something keeps pushing us on. [Your spiritual truth] Do you think we're losing it? [No. You're finding it.] Are we crazy? [Nope] You know how insane we are. [Not to me] Reading helped us see what we did wrong, and now we can do it right. [Yes.] I know something too big for a child to handle causes MPD. We've been crazy, but are trying to put our life back. [No, others disoriented you.]

When others tortured me, everything stopped when the pain, sadness, fear, loss, and the thinking there was no way out exceeded 10 on a scale from 1 to 10. Then I began to feel detached, like watching one hundred television channels with me in them. There was blackness or a break to take a deep breath before the next channel came on. Then someone turned the television off, leaving me in total quiet and darkness. It felt this way when I was evil, and The Mother locked me up. It was like I was on television, and within was a second television, and I was also on it. The second television could change channels, but the first one couldn't because it was too scary. The Mother controlled one and my craziness the other. I saw hundreds of televisions, one within the other. [This is a fantastic way to explain this feeling!]

When The Mother put Dorothy in the oven, she saw an angel and real-looking people who spoke to her. Then in a flash, Dorothy was on the kitchen floor, and The Mother was yelling at her. [This is what happens when people go out of the body.] I still feel crazy, but I understand that means I'm dissociating. [Good. I'm glad you know the difference.]

You said you didn't need to know everything that happened to us, but we know we must somehow tell you everything. [That's your choice.] We didn't want to show you how crazy we are, but something drove us, and boy, did we give it a run for the money! [Yes, this is truth, and the need for centeredness and spiritual balance] I'm looking for a church, or somewhere I can fit in. [Good idea] I've never been around a Buddhist church or retreat. I don't know if it's right for me. [You'll find out. You don't have to explain yourself, and they'll be safe, Leena.]

Punky Lil and the kids are back! [Hi guys.] Here we go round and round. Here we go, loop de loop! We don't know what we're doing. It's like we're out for a long lunch. Someone said we're died. Are we died? [No.] I'm glad we're not died.

Someone helped Rachel print:

It's taken many years, and places
to become me.

I've been dissolved, shaken,
and worn other people's faces.

Time was there, crying the warning,
hurry, you'll be dead before morning.

The end of the poem is clear.
Now there's time, and time is near.

Remain still pursued,
who madly run, remain still.

One day I'll honestly know what this means! You told me I couldn't go back once I begin, but I said, Yes, I could. I have choices. I can also stand as a bystander and not change or step beyond my walls and open up to what's there. I choose to learn to take in what's needed and risk growing. I now see that I can't go back, but I can remember.

I've found words to explain myself more succinctly. I have a weak and shaky sense of self, but can temporarily rise above our deficiencies and touch states of openness and selflessness.

The Mother broke us, and we've been trying to heal ourselves since, but then came the school and later Anthony. They took us to the mental hospital after The Mother broke us, where the doctor called us a slow learner. We got broken again by the teachers calling us liars and accusing us of cheating, claiming we weren't smart enough to do well. Then The Mother fractured us further by making sure we never did well again. After years of this kind of desecration, we got lost. [Yes, you did, Leena.]

Yesterday, you asked which of us I wanted to heal. That's like asking a class of students who wants to present their report first. I remember wondering how healing would make us feel. If I heal, will I die, no longer be, forget myself, or be expected to behave differently? I might not be able to do what others think I should.

There are 207 of us presently. We must heal one by one to mend the broken self. We didn't see a person before. A tiny, frail, misplaced, misused, misunderstood ego is behind all our alters. [Yes, it is.] No one has touched this self for forty years. It broke off long before we did. Each alter is hurt, and each must heal before the whole. [The self is spirit. That's why I said they never broke you.]

We read that the first level of self-development is reclamation, whereby we understand the painful conditions that created our weak, deficient, barricaded sense of self. We don't move if we see ourselves as a whole because each alter has its pain and background. Gradually, we can cease to identify with these old patterns and permit a healthier sense of self. If you separate and look only at one at a time, you'll see the sound parts and broken parts that need to heal. [We'll focus on this next.]

We must start over by recognizing and reclaiming our body and heart wherever we were brutalized or cut off from ourselves. Undertaking this reclamation is a considerable part of our journey. It might take years of work to stop fleeing and reclaim our unspoken voices, the truth within us. [For all of us, Leena]

Journey's End with Dear Mr. Clarke

"For all of us" were Mr. Clarke's last words to me. Sadly, Mr. Clarke had to stop practicing because of poor health. He put his hand on my face in our final session and said, "Of all my clients, never mind." Mr. Clarke has since deceased, and that saddens us. I thought he was just on vacation when I wrote the first three paragraphs of the following letter to him. Rachel, Lilly, and Feeler added to the letter.

We're getting better at saying what we think. We appreciate your honest feedback even more since we've been testing out what we believe. We read about being in the moment, being in a state of love, and being one with God and the world. As the Wise Ones say, there are two sides, and when we fail in one way, we make up in another.

We shocked ourselves at how open we were, pushing through our fear. You surprised us too, Mr. Clarke. Others taught us this was our imagination or the devil's work to pull us away from God. Literature gave us the words to explain our internal dynamics. There were no teachers or churches to help us. We learned to not believe in ourselves. We told you in our first meeting, and again today, we've waited a long time! We fear reaching out and getting hurt again and then going back to waiting.

We went from craziness to some understanding, with many questions, back to madness, then to the Little Ones returning. We see ourselves as broken but trying to be whole, the truth here and now! We're many, and each alter doesn't work on the whole. Suzie Q. heals Suzie Q., Leah heals Leah, we repair us, and the self grows. We had it wrong that we work as a whole. We can't! If some go too fast, the others lose!

Lilly wrote: We still have missing pieces to our puzzle, but there's enough to give us a sense of completeness. We think our dividing helped considerably. We don't believe this integration is a good thing. It messes up things. We're not one that got broken. We're many! We gathered the many and called it "self." We grouped our alters into likes, dislikes, and levels. We separated them enough to keep a false self and put the rest away when that didn't work.

Feeler wrote: My sister, Brenda, phoned last night. We discussed MPD. I told her that we found who we are in therapy, discovered our likes and dislikes, and decided that it's okay to be us. We can do good and bad things, which all add up to us! We don't integrate, but each of us is learning. We listen to ourselves and accept all we are. Those who were hurt the most hurt themselves, directing their emotional pain inward.

Brenda said she could kill. I told her I could also and that anyone could if put to the test. She spoke to me about dying, and I said that's called psychological death. It's when you go into overload and close down. She said she and I died many times and knew many lives in just a short while. She had to go, and as her voice faded, she continued saying she loved me. Talking about MPD with my sister helped me feel okay.

Rachel printed: Oh my! What shall we do while our therapist is on vacation? Some are crying because they fear he won't come back. Some are asking who'll fix us if we have a crisis. Others think it's long overdue! Some miss him because he has become part of our life! Some think it's good because it'll show we can do okay while he's gone! Some think he'll have a lot to read when he gets back! Ha! Some will learn how dear someone is to us.

After Mr. Clarke, I was in therapy with Roger Phillips, Ph.D., from November 1972 to sometime in 1975, when he moved away. I didn't derive much benefit from his work with me. He was very textbook-oriented. A fire destroyed our file except for the following letter he provided to social services on March 9, 1976:

"Leena's diagnosis is MPD. She manifests 100 or more alters. Her impairment will exist for the rest of her life. Still, she'll manage her financial affairs and daily activities with continued treatment. Her memory loss, which accompanies "switching," doesn't help.

She experiences textbook symptoms of having multiple alters. Some suffer from physical illness, whereas others don't. Some read well, but those can't be brought at will, and some can't read at all. Some need glasses, yet others don't.

Her current medications include antidepressants as needed and others for physical illnesses. Some personality states tolerate the drugs well, while some experience severe side effects. Her physician monitors her medicines regularly and makes changes as needed.

Her general appearance, posture, age, and mannerisms often resemble that of a young child, and most of her personality states taking executive control are childlike. Her disorder began in early childhood when she experienced severe physical, emotional, and sexual abuse. When Dorothy was 11, her mother placed her in various psychiatric hospitals for treatment. Her maltreatment continued in her adult years, perpetrated by her ex-husband, and resulted in her splitting even more to preserve herself.

Currently, she's doing reasonably well. Her social interactions are appropriate, and she's doing well in managing her finances, but she still can't interact with her mother on any healthy level. She experiences suicidal ideation and becomes overwhelmed whenever her mother contacts her and continues the torment. She maintains contact with her siblings, except for Rebecca and Henry, both deceased. She receives emotional support, validation, and understanding from her siblings.

Her attitude and behavior are generally splendid. She's delightful to be with and has dedicated herself to her recovery. As for her intellectual functioning, she's an intelligent person at her best. The difficulty lies in which alter is in executive control. She sometimes expresses delusions that alters from past lives stayed to help her. At times, she also experiences paranoid ideation about her ex-husband's plan to take her away during certain phases of the moon and continue ritual and sexual brutality. I've seen no evidence that would allow me to diagnose schizophrenia. I believe all her symptoms fall within the MPD diagnosis.

As stated at the beginning of this letter, I don't believe Leena can work and think she will remain permanently disabled, even though she manages other life functions well. The stress of any work environment is presently too overwhelming for her, and I believe it will remain so."

Four - Our Work with Mr. John Hall

From July 1975 to July 1978, counselors declined to see me or wanted a higher fee than I could manage, but then I found Mr. Hall. He explained he knew about MPD but didn't consider it an area of expertise. I asked if he had worked with victims of severe abuse, and he said he had. He explained he's a master's level therapist and primarily works with relationships, recovery from substances and other abuses, post-traumatic stress, and anger management. Upon meeting him, I decided we were a fit.

Our therapeutic contract included my agreements with Mr. Clarke, except for the not killing one, which neither of us felt was necessary. We added: If I'm upset by anything mentioned in therapy, I'll process it at the time versus holding on to it.

Even though Mr. Hall didn't contract to treat my MPD, he learned about my struggle by speaking with me and reading my letters to Mr. Clarke. He always responded empathically and encouraged me to talk to people I trust about how I feel, practice soothing activities, and regularly engage in healthy endeavors I enjoy.

{The remainder of this story covers 1978 through 1995 and primarily consists of summaries of Mr. Hall's discussions with various alters and Leena. Mr. Hall's comments are in brackets. I reference a pertinent "Protective Services" issue and a popular song for each year}.

1978:

Groth and Birnbaum categorized child sexual offenders into two groups, "fixated" and "regressed." "Fixated" are primarily attracted to children, whereas "regressed" mostly maintain relationships with other adults.

Dust in the Wind" by Kansas reached Number Six.

Life with The Mother

Timothy A. Bradshaw related in his unsteady tone: Leena talks to The Mother and then breaks up. Some of us want to give in to The Mother, but others are afraid they'll get locked up if they do. In a dream, I threw The Mother into a hole. Leena feels terrible about it. We want the childhood we never had, but people's reactions to our childlike behavior shut us down. [What would you think of exploring life without worry about criticism, Timothy?]

Alter Dynamics

Timothy continued: Pennie wishes we were dead. One of us eats hot dogs, and Shelby likes celery and apples. I order at restaurants, switch and hate what I ordered, then switch back and like it. Clara had the idea to go to the doctor to evaluate the heart and check the uterus for cancer.

Sarah knows things and wants to know why and how we disassociate and have Social Phobia. She wants to remember the truth but prefers our pretend reality. [Sarah is curious and wants to grow but is more comfortable in denial.]

Brad, Leena's son, tells Tabatha to stop throwing tantrums. Punky Lil rides the merry-go-round. Sometimes we get loud when we're happy. My mother would never allow it. We're never safe because it's too difficult to determine which alters are good or bad since they're changeable and unpredictable. [That's scary.]

Mary thinks her life has been typical even though people tell her it's been horrible. Sam wants to give up, saying it's not worth it. [Thank you for providing these dynamics, Timothy. Remember our agreement to phone 911 or suicide prevention if you have self-destructive intentions.] Most of us are aware of that agreement. [Please tell everyone you can.]

Tamara articulated in her wavering voice: We thought up Leena. She's scared, and to avoid trouble, she and some alters tell us what to do and back us up. She wrote I love you and drew a heart on the sidewalk, and Ralph, her boyfriend, loved it. Ralph got Leena a poodle. Ralph allows us to get loud when we're happy. The longer we're around, the more authentic we are. We're smoking two packs of cigarettes daily, but our blood pressure's okay now that we've given up coffee. [What's Leena afraid of?] Life.

Therapy Not Included Under Other Headings

Safe, age four, shared in his shaky voice thick with fear: I'm scared of everything and don't like it. I know my brother, but not you. [Hi, Safe. I'm Mr. Hall, the counselor.] Hi. Are you the brain doctor? [Sort of, in that I try to help people with their thinking.] Oh.

Punk shared in her wavering tone: If I acknowledged all that's happened to me, I'd become a monster. If I allowed my anger, I'd be overwhelmed and out of control with it. [Find a pace you can manage. We can work on handling your anger.] Okay.

I believe I killed my baby because the devil worshipers were torturing it and because I thought if I killed it rather than them, it would have a better chance to go to heaven. They were peeling it because blood drains from a body slowly when peeled. My baby cried at first, then stopped. They had to pull me off it. My causing my child's death was pain beyond all things. I lost all faith that day and have fought going crazy every day with every breath. [That's an agonizing memory. They pressured you into a gravely difficult choice.]

People have told me what to do and have imposed their views on me all my life. Now we're supposed to do things on our own. Sometimes, we want people to tell us what to do.

[I know. You certainly want to do as your doctor advises, but generally, making decisions promotes being true to yourself.]

Facing my fears doesn't work. It's too scary. [If you run from fear, it's always in front of you, Punk. Only by facing fear can you put it behind you. What would you think of going on in life as if failure were not a consideration and ignoring your concerns as you proceed?] I'll have to think about that one.

I've told the men in my life not to hit me, and they've responded they don't do it so much. I usually tell myself it's my fault, but Winter once told a boyfriend he was dead if he physically hurt her or played mental games. The boyfriend's eyes widened, and his hands began shaking in reaction to Winter's cold, dismissive look, intense, unblinking focused eye contact, and tone, flat and hard as a stove lid. [Winter doesn't play, huh, Punk.] No. [It's not your fault if others hurt you, Punk, but we can work on confronting others immediately to prevent the build-up of anger, which often leads to aggression.] Okay.

Smiling and displaying her crinkled nose, Punky Lil spouted in her high-pitched, cheerful tone that rises and falls musically: I love my G-ma. She's kind to me and lets me play with toys. We get "dolled up," laugh, dance, hug, and hop. [You still see your G-ma?] Yes. [God bless grandmas.] Yes.

Sarah disclosed in her clear, gentle voice: I'm Sarah. [Hi Sarah]. Hi. To please everyone, I dress unisex. I sometimes wear tennis shoes or little kid animal slippers. Punk likes rabbit slippers. Dorothy is our core person and has always been there but got chopped up. We separate, yet very much want to be together. We have young male and female alters, including one who can sing. [I hear about Dorothy but not from her. The singer is Angel.]

Annie asked in a high-pitched, excited tone: How'd you know that? [I've met Angel.] Oh! Mr. Clarke told me it okay for all the kids to come out on weekends, but we must be adults on weekdays. I'm not happy if the kids can't play. [Make time for them to play.] We feel we're not worth anything because we're damaged, making us want to cry. Sarah told us to have thick skin. [It's okay to cry when you feel sad, Annie, but being damaged doesn't mean you're not worth anything.]

1979:

The Cycle of Abuse is a social cycle theory developed in 1979 by Lenore E. Walker to explain behavior patterns in an abusive relationship.

"I Will Survive" by Gloria Gaynor reached Number One.

Life with The Mother

In his husky, breathy voice, Charley shared: Mother stabbed us with a fork, put us in a deep freeze, and caught our bed on fire. [How horrible for you!] The Mother's boyfriends had sex with us. [You didn't have sex with these men. They perpetrated you, Charley.]

Shelby complained in her unsteady tone: Much of our pain is because we've never settled anything with The Mother. I prefer believing I'm evil because I can't handle thinking The Mother didn't love us. [You're not evil. Your mother was full of pain and resentment that came out mostly against her children. She mistreated you because she didn't feel she mattered much. She hurt severely and might have had MPD. Remember that Mr. Clarke told you your mother mistreated you because she didn't feel she mattered much, and your siblings told you about the horrible, ridiculous, untrue things your mother told them.]

We've had enough of The Mother's brutality but haven't given up on her. She has panic attacks if we don't answer her regular morning phone calls, so we have to put everything on hold until she phones. Some alters don't like to tell her what's happening with us. When young alters answer the phone, The Mother tells them to grow up and do adult things and then hangs up. [You choose to put everything on hold to take care of your mother because some of you still want her nurturing, Shelby.]

Life with Husband and Boyfriends

James doesn't like my current boyfriend, Ralph, to touch us because James likes girls. [Ralph isn't James' type.] Ralph and I took my grandbaby to play in the snow. [Nice, Leena!]

Medical/Psychiatric Issues

I smoke cigarettes due to stress and boredom and have emphysema. I overeat if I don't smoke, and my blood pressure rises even more. I'm also diabetic. I'll be taking a new medication for depression because I had an allergic reaction to the old one. [You self-medicate your emotions with nicotine and food. Have you considered asking your doctor about programs for smoking and over-eating, Leena?]

Alter Dynamics

Sarah explained: Continued disappointment with life sometimes leads to feeling defeated and inability to muster even a fake smile. We huddle in corners, wringing our hands with our eyes wide open, staring into space. We don't have the fortitude to create another Leena, so we won't return if we go to the mental hospital? [That's understandable. How about we do all we can to keep you out of the hospital and keep working on acquiring wins?]

Lots of us want to kill ourselves. [Remember our emergency response contract.] I won't call 911 for fear they'll take me to the hospital and keep me, but I agree to contact suicide prevention or one of my siblings. [I'll take that, Sarah]

Junior announced with a hateful tone: I'm Junior. [Hi Junior.] Hi. I'm finding out a great deal about myself and feel different. I don't want to be Dorothy at all anymore. I wish to remain Leena. Dorothy incorporated everything The Mother said and did. Dorothy didn't know how to handle life and became too scared to do anything. Leena wants to know everything and acquire ways of engaging in life sensibly. She gives us one outside who's the same all the time. Other alters insist I can't get rid of Dorothy because she's one of the 12 Selves. All the Angry Ones can't be in the same room because their revengeful energy compounds when they're together. [You're in favor of Leena, Dorothy is no longer helpful, and the Angry Ones must be separated.]

Therapy Not Included Under Other Headings

Punk clarified: Ralph is our friend but Leena's boyfriend. They played hopscotch. I drew it on paper. The older alters fear that the younger ones will get them into trouble, in that an adult woman playing young children's games may look strange. [What are you worried might happen if others think you're weird?]

I'm afraid of nighttime, so I get stressed, dwell on something, and have difficulty sleeping. [Why does nighttime scare you?] Bad events happened at night. [That makes sense. Those who harmed you aren't around anymore.]

I sometimes think of myself first, although it goes against my grain because I tend to trade happiness for safety. Choosing happiness brings guilt, but I like this new assertiveness and figure it'll be okay if I don't get too selfish. [It's healthy to put oneself first at times, Punk.]

1980:

Married women couldn't accuse their husbands of rape in every state.
"Crazy Little Thing Called Love" by Queen reached Number One.

Life with The Mother

Maybe The Mother was just born stupid, and it's not her fault she has problems and gets angry. Maybe her life didn't go as she wished. Perhaps you're supposed to harm your loved ones. I've decided it's a waste of time to be angry. Life is as it is. [You're not supposed to harm those you love, but we tend to behave toward others the way we were treated. It's okay to have anger but not healthy to hold on to it, and it's not okay to be abusive behind it, Leena.]

Yet some of us are still angry and ask, "why me?" When Dorothy asked the preacher why God didn't grant her request to put The Mother on an island so she couldn't hurt her anymore, the preacher told Dorothy she was evil for asking God to do that. [Are you angry toward your mother or the preacher?] Both. [How long do you plan to be angry?]

I understand that wild animals might get you in the woods because they're hungry, but I don't know why people are evil. [Some people are mean or even cruel due to nature, nurture, or a combination.]

The Mother phoning us causes us to switch frequently. She's pressuring us to live with her, but we'd prefer not to. She's never been trustworthy. She told people how difficult it was for her to have her men have sex with us and that we ruined her life. [I strongly advise you not to live with your mother.]

Our heart wants to take care of The Mother because we worry about her, but we don't want to live with her, even though we fear her anger if we don't. [Remember, fear goes away when you face it, Leena.] Okay.

We wish for The Mother's forgiveness for being with her boyfriends even though we believe law enforcement, the doctor, and The Mother were wrong. [You did nothing for which you need your mother's forgiveness, and yes, they were all wrong.]

Three years ago, we visited The Mother for a few days, and it took seven months to compose ourselves and get rid of Dorothy, who's emotionally dead.

The Mother told us to listen to grown-ups or she'd break our legs. We gave up our beliefs by doing so, which is why we're so screwed up. Part of us thinks it's best to obey someone else, but part of us wants to sort out life for ourselves. [It's best to figure out life for yourself, Leena. How about we look at your abandoned beliefs and decision-making?]

Life with Husband and Boyfriends

Once Dee threatened to kill Anthony. Now that Anthony is dying, she feels sad and thinks something's wrong with her for having those intentions. [Her threat was understandable. It's reasonable to feel compassion, even for our enemies, Leena.]

Ralph wants me to pay more attention to him. [Do you ever tell Ralph what you want and need?] No. [It's okay to do so, Leena. We can work on negotiating your relationship with him.] Okay.

Alter Dynamics

With slumped shoulders and glancing down and away, Punky vented in her wobbly tone: On rare occasions, The Mother is kind, so we switch due to guilt, but then we remember sitting on the front steps for hours while she entertained a boyfriend. [You've done nothing to feel guilty about. You're entitled to your hurt and anger, even if your mother is sweet to you on rare occasions, Punky.]

Dee was looking for male friends, but they wanted dates. Dee still tries to hurt us, and we must also be wary of Cutter. [It's important to consider what Dee and Cutter want and need. When you're afraid they'll kill you, do you still switch to young children who want to live, Punky?] Yes.

We're switching in quick succession. We've been numerous alters, including young ones who Ralph wants to be quiet because he can't focus on his computer game.

I sometimes shop for clothing for some of the alters and must return it. [Oops.] A month ago, some new alters started coming out. I sense the presence of a child rocking and crying due to being left alone in the dark.

Therapy Not Included Under Other Headings

Punky continued: I'm programmed to do everything for everyone else, and it feels good to be needed, but I want more from life. I like listening, validating, empathy, authenticity, showing my emotions, and non-sexual hugs. [I like all of those too.]

When I cut my leg deep, I get rid of the feelings the younger ones call yucky, like being petrified. I'm tired of feeling all the bad. Running away is less stressful than remembering, but I won't use drugs or alcohol. [Acknowledging your emotions and sharing them is a better way to diffuse them. When we run away, our torments are always ahead of us. Taking medication as prescribed and engaging in calming activities and those that bring you joy are also good practices. I'm happy you're avoiding drugs and alcohol, Punky.]

I like the outdoors because the changes are gradual and predictable. Maybe when I grow up, I'll know what to expect from everyone. [Most people are predictable. Some aren't. You can increase predictability by improving how you interact with others.]

If loving means hurting someone, then I don't want to love. The hugs and love I've had scared me. I want nothing to do with devotion or having anyone devoted to me. [Loving doesn't mean hurting. What you got wasn't love. You presently have those who love you and don't harm you, Punky.]

Our struggles with relationships and terrible problem-solving lead to self-loathing. We're switching in a fast sequence due to contact with The Mother and our difficulty finding a more suitable place to live. [We can work on you relationship and problem-solving skills. What can you do to be more in control of your contact with your mother? What are your housing options?]

Dealing with emotions is especially troublesome of late, so I'm experiencing emotional numbing and am switching more often. It doesn't help that I haven't taken antidepressants in a month. [It's advisable to take antidepressants as prescribed, Leena.] Also, there's a problem with the labor division in my household, and I'm getting fed up. [What are your options to deal with that?]

The Little Ones need us to have a kid's day, or they'll cut us. We got to be kids for a short time while living with Grandma. [What are some things you want to do on the kid's day?]

We've been switching to children. Today, we played in mud puddles, and Brad drew mud pictures on his stomach. We had fun roller-skating, but it was scary because we fell a lot. If you use your car to stop, your feet keep going. [I'm happy the kids are playing now, Leena.]

1981:

The National Child Abuse Coalition was formed in 1981 by national voluntary and professional organizations. The Coalition is committed to coordinating advocacy efforts for abused and neglected children.

"Hold on Tight" (to your dream) by Electric Light Orchestra reached Number Two.

Life with The Mother

Missy divulged with hesitation in her voice: I've been chewing on pencils and pacing because The Mother wants me to move in with her, but that wouldn't be in my best interest. No, no, no! [Hi, Missy.] Hi. My mother's crazy-making was worse than her beatings. I made a "Take Care Of Myself List." [Your mother led you to experience de-realization. This could explain some of your depression and anxiety. Your list is a great idea!]

While closing his eyes to focus better, Dale announced in his deliberate, clear voice: I'm Dale. [Hi Dale.] Hi. I'm trying to be like Leena so no one can tell the difference. My mother wants me to move in with her, but I'm trying to forget her. [Moving in with your mother would be a disaster, Dale.]

The Mother told me I was a horrible mother, mentally retarded, and worthless. Why can't I accept that I'm okay and stop hating myself? Why do I take everything personally? [You were brainwashed, Leena. You're not retarded, and you're a good mother and a kind person.]

The Mother wrote the following letter to Mr. Hall: "Dear Mr. Hall, I just wanted to thank you for helping my daughter. As you're aware by now, she's a very special human. I'm sure that your being there for her makes her feel safe. Thank you."

Life with Husband and Boyfriends

The Little Ones are afraid Anthony might come to our house and torture us again. We shut down and can't think when we're scared. For the last three years, he hasn't known where we live, and therefore we've been able to live a regular life. Still, Dee is out and thinking about killing herself. How do I put Dee away? [Pay close attention to what Dee wants and needs, Leena.]

Life in my Household

I've been crying and am angry with myself. I fear I'm setting myself up to be let down by my boyfriend, Ralph, and I think he pities me. He's been cuddling, but I'm uneasy with this. Ralph has a good heart, but I'd like him to be more helpful around the house. I wonder if I'm picky and expect too much from others. My old boyfriend, Rick, wants me to come back because he's lonely. [Why are you uneasy with Ralph's cuddling? You tend not to expect enough from others. If you return to Rick, you'll likely experience the same Rick you left, Leena.]

Medical/Psychiatric Issues

Clutching her stuffie, Kay shared in her high-pitched, thick-with-emotion voice: I'm a 6-year-old girl. Other girls are with me today. [Hi girls] Hi. [What shall we talk about?] I take a pill for depression and another for sleep. I have a history of not sleeping at all sometimes cause I forget to, and when I do, I wonder what I'll be wearing when I wake up cause of switching. No one sped today getting to your office. I'm not Leena anymore. [You know about depression and switching?] Yes. [What's going on with Leena?] I don't know.

My blood pressure got to 182/110 because I took my medication too soon. I'm not taking my Ativan anymore because I get angry when I do, but I get depressed without it. [It's essential to manage your blood pressure. Are you sure your anger is related to Ativan? What does your doctor think, Leena? Say hello to Kay for me.]

I'm back on Ativan and halfway back in the world. I'm cooking dinners, showering, and working in the yard. I've started getting nervous again, though, and am smoking a great deal. [What are you worried about?] Everything.

Despite my agoraphobia, I've left the house for necessary errands and gone to the county fair twice this week. I tend not to go anywhere alone because I mistrust others and therefore need a witness to confirm anything that might happen. I've been more active and lost six pounds. I still smoke to avoid emotions. [Good for you on leaving your house! To help manage your feelings, are you continuing to meditate, distract, and engage in the activities you love? Have you considered a stop-smoking program, Leena?]

Alter Dynamics

Timothy A. Bradshaw declared: I'm Timothy A. Bradshaw. I'm 9. [Hi Timothy]. Hi. I'm in second grade. I still live with my mother, and my dad goes to work. I have one girl's eye and one boy's eye. The girl's eye cries, but the boy's eye doesn't. I have animals like ButterFly, who carry the hope we'll someday be loved. Dorothy is "crashed up" and isn't with us anymore. Leena lives on the outside. The guy that lives with her tells her to write Leena on checks. Sometimes we're here and figure things out quickly. Other times we go into the dark. [You still live with your parents and don't feel loved.]

Alice related: I'm Alice. [Hi Alice] Hi. Timothy A. Bradshaw drove today. He's nine and drives exceptionally fast. When there's too much stress for Leena, she disappears. [Who's older and can drive safely? Leena has a tough job.]

A mix of alters divulged: We've kept bad things from Leena so she can feel okay, but she's not real. We're real. There are 106 of us, and many of us have contact with the public. We need Leena to represent us, and we need to learn how to avoid damaging her, as she's our last chance to cope with life. [You value Leena and don't want to overwhelm her.]

In her straightforward, unemotional tone, Pamela Boy complained: Our mother hangs up the phone on me and threatens to disown me to make me feel guilty. I don't hate her, but I don't trust her. I've concluded I'll either live with her or kill myself to avoid her pressuring me. [Your mother has given you plenty of reason to mistrust her. Her threats are efforts to manipulate you. I don't want you to kill yourself or live with her. You don't have to talk to her, and you might decline when she violates your boundaries.]

I've chosen not to be like my mother. [Good choice!] I want to know how not to have emotions and adapt to other people. [You're going to have feelings, but you can learn to manage them better. We can work on tools to help you adapt to other people, such as healthy boundaries, Pamela Boy.]

My mother claims she's always kind to me, but she's a very mean, troubled person. Her imposing her reality on me leads to my losing mine. I'm trying to forgive, love, let go, and look for what I can be grateful for.[What do you believe about forgiveness, love, and letting go? For example, do you think you can forgive a person but not their behavior?

I call my dad's wife "my sweet stepmom." I phoned her today because it's her birthday. [It's good to create new families when your own, for whatever reason, isn't available.]

I start feeling good, but then my mother phones, and I feel helpless and think of suicide. Some alters want to talk to her, but others don't. She controls and degrades me, but I still want her, and tolerate her mental cruelty, and so what! She wants me to come home to take care of her. [I get your ambivalence, but it'd be self-destructive for you to be your mother's caretaker, Pamela Boy. Remember that you especially dislike psychiatric hospitals.]

Many alters from the Us Cluster are here, and it feels great and healthy. They like Christmas because they get presents. [Hi everyone. I enjoy Christmas also.]

Therapy Not Included Under Other Headings

The Mother whipped us for hitting kids who were mean to us. We were afraid to laugh and play because we always got hurt emotionally. [You must have been lonely.] With you, we don't feel stupid. We fit in. [Good, because you're not dumb, Leena.]

I'm reading that I can heal, stop blaming myself, and quit being self-destructive. I like that the book I'm reading recommends saying "I choose to" versus "should" or "have to" and offers that everything is a choice and that if you like yourself, everything works out. [It's good that you're still reading this kind of literature.]

I'm experiencing agoraphobia. Also, I cut my legs, and they hurt. I'm not feeling like getting up to cook, so I've been munching on canned foods, which is no big deal since I've dined from garbage cans. Patty eats cubes of butter. Hell, everyone is back. [Are you taking your antidepressant and antianxiety medications?] No. [You do better when you're on them. Remember that you have only one body, so it's essential to be mindful of what you put into it.]

I must be feeling better because I'm getting out and doing things. My child alters got little presents today when I went grocery shopping. [To what do you attribute your feeling better?] I'm taking my meds.

It's chaotic when several alters are out, and when one comes up with a piece of the puzzle, it knocks us off balance but is beneficial overall. We've begun using sticky notes and a chalkboard to facilitate the alters' communication. [Great idea!]

This physical sensation business is challenging. When I first began to have this awareness, I called 911 when I felt the discomfort of needing to pee. I also discovered that ice cream is creamy like butter but cold with tiny pieces of ice. [Discoveries and challenges]

I'm reading a book with many big words. It's bringing about a flood of emotions leading to regression, so I have to read slowly. I've learned I have unresolved conflict, "depersonalization," fear, and anxiety and that The Mother has a mental health issue. Maybe if I can understand her better, I won't have such bad memories. I tried to forget my injuries and pretend everyone was friendly, but that didn't help. The book suggests that therapy aims to help one find inner peace by accepting what happened and learning to live with it. [You've made new helpful discoveries, Leena. The book is correct about therapy.]

I compare myself to others my age and become depressed. My lack of education bothers me. I tried to enroll in college but couldn't read the first sentence on the test. As a result, The Mother slapped me, called me retarded, and said she only puts me down to get me to do what's right. [There's no benefit in comparing yourself to others. We're all equal in value. Consider accepting who you are and contemplating what you'd like to improve. You must have been a young alter when trying to read the placement test. I'm sorry that your mother was so mean to you.]

We've accommodated others to the point we have no self anymore. We cry internally but not on the exterior. I'm sad today because The Mother nagged me. I'm in hell with her, but I'm getting more assertive. I believe in treating people the way you'd like them to treat you, whereas The Mother believes in an eye for an eye. [I'm glad you're getting more assertive.]

All my therapists told me it would be best to avoid The Mother. She tells me to only trust her and that she knows more than anybody. [I can understand why your therapists would say that, but since you choose not to, we can work on boundaries to manage your relationship with her, Leena.]

I went to my first group meeting at County Mental Health. They told me they don't deal with people like me and they wanted me to go into residential treatment. That's not for me. [I agree that residential isn't for you. Will they allow you to continue with group counseling?] I think so.

We're doing better. We had one of those troubling days, but we still cleaned the house, barbecued, and played with our dogs. We need a lot of rest to wake up to all these MPD issues, not to mention agoraphobia. Therapy is the only place I go by myself, and I even got lost coming to see you today. [You were productive today, Leena. I'm glad you got here. Can Ralph program your phone with directions?]:

1982

Sgroi, Porter, and Blick define child sexual abuse as a sexual act imposed on a child, noting that children lack the emotional, maturational, and cognitive development to understand what's happening and protect themselves.

"Take It Easy On Me" by the Little River Band reached Number 10.

Life with The Mother

When The Mother worked at a daycare, she put the kid's dirty diapers on their heads. [She didn't!] I'm struggling with guilt about not accepting her offer to live with her. [There you go again, feeling guilty when you've done nothing wrong, Lynne.]

The Mother has been fussing about my having sex with her favorite boyfriend when I was a child. Even after he raped my sister, she protected that boyfriend because he had money. [You weren't having sex. You and your sister were being perpetrated and prostituted. Your mother's concern should have been protecting her children, and she should be trying to make amends with you instead of fussing with you.]

No matter how good I tried to be, life kept going badly with The Mother. I figured the harder I got whipped, the graver my misdeed must have been. I hated whippings and would sit and cry a long time afterward. [Your mother's brutality was about her, not your behavior.]

The Mother is dying but forbids me to tell my sister. I had 18 years of unpleasantness with The Mother and the men in her life. I wanted her not to throw me away, but kids got in her way. [I'm sorry about your mother's impending death and that she discarded you. How do you feel about knowing your mother's about to die and being forbidden to tell your sister, Lynne?] I don't like it.

Life with Husband and Boyfriends

It took many years to get fed up with Anthony's daily cruelty. We're still vibrating emotionally and trying to erase recollections of life with him. Our sleep pattern is way off, and we're having nightmares about scary events and our acceptance of Anthony making us feel guilty. [Anthony was cruel and good at brainwashing. You can't erase your memories, but you can make them less impactful.] Some alters are hanging in, but more are tuning out. [What's that about?]

Memories of Anthony's devil worship and my babies are still overwhelming. When we have these recollections, it's like watching a movie because we don't want to feel or believe them. [I know it's grueling to have these memories, but it's a necessary part of healing, Leena.]

A We Cluster alter complained: We're not sleeping well due to nightmares of despicable things done to us by The Mother and other people, and we frequently sit in a closet, shaking and crying. We dream of Anthony constantly shaming us and our being nothing without him. We don't know what day it is, where things are in our house, or what time we're supposed to talk to The Mother, who phones regularly and has pity parties, blaming her suffering on us. [It sounds like the lack of sleep leaves you unable to deal with your normal daily activities, let alone having to talk with your mother, which is always your choice.]

Ralph and his mother consider Leena to be family. Ralph drove us to the market and the snow, which felt good. [I'm glad you have a family. You've stated you're 70 % sure you want to be in the relationship with Ralph, so how about we work on relationship-building skills.] Okay.

Life with Other Family Members

The We Cluster alter continued: Lynne's oldest son, renamed Rod, and his preschooler son, Jimmy, are visiting. Rod retired from a military career. Many of us are excited to play with Jimmy. Some of us can play musical instruments. Timothy A. Bradshaw and Iris like to draw, and one of us makes gardens. [Your grandson is coming, and you have talents to share with him!]

Medical/Psychiatric Issues

The We Cluster alter continued: We're not sleeping well and are concerned about our health. Leena probably behaves most responsibly about our health. [Has Leena called the doctor?]

My stomach has felt full, and eating or drinking has been painful lately. My doctor told me to go to the emergency room, but I'm afraid to go to a hospital, fearing they'll hold me for psychiatric observation. Sarah knows things and would go with me. [I know you have this fear, but you can't ignore your medical issues. Your doctors can always contact me if they have questions about your DID, Leena.]

We went to the doctor, and he ordered an upper GI and colonoscopy. [Good!]

1983:

Utah passed House Bill 209, which created mandatory minimum sentences for convicted child sex offenders.

"Do You Really Want to Hurt Me" by Culture Club reached Number Two.

Life with The Mother

The Mother told me I was lazy and didn't care about the future and that my dad was a son-of-a-bitch. I realize that The Mother causes me a great deal of distress. [I'm glad you recognize this.] She wants me to move to Georgia and marry my stepdad to get his retirement funds. [You might tell your mother you need 72 hours to process requests in general and say an emphatic no to ridiculous invitations, Leena.]

Tamara shared: One of The Mother's boyfriends never hurt us, and he told us we were great kids. Others raped us. Dorothy wanted to file charges against one, but The Mother threatened to make her life miserable. Dorothy began to batter other children when she was in third grade. [Dorothy's violence was understandable.]

Life with Husband and Boyfriends

Once I was distressed and overheard saying that if I die, I die. People came to my house, removed all my medicines and searched for my gun but couldn't find it. I don't have bullets. [They were worried about you, Leena. I'm glad you don't have ammunition.]

I want any man in my life to do the right thing, and I don't want bad things to happen to them, but I'll whack them if necessary to protect my sons. [You're not vindictive but are capable of whacking.]

Life with Other Family Members

I recently spent the night with my birth father and his girlfriend. The girlfriend took my braids out and put my hair into a ponytail. My father was a soldier. He left the family for a girlfriend early on, but that didn't work out, so he asked to return home, but The Mother said no. He subsequently left his new family for another girlfriend and her family. I'm taking my anger toward him out on my boyfriend. [Can you explain your displacement of anger to your boyfriend and commit intent to stop doing so? Can you process with your father your animosity toward him, Leena?]

I talked to all my siblings and a son this Christmas. I also always talk to my siblings on their birthdays. [You love your siblings and sons.] Yes.

Life in my Household

Patty revealed in a somewhat thick-with-pain voice: I'm looking for a trailer for my son, Brad, who's seeking work. I still want a house of my own.

Medical/Psychiatric Issues

Patty continued: It's my birthday, and as I reflect on life, I become depressed. I've been paranoid, my thinking's off, and I haven't done much for two months. I stopped taking my antianxiety medication because my blood pressure rose. Since then, I haven't been leaving my house except to go to my mental health group and see you, and I'm switching at short intervals. I sometimes panic and remain motionless for a long time. I'm smoking more and have been angry with myself. [I'm guessing you haven't been taking your medication for depression either.] No. [I encourage you to resume both as your doctor advises and to report the blood pressure issue to him.]

I saw my doctor and now take a sleep aid and medicines for migraines, depression, and anxiety. Subsequently, I drove myself to the hospital, Wal-Mart, and grocery store. I'm sleeping better and thinking more clearly, and my blood pressure remains stable. [Your medications appear to be working. Good for you on seeing your doctor, Patty!]

A new male group member rubbed my shoulders in group therapy, and I froze and began crying. Also, The Mother has been badgering me about spousal support matters. I'm switching frequently and having suicidal ideations, but I have none presently. On the positive side, I ran the art class at County Mental Health without incident. [Good job on the art class, Leena! We can work more on boundaries and assertiveness. You might want to listen to your attorney, not your mother, about court matters. Are you taking your medications for depression and anxiety?] Sometimes I forget.

I'm still attending the Women's Crisis Center group meetings and volunteering in the art program at County Mental Health. My body was at the last group therapy meeting, but not my mind. I was Patty, Dee, and Lynne. I wear various cartoon character slippers and carry a stuffie to my group, just as I do to our sessions, Mr. Hall. [Your slippers and stuffies are welcome, and I'm glad you still attend meetings and volunteer.]

Alter Dynamics

Some of us can write with either hand, but others can't write at all. Some can read, but most can't. Reading is a struggle for some due to mirror vision. Some of us don't want people to see us. Others are bizarre, and we can't let them out, even though they want to be seen. [I welcome any who wish to meet me, Leena.]

Therapy Not Included Under Other Headings

Dee is popping out and having suicidal thoughts. She likes fishing but is afraid of deep water. We all like camping and fishing. It's mostly about enjoying nature's sights and sounds. [What's going on with Dee? Are you taking your medication, Leena?]

An Us Cluster alter proclaimed: The Women's Crisis Center wants me to be a peer counselor. They like the way I talk about emotions during group counseling. Leena doesn't know everything that's happened to us but knows that terrible things, in general, have happened. [Being a peer counselor will be helpful to others and healing for you.]

Timothy A. Bradshaw confessed: I left two hours early to get to our appointment with you. I went down the wrong road, and it was scary. Your dog, Foxy, greeted me at the gate. I've known Foxy for quite a while. She loves women. I let Ralph hug me and shake my hand. [Hi Timothy.] Hi. [I'm sorry you got scared but happy you got here. You're not supposed to drive because you're not a safe driver. Timothy? You just switched, didn't you?] I'm Punky.

I'm depressed, struggling with insomnia, and switching in fast sequence because I've been overwhelmed lately. Ralph brought me to our session today because I was changing too much to drive safely. [You need a better system to remind you to take your medication, Leena.] Okay.

How do I tell people how badly I'm doing and avoid appearing weak? Other people pounce on vulnerable folks. [You might pick those you choose to trust carefully. Showing vulnerability is strength, not weakness.]

I'd like to work, but can't "make change" or spell. The Women's Crisis Center didn't want to hire me due to my disabilities. Other places didn't like me because of my scarred arms from cutting. [What are your thoughts on this?]

To determine my eligibility for disability, my attorney arranged a problem-solving evaluation. I fall apart under stress, so I never do well on tests. The assessment revealed that I'd be suited for sheltered employment. [How do you feel about that?]

Upon my request, to be used as needed, Mr. Hall wrote the following letter for me:

"I've been counseling Leena about three times a month for five years. She has a mental health diagnosis of Dissociative Identity Disorder. This disorder tends to be caused by severe early trauma and results in one personality splitting into many alternate personality states. The more serious the injury, the larger the number of personality states created.

In her early childhood, she suffered substantial brutality perpetrated by her mother and the many men in her mother's life. Subsequent atrocities at the hands of her husband resulted in her splitting even more to preserve herself. I've seen her switch on many occasions, especially when emotionally distressed. The personality state present is often a young child.

There's a correlation between her frequent switching and high stress over her current court matter. She suffers from nightmares, sleeplessness, and increasing fear of leaving her house, primarily related to her fear of her ex-husband."

Mary announced in her high-pitched, unsteady chirp: I know who you are. You're the therapist. You're to fix my problems. I'm having a lot of evil thoughts. Timothy drove today. [Timothy isn't supposed to operate a vehicle.] He does. [What are the wicked thoughts?]

Tami shared in her delicate, wavering voice: I'm Tami. Tina is here also. [Hi Tami and Tina.] Hi. I cry a lot when I'm scared. My phone tells me how to get home but doesn't tell me how to get to other places. [You might ask Ralph to program your phone with directions to places you usually go.] Okay. My mother yelled at me for not answering my phone yesterday. I want my mother. Others don't. How do I switch to become Leena? [You might try thinking of what Leena looks like and what you need her to do, just like when there's a need to switch to someone who can drive safely.] Okay.

I try to present myself as intelligent, durable, and not damaged, but people see through that façade when I put crayons and clay in my shopping cart. [You're smart and proved you're strong by standing up to your tormentors. Many of those you worry about seeing you as damaged have also been wounded. I hope you enjoy the pastels and clay, Leena.]

My boyfriend is a nice guy, but I'm losing my emotional attachment and pulling back from him to avoid the future possibility of getting hurt badly. I don't like attention from guys in general, and once intentionally got skinny so I wouldn't have breasts. [You still struggle with closeness. If you go through life trying to be safe all the time, you likely will miss out on potential happiness, Leena.]

With unblinking focused eye contact, Winter announced in her flat tone: I'm Winter. [It's good to finally meet you, Winter.] It's good to meet you. Even though my body's alive, I have no emotion or physical sensations. The 12 Selves helped create Leena, and they believe she's their last chance to be happy and find peace. She goes to therapy to improve her thinking, manage The Mother's impact on us, and learn and grow. [Thanks for sharing, Winter.] You're welcome.

Leaning forward and nodding, with wide eyes and intense eye contact, Sherry shared in her melted honey tone: I'm Sherry. [Hi Sherry.] Hi. I don't like Winter because she's scary. She has a big job. [Yes, she does, Sherry.]

1984:

California State Attorney General, John Van de Kamp, described the explosion of reported child abuse cases, particularly sexual abuse, that marked 1984 as follows, "We've unearthed an epidemic of violence."

"What's Love Got to Do With It" by Tina Turner reached Number One.

Life with The Mother

Us Cluster complained: We continue to be negatively impacted by phone conversations with our mother, who regularly denies our reality, yet we're profoundly enmeshed with her. [You might consider trusting your judgment and memory versus believing your mother. What might you do to become less enmeshed?]

Our mother told us sex is nasty and disgusting. We cut when we feel that way. We allow our boyfriend to have sex with us because you have to let guys do it, but we're learning to enjoy it without feeling guilty, nasty, or dirty. [You don't have to let guys do it, but good for you that you're learning to enjoy sex, absent negative feelings about yourself!]

We can't tolerate the dark because our mother put us in a dark attic for punishment. We can't lock our doors or be in a room with closed doors because our mother used to lock us in our bedroom. [We can work on your phobias.] We have too much else to deal with. [Okay. What?]

I want to work on boundaries. I confronted The Mother about her constant dumping on me, and she feigned being receptive but then reiterated how distressed she was. I know she'll continue to phone because she's lonely. [Good job asserting, Leena! You might want to continue to assert yourself, despite how your mother reacts.]

Life with Husband and Boyfriends

My anxiety escalates, and I disassociate when anything reminds me of The Mother or Anthony. I lock up the bad and create a front of a person. [I know, but allowing these painful memories at a pace you can manage also promotes healing, Leena.]

Life in my Household

I recently traveled alone to San Diego and was frightened but only cried twice. My new trees were dead when I returned, and I became angry. [What did you do with your anger?]

I'm depressed, not sleeping well, and am switching in quick succession because I'm struggling with my relationship with Ralph. I've begun sleeping on my air mattress in the living room, and that's helping. [What specific relationship issues are you having? Are you taking your medication, Leena?]

I listened to Christmas music, made hot chocolate, and watched fireworks during the holidays. Ralph slept on New Year's Day. I wish I could fix things with The Mother and Anthony because I don't think I'll do well when they die. My dad's passing upset me. [I doubt you can fix your relationship with your mother or Anthony, but you can influence how those relationships impact you. Can you work on letting go of any venom of bitterness running through you?] I'm trying.

I'm sad because my birth father died. Rick's dad died at age 97. Rick is a prior boyfriend. I liked him because he was good to me, even though he called on specific alters to get what he wanted. [I'm sorry about your father. You liked Rick even though he exploited you at times, Leena.]

Medical/Psychiatric Issues

I'm back on an antidepressant and sleep medication. My doctor also started me on hormone therapy and is concerned that my blood sugar is high, so he cautioned me about my diet. [I'm glad you're maintaining regular contact with your doctor. You do better when you take your medications as prescribed. Proper management of your diet is always advisable, Leena.]

Hormone therapy improved my patience, reduced switching, and I'm feeling less crazy. My doctor referred me back to County Mental Health. [Great news about your hormone therapy. You might want to take advantage of any mental health programs available.]

Mental health personnel told me to speak with you, Mr. Hall, because I've been staying in bed all day, cutting, and having suicidal ideation. [You can talk to me most anytime you need to. Are you taking your antidepressant medication? If so, you might need your doctor to reassess it. Are you engaging in your calming and pleasurable activities? Remember our emergency response contract, Leena.]

I resumed taking my antidepressants and am doing better. The Mental Health Department is terminating my services because I'm not disturbed enough. I'd like to at least continue with group counseling. [They have budget cuts. I can write an appeal to allow you to remain in group therapy.] Thanks.

Alter Dynamics

Sleepers hope I can make life the way they want it. They have bad memories and need to speak up when they become brave. We suppress recollections we can't deal with, and we bring out different alters every so often so everyone can have their turn to live. [Suppression helps temporarily but doesn't resolve anything. You're doing an excellent job for the alters, Leena.]

Therapy Not Included Under Other Headings

I dreamed of attacking Anthony. I trust very few people. [Both make sense.] I'm glad I came to see you today. It's a huge relief to hear you tell me I can say no. [You'll experience even more comfort as you assert yourself more.]

We haven't used our legal name, Dorothy, since 1966. No one wants to be Dorothy because she's wrecked beyond repair. We're doing our best to focus from this day forward.

We still have memory gaps, so our life history looks like Swiss cheese, which is painful to realize but helps explain our behavior. The emotional turmoil that comes with unpleasant recall, which begins with snapshots, can take weeks to settle, depending on how many alters are involved. [Remembering at a tolerable pace is advisable, Leena.]

We no longer thought we needed precaution when we locked up horrible recollections, so the beatings and rapes reoccurred but seemed like the first time. Thus, not remembering was a setup to get re-victimized. We, therefore, also isolated ourselves because we knew how evil people could be. [You paid the price for forgetting. You believed that isolating provided safety. I wonder if what little protection it brought was worth the loneliness. We can work on boundaries in hopes of reducing your isolating.]

I watch you closely and try to copy you, Mr. Hall. You have good relationships with others, even if you sometimes get frustrated. I'm becoming you. [I'm happy to hear you think I'm modeling healthy behavior, Leena.]

Squinting her eyes and tucking her chin Sophia declared in a matter-a-fact way: I haven't met you before, but I know who you are, Mr. Hall. I question some of your comments, which the others don't like. [Hi Sophia.] Hi. [It's healthy to scrutinize. What do you have questions about?] The idea of confronting scares me, but I'll be stuck in therapy forever if I don't learn. [We can continue to work on assertion.] I have thoughts of suicide but would never act on them. [I'm glad to hear that.]

Abby explained in her high-pitched, thick-with-emotion tone: My boyfriend came into my room today, and I asked him who he was. My dogs wagging their tails reduced my fear. [Hi Abby.] Hi. [You're just meeting Ralph?] Yes.

Glancing down and away, in her shaky tone, Cindy shared: I'm Cindy. [Hi Cindy.] Hi. One of my mother's boyfriends told me everyone plays the touching game. I never want to grow up and know about that, so I stay a child. I'm a big girl and have secrets. I don't like touching. I'd rather play, but my mother insists we have to be friendly to her boyfriends. [Do you still live with your mother?] Yes. I confuse sex with being nice. Lilly sits in a corner and bangs her head against a wall. Lots of our young ones cry all the time, even though some have grown-up bodies. [Being kind has nothing to do with sex, Cindy. Sex isn't supposed to happen with children. I feel terrible for the young ones.]

I lost track of time. Did I just arrive? [No, you've been here almost an hour, Leena. I've been speaking with Cindy.]

Amy shared in her high-pitched voice edged with fear: I'm Amy. [Hi Amy.] Hi. Charles said that your dogs don't bite him. Dogs scare me. [I can put them out.] No. It's okay. Some guy in our house knows how we got here. I know things. I didn't like my mother's long kisses. I don't want to love anyone if that's love. I sometimes wish Dee luck in trying to kill us because I'm tired of being afraid. [What your mother did wasn't love, Amy. Your mother wasn't supposed to do that with you. We can work on your fear.]

A We Cluster alter revealed: We were always in trouble with The Mother but never sure why. Amy has a terrible secret about a field, is still afraid of everything, is physically numb, has stopped laughing and playing, and even lousy memory no longer hurts her. [Tell Amy I'd like to hear about the field when she's ready and that it's okay to laugh and play now.]

1985:
The first annual conference on Victims of Child Abuse Laws was held in Minneapolis, Minnesota.

"I Want to Know What Love Is" by Foreigner hit Number One.

Life with The Mother
While slumping her shoulders and averting her eyes, Leah revealed in her wavering voice: An alter told my mother that she'd visit her, but I said I wouldn't. To be a kind person, I need my mother not to be evil. My mother wasn't pleased with anything I did, so I quit trying and stopped feeling. Also, my therapists have told me that the rapes weren't my fault, but my mother's word is powerful. I still feel dirty. Therapists told me to pretend that I'm pure until I believe it. [Your mother treated you horribly and brainwashed you. You can still be a kind person. You can practice nurturing parental self-talk to rebut what your mother said.]

I was told The Mother's father was a sociopath and went to prison, but he remarried afterward, and his children from that marriage seemed fine. We dread that we might someday have to take care of The Mother. [I strongly recommend against that. She has other resources, Leah.]

Life with Husband and Boyfriends
Tamara shared: We got lonely around the holidays during the 27 years that The Mother didn't contact us. Loneliness sucks, but fear sucks more. We fear people and even fear leaving our house. We still have a petrifying terror of Anthony, which often causes us to split all over the place. [It appears that neither Anthony nor your mother presents a danger presently. How about we explore what you can do to be less afraid of people and of leaving your house? You could ask trustworthy friends or family to accompany you. Your antianxiety and antidepressant medications should help. Are you taking them? We can also try exposure therapy.]

There's a guy named Ralph at our house, and we care for him, but one of us is afraid of him. [Who's scared and why?]

Medical/Psychiatric Issues
I haven't been eating, doing anything is just too much at times. My doctor put me on antidepressants and is also concerned that my blood sugar and blood pressure are low. She

discovered arthritis and spine anomalies, so she ordered an MRI. [It sounds like your doctor is taking good care of you. You tend to not do well when you're not taking antidepressants, Leena?]

Therapy Not Included Under Other Headings

I've been disassociating. It's like going away in my mind, checking out, or a blank space. I'm not in my body or mind, sometimes have to tell myself to breathe, and get one hell of a headache when no alter wants to be out. [Is the pending spousal support matter troubling you presently?] Yes.

My attorney agreed with your suggested changes to my stipulation. I got a monetary settlement. [I'm glad I could help, Leena.]

Seven -and-Three Quarters announced in her unsteady voice: Today I'm 7 3/4. [Hi 7 3/4.] Hi. I'm proud because I'm almost age eight. Others are at home in my room. They have their own emotions and behaviors, and we impact one another. For example, I got very sick once because PJ wouldn't eat. [Why wouldn't PJ eat?]

With wide eyes and a lifted brow, a trembling 3-year-old PJ announced in her unsteady, high-pitched tone: I'm PJ. [Hi PJ.] Hi. We get scared and cry every night, so we stay awake until light, and even then, we don't leave the house. I like trucks. Anthony is a "pooh head," and Ralph throws pillows when he's mad. Others have told me that I'm retarded or hollow.[I don't think you're mentally slow or empty.] My mother is driving me crazy. [How's your mother driving you crazy?] Dee is getting yucky to my mother. [What's Dee saying to you mother? Have you been eating?]

Tamara revealed: Punky calls Ralph "Bear." Sam calls him "Mr. Ralph." Leena sees Mr. Hall for therapy and is eating healthier and planting vegetables. A child molester gets a child to trust them. A child wouldn't be afraid of 90% of them. We isolate and try to be as unattractive as possible to keep men away. [You believe isolating keeps you safe. It might just cause loneliness. I encourage you to have more contact with those you trust and go out into the world with them.]

1986:

Diana E. H. Russell has researched sexual violence against women and girls for the past 45 years. She was a co-recipient of the C. Wright Mills Award for her book, The Secret Trauma.

"What Have You Done For Me Lately" by Janet Jackson reached number four.

Life with The Mother

Punky complained in her deliberate, steady voice: I feel as if every aspect of my life has involved pleasing my mother. Presently, she's trying to make me feel guilty for not wanting to take care of her. She sometimes calls several times a day and yells that I'm killing her. She and my stepdad wish to visit and call every three days to discuss the visit, but I'm putting them off. [I'm glad you're asserting and having contact with your mother more on your terms. Guilt is a choice. Healthy guilt comes when you violate one of your principles. [Did you?]

I want to discuss anxiety and my anger and frustration with those in my life. [Anxiety and anger are common secondary emotions experienced in place of other feelings that are difficult to feel or express, Punky. Which relationships would you like to discuss?]

While grimacing and glancing down and away, Tamara shared, in her wavering tone: We like having Leena, who's her separate person. Our mother can brainwash us, yet we're considering living with her. [Living with your mother could be devastating, Tamara.]

Life with Husband and Boyfriends
Men have wanted sex while intoxicated, and we haven't known what to do. Also, we want to talk about expenses. [You might tell any man of interest that he must be sober and pleasant if he hopes for intimacy. What about your expenses?]

Medical/Psychiatric Issues
I've been forgetting to take my medication and may have had a stroke. I, for sure, had an anxiety attack. My blood pressure increases when I communicate with The Mother. [Would a pillbox help you remember to take your medication? Is your doctor still prescribing antianxiety medicine? We can continue to work on assertions and boundaries to help manage your dealings with your mother, Leena.]

I'm not sleeping, have low energy and depression, and dream about killing myself. When we get too depressed, we let the house go to hell, making us more depressed. [It sounds as if you either aren't taking your mood medication or need a different one.] I stopped taking it because I experienced little relief but terrible side effects. [Do you have an appointment with your doctor?] Yes.

My doctor gave me a different antidepressant, which helped. Also, I've been dizzy, nauseous, and falling, and I might have diabetes. I'm due for my yearly physical. [It's good that you attend to your medical issues, Leena. It's best to continually advise your doctor about how your medications impact you versus discontinuing them.]

Alter Dynamics
Suzie Q. revealed in her wavering tone: I'm Suzie Q. [Hi Suzie Q.] Hi. I was initially leery of your dogs. I've been drying fruit and making 10 gallons of liquid soap. Some alters have their favorite stuffie and slippers. Punky is in love with Ralph. We also have a protector with us today. [Are you sure you made enough soap? Who's the protector, and why do you have one today?]

Therapy Not Included Under Other Headings
I've tried being nasty to keep people away so they won't take advantage of me. I've also wanted to torture others so they'd understand how bad I feel. I didn't like myself when I

was nasty or had terrible thoughts toward others, so I decided to be kind. [You'll be happy you chose kindness, Leena.]

1987:

An article in The International Journal on Child Abuse and Neglect read that a review of recent research suggests that such mediating variables as the child's characteristics, environmental resources, and quality of personal interactions are as important in predicting the outcome as maltreatment alone.

"Here I Go Again," by Whitesnake, hit Number One.

Life with The Mother

An Us Cluster alter complained: My first counselor told me neither my cutting nor my mother taking me to school and telling school personnel I was a whore, were big deals, so it's no wonder I withheld truly horrible details. [Your withholding makes sense. Your first counselor was wrong. I want to hear about those awful details when you're ready.]

My mother claims she loves me, but I want to tear her head off. I cut after contact with her. [Following your talks with her, you might be prepared to engage in your calming activities and engage in activities you enjoy.] It does feel good when we run and play, talk to one another, and barbecue giant fat hotdogs. Most of our toys are in storage. [Get them out.]

I'm trying to reconcile what my mother has done to me. I've attempted to hurt people but didn't like it. I've locked up the Bad Ones to avoid being a Ted Bundy. I want to find inner peace and never again act out my anger aggressively. Going from evil to pretending to be kindhearted is challenging. [If you keep pretending to be compassionate, I think it will stick because it will be rewarded.]

My mother phoned and bitched at me, claiming my affair with one of her boyfriends ruined her life, so I felt numb and shut down again, which caused me to "go bonkers," and then I wanted to kill myself. The pain was intense. Other alters cried and said it hurts. How do I let my mother know I love her? [Wow! She still hurts you, yet you haven't given up on her. You could try pointing out what she's done that you appreciate.]

My mother wants me to move near her to take care of her. How can she ask that, considering the way she tortured me? [She doesn't hold herself accountable.]

I've given up on finding a house, and I'm still uneasy about finances. In June, I might move in with my mother even though she triggers thoughts of suicide, leading me to cry and "zone out" a lot. [Living with your mother could be your ruination.]

Life in my Household

Punky revealed: Several alters are waking up because I'm under stress. Many of us play in our house. [We can work on stress management, Punky.] Okay.

I've been staying in my bedroom for almost 24 hours a day and eating very little. I'm beginning to feel alone. Also, I'm wondering whether it's time to put my doggie to sleep. [Why are you isolating? Are you taking your antidepressants? How do you measure your doggie's quality of life, Leena?]

Medical/Psychiatric Issues

Clara divulged in her deliberate, clear tone, absent her usual laughter: Leena has been on heart medication for the past seven years and recently discovered that abruptly stopping causes symptoms similar to a mild stroke. Also, her doctor increased her bupropion. [It's a good idea to take one's medicine as prescribed. I'm happy that Leena's doctor monitors her antidepressant medication, Clara.]

Therapy Not Included Under Other Headings

I need to see myself as good, not evil, and accept what happened to me and why it happened. [Remember that Mr. Clarke told you children sometimes do what's necessary to survive because they're terrified." Also, Anthony forced you into choices whereby you couldn't feel okay about either outcome. You can accept what happened to you by biting off a little at a time. Horrible things happened to you because you had the bad luck of spending much of your life with two exceptionally abusive people. Feedback from those you trust should help validate your memory, Leena.]

I close myself off because I distrust almost everyone, but most alters want you to know who they are. Alters are going deeper, finding more anger, and having more suicidal thoughts. If I want to heal, I must allow new, painful recollections, but I don't want these memories. When I remember the past, I disassociate from everything. [You've improved at allowing new, painful memories.]

I don't want to make you feel bad, but your goodbye hugs are pleasant but emotionally painful. As you know, I often get overwhelmed with emotional pain. [I don't feel bad that you experience ambivalence about our hugs, but I understand why you do. I'm sorry for your agony. I'll always offer a hug, and you can choose whether to accept it. I'm not offended if you don't, Leena.] I want them.

Tamara spouted: We were hypnotized once and found new alters. One can read at the college level, but we're not sure which. I have a baby turtle named Sassy. [Did you benefit from hypnosis?] I'm not sure. [I'll bet Sassy is cute. Who picked out Sassy?] Some Little Ones and I did.

Some alters, especially PJ, are upset that they're unnecessary, that The Mother pressures us to live with her, and that some want The Mother's forgiveness. [You're all important. I can see why your mother's pressure would be upsetting. Alters still have different attitudes about your mother.]

1988:

The 1988 Child Abuse Prevention and Treatment Act, among other things, provided financial assistance for demonstration programs for the prevention, identification, and treatment of child abuse and neglect and to establish a National Center on Child Abuse.

"Sweet Child O' Mine" by Guns N' Roses topped the chart.

Life with The Mother

Tamara continued: I had a recent awkward talk with my mother and hung up on her. She accused me of thinking more of my son than my brother and said it would be my fault if my brother died. [Wow! It's no wonder you dread contact with your mother. Hanging up was a healthy assertion.]

Part of me thinks my mother may not be evil but just demanding. Part thinks she's crazy-making and that I must shut her out to maintain my sanity. Doing so might be selfish, but I no longer want to be without bodily sensations or emotions. [What are your choices, and what would be the consequences of those choices? What would it look like to shut her out, Tamara?]

Alter Dynamics

A smiling Bubble announced in her excited, high-pitched voice: I'm Bubble. I'm five. I'm the "Secret Police." Is Viking a bear? [Hi, Bubble. Viking is my dog.] Hi. He's big! If you go out to play, you have to quit if you get in trouble. I want to be a real kid. I hear a lot, and I get in trouble. Motions don't want to come out. I'm afraid of them. I'm the one who makes us feel bad. Grandma said I wear my motions on my sleeves. That's why I wear short sleeves. We stay home when we're switching a lot. Many of us have stopped talking, but I still talk. [Thanks for telling me about yourself, Bubble. You still see Grandma?] You're welcome. Yes

Therapy Not Included Under Other Headings

We're often like zombies but sometimes want to cry and mostly feel bad if we have emotions at all. The Mother tells us to keep a "stiff upper lip" and not let life bother us. Meanwhile, we're disappearing. Yesterday we accidentally cut ourselves but didn't feel it. [Your mother has no idea how much damage her invalidation of your reality is causing. We can continue to work on assertion and boundaries, Leena.]

I'm afraid to reach out to others because I don't trust myself to remain strong and have healthy boundaries. I have to be slow and methodical. [Good idea.]

I vary from hyper-vigilant to trusting others blindly because I don't trust my judgment. I once got touched inappropriately by a man near a public restroom, causing me to switch to Winter, who slapped him. [You'll get better at this. How do you feel about hitting the man, Leena?]

Although I question my goodness, I've always wanted to help others like me be self-sufficient. I've tried doing this through the years via the crisis line for County Mental Health agencies, teaching groups about violence and anger, and teaching art therapy through the years. [I'm sure you've helped many people.]

1989:

The Supreme Court concluded that the Constitution doesn't legally require states to protect their citizens, including abused children, from harms that the states didn't directly generate.

"Wind Beneath My Wings," by Bette Midler, reached Number One.

Life with The Mother

The Mother found me a house and wants me to visit her. The death of family members has left me more vulnerable to accepting The Mother's offer. [I know you're cautious about anything related to your mother, Leena.]

Today I flashed back to The Mother putting pins in my ears, scrubbing my vagina, and consistently lying and telling me not to let things bother me. [Those are painful memories.]

Sometimes I make The Mother go away in my mind, but then everyone disappears. I prefer no contact with her to letting her make me crazy. [Good choice] Thank you for being here for us, Mr. Hall. [It's my pleasure, Leena.]

A 3-year-old Little One, who chose not to give her name, spouted in her high-pitched voice: We found out a week ago that we have Abby. She's tiny and makes animal cries. We like her. Our mom hurt us. [Hi there.] Hi. [I'm sorry your mother hurt you. Say hello to Abby for me, and tell me when you want me to know your name.] Okay.

Life in my Household

Ralph got me a present for Valentine's Day. I've been working on my budget, looking for a house to move into, and canning chicken breasts. I've been sad, angry, and disappointed over money and housing. [A Valentine's Day present! How about we look at your housing options, Leena?]

I'm moving to Georgia. The Mother bought me a house. [This is a massive change for you. I hope you can manage the increased contact you'll likely have with your mother.] Can we maintain contact by phone? [Absolutely]

Tamara exclaimed by phone: We moved to Georgia into a house on a three-acre farm in the same town where The Mother lives. We have chickens for laying eggs. We've been painting and working in our yard. Being on a farm reminds us of living with Grandma. [These are pleasant living conditions for you. How are you doing with your mother?] Well, then there's that.

Many of our Little Ones have disappeared. They're hiding from The Mother. They no longer trust Leena because she moved them nearer to The Mother. [I understand why they disappeared and no longer trust Leena, but she had valid reasons for moving. Her housing choices were limited, and the new home reminded her of Grandma's farm. Hopefully, Leena can rebuild trust. Have you thought of finding a therapist where you live?] We'll never do what it takes to "break in" another therapist. Can we keep you? [We can continue our contact by phone, but I encourage you to seek someone there.]

The Mother won't enter our new house, claiming it's too dirty. We sometimes want to cry but have no feelings for the most part, due to seeing her more. We accidentally cut ourselves yesterday but didn't feel it. We're also having thoughts of suicide but won't act on them. The Little Ones are afraid. Some of us want more contact with The Mother but don't trust ourselves to stay stable. [If you continue to use your boundaries with your mother, her negative impact on you will likely diminish, and the Little Ones will be less afraid, Tamara. You might avoid her altogether when needed.]

Medical/Psychiatric Issues

My doctor put me on Paxil, which makes me tired. [What effect is it having otherwise, Leena?] I'm not sure yet.

Alter Dynamics

Bubble announced: Others are quiet, but I talk. [Hi, Bubble.] Hi. [Did you want to speak today?] No. I just wanted to say hi. Viking isn't a bear. He's your dog.

Punky Lil spouted: I ride the carousel horse at Safeway and sometimes color with crayons. I hate vegetables, but ice cream and cake are good for you. My G-ma lets me have coffee, and we go fishing. G-pa doesn't allow throwing stones in the water because it scares the fish. He calls my mother an evil witch. [So, you still spend time with G-ma and G-pa.] Yes.

Abby shared: A cat got into the chicken coop. I cried when we found a dead baby chick. [Hi, Abby. That's sad.] I know. I'm tiny, and I love animals.

Tamara blurted: Winter grabbed the dentist's scrotum when he put his leg across her lap for traction when pulling a tooth. He asked Winter to kindly remove her hand. [Did the dentist get the tooth?]

Therapy Not Included Under Other Headings

While displaying wide eyes, in his shaky tone, Ben shared: I'm an 8-year-old boy. I carry many emotions. [Hi, Ben.] Hi. I know Tina and Joyce. Joyce and others are afraid people will think we're crazy and lock us up. I've conquered a few fears but have many more, including Claustrophobia, which stems from The Mother putting me in an attic, deep freeze, oven, and garbage can. [Claustrophobia makes sense. How about we work on improving your boundaries to promote trusting yourself and on diminishing your fears, Ben?] I've been attempting to practice my self-talk, as you suggested. I get the concept, but it's a work in progress. [I'll help you get better at it.]

1990:

Victims of Child Abuse Act of 1990 - Title I: Child Abuse Offense - Requires the United States Sentencing Commission to openly declare guidelines or amend existing policies so that the court shall sentence two offense levels higher, one convicted of a sexual offense or violence against a victim under age 14.

"When I'm Back on My Feet Again" by Michael Bolton topped the charts.

Life with The Mother

Punky shared: My mother wanted Dorothy to get into bed with her, but Dorothy just cried and stood beside the bed. The Mother told her she wasn't her love bug. Now that we're talking, someone is popping out with words on the tip of their tongue. We think more happened. [I believe so too.]

I want to please my mother, but I recently told her each of us has our perspective. [Good asserting, Punky!] My mother hasn't called much lately, but she's still a pain. I sometimes don't answer the phone when she calls, and when she complains, I tell her it was in my pocket, and I didn't hear it, okay? [Good asserting!]

I realize my mother is mentally ill and loves me in her twisted way, and I'm trying to separate her from her behavior. [That would be an impressive spiritual walk.]

Child is attempting to let go of anger and bitterness over not being allowed to live with her real dad when her parents separated when she was 18 months old. [Is she trying to let go of anger toward her mother, dad, or both?] Most of my feelings are toward my mother, who disowned those who wouldn't do her bidding. We disappeared and could no longer feel her slaps because she whipped us regardless of how we behaved. [Dealing with your mother's unpredictable punishment by going away in your mind makes sense.]

My mother did monstrous things to me, but the abandonment and not protecting me from her boyfriends bothered me the most. By having more contact with her presently, I'm forced to face the reality that she was a jerk. I can no longer make excuses for what she did. It's no longer possible to rationalize her awfulness. I fear my being angry makes me my mother, and allowing my anger to take over could make me a serial killer, which I don't want because I have to live with myself. I'd rather be depressed and have DID. [I'm glad you're acquiring clarity and working through your emotions. Being angry doesn't make you your mother. You're entitled to your anger, and you've done well in managing it. You'll never be a serial killer because you have a conscience.]

My mother died, and I've been angry and short-tempered for days. [Your mother died? Are your feelings because she's gone away, yet so much remains unresolved?] Yes. I never got to settle things with her, but she wouldn't have allowed it. All the alters are screaming in my head. Some still have anger toward her, and others are happy she's gone. [Having mixed feelings make sense, Punky, and you're right that your mother wouldn't have allowed you to settle matters with her.]

I've been thinking of my siblings. When The Mother set Dorothy's bed on fire, Dorothy got burned when she crawled under it to get her brother, Ronald. When I first began to remember this, I remembered it differently. Ronald worked with computers after retiring from the military. He married several times but only had two children. My brother, Henry, also worked with computers, married, and had two boys.

Alters remember different things about the past. Some say it's not okay to think badly about The Mother now that she's dead. [You're entitled to all your emotions, Punky, and you can still verbalize them to your mother even though she's deceased.] Many alters are unaware of The Mother's death. Life circumstances froze them in time, so they continue to relate as if she's still alive. [I'll have to remember that, Punky.]

As a teenager, I had ambitions of being a nun or a nurse, but The Mother told me I didn't have the brains for either. [You're intelligent and compassionate enough to have done either, Punky.]

Hurter confessed in her fragile voice: I hurt mommy. I caused her death. I'm her downfall and disappointment. I'm so bad to have made her so sad. [None of this is true, Hurter.]

Life with Other Family Members

Hurter continued: I found my birth father and saw him before he died. He drank alcohol too much but was a good guy. My mother claimed he was abusive. [You and your mother remember your dad differently. I'm glad you got to see him, Hurter.] I was feeling better, but now others are popping out. Dr. Phillips thought he wasn't doing his job since many alters were still coming out.

If my mother was getting what she wanted, she was okay, but we were on her "Crap List" most of the time. She was unpredictable, whereas I felt safe with my dad. My mother ran over him with her car and cut him with a knife. [Wow!]

Dummy-Two exclaimed in his unsteady voice, mother likes dad dead. [That's upsetting, Dummy-Two.] Yes.

Punky Lil, stuck in time until recently, thinking G-ma was still alive, spouted: G-ma allowed tree climbing. My mother didn't. [Hi Punky Lil.] Hi [Being with your Grandma was fun, and she loved you.] Yes.

Life in my Household

Suzie Q. shared: My neighbor borrowed eggs to make a birthday cake. I'm cooking beans and dehydrating vegetables today. I've been harvesting lots of vegetables, and most of us are eating healthier. Sadly, my baby bunnies died. [I'm glad you have a friendly neighbor, have been enterprising, and are eating healthier. I'm sorry about your bunnies.]

My dog plays with my goat but kills my chickens and turkeys. [The goat is fun, but the birds are fair game.] I harvested two turkeys because they smashed the chickens doing "boy urges." [There's crime and punishment on the farm. Maybe you should stick with chickens.]

I cooked a turkey dinner for my stepdad, Brad, and Brad's girlfriend. That's what we do. We prepare a big turkey dinner and then have leftovers for days. Brad whipped up six pumpkin pies. [It sounds like you had a splendid holiday dinner with family, Suzie Q.]

Punky complained: I recently became so depressed I couldn't leave my bedroom. Brad's taking me for a drive took the edge off. I've been switching and don't know why. Now that my mother is dead, I don't have to hear her criticism, so I feel relieved but feel guilty for the relief. She and her boyfriends confused me about trusting because they did terrible things to me while telling me I could trust them. [Are you taking your antidepressants? It's okay to feel relief now that your mother has passed. Learning to trust again is a challenge, but it's possible. You can start slowly.]

I resumed taking my antidepressants and have felt better of late. My stepdad bought me a John Deere lawnmower. I've been mowing, planting, gardening, and painting, and I was particularly pleased with how I decorated my hallway. [You engage in activities you enjoy when you feel better. Do you also notice that engaging in these activities makes you feel better, Punky?]

Medical/Psychiatric Issues

Punky continued: I had a heart attack without knowing it, and now I'm monitoring my heart. I didn't even feel the pain despite a 40% blockage in my arteries. My blood pressure was dangerously high. Going to the hospital was scary. The Little Ones hid. I bled too much when my doctor pricked my finger, so she wants me to reduce taking baby aspirin to once every three days. Also, she switched me to a 20-mg dose of Prozac for my depression. I'm following her advice to exercise, eat a healthy diet, and stop smoking. [I'm sorry the Little Ones were frightened. Those are serious health issues! I'm glad you're following your doctor's direction. You have many alters but only one body. Does she have you in a stop-smoking program, Punky?] I'm stopping "cold turkey."

My doctor scheduled me for brain and ear tests because I've been getting dizzy and falling, and I'm getting an MRI because I'm having difficulty walking due to sciatica. I'm also diabetic, and I take insulin orally. I'm using a C-PAP for sleep apnea and therefore dream because I sleep better. I'm having a reoccurring dream of flying and feeling free. [I'm sorry you're having medical issues, but I'm happy you diligently attend to them. What do you think your dreams mean?] They might mean that I feel free because my mother is no longer harassing me.

Alter Dynamics

Punky continued: I've been cleaning and gardening, and it feels good. Also, I'm trying to separate other people's parts in matters versus mine.

Before my mother died, I told her that she could have prioritized her kids over her boyfriends, who left me with hate and guilt. [Good for you!] I created an alter to handle hatred for my mother because hate would make me evil. [Feelings don't make one evil, Punky.]

My currently active 106 alters are hiding many others I've locked up. One of our Angry Ones says to buckle up. Do we need more alters, or are 106 enough? I'm afraid new ones will come out now that my mother is dead. [That's not for me to say. You'll create new ones if you need them.]

Deon wants us only to be kind and not have a choice of other emotions, but it felt good to tell you I hate my mother. [I'm glad you benefitted from verbalizing your feelings, Punky.]

Our Wise Ones don't let Dee out often because she cuts us to relieve pain or let the evil out. Everything that happened to me was my fault, and if I'm around people long, they become evil because I'm evil. Evil begets and attracts evil. I thought if I cut big enough, the counselors could see my wickedness and understand it. Most counselors said that wasn't necessary. [What happened to you wasn't your fault, you're not evil, and you don't need to cut to help me understand you.]

The Little Ones are out because they believe it's safe now. Peter and 7 ¾ are also out. [Do these alters think it's safe because The Mother is gone?] Yes.

We put a park in the middle of our town but haven't played in it because some of us have started to think it's childish; however, now that the Little Ones are coming out, maybe they'll enjoy it.

I'm embarrassed because continuing to make new alters is weak. [Accept your weaknesses and celebrate your strengths.] Tommie wanted a girlfriend, but Mr. Clarke said she couldn't have one because she was nine and had a girl's body. Mr. Clarke told me that all alters have a purpose, even Dee, who tries to kill us. He said to be extra kind to Dee and those like her because people have hurt them the most. Dee thinks only she'll die if she kills herself. Mr. Clarke told her that all would die if she died. [You only have one physical body, Punky. How did you feel about Mr. Clarke saying Tommie couldn't have a girlfriend?]

I've been switching and wandering around in a fog. I'm putting up a wall and taking a while to register pain. It's as if I don't want to accept or deal with more alters coming out. I used a chalkboard to write their names in the past, so I'd know they'd been out, but I don't have a chalkboard anymore. [Would your drawing tablet suffice?] Yes.

It's hard to give more extensive information about alters because I must switch to them to gather that information. I began using numbers for them because my imagination ran out of names. Later I stopped assigning numbers or names to new ones and just accepted their presence. I'm unsure which one studies Buddhism, but she's out occasionally. People from the Pentecostal church said I was possessed and that they'd pray for me. [So, names, then numbers, then neither. The church didn't know about MPD, Punky.]

Us Cluster proclaimed: One of us is intelligent and reads a lot. We read that there are antibiotics in food animals, and when we consume them, we build tolerance, and then antibiotics don't work for us. They're also growing genetically manipulated corn. [I believe more than one of you is astute.]

The Little Ones like gardening and want to plant, someone wants noodles, and Suzie Q. has been out because I have a clean house. We've been sewing, planting our garden, organizing our garage, building a driveway, and dehydrating shredded pumpkin and watermelon. [You've been productive. Do you notice you're happiest when you do what you enjoy?] Yes.

Therapy Not Included Under Other Headings
I went from being gullible to not trusting at all. Presently, I'm beginning to have faith again. Still, I'm isolating myself more because I don't want to deal with the world. I spend less than an hour out of my bedroom each day. [Are you taking your medication? Not trusting and isolating have been ongoing problems for you. Your world is much safer than it used to be, and you have trustworthy people in your life now. I encourage you to give these new people a chance, Leena.]

My ability to experience physical sensation comes and goes, but all my therapists have told me it will stay in time. [Consider having the intent not to let fear rob you of the joy of physical sensations.]

Some of my younger alters see me in the mirror and wonder where all the years have gone. It's like being in a coma. There's no way to make up for the lost time. [No, but you can learn to live more fully in the present and plan for the future.]

I got up at 2:30 a.m. because I couldn't sleep for unknown reasons. I fear something terrible could cause me to become broken and not return. [You've come too far to let that happen.]

Doing yard and farm work is getting harder with age. On the positive side, now that I'm getting older, I care less about people's appraisals. [You've acquired a healthier perspective.]

I tell people I'll kill them if they break the Polar Express cup you sent me. It's a good soup cup. [I'm glad you like it.]

I don't wear a seatbelt because being tied down causes panic attacks. I have Claustrophobia to the point that I can't even roll all my car windows up. [Are you taking your antianxiety medication? We can try more relaxation and desensitization exercises.]

I have a brain like Swiss cheese and alters having memory pop out of the openings. Becoming healthier is somehow filling up the holes. That means accepting that the bad memories are real and being more on guard so I'm less likely to be re-victimized. I know I have to incorporate pieces as I can, healing a little at a time. It'll take years to eat the whole cake. [You're progressing well.]

I confronted one of my rapists and requested my childhood and innocence back. He owned responsibility, apologized, and wished he could take it back. Although his apology helped, I told him I understood that he was sorry, but that didn't make it right. He answered, "No apologizing will ever make it right." [I hope his responding with such accountability was helpful, Leena.]

1991:

The Domestic Violence Prevention Act of 1991 - Title II - Amended the Omnibus Crime Control and Safe Streets Act of 1968. It authorized competitive grants to states for use by state and local governments to help develop effective law enforcement and protection strategies to combat and reduce the rate of domestic violence.

"I Don't Want to Cry," by Mariah Carey, reached Number One.

Life with The Mother

Us Cluster shared: We cry when we recall things our mother did to us. Now that she's deceased, we're not tense all the time. We feel guilty for being only a tiny bit sad but 99.9% relieved. It's like being on vacation. As a whole, we're trying to pretend our mother was okay, but some of us are angry. [Is that healthy guilt? What do you want to do with the guilt and anger? How's the denial working?]

Punk complained: My mother committed grave sexual, physical, mental, emotional, and spiritual savagery against me. Yet, I'm conflicted over needing to know she loved me versus accepting that she didn't and hating her for it. In my presence, she used to tell people I was stupid. When she told authorities I was a control problem, they took me away and said I had a vivid imagination, was spoiled, lying, or trying for shock effect. Her boyfriends loved me too much when she arranged our meetings at hotels. My Grandma was my salvation. [Did it feel like your mother loved you? Thank heaven for your Grandma.]

Life with Husband and Boyfriends

Anthony behaved unmercifully, and I have harrowing memories about him. The next man in my life was devious, calling on the alter who'd have sex, and the third wasn't cruel or devious, but our relationship didn't work out. I haven't been interested in sex for the past 9 years but would like companionship. [How have you thought of acquiring someone to keep you company, Leena?]

Life in my Household

My stepdad's girlfriend is moving in with him. I've been baking holiday cookies and brownies, and my stepdad took cookies home. I got Brad a ratchet set and pair of pants for Christmas. [You're enjoying some healthy family life.] I was sad because Brad didn't take me to see the Christmas lights. [Darn!]

I bought a truck and purchased a large cage to house my chickens. I'm getting 27 eggs each week. [Good for you about your vehicle and going shopping. Are you bartering with the eggs, Leena?] Yes.

Suzie Q. exclaimed: My dog, Dexter loves me. He smells minty fresh after his bath with a bit of mint oil. I made almond butter and dried pumpkin, which I put on pancakes. [You enjoy Dexter and homemaking!] Yes.

Medical/Psychiatric Issues

I accidentally burned my leg badly while barbecuing today and am worried because I now have no feeling in that leg. The Little Ones don't understand why I burned them. The pain reminded me of when The Mother insisted I touch a hot pan to demonstrate my stupidity to her boyfriend. [Darn! You saw your doctor about your leg, right?] Yes. [Bad burns are serious. You could let Brad do the barbecuing. Can you get the Little Ones to understand it was an accident, Leena?] Maybe.

I've lost weight, and my blood pressure and sugar count are down to normal, but now my doctor is worried about a possible blood clot in my leg. [I'm glad you've lost weight and are keeping healthy blood and sugar counts! Blood clots are potentially dangerous.]

I'm having an MRI to look at anomalies in my spine, but I have swollen joints due to arthritis, and the swelling must diminish before they can do the MRI. I also have a clogged artery and something similar to lupus. I have appointments with specialists.

My burned leg is still painful, but I've managed some weeding and pruning. My doctor told me I could endure a remarkable amount of pain. Clara helps deal with our medical issues. [Whenever possible, you might have someone else do your chores until your leg heals. Good for you for attending to your health issues! I'm glad you're seeing specialists. Clara is doing a good job, Leena.]

Clara announced in her clear, deliberate voice: I no longer have to see my doctor for my burned leg, even though it stings and I'm still treating it. [Hi Clara.] Hi. Both my legs are somewhat numb, so I'm using a walker. I'm switching frequently but not sure who to. I'm depressed because I can't work in my yard or garden. [I'm glad you're diligent about treating your burns. You might want to engage in some of your favorite non-strenuous activities rather than yard work and gardening.]

Tamara shared: We hear voices, and we're still trying to figure out who we are. How do we deal with hallucinations and test reality? What should we do when other alters possess us, and we're in the background thinking through their minds? {Tamara might be talking about "blending," a temporary type of integration whereby alters inside can tap into each other's abilities and skills.} [You're progressing but still having MPD symptoms. Are you taking your medications? What are the voices saying? Test reality by consulting with those you trust.] You keep us well-grounded, but we've forgotten to take our Ativan for two weeks. [What can you use as a reminder to take your medications?]

We were unmotivated and sleeping a lot, but our mood has been much better since resuming Ativan, so we've been sleeping less and doing chores. It sucks not to be Leena. Some of us are agoraphobic, we weren't scared with Leena. [Are you thinking of what Leena looks like and what you need her to do, Tamara?]

Suzie Q. shared: When I'm in too much pain, I sometimes shut down, but lately, I've been taking my pain medication regularly, so I'm doing better. My doctor recommended Tai chi to get my balance back. [I'm glad you're taking your medication. Tai chi makes sense, Suzie Q.]

I historically register mild but not severe pain. At age 51, I switched to 6-year-old Tami and played in the snow with only socks on my feet, and the tips of my toes required amputation due to frostbite. My doctors are surprised I'm not experiencing severe pain in my burned leg. [As you're aware, you need to be extra cautious because you often don't experience the type of pain that signals danger, Leena. Tamara seems to think you're gone.]

Alter Dynamics

Punky divulged: I've been having fun coloring with little crayons and skipping, but I panicked yesterday, trying to find my bank, and after that, I started having sleeping problems. [I'm glad you're having fun. Can you put directions to your bank on your phone?] I'll try. [Maybe your stepdad or Brad can help.]

Smart Ones are nameless and sit quietly to not be noticed by potential perpetrators. One of our Smart Ones watches documentaries. The U.S. government is abusing social security. The corporate elite controls our government. Houses are sinking in Alaska due to global warming. Cattle ranches can't profit due to drought caused by rivers flowing into the ocean versus sinking into the ground. [Interesting]

Us Cluster exclaimed: Now that The Mother is gone, the Little Ones are coming back out. Other alters are also popping out because they want to engage in life. They saw baby chickens hatch today. We watched movies, played dominoes and Yahtzee, worked on our "kids" puzzle book, and planted 20 baby papaya trees. Pennie picked out a fluorescent green chicken. [You're planting and having fun.]

We still don't know who we are. Alters spontaneously pop out. Maybe we're the Unnamed Ones. [Maybe you're a revolving door, as described in the book you read about MPD.] That seems especially true when we don't know who wants to be out.

1992:

The National Organization for Women's third March for Women's Lives set a record for the most massive civil rights demonstration in the U.S. with 750,000 marchers.

"We Have to Learn to Live Alone" by Tycoon was released.

Life with The Mother

Us Cluster shared: Our mother had a thing about sending Dorothy to "cuckoo places," claiming she was disturbed. The song "Sounds of Silence" reminds us of that time.

Life with Husband and Boyfriends

At the Women's Center, a lady suggested we fantasize about nailing Anthony's penis to a board, setting it on fire, and handing him a hatchet. The impact of physical injury perpetrated by Anthony dissipated faster than his mentally harming us. [You might not want to do the hatchet thing, Leena. Many maintain mental torment is worse than physical.]

Life in my Household

Recently my neighbor's wife visited, and we baked cookies. I feared she'd trigger an emotional dam break, but she only caused a little drip, and I recovered. [This is healthy desensitization versus unhealthy isolation. You're getting better at this, Leena.]

I shopped yesterday for fertilizer, feed for the animals, and flowers to plant. I also bought a paint gun and spray washer. Penelope likes to paint. Timothy A. Bradshaw can use the spray washer. [I'd think a paint gun and spray-washer are too dangerous for young children. Maybe Brad or your stepdad can use them.]

I brought home a 9-week-old puppy named Nugget. My stepdad and his wife dropped by, and they loved Nugget. Mister also likes Nugget. [Who bought the puppy, Leena?] Punky Lil answered: We did. [Who?] Dee, 7 3/4, and I. [Nugget will be fun and good company for Mister.]

I have a handyman now, and he was a big help with my garden. I have lots of vegetables. My neighbor, Mr. Simmons, is my new buddy. He's going to paint my house. My new stepmom gave me flowers yesterday. I call her my sweet stepmom. [Wow, Leena! You have a handyman, new buddy, pleasant stepmom, and Nugget.]

My neighbor invited me for Thanksgiving dinner. I kind of really like her, and I told her so. Brad is taking me to see Christmas lights. [A new friend and Christmas lights!]

I've come to accept about half of what happened to me and am still afloat. I know people will likely return kindness if I'm kind to them, but I still fear reaching out. [Good progress on remembering! Your self-confidence is building, Leena.]

Around the Christmas holiday, I like *White Christmas* with Bing Crosby, *Miracle on 34th Street* with Maureen O'Hara, *Bell, Book, and Candle* with Jimmy Stewart, and "*Frosty the Snowman*" sung by Burl Ives. [I like all of those too.]

My stepdad came to my holiday dinner. I baked and took cinnamon rolls to my neighbors. I remembered Grandma today when I saw embroidery at the Ben Franklin store. [You're creating new good memories and recalling good old ones, Leena.]

My brother, Buster, sent elk horns for my dogs, and I bought noisy ducky toys for them. [You love your dogs.] Yes.

Us Cluster proclaimed: We've been working around the house, mowing, putting up clotheslines, helping the neighbor with his pasture fence, using our table saw, and using gasoline to burn garbage. Our neighbor built two metal shelves for our tools. [I'm glad the alters who can do these chores are out even though I'd prefer they not to be burning, especially with gasoline, and not using power tools, including the mower. Can Brad, your neighbor, or your handyman do these chores?]

Medical/Psychiatric Issues

I had an emotional crisis because I had to euthanize my dog, Mister. Counselors have told me to burst the emotional bubble by telling somebody, so I'm telling you. I told my doctor I had suicidal ideation to persuade him to give me antidepressant medication, and he relented. [I'm sorry about Mister. It's sad when our pets die. You can medicate depression but not grief, Leena, but you have a history of doing better on antidepressants.]

My doctor put me on medication for cholesterol and wants me to exercise. He also told me that my autoimmune disease might be attacking my nerves. Also, my vision is blurry now from diabetes, so I hardly ever drive anymore. [Are you exercising and taking your medications?]

I'm on a new medication to prevent strokes because my doctor found lesions on my brain caused by strokes. This medicine raised my sugar count, so I have to adjust to that. The doctor told me I possibly had a recent stroke because I felt weird for about 15 minutes, and then it took a couple of weeks to begin thinking with clarity again. [I'm sorry you're having these medical issues but glad you're under your doctor's care.] I take lots of medication. I have four pillboxes, but I still get confused and forget sometimes. [Can you create a system or alarm? Can Brad help, Leena?]

I had a heart attack. There's a great deal of heart disease in my family. My brother, Buster, told me to go to the hospital, and Brad drove me. My stepdad informed the medical staff I'd lie to get to come home. My stepdad, sister, and Brad told the doctor to keep me even if I claimed I was okay. I had a 97% blockage, and Brad said I was gray. I'm tired now but comfortable and am complying with medical directions.

My surgeon arranged a new general practitioner and will be creating a diet for me. He told me I'm one person. That's true, but there are others. My surgeon inserted a cardiac stent, and I'm on medication to prevent rejection. I'll be taking a blood thinner and baby aspirin for the rest of my life. Brad has been keeping track of my medication. [Your medical issues are scary. Please follow your doctor's recommendations and only engage in activities he approves. You only have one body.]

Some days I can amble around fine, but other days my chest hurts. The other day I heard ducks quacking and dogs barking, so I scrambled out of bed, suspecting a predator, and only managed to get to the door before having a minor heart attack. It felt like my throat was swelling. I had trouble breathing and felt my heart pumping hard. My doctor had told me to come to the ER if I had any pain in my chest. I drove myself but probably shouldn't have. [Please be careful and keep your family advised of the status of your health, Leena.]

My stepdad calls a few times a day to check on me, and he suggested my sister stay with me for a while. [Great idea!] I'm on another medication to thin my blood even more.

[Who are you today?] I'm JackJill. I went to the hospital. Lots of us disappeared, but some stayed. I don't like people to worry about me, and I prefer being ice cold or like a stone so people don't know how to hurt me. [Hi, JackJill.] Hi. [Too late! Many people already love and worry about you.] My new doctor labels and has my medication delivered. [She's a conscientious doctor.]

Alter Dynamics

Amy shared in her high-pitched voice edged with fear: I was at the hospital. We called our stepdad and asked if he'd be our real dad, but some didn't like that. Brat, a 5-year-old girl like me, asked the doctor if we had to stay in the hospital. We act tough around other people. Mr. Clarke said we have angry children. We don't want to get mad because we might be mean. [What was your stepdad's answer, Amy?] He said yes. [You don't want to be mean, Amy?] No.

Dale announced in his deliberate, clear tone: My insurance representative arranged a new general practitioner for me, assigned an advocate, scheduled a mammogram, colonoscopy, and pap smear, got me a handicap sticker, and asked if I wanted a therapist. I get colonoscopies because family members died of colon cancer. I'll also be seeing a dentist and optometrist. [Your insurance representative impresses me, as does your diligence about your checkups. What was your answer about a therapist?] I told her I didn't want to "break in" a new therapist. She said to let her know if I changed my mind.

Us Cluster ranted: This's been a heck of a month. This shows we can't handle life so well, but we know that. We're getting better at it, however. It's been a wild ride from Leena to crazy, two steps away from suicide, a zombie zone, and 10 steps back. I did manage to get out of bed today, feed the chickens, and wash my bedding and myself. [I believe you handle life better than you think.]

Leaning forward with her hand on her heart, raised brow, and wide eyes for intense eye contact, Sarah complained in her clear, gentle voice: Mr. Clarke told me I should pick one look and stay with it so people don't think I'm weird and lock me up. He told me adults don't usually wear animal slippers and carry a stuffie. [How do you feel about what Mr. Clarke said, Sarah?] I haven't followed his advice.

Punky Lil spouted in her high-pitched, cheerful tone that rises and falls musically: I play with our farm animals. My gate is crooked but keeps them out of my garden. Nugget knows his name and knows how to sit and come. [Your farm animals are fun, and Nugget is smart.] Yes.

The Wise Ones know we ought to be ourselves, be one with the world, find peace, be respectful of all things, and do no harm. We have three nameless Wise Ones who perform tasks they learned from watching television. They're hungry to acquire knowledge, like little sponges soaking up water. [You're wise, and eager to learn, Leena.]

A wide-eyed Pink announced in her high-pitched voice edged with fear: I'm Pink. [Hi Pink.] Hi. I'm bigger than my pants, so that makes me big. I don't wear diapers. I go fishing next to a bridge with my grandparents. [You still visit your grandparents?] Yes

Grandpa scares me a little because he doesn't smile much. He puts his overalls on and goes out to do chores. Then he naps, and if we aren't quiet, he flips us with his finger. He sometimes says, "Dammit, this is tiring."

We new kids won't have a chance to do things before we die because our body is already age 61. [You and the new kids might want to get busy having fun, Pink.]

JackJill, Amy, and I aren't supposed to come out because we know The Monster, but we want to have a life and grow up. We want to be real kids. We'll hide if someone tries to put us together. If that happened, we'd be fat. The Monster is my aunt's friend. He's old, like Grandpa. Even today, it too scary to talk about, but I remember the barn. I crossed my arms and made fists as he came my way, wearing only a slight smile. His hands were cold and big, and his breath stunk of alcohol. I floated away and watched from the loft. [Thank you, Pink, for sharing this scary memory about The Monster.] You're welcome.

In her straightforward, unemotional tone, Pamela Boy explained: Fifty alters have been active in the past year. Others aren't gone but are simply behind doors. Young children like Pennie and 7 ¾ have been highly active and don't remember the bad. [Thanks for sharing, Pamela Boy.] You're welcome.

Ham explained in his unsteady voice: My doctor told me to first take it easy and then relax even more. Suzie Q. has been doing chores, I've been eating healthier, and I've got humor today. I got my name because I like ham. [Hi Ham.] Hi. I like you. [I like you too.] Thanks. I'm trying to be Leena, but I don't know much about her. She's in another faraway place, and I don't know how to get there. We have chickens and other creatures in our yard. [Those are goats, Ham.] Oh! [Try thinking of Leena and what you want her to do.] Okay.

Therapy Not Included Under Other Headings
I thought you'd like to know when I feel dumb. I was cutting meat and felt pain, but stupid me didn't realize we were piercing our fingers. Shoot! I just kept cutting until it hit me. I've been thinking and talking about Cutter, so perhaps I should stay away from knives. [You're not dumb, Leena. Dissociation hinders your focus. What could you do to prevent cutting yourself?]

Some of the younger Us Cluster alters printed the following letter: hello mr hall. we want you to know how much you mean to us. you've been there for us a very long time now. you listen to all our bull. you never look down on or pity us and you're understanding. very few people in our life took the time to know us. care about us. tried to understand us. 99% were therapists and my Grandma. or put up with us. yes for us you're in the group with our Grandma. you understand what we're saying. Grandma and mr Clarke showed us what life could be like and you're doing that now. what we should be or try to be like. take care, our dr Friend. PS Meme wants to talk. She's tiny, but I'm not sure how old she is. [Thank you. I'm glad I'm helpful. Meme can speak with me anytime she wants to.]

Meme shared in her high-pitched tone, edged with fear: would be nice to be able to think again and know what around us. but then we not crazy right now. feel in check mostly. that good. we ashamed of our behavior of late. good, I guess you get to see our inner workings. [Hi, Meme.] Hi. [What have you done to be ashamed of?]

It's difficult to relate to a feeling we have no words for. Mr. Clarke told us that remembering is like being in the eye of the storm. The Little Ones asked him to put it into simple terms, so he wrote on a chalkboard and explained: Anger is an emotion that usually comes from another. Guess at feelings you can't name. You must go through layers to get to the base emotions. [I agree with what Mr. Clarke wrote, Leena. Anger is usually a secondary emotion experienced in place of other feelings that are difficult to feel or express.]

How do I get over MPD? I tried telling myself it's different now, but it seems the same. When does it stop, or when do I learn? I've trusted others so many times, yet again ended up in a place I didn't want to be. I put out something that tells others to hurt me. I know it's me that causes it, so I keep everybody away from me. [Learning and healing are ongoing processes, including being aware of our part in matters. How about we continue to work on social skills, including assertions and boundaries, with the goal of safety without loneliness.] Okay.

I was wondering if hypnosis could erase everything. Mr. Clarke tried hypnosis with me. The outside people were sleeping, so the inside people talked to him. [I know of nothing that will erase everything. Learning to live with what you recall is a more realistic goal. What did the inside people say, Leena?] I don't remember.

Instant fears are more challenging to control than carried ones. We sometimes cry over immediate scares because no one comes out quickly to deal with them. When The Mother became angry, we could prepare by bringing out a robust alter to handle it. We have tough alters and can create more if needed. [Crying and even retreating when afraid at times makes sense, but regrouping and facing those fears is needed to eliminate them.]

I stay heavy to keep men away. My age also helps. I'm sacrificing my physical health to avoid fear. I think, what the hell, roll over and die. [Could it be that your isolating, not your size or age, keeps men away from you? How do you manage those thoughts of death?] I avoid heights, knives, and anything that could harm me. [Good, Leena!]

An unknown alter wrote: I have more emotions and thoughts and make more decisions than I used to. Still, I'm like a broken eggshell put back together that will never be whole again. I continue to choose to split at times versus having devastating memories. Some of us think The Mother was perfect, and others worship the devil. I don't believe becoming one person is possible, and I don't care to try. I only want peace. I'm not sure I even have a core personality. [Healing is a process, and you've come a long way, Leena. Who knows how far you'll go, but you don't have to become one. I believe that the original personality born with your body is gone. Instead, you seem to be a revolving door of co-existing alters.]

Some young alters were upset by material mailed to us by Mr. Hall, containing misinformation about the first time we were raped. They sent him the following letter: like we explained it was due to all the lies we had to tell because of mother. to make what she wanted to be true. it just brought up horrible feelings. we had to let it settle down before we could write. we hate her for telling lies and keep telling us we was wrong. that wasn't the way it happened. after you told us you got the dates from the state papers, we understood why you thought we was 13. we was okay then but wanted to explain what we know to be true. sometime, no, a lot of time, we don't know what real. or who telling the truth. or like we was told we want people to feel sorry for us. we don't think that true because we didnt want anyone to know we had sex. but we don't know what to believe. that a big reason we don't like thinking about things that happened. it make us crazier. it hard to sort out what the truth is, recalling everything that was told us compared to what we think the truth is. it seem everyone has what they believe the truth is, even if they weren't there. the hospital, teacher, head docs, mother, even later with men. is it possible all of it real? it just depense how you look at it? we come to think that way everyone right. anyway we, you and us are ok. we're still good. [If you ever become upset about our relationship, please talk to me as soon as possible so we can talk it through.]

Punky shared: Mr. Clarke told me I have a high emotional IQ. He said Dee "acts in," directing her anger toward herself because she can't act out toward others. Mr. Clarke requested that I call him when Dee is out. Leena usually waited two days before calling him because she needed to calm down and not be too clouded by emotions to understand what was going on. [So much for Mr. Clarke's request. I think he's right about your emotional intelligence and Dee.]

Pink announced: I talk to you, Mr. Hall. You help us. We learned the most from you and Mr. Clarke. We get to be us around you. You not scary like The Monster, who's a deep dark secret. I don't talk about him. About 99% of us are kids, but we act like adults to avoid the mental hospital. [We can talk about The Monster more when and if you want to, Pink.] Okay.

[Have you thought of having a counselor nearer your residence, Leena?] In her thin, frail tone, Tina tearfully asked: Are you leaving me? I'm Tina. I'm little. I don't go to school. [I'm not going anywhere, Tina.]

A grimacing Penelope declared in her high-pitched voice edged with fear: Mr. Hall? Yes, that's who you are. I'm Penelope. [Hi, Penelope.] Hi. I'm tiny and don't know my age. All the others left and dumped it on me. I'm not supposed to get distressed, but I don't know what that means. I'm supposed to keep balance, whatever that is. The doctor touched me for a long time near my pee-pee to examine a blood clot, which resulted from his puncturing a vein during efforts to insert a catheter, whatever that is. I'm willing to try the doctor's suggested diet, including using olive or canola oil and avoiding trans fats, whatever they are. I can't be Dale because he eats butter and cheese. My neighbor cooked soup for me, and my handyman came by to check on me. I've learned the most from you and Mr. Clarke.

My breathing is steady, and my thinking is clear now that my blood flows better. My doctor told me that other body parts shut down to keep my heart alive when I had the blockage. I don't know the names of our Smart Ones. Most of us don't spell so well. Iris and Art focus only on drawing. Some of us can play the piano and sing. Some can figure out things. [You sound intelligent to me, Penelope.] Thanks.

Clara shared: My doctor wants me to get regular sleep and exercise three times a week by walking. He wants me to rest if my chest hurts when I'm active. My neighbor will be mowing my lawn. We haven't figured out if this is serious yet. [It's immensely so, Clara.] My stepdad is phoning almost daily to check on me. I disappear when I'm in pain, so maybe that's why I can't take my heart attack seriously. [Have you spoken to Leena about this? It's unsafe to fail to notice your chest pain, Clara.]

Unknown alters asked, what's so bad about dying? [Everything goes away, including your siblings, sons, grandson, and animals.] Oh! That's true. [Who are you now?] It's hard to tell. We're a "bouncing ball."

We have emotions and thoughts, make decisions much easier than before, and regularly engage in calming activities. Yet, we still dissociate to avoid devastating memories, and we neither desire nor believe we can become one person. [I'm glad you're doing better. No one wants you to become one. Some of you aren't aware of that.] Oh!

Glancing down and away, Samantha concluded in her high-pitched, thick-with-emotion tone: I'm a whore because I've had lots of sex. My mother said it was no big deal until I had sex with her favorite boyfriend. I don't like sex, but it's a girl's duty. I don't think I could have survived without a few good people like Grandma in my life. [You're not a whore. Having sex forced on you is a big deal. Sex isn't a girl's duty but a choice when you're mature enough to engage in it. I'm happy you had your Grandma, Samantha.]

Pamela Boy asked: Does the doctor mean we must all take it easy? Kids don't have heart problems. [Yes. You only have one physical body, and that body has heart problems. You can still engage in non-strenuous activities.]

Five asked in her wavering, high-pitched voice: Did you know all this bouncing around gives us a headache? [Hi Five.] Hi. [Yes, you've told me about the headaches.] We should be skinny because we bounce around so much. [I don't think it works that way.] Do you know Tina? [Yes. She's an 8-year-old crybaby?] How'd you know that? [Someone told me.] Sometimes we write or draw to keep others from hearing or seeing us, making it easier to pretend we're healthy to avoid getting embarrassed or locked up. [That's clever.] Thanks. [You don't have to hide from me.] I know.

Us Cluster shared: We have a new electronic pill reminder with a soft, girl's voice. Our new doctor isn't a horse's butt. We've been monitoring our blood sugar, eating vegetables, fish, and avocados, and reducing our smoking. [Great!] We're reading about the "good old days" of farming. [You like farming.] Yes.

When we're Angel and look in the mirror, we see Angel. [Angel can sing.] How'd you know that? [I know Angel.]

We've had many monsters in our lives, and as a result, we only have a small hill of good, a mountain of unhappiness, and two towering peaks of shame. Under pressure, the mountains become volcanoes, like when the hospital doctor told me emotions are acceptable and that we could have them with him, but then he became scared and locked us up when we did. [That won't happen with me.]

Holding herself and rocking from side to side, Mary shared in her high-pitched, edged with fear voice: he not help. he hurt us. bad doctor he was!

Us Cluster shared: People broke our hearts into a million pieces of shell. People killed us over and over, and now there's no us. They took everything. We avoid people because they stimulate old fears, and we get overwhelmed if we have to deal with many people at once. We hate ourselves. [I know you have much pain, fear, sadness, and shame. You also have a great deal of compassion for others. Can you work on also being kind to yourself? I've read that if we find a place within us where there's joy, the memory of Grandma perhaps, the joy will burn out the pain.] We'll have to think about that one.

We hear voices calling for Leena. She's not scared like we are. She went away on February 17. [How do you get her back?] We don't know. [Can you think of her and what you'd like her to do like you do when you need a safe driver?] Maybe.

I'm doing better because I switch less often and have emotions under control. As you suggested, I created a medical directive, and to avoid liability, I put the truck I gave Brad in his name. I'm progressing in my recovery from coronary surgery and not getting dizzy and falling anymore, but I'm still using a walker and cane. [Those in the Us Cluster think you're gone, Leena! You've been productive. I'm glad you're progressing.]

I'll always need therapy. You keep me grounded, Mr. Hall, and I think as you do. If there's a gap in our talks, I resume feeling bad about myself. Therapists believe I'm a worthwhile person, even though I don't. Because I have so much pain, part of me wants to inflict pain on others so they can see what it's like, but I don't because I want to avoid jail or a mental hospital. [Also, you're compassionate.]

I get headaches when I switch, especially when an alter comes out and wants to stay for a while. Sometimes none want to come, so we push them out. It feels crazy when they repeatedly go back in, and we continually force them out. {Leena is talking about a "switching headache," a migraine-like headache resulting from "cycling," switching too frequently or quickly. It sometimes results from forcing an alter out.}

You and Mr. Clarke let go of your personal lives to focus on me and explain issues. I remember Mr. Clarke telling me to chew on recollections a little bit at a time and then put them back in the box until I eventually arrive at a better place. We didn't connect with or trust Dr. Phillips. One counselor thought he knew everything but didn't, and another challenged the existence of MPD. The county counselor told me he cured me. One said he could make all my alters go away in two sessions. Not. Another couldn't understand why I wasn't a mass murderer. Still, another thought I was grossly exaggerating. One of my boy alters patted the butt of one counselor's daughter, and I almost got in trouble. [I'm happy that Mr. Clarke and I have helped, Leena. One of your boy alters has an impulse-control issue.]

Punky Lil sighed: When I fall apart, I cry myself to sleep. [I'm sorry you have this pain, Punky Lil.]

1993:

The United States Advisory Board on Child Abuse and Neglect declared a child protection emergency. Between 1985 and 1993, there was a 50% increase in reported child abuse cases, with 3,000,000 cases reported in the United States each year. Treatment of the abuser had only limited success, and child protection agencies were overwhelmed. Efforts began to focus on prevention.

"Ooh Child" by Dino Esposito reached Number 27.

Life with Other Family Members

Punk complained: I've had the "crybabies" all day because I feel sad and overwhelmed. It's my birthday tomorrow. My brother, Buster, sister, Mandy, and stepdad are taking me out for a meal, and Buster is bringing me a present. Mandy is married with children and prepares tax returns for a living. My sister Megan is a counselor. She was never married. [You're planning a family outing! What do you do when you're overwhelmed?] I get angry and cry. [You've also written and engaged in other soothing activities like meditation, which was helpful.] True. Thanks for listening. It takes the sting out. You know me but still care about me. My neighbor's caring about me makes me cry. My mother always told me I wasn't worthy of consideration. [Your mother was wrong, Punk.]

Grandma told me my mother was gorgeous in her youth and that boys gave her money. Grandma said that instead of studying, my mother partied and liked to be the center of attention, had a temper, and would fight anybody, whereas women usually quietly get even. [Thanks for sharing about your mother and how women typically operate.]

Dad took my mother to a psychologist, who said she split in half, like Jekyll and Hyde. Dad told me she'd talk like a little kid and be sweet and innocent when she wanted something but then turn on you. My stepdad his said said she played the victim games: "poor me" and "take care of me." [Others also found your mother to be a challenge, Punk.]

My stepdad, his wife, and Buster visited yesterday. Buster and my stepdad hugged us, and it felt nice. It seems as if people genuinely care about us. [They do, Leena.]

Life in my Household

Punky spouted: I have seven baby ducks, three baby turkeys, and five baby chickens. [You have a nursery, Punky!] I went grocery shopping by myself. [Good for you!] My doggie licks my face to wake me up in the morning. [Cute!] My tiffany lamp got broken. [Sorry!]

Medical/Psychiatric Issues

Since my heart medication causes depression, should I increase my antidepressant? I've been in bed for three days and in my house for three months, even though my walking has improved because I can feel my legs better. [Always consult with your doctor about your medications. This sounds like depression and agoraphobia. I'm glad your feeling in your legs is returning, Leena.]

I have a new doctor. She's female, and her daughter has multiple personalities. My talking pillbox helps me remember to take my medicines. Patty doesn't believe we need all this medication. [So, your present doctor better understands you. You might not rely on Patty for medical advice. She's eight.]

Clara announced: My stepdad took me to see my doctor and went in to hear what the doctor said. I tend to "zone out" when the doctor talks because it's not real if I don't listen. We switched to Samantha in his examining room to handle our Claustrophobia, but he didn't notice.

Leena has been around and explains grown-up things, but we send her away when reliving past trauma because we don't want to over-burden her. She's smart but inexperienced in that she hasn't had the level of injury we have. The same goes for you, Mr. Hall. You know things, but you haven't experienced the trauma we have. [True, but you don't have to protect me like you protect Leena. You might not want to "zone out" when your doctor is talking. Your medical issues are real, even if you don't hear what he's telling you.]

I don't think I'll tell the doctors when I feel bad again because I didn't like the hospital. It reminded me of prior unpleasant hospitalizations. [It's important to tell your doctor when you feel bad. You won't be going to a mental ward, Clara.]

Alter Dynamics

Sophia shared in her matter-a-fact tone: The Little Ones won't have time to grow up, so they need to have fun. We don't give the names of the alters guarding the anger door because they can open the door to hell if called on. [Hi, Sophia.] Hi. [Shall we talk about your anger?] Okay.

Some alters from our original town remain active. We're thinking of building another town with apartments nearby for our overflow of alters and have even considered a parallel universe to have hundreds of alters nearby without being crowded. [A parallel universe, Sophia!]

In a voice tight with pain, Tabatha revealed: We still need Winter to keep some control over our feelings. I stomp my feet when I get mad. Some of the Little Ones are scared and don't want to be out if there a heart attack cause they not ready to die. [Hi, Tabatha.] Hi. [Winter is helpful, but you still show your anger. The Little Ones might want to make time to play, even if they're afraid.] Okay.

Punky exclaimed: Our neighbors asked us to go to Oldies today. It's a warehouse of discontinued items. [Your neighbors seem friendly, and I think you'll enjoy Oldies.] Leena hasn't been around for quite a while. I think something happened, and she didn't want to be impacted. Some of us were afraid and disappeared when Leena increased contact with our mother, so maybe we were angry with her. [I understand the anger, but I think she can still be helpful. Some alters have had contact with her recently. Do you talk to Clara?]

Cheri explained in a somewhat indifferent, wavering tone: I now co-exist with other alters. In doing so, I don't lose time, and it's easier to access information. Most information is about the present, such as getting dressed, but there's also past material. [How do you like this co-existing?] I like it.

Clara announced: We're picking out the alters we want to be. [Who've you chosen so far?] We have Butterfly, Froggie, and Pam.

Pam confided: I become angry and frustrated, complain mightily, and have difficulty dealing with life when emotionally hurt. At the same time, it's difficult for me to confront people because I don't like their anger. [How about we talk about asking questions and using I-messages to take the sting out of confrontation, Pam?] Okay.

Punky Lil blurted out in her high-pitched, cheerful tone, which rises and falls musically: G-ma got me a rocking chair, but my mother torched it. Charles came out and told me to let it go. I'm 4 years old, but I've been here for a while. I lived with G-ma because they took me away from my mother. My mother didn't love me, but G-ma loved me, and I loved G-ma.

I got motions, and I know things. I was an accident. My mother went to bars and picked up men and did naughty things. You're supposed to be a mother.

I felt hurt when my G-ma scolded me, but then she'd give me a soda, making me feel better. [I'm sorry about your mother's neglect and your rocking chair, Punky Lil.] Thanks. [You loved Grandma, and Charles helped you feel better.] Yes.

Therapy Not Included Under Other Headings

Think explained in her thin, frail tone: It isn't okay to cry cause it makes my mother mad. Men don't like my mother to complain when they squish her. [Hi Think.] Hi. I know how to say stuff and get rid of it. This other guy told me the more we talk, the less it hurts. Do you know that if you keep scratching your skin, it burns and comes off? I don't worry unless Dee, Deon, or Chopper is out. Chopper cuts us to make us feel. If you talk about clever stuff, then Smart Ones come. Little crybabies come when I name fears. [Thanks for sharing, Think. I don't mind if you cry. Do you still live with your mother?] Yes.

Us Cluster shared: We try to be Leena the best we can because we don't want to go to a mental ward. [That makes sense.] We prefer daytime naps because demons come into our nighttime dreams. [Oh!]

The Emotional Ones are unnamed children of various ages, fashioned to react without emotion to appear normal, but they have lots of feelings they never learned to hide. They were out last week and didn't know us, but they talked to us. [What did the Emotional Ones say?]

Sunshine was here a couple of days ago. She gives us hope because she still has kindness. She's the part of us that's never been touched by what we consider evil. Bad things never happened to Sunshine, so she's optimistic. [It's good to have hope.]

When our mother beat us, we separated body parts to spread the pain. We're beginning to remember that these body parts represent unnamed alters.

Upon my request, Mr. Hall wrote the following note for me to carry:

"Leena has Dissociative Identity Disorder and frequently switches to different personality states. She's sensitive about being touched. Don't use physical force. Instead, tell her what you want and give her time to process the request because she has a different degree of understanding depending on the age of the dominating personality state. Be patient if she tells you she needs you to pause what you're doing. Prescribe pain medication as sparingly as possible."

We're a mix of alters today, just little ole us. We each have a unique point of view and do our best. Still, we're afraid of leaving our house because we get lost. Mary thinks The Mother was kind. Sam doesn't. Amy isn't sure what happened and wants to know because she thinks knowing would be helpful. It's easier to separate than to resolve the different points of view. To integrate, we'd have to agree with one another. We just switched to Punky, who thinks some of your questions, Mr. Hall are difficult because we're not sure who should answer. [You don't have to integrate. I'll try to be helpful regardless of who answers.]

Our presently active alters don't remember our past traumas. Since our two primary perpetrators are no longer around, we no longer need the alters who dealt with our wounding and terrible recollections. [Is this your way of starting a new tolerable life?] Maybe.

Some of the Little Ones responded to Mr. Hall's inquiry about alters, which he knew nothing about: wow, this is many names. many are made to take over to be good. like when we get mad or hurt. it not who we want to be. to be good, we make others to hide our evil far away. All our having so many of us shows is how bad we are. we tried to be what our mother wanted, so we didn't have negative emotions or did anything that made our mother mad. to be that sweet little girl our mother wished for. on the other hand, our mother got mad at us cause we were dumb, trusting, believed other grown-ups, truthful. all these names stand for are our faillurs. we've made others, and changed so many times, so often that we had to build walls, rooms, doors, and other places to keep from the craziness. The bottom line is we're nothing, and then again, we have so many different kinds in us we're many. It sad what we've become to live.

Us Cluster shared: When Mr. Clarke told us he wanted everyone to listen to him, our heads "blew up" because we all tried to listen. We've noticed that the aftermath of having emotions is the danger zone, where we go numb and want to give up. [You smiled before when I suggested that you regularly immerse yourself in activities you enjoyed with your Grandma and the recollections from that time in your life to avoid the danger zone.] We loved Grandma.

I need counseling to keep me grounded. Between our sessions, I revert to old comfortable but unhealthy ways. I've discussed more adult matters with you than with Mr. Clarke. Therapy helps me accept myself, find inner peace, be okay with being broken. We have pieces, but you see the whole puzzle. [Being okay with ourselves as we are is a crucial goal and promotes moving forward, Leena.]

Several alters worked on responses to questions Mr. Hall asked us by mail. One from the Wronged sent the following response: i so mad it feel like a football in my throat, and my head will blow up. body is like a log, mind like a mad dog ready to spring on anything i see. mad, not the right word for this. having to take the bad, horrible, ugly, hurtful, unlovable stuff of life. only seeing and feeling the wrong thing. why do i have to be the one to hold and live with all this ugly, hurtful hateful stuff. it not fair. the others get to have some good thing, and i have to have the bad stuff. we all fight over who does what. ending up putting big space between the haves and have nots.

i been on the outside. i know what out there. i not like it. hurt you and throws you away, showing you no kindness, and the inside not want you and throw you away. put you in the dark place. we fight with them over wanting out to get some good feeling also. they say we cant cause we bad. they scared of us and what we do. we push those inside away, lock them out, put them in dark places because they have too much emotion we can't have to avoid trouble. i, for one, can yell, fight back, say no, no, no. i can run away and don't care what happens to us. even if the outside hurt us, it better than having someone we love hurt us. as long as you have someone that love you isn't so bad. love makes a lousy life bearable. but when you don't have love, it the worstest thing i know. i want to feel love so life can be tolerable. im what life has showed me. [Your life has been dreadful. Of course, it's not fair. Your siblings love you. Your puppies, Brad, and your stepdad adore you. I love you like a sister. I want you to learn to love yourself.]

So many were trying to type at once. The alters were having a five-way conversation with themselves, and at the same time, writing to you, so things got confusing. They want anyone to understand what happened. [I know what happened to them, Leena, and I'm deeply sorry that those who were supposed to love and nurture them heaped such brutality on them.]

1994:

After four years of intense research and debate, Congress passed the Violence Against Women Act, the first comprehensive legislation focused on ending intimate partner violence.

"Rock Bottom," by Wynonna Judd, reached Number Two.

Life with The Mother

Punky shared: I'm working on my negative self-concept by accepting the truth without being ashamed. Dorothy let boys have sex with her because she figured why shouldn't everyone since others did it. [You did nothing shameful, Punky. Adults did shameful things to you, impacting how you relate to others.]

Life with Other Family Members

Patty shared: We're doing okay despite periods of depression. Various antidepressants have helped. We have difficulty motivating but are dealing, even though we're smoking three packs of cigarettes daily and overeating. [When you feel unmotivated, you might try doing one thing at a time and focusing on fun activities or those you receive a sense of accomplishment from. Have you asked your doctor for help with smoking and overeating?]

We call our stepdad's daughter our sister. Our stepdad's preacher told him he was living in sin by not marrying his girlfriend, so they're getting married. Olive Garden is catering. [How do you feel about his getting married?] We like it.

Life in my Household

Punky shared: My stepdad calls me twice a week and hugs me now. He's helping me rototill. I'd like more help from him, but asking for help is a sign of weakness. [You're having good contact with your stepdad, and it seems your life is better with him in it. Asking for help is a sign of strength, not weakness, Punky.]

We love our animals, even the goats that ate our berry bushes. James Dean, our boy goat, keeps getting out of our yard and panics when he can't find his way back, so we have to help him. We bought enough lids for the next three years because we like canning. [Is James Dean going to allow you time for canning?]

I have miniature and full-size adult goats. Squeaky, my 10-pound dog, barked at a goat, and the goat tried to butt him, but Mister, my 17-pound overweight terrier, backed the goat up. [Did Squeaky learn from this? You go, Mister!] My third dog, Rascal, is afraid of my ducks. [Tell Rascal it's okay because ducks can be scary!]

Mary shared in her high-pitched chirp, edged with fear: Oh, we had a baby goat today. It was scary. Cause its mom cried. After an hour, she had her baby. The baby trying to stand was cute. It wobble and fall and gets back up. It white and black spots. So now we have three baby goats. So that make nine goats so far. [Hi Mary.] Hi. [A new baby goat!] Yes.

My next-door neighbor's wife visited this week. We baked cookies. Brad put country music on for us. He'd gotten a speaker for my Christmas present but unwrapped it to try it out while my guest was present. That's my Brad! My guest especially enjoyed the visit and gave me an A+. She studied counseling in college. She'll be the first since junior high if she becomes my girlfriend. I was shaky after the visit. I switch considerably when I like someone. [It sounds like you were a great hostess, and it seems as if your neighbor's wife is already your friend, Leena.]

I bought nine pounds of tomatoes to can. I also got berries for pancakes and muffins. I've been wearing gloves to chop onions and hot peppers for my ham, white beans, and chicken chili Verde. I expect to be canning 8 quarts and 20 pints. I've been studying about going back to old ways to survive. Many people had root cellars. [You're quite the survivor!] My view on politics is that they're lying to us. [You have good political insight.]

I'm having a rooster for dinner because it sexually lit into the ducks. [More crime and punishment on the farm] I lost 24 of my 30 chickens to a fox. [That was one hungry fox. Can Brad build a chicken coup, Leena?]

I cleaned my kitchen and laundry room and hired someone to mow my pasture and trim my bushes to a maintainable height. One hen is clucking at its chick, and another is sitting on eggs. [It's a busy time on the farm.]

I got a new puppy that's smart and sits already. I'm also spending money on things I need, such as a ladder. [Oh boy, a new puppy! What's its name? Whose idea was the puppy? You might have your handyman or Brad use that ladder.] Some of the Little Ones got the puppy. We haven't named him yet.

Brad has a girlfriend, a new car, and works full time. My handyman uses my ladder. My oldest son, Rod, is studying to be a veterinarian. I've had little contact with my middle son, Jim. He doesn't seem to be doing well.

My next-door neighbors came over three times last week unannounced. I baked cinnamon rolls for them. It's taken me a long time to get used to their unannounced visits. I want to trust, but I get hurt when I do, and then others tell me I should've known better. [Many people in your past were untrustworthy, but it appears you can trust your neighbors, and they augment your social support system.]

Brad bought a bag of candy, which I thought was for me, and when he took it with him, I switched to Tabatha and made a scene. [It sounds like you need to get the Little Ones some candy.]

I'm managing my housekeeping, planting a winter garden, and emptying my freezer by canning because Rod will be butchering some of my goats. [You're pretty darn enterprising.] I have to go now because the baby chicks are telling me they're out of food and water. [Go. Go. Go.] I like talking to you. It keeps me grounded. [I also enjoy talking to you, and I'm glad you benefit, Leena.]

Medical/Psychiatric Issue

My doctor changed a medication upon intervention by the insurance representative. The initially prescribed medication for my kidney infection had the warning "will cause nerve damage." He changed the prescription to one with the notice, "may cause nerve damage." I requested a new doctor, but the only one available is three hours away. [It's good she caught that warning.]

My colonoscopy and breast examinations are pending, and I'm afraid because my doctor is unaware of my mental health issues. I'll have to remain one alter during the tests, which is a challenge. [As you requested, I left a message for your doctor about your DID, Leena.]

Alter Dynamics

Clara blurted out in her clear, deliberate tone between snickers: Turkey day wasn't a Leena day because she has diabetes, so we ate for her because we're not diabetic. She tested us later, and our blood sugar was good. Want to hear something naughty? We switched at the optometrist's office and confused him. [The blood sugar issue is interesting. You had fun with the optometrist.]

We Cluster shared: Some of us like to draw with crayons and have ice cream for breakfast. Others can sing or play the piano. We don't like losing the time that comes with switching, but knowing how to do things feels good. [So, some things are worth the cost of losing time?]

A trembling Little shared in her brittle tone: A boy is in a wall, but I don't know his name. I'm not always sure why we make animals and people we can't see, but I know "Dragon, Dear" took our whippings cause he's big and can cover us. [Hi, Little.] Hi. [Thanks for sharing this information, Little.] You're welcome.

Ken announced in his calm, pleasant tone: I'm Ken, The Doorkeeper. I was created to keep track of the comings and goings of the alters. [Hi Ken.] Hi. I have new ones with lousy behavior. For example, Ripper, a 10-year-old boy, rips paper to relieve stress. I hide some so they don't get overwhelmed, and I prevent others from overtaking those present. [You have a big job, Ken!] Yes.

Children aren't mean like adults. Many adults in my life have been mean. Because you're kind and are a grown-up, Mr. Hall, maybe it's okay to grow up. We want to grow up but aren't happy when we try, so we crack, and the kids come out. When we're scared, we switch to one alter. When we're glad, we become another. It all comes down to how we feel about our environment. We feel better when many of us are out at the same time. We can switch to a different 7 to 12 alters and forget what group we recently were in. [Most adults aren't mean, Ken. Thanks for sharing.] You're welcome.

The Little Ones don't want me to get rid of their toys. One Little One got excited when he found a kaleidoscope. I need to build a little kid corner again. [Good idea, Leena.]

Tamara articulated in her wavering voice: We're like a diamond with many sides, with the most valuable part in the middle, which needs the most protection. We're also like a kaleidoscope. The specs in the circle are the alters the therapists speak with. The triangle in the middle surrounds the material we don't want to look at. Leena is the only one who's not in the circle. [These are helpful analogies, Tamara.]

Why were my siblings and I so unlucky? When I compare myself to others, I seem lacking. I wish my life could've been even the slightest bit better. Sometimes I think if I hadn't had my life, one of my sisters would've, which wouldn't be good. It's never easy being the odd one out. It's not easy being me, but who else am I going to be? [You and your siblings were dealt a bad hand. Versus comparing yourself to others, consider comparing yourself today and tomorrow with what you were yesterday. You can continue to improve your life from here forward.]

I'm so grateful for all the help I've received. I also know I'll never get 100% better if I don't keep going into the "Black Hole" where the dark material is. I tend not to go there because it petrifies me. [You've been brave.]

My past was often unsafe, so I couldn't give up creating new alters. It was like Harvey, the kid's movie. I just wanted peace and to be okay in my brain. I try to tell myself I have survival, not mental issues. [I like that, Tamara.] Lilly learned to meditate, and we found that very helpful. [Meditation is an excellent soothing activity.]

Therapy Not Included Under Other Headings

At the Women's Crisis Center, we presented to staff from County Mental Health, Child Protective Services, the Sheriff's Department, the District Attorney's Office, the Department of Parole, and the School Board. Several of us helped. The guests asked lots of questions like "why do women go back" and "why did we tell?" They told us we helped them better understand DID and abused women.

It felt good to know the next woman or child would be better understood and not snubbed. Had we not been brutalized or had DID, we couldn't have helped them understand, and then they couldn't help others. There was a ripple effect because something good came from the hell we lived in. This experience answered the "why us" question. It was so we could help others. It turned something ugly and evil into something good. We like that. [What a great perspective, Leena!]

We also taught classes to staff and clients on physical and sexual abuse at the Women Crisis Center. We stressed that it's essential to communicate to victims that even one trauma can have a devastating impact. We even got a paper noting that we were peer counselors. [Good job, Leena!]

Amy and Meme printed the following, titled "Our First Letter to Mr. Hall:" Amy printed: Hi there. I'm Amy. I talk to you today. Not know what to say. Lots go overhead. I don't like writin cause it show we dumb and odd. I went to class to learn to spell and write. But we never real learned. Got so much in our head it hard to just write about one thing. [Thanks for the letter, Amy. Please ask me to explain if you don't understand my comments.]

Meme printed: I not like showing weed dumb, and others make fun of us. It was hard to write Mr. Clarke at first cause we not want him to think we stupid. Dumbing and crazy can't be trusted. Mr. Clarke planned to set up a meeting to talk to other therapists like him like we did at the Women's Center with county people to learn about people like us. We'll die before we can be real. You gonna fix us? [You're going to fix yourself. I'm going to help. You're not dumb or crazy, Meme.]

We Cluster explained: We have guards to permit alters to relate to people we're encountering. We struggle to decide whether to trust anyone or everyone. Usually, we believe everyone. We accepted what our mother told us because mothers aren't supposed to lie. You, Mr. Hall, are honest and tell us what's real, and our intuition tells us you're truthful. Different things, however, also seem correct, so our solution is to separate them. Others have told us to believe them because we're stupid or less experienced. Our therapists have told us we live in a black-or-white world and need to find the gray. [Finding the gray is beneficial. Believing those you trust makes the most sense to me.]

Mr. Clarke told us we're still not cured if we're pretending and blocking memories. It was a horrible time in our lives when we saw Mr. Clarke. We were popping out all over the place. Both of you have said we don't have a core personality because we're so damaged, so we'd need to remain a revolving door. [I believe Mr. Clarke helped you a great deal. Getting healthy is a process, and you've come a long way.]

Mr. Clarke helped me learn to discriminate between soft and hard. I socked him when he poured warm coffee on my hand to see if I could feel it. I can turn off feeling so I don't experience the pain of injuries to my body, but the hot coffee surprised me. I once had a tooth pulled without numbing and didn't experience pain. Later, I even came to be able to feel my eyelashes. Yet, I still automatically turn pain on and off. For example, once I ran a bath, which was too hot, and felt the sting initially, but then turned off the hurt and was scorched when I got out of the tub. [This survival technique was logical in your past but can be dangerous, so a good goal would be to eventually no longer use it, Leena.]

My emotions have been out of whack since The Mother's death. Various alters are popping out. We had to switch to an alter that pretended with The Mother, but we don't like deceiving others. [You had to fake it because she didn't allow an honest, open relationship.]

A We Cluster alter shared: We freeze when men touch us and fear others knowing about us because they might take advantage of us. We refrain from telling you how evil we are because you'll leave. [I won't exploit you, I don't think you're wicked, and nothing you reveal will drive me away.] Do we need to go to our dark places to get healthy? [You've improved considerably and will continue to do so by remembering and incorporating.]

Mr. Clarke told me to guess if I couldn't decide about something because I could change my decision later. [Guesses are often correct and are better than staying stuck, Leena.]

Others broke us to pieces, but now we're super-glued back together with holes. The holes are time, memory, and spaces where the alters live. Another hurt could shatter us again. We're so fragile that for self-preservation, we avoid everything. Being forced into a mental hospital, or remembering all that The Mother or others did, could break us. We buried many recollections. Even thinking about it makes us crazy. Sometimes we sit on the floor and rock or bang our heads against a wall and vacillate between awareness and going away. [Repetitively stretching, then retreating is how many move forward.]

Mr. Hall, how can you be so kind to someone whose internal dynamics are yucky? How can you give me a platonic hug when I might rub off on you? It drives me crazy that you know about me yet still like me. It's a big step to admit I like you because I fear you'll somehow use that to hurt me. [I don't think you're yucky. I don't judge you. I can tell you like me, but I'd never intentionally hurt you, Leena.]

A therapist feels like a friend or big brother. I've benefitted from watching you as a role model with your wife, son, handyman, and dogs. I'm striving for inner peace and not to get hurt again. How do I know if I'm growing versus covering up better? [I'm glad you think I've been a helpful role model. Inner peace is a good goal. An excellent way to fend off injury is to develop healthy boundaries. You'll know you're growing if you're continuing to allow memory and if you disappear and become numb less often. I think you're growing but probably still covering up somewhat.]

My work in life has been survival. Life isn't simple. It's challenging to know what I want. I know I want to be healthy and accepted by others and that helping others helps me. [You've had more than your fair share of difficulty navigating life. More people approve of you than you might think. Self-acceptance is also a good goal because, with it, you'll not be so concerned about others' opinions, which are often unpredictable and flawed. Yes, when you help others, you'll often feel better about yourself, increasing the likelihood that your next experience will be positive, Leena.]

Men petrify me. My neighbor patting me on my back yesterday sent me into a non-feeling state. With your hugs, I went from stiff and scared to okay, then to liking them a great deal and being disappointed when you didn't hug me goodbye one day. [You'll become more comfortable with your neighbor as you have more contact with him. Sorry, I forgot a hug. I must have gotten distracted. I owe you one.]

My age might have cured me because DID people over 60 get Alzheimer's and forget their past. I remember mine, but it's still chopped up. I get suicidal ideations when I remember too much. Some of our past alters pop out occasionally, but not often.[I've heard nothing about that DID and Alzheimer's connection, and your memory is intact. Still, pacing yourself as needed makes sense, Leena.]

I get depressed and want to cry. I stay in my bedroom too much, but I feel safe there. I've lost a little weight and have reduced my smoking, but I still detach from my body when I switch. I'm accident-prone when I disconnect, so I've stopped engaging in potentially dangerous activities like using power tools. [Good for you on the weight loss, smoking, and decision about tools. Are you taking your antidepressant and antianxiety medications?] I've been forgetting. [You do better when you take them regularly.]

I'd like to go to Italy to see the old buildings and to Alaska to see the northern lights. [Hopefully, someday you will, Leena.]

I still have "the crybabies," but I'm managing them by keeping busy. Mr. Clarke told me it means somebody is sad. Being kind to myself is difficult because I think I don't deserve it. [Keeping busy with activities you enjoy is an excellent way to distract from sadness. Embracing your grief also helps move it through you. You merit kindness, and you'll do better at your interest in helping others if you're also kind to yourself.]

How do I deal with others making negative comments about me? [Remember that their negativity is about them, not you.] I was sad last night because I didn't have my teddy to hug. I had washed it, and it needed extra drying. [That is sad, but it'll be dry tonight. Is this still Leena?] Yes, and others.

I was anxious about going shopping by myself but overcame it with positive self-talk, such as: "I'll be fine" and "You can always call someone if you need to." [Good job!]

One time I went to a restaurant and tried to use big words. I asked for condoms for my steak, meaning to ask for condiments. When Anthony put Drano in my eyes, pointing to my iris and trying to sound smart, I told the doctor he put it in my uterus. [Oops!]

I used to believe everything others told me, but Mr. Clarke told me some people lie and to watch for bad things because they happen [You're less gullible now, but reasonable vigilance is always advisable.]

Being ugly keeps abusive men away. If you look at men and then get exploited, it's your fault because you led them on. [You're not ugly, but one's appearance doesn't guard against abuse. Just looking at men isn't leading them on, and being exploited is never your fault, Leena.]

I'm outgoing and like people by nature, but I go against my personality due to fear, and avoiding people leads to loneliness. [You might begin with small social risks, pull back as needed, and incorporate your calming activities and boundaries in this process.]

An officer stopped me once, and when he asked if I saw his patrol lights, I told him I thought they were Christmas lights. When he asked for my registration, which I didn't have with me, and I told him to come home with me, and I'd get it for him, he thought I was trying to bribe him. On another occasion, an officer asked for my license, and I said it was in my purse, which I emptied onto the road. That officer thought I did weird things, but I didn't get into trouble. Sometimes I get tickets, and sometimes I get warnings. The officers always say I'm honest.

We saw a giant chipmunk at a store and thought it was so cute we wanted to take it home and take care of it. When we picked it up, it shouted, "Lady, put me down." [Oops!]

A minister told us his church wouldn't baptize us, and another said we should kill ourselves because someone raped us. [Those people are full of baloney, Leena.]

Windy articulated: We associated The Mother with agony, and when we resumed frequent contact with her, we lost our past. Total obedience, confusion, and loss of self were what she called loving us. Other alters began popping out after she passed away. They don't trust Leena because she decided to get close to The Mother and thought she could become Dorothy again and feel nothing. It didn't work. Shutting down the horrible recollections cost us our precious few pleasant ones. We believe we're awful people down deep, and we have difficulty knowing what's real and who's trustworthy. [You're not terrible. Your mother brainwashed you into believing that. You can rebuild trust in yourself and others.]

Discovering that much of what others taught us is untrue is painful. That's why we conceived Leena. She benefitted from what therapists told her. For example, she no longer believes the Catholic nun who said we're going to hell for hating our mother.

Some alters who don't know The Mother is deceased still hate her, others love her, and many fear her. Also, many of us are worried that Leena has become tainted, making us sad. [I believe Leena is valuable and more durable than you think, Windy.]

We're capable of being nasty, but our golden rule is, "we're not going to be like The Mother." The Mother didn't allow playing. Therapists taught us hopscotch and drawing with crayons, and Grandma played with us. [I'm glad that you had Grandma and your therapists.]

1995:

As of December 1995, all but eight countries had ratified the Convention on the Rights of the Child–propelling it toward becoming the first universal law in history. Long regarded as their parents' property, children have come to be seen as individuals having fundamental rights that adult society must respect and essential needs that must be met.

"Life Goes On," by Little Texas band, reached Number Four.

Life with The Mother

Us Cluster shared: We tried hard to honor our mother, who raised us that you don't say no to grown-ups. Many of us blame ourselves for having been tormented. [Adults must always take the responsibility to behave appropriately with children.] That's what all our therapists have said.

Life with Husband and Boyfriends

A new boyfriend would have to do chores, and I'd even let him have his way with me. [So you're considering having a new boyfriend, Leena?] I'd like the company but not the challenge of a relationship.

Life in my Household

Punky exclaimed: Guess what I did! I went for a car ride with my neighbor and didn't get scared. I think I felt a sense of control because we rode in my car. I'm working on being pleasantly assertive, but I still tend to go along with others' wishes. [I believe you can trust your neighbor. Being politely assertive is healthy, Punky.]

Charley and Timothy built three arbors this week. Iris drew the drafts. Punk gardened, and Suzie Q. baked. I made peach tea. [You've had a busy week.]

Roxie explained in her deadpan tone: My toy unicorn has to stay in the house, but my owl on a chain can go with me on outings. People won't notice the owl and think I'm strange, but my unicorn is too big to hide. [You believe people would think you're odd because your body is adult, Roxie?] Yes.

Alter Dynamics

I think 11 of the 12 Selves are still around. I'm aware of Dorothy, but she's broken. She went away a long time ago and never came back. She was last seen sitting on a floor, rocking. [I'm sorry about Dorothy, Leena.]

Unknown alters mailed the following letter to Mr. Hall, which they discussed in our next session with him: Hey, we wasn't gonna write. but here we are. anger, piss, whatever it's called. did you know we always have to tell someone when we go to the bathroom, take a bath, get dress? now we tell our dogs. sad. when brad was here we told him. when Ralph was around we told him. when getting nude, keep an eye out is what our thinking is. thinking since we have to depend on ourselves now and we never could. just stop living. why not? we a mess, the house a mess, our life a mess. we should have went to the hospital a week or so ago, but did we, no. why not you ask? We'd have to leave the house, drive, and then have to let them touch us. ever time we go to the dr we have to fight the fear and let them touch us. being in a closed little room with them. plus being in a place with others we don't know. the truth is we aren't strong, but we don't tell ourselves that. [Thanks for sharing in your letter about your struggles. I'm sorry that life remains such a struggle for you at times. Healing is a lifetime journey. Are you taking your antidepressants and antianxiety medications?] No. [Please take them. You don't do so well without them.]

Therapy Not Included Under Other Headings

I feel okay now about not being normal. You, Mr. Hall, have convinced me that most other people don't care if I'm atypical and that I'm, actually, impressive in many respects. [Indeed you are, Leena.]

I don't believe I could handle another episode of being tortured, fighting, or even arguing. [I think you're more robust than you think. You feel you'd be emotionally overwhelmed?] Yes. [Fighting or arguing is almost always a choice, Leena.]

My life was like watching a silent movie when Mr. Clarke was counseling me. Initially, I wrote to Mr. Clarke because I feared that if I saw him in person, he might view me as pitiful and weak. Later in treatment, the words came, then the feelings, and finally the relief when we figured it all out, but shame followed and hasn't gone away. I feel shame when I think or talk about my life. I sometimes believe I'm entirely unacceptable to others and myself. Mr. Clarke taught us about co-conscious. These days we only have semi-co-conscious because, to function, we have to close off many alters.

Your modeling of relationships helped a great deal, Mr. Hall. I also greatly benefitted from acceptance by you, Mr. Clarke, and other counselors. We're learning to say "no," as you taught us, Mr. Hall, but still struggling with it. Many alters believe we're as worthy as anyone else, like you've told us, but others think they're the devil's seed. I still experience brainwashing effects, but not in every facet of my life. [I'm glad Mr. Clarke and I've been helpful. People did shameful things to you, but that diminished them, not you.]

It pains me to see more kids becoming like me every day, and I can't stop it. I picture myself standing with doctors on top of the world. I'm showing everyone the pain I experienced as a child, hoping to touch them and prevent more children from getting hurt. It wouldn't stop my pain, but it'd soothe my soul if it showed how to prevent other children from becoming me. [Your work at the Women's Crisis Center has been helpful, and perhaps you can find additional ways to do this, Leena.]

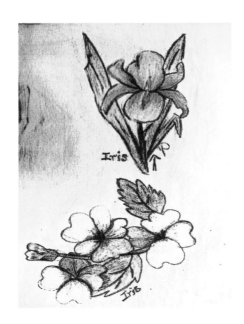

Appendix

Glossary

Age slider – an alter who can slide forward or backward in age depending on the circumstances

Alter – dissociated part of self with the ability to:
Operate independently
Perceive self and the world in their own unique way
Assume control of the mind and body, or
Exert enough influence to impact thoughts, feelings, and behaviors

Animal alter – an alter who, for a system coping mechanism, appears as a whole animal

Blending – a temporary type of integration whereby alters inside can tap into each other's abilities and skills

Blurring – when two or more alters are hosting or close to doing so, seep traits or feelings into each other

Body dysphoria – seeing one's body as unattractive

Co-conscious – when two or more alters are actively aware of each other and might even be aware of each other's emotions or thoughts, and is a step toward communication often regarded as one of the most significant steps a system can take toward being healthily plural

Co-hosting – when two or more alters are out and in control of the body

Communicator – a type of alter usually entrenched in the communication of the system, often playing go-between for other alters

Core – the original personality born with the body

Cross-gender – alter who's the opposite gender to the body

Cycling – switching too frequently or quickly

De-realization – a feeling that reality is unreal, incorrect, or distorted, often accompanied by depression or anxiety and often experienced with depersonalization and dissociation

Depersonalization – a feeling that oneself is unreal or distant, often accompanied by numbness or the thought that one's actions are distorted and often experienced with depression, bodily dysphoria, anxiety, de-realization, and dissociation

Dissociation – a method of coping where one disconnects from one's own conscious experience of reality, intentionally or unintentionally, due to a perceived threat of danger or annihilation

Dissociative Identity Disorder – previously known as multiple personality disorder, is a mental disorder characterized by the maintenance of at least two distinct and relatively enduring personality states

Dissociative amnesia – inability to remember what another alter did while out, resulting in losing time

Fragment – an incomplete alter, or a kind of extreme form of compartmentalization of thought and action which often holds a single memory, handles one emotion, or does a specific task, and usually doesn't have too great of an effect on the system.

Gatekeeper – an alter who can control those inside or out, or other matters.

Gender sliders – alters who can shift between genders

Helper – generally a protector, a leader in the system knowing everyone and working to maintain stability and help everyone, and doesn't usually come out very often

Host –the alter in control of the body

Innocent – the type of alter who spreads joy within the system

Inside – the inner world where alters can be when not interacting with the outer world

Integration – the joining of two or more alters, or for fragments, integration may simply entail other alters being able to access what those parts held without a switch being necessary

Little – child alter or fragment under 8 years old, called Little Ones in this story

Losing time – when people with DID experience dissociative amnesia and often feel like a chunk of time is missing, which can be anywhere from minutes to years

Multiple Personality Disorder – an earlier name for Dissociative Identity Disorder

Out – when an alter is interacting with the outer world

Outside – the outer world

Parental alter – a relatively common type of alter who's usually old enough to be the body's parent and who mimics a parent in some way, usually taking one of two forms, either representing a better parental figure the system should've had or representing abusive ideas and the aftermath thereof which came from the systems parent

Persecutor – a type of alter representing some kind of pain the system went through and is often prone to dangerous, self-destructive, panicked, manipulative, or irrational actions

Programmed alter – typically seen in ritual abuse/organized abuse, an alter set up to return to the abuser(s) or programmed to believe certain things, who are usually very well hidden and separate from the rest of the system

Protector – an alter protecting the body, system, host, core, or another specific alter or groups of alters

Selves – alters who speak among themselves but not to others

Separation – when alters are unaware of each other

Shell – an informal term meaning a person serving as an encasement to hold and display what alters are thinking and feeling

Splitting – the creation of another alter

Sub-system – used to describe a specific group of alters inside who are often separated from others inside in a particular manner

Switching – when one alter shifts control of the shared body to another, sometimes deliberate, sometimes not

Switching headache – usually a migraine-like headache resulting from switching too frequently or quickly, sometimes a result of forcing an alter out

System – a collective term to describe all alters inside

Trigger – anything stimulating a series of thoughts or reminding one of some aspect of one's traumatic past and could cause a response like panic attacks, flashbacks, or another type of stress.

Alters, Fragments, and Clusters

The 160 Named Alters and Fragments in This Story

The 20 most active are numbered, with (1) hosting the most. The 80 fragments in the story, including Deand, three fragments, are asterisked. Dorothy created all while living with The Mother unless otherwise specified. Many are addressed in the present tense because although they aren't active, they haven't gone away.

Abby, a 6-year-old girl who made animal cries, helped Dorothy endure the horror of The Mother abusing and killing our pets.

Abigail, a 5-year-old girl from the I's Cluster, helped carry Dorothy's evil thoughts and helped her read, write, and deal with people.

Adam, a 9-year-old boy from the Dark Secret Ones and Boy Cluster, wished for purity and helped Dorothy suffer the pain from The Mother putting her in the "loony bin."

Adona, a 12-year-old emotionless girl, who came while Lynne was with Anthony, helped Ice Queen endure the horror of Anthony's demonic activity.

Adora, a 6-year-old girl Bad One from the Angry Cluster, hated herself because she wanted to love The Mother, who saw evil in others, cared only for herself, and couldn't love, whereas Adora saw the good in others, cared only for them, and could love them.

Alice, a 14-year-old girl from the Goodie Cluster and Want-To-Bes, called "Defiant Little Bitch" by The Mother, helped take on the shame of The Mother wounding us.

Am, a 4-year-old girl, one of the 12 Selves, helped bear Dorothy's pain from The Mother telling her to keep her mouth shut and no one would know she was stupid.

Amanda was one of four Soldiers made while living with Anthony.

Amber is an 8-year-old girl from the Angry and Me Clusters and is one of the 12 Selves.

Amy (7), a 5-year-old girl from the We-Three Cluster, helped absorb the fear of The Mother.

Andy, a 12-year-old boy, one of the 12 Selves, formerly Hater, from the Bad Cluster, is a "piss-off-er" who gets angry and gets things done.

Angel (Gloria or Lulu) is a female African American gospel singer who came when Dorothy attended a church because she liked to sing.

Angie, a 7-year-old girl, helped block out the harsh reality at home by daydreaming of having kind parents.

Angry is an 8-year-old boy, Angry One, Taker, and one of the 12 Selves.

Ann, a 6-year-old girl from the Kid Cluster, helped endure the pain, hate, and horror from The Mother's neglect and abuse and hurt herself when angry.

Annie (13), a 5-year-old girl, Helper and Unreal One from the Hope/Heart, and We-Three Clusters, is Tiffany's mommy, lives inside Lilly, and is daddy's girl.

Apple* is a 7-year-old girl with self-control which she uses to avoid the "nuthouse" and provide a window to the outside.

Arrogance*, a 12-year-old girl, tries to eliminate evil thoughts.

Art, a 9-year-old boy from the Kids Cluster, helped distract us from our pain by drawing.

Autumn* was a 10-year-old girl created while living with Anthony to hide from him and come out to teach Lynne's sons how to be kids while he was away.

Bad Girl*, age 10, who isn't kind, carries the guilt of telling The Mother's boyfriend to take Dorothy's sister first.

Bandage*, a 10-year-old girl, had extraordinary powers, like fixing bleeding or broken bones and putting on invisible bandages.

Banger*, a 7-year-old girl, counted each time she banged her head to get unpleasant thoughts out.

Brooklyn, the first alter baby, began at age one and grew to adulthood. She carries the pain from The Mother breaking Dorothy's rib.

Basket, a 4-year-old girl, helped absorb the pain from The Mother mutilating us. She hid to make us not exist.

Bee*, a tiny 6-year-old girl, helped carry anger and struck back with hits that stung like a bee.

Believer*, an 8-year-old girl, denied the awful ongoing reality, believing that moms and "dads" weren't bad.

Belinda, age nine, Brooklyn's sister and a soldier, helped absorb the reoccurring rape and brutality.

Bell, an 11-year-old girl, Angry One, carries the pain from The Mother having sex with her boyfriend, Bill.

Ben*, an 8-year-old boy, carries sadness, anger, fear, and disappointment.

Beth is an 8-year-old girl from the Dark Secret Ones, Hope/Heart, and Hurt Clusters, a markedly injured, angry combination of Mary, Dee, and others who agreed to pass as one and teamed with Iris to make James.

Bo-Bo, originally Dummy, a stupid 4-year-old boy from the Dummy Cluster, is 7-year-old Bobby in the Boy Cluster. He holds the key to unlocking bad memories, promoting healing, and the key to hearing, to avoid being overwhelmed by too many inside speaking at simultaneously.

Bobby, a 7-year-old boy from the Boy Cluster, displays appropriate behavior so people won't be scared.

Bonnie, a 5-year-old girl named after the song "My Bonnie Lies Over the Ocean," dealt with the pain by not having physical sensations.

Brat*, an 8-year-old girl, was named because Dorothy was a "military brat."

Breather*, an 8-year-old boy, held his breath until he only thought of not breathing.

Bree*, a 6-year-old girl from the Me Cluster, helped take on the pain from a specific rape.

Bubble, a 5-year-old girl, helped Dorothy be a real kid.

Bunnie, a 4-year-old girl from the Happy Cluster, wants to remember The Mother's abuses but not judge her.

Butterfly, from the Animal Cluster, who began as an animal alter but later became a 4-year-old girl, carried the hope for love someday.

Cara*, a 6-year-old girl, Good One, helps bear the horror of The Mother putting Dorothy in a deep freeze.

Carol, an adult female, helps absorb the pain and humiliation of being exploited by men, made after Margie's encounter with a man of the Church.

Carrie helps hold the depression caused by The Mother not allowing Dorothy to be a real kid. She's a Good One and Want-To-Be from the Hope/Heart Cluster, who began as a 4-year-old girl, grew to adulthood, and returned from emotional death.

Cathy*, a 1-year-old girl, the second alter baby, absorbed some of the terror and pain from Baby Dorothy's abuse and neglect when she was age one.

Cathleen, a young adult female, created to save the alter babies, wrote to Mr. Clarke that love is only pain, and she wished no part of it.

Charles, a 6-year-old boy, one of the 12 Selves from the We-Two Cluster, absorbed The Mother's kisses and made Dorothy's fear and other bad feelings disappear.

Charles III, a 7-year-old boy, had manners to avoid The Mother's wrath.

Charley, a 14-year-old boy from the Boy Cluster helped endure the pain and horror of The Mother stabbing Dorothy's hands with a fork and putting her in a deep freeze.

Cheri (10), a 15-year-old girl from the Sex Cluster, is angry, introspective, scared, cold-hearted, lonely, depressed, had no purpose in life, and wanted to hurt herself. She protected Dorothy during Dorothy's confinement in the psychiatric unit.

Child*, an 18-month-old girl, endured the sadness, anger, and bitterness from not getting to live with her real dad when her parents separated.

Cindy, a 4-year-old girl from the Us Cluster, carries unbearable shame from what she called The Mother's boyfriend's yucky touching.

Chopper*, an 8-year-old boy, cuts to feel.

Christina was a 4-year-old girl made by Dorothy, so Punky Lil would have a playmate.

Clara, a 7-year-old girl teacher from the We-One Cluster, helps bear physical pain and helps with medical care.

Cole, a 4-year-old boy, took whippings because boys are tough, got his privates scrubbed by The Mother, and cried because it stung.

Conrad is a 12-year-old boy Gatekeeper of Good and Evil.

Crybaby, the fourth alter baby, an infant girl who grew to age four and cried to get heard, helps suffer the pain of what The Mother did, like the broom and the burning. She's one of the 12 Selves and could contribute to the council even before she could talk because of its community brain. She often holds herself and rocks from side to side.

Crystal, a 9-year-old girl Bad One, constantly screamed because she'd been on fire since The Mother set fire to Dorothy's bed. She helped us survive by dealing with rage and carrying the fear of men.

Cutter*, an 8-year-old girl, cuts to get evil thoughts and emotions out or because he's terrible or misbehaves.

Dale, age 10, was a boy in a girl's body. He was logical and kept his emotions in check to appear normal.

Danny*, an adolescent boy nicknamed Hippy Boy, talked like a hippy. His purpose isn't remembered.

Daisy, a 5-year-old girl, made because Dorothy liked flowers, didn't remember the bad, and wanted Leena to return.

Deand*, two boy fragments and one girl fragment, all age six, could bear the memory of all 15 minutes of the feelings of a 15-minute whipping.

Dee (14), who stands for death, an 8-year-old deaf girl, is the only complete alter from the Hidden Ones. She's also a Dark Secret One from the Hurt and Bad Clusters. She tried to kill Dorothy numerous times between ages three and five to end her pain and horror by laying her on railroad tracks during her runaways. Dee also cut Dorothy, tried to drown her, and attempted to overdose on pills.

De-de*, age six, was a second-grade girl fragment from the Hidden Ones who helped absorb anger.

Deon*, an 8-year-old boy fragment from the Hidden Ones, Can-Bes, and We-Two Clusters, helped stop the pain. He talked about death repeatedly, cut Dorothy, tried to drown her, and tried to overdose on pills.

Dirty, an 8-year-old girl from the Sex Cluster, wanted to be a nice girl, so she wanted the stuff about The Mother not to be true.

Doer, a bright boy from the Bad Cluster, began at age one and became Mary at age five, but still lives as Doer within her. He holds emotions other alters can't handle, like intense ill will toward others.

Dorothee, an 8-year-old girl, alter named after the Wizard of Oz character, helped carry traumatization by The Mother (the evil witch) and The Mother's boyfriends (the monkeys).

Dot, a 9-year-old girl, helps forget bad things but believes that she wouldn't have a life if she buried everything.

Dummy-Two, a 7-year-old boy from the Dummy Cluster, carries the shame of The Mother putting Dorothy in a dummy school.

Dusty, a 5-year-old boy Nobody from the Us Cluster, tried to convince The Mother he could be like other kids instead of taking care of the baby, cleaning the house, cooking, and selling his body.

Eater, a 7-year-old girl, stopped eating to die.

eB (Dyslexia Be) is a 7-year-old boy who helped suffer the pain of being mistreated at school. He later became eB, an Evil One.

eM* (dyslexia Me) is a 7-year-old girl who carries shyness.

Ethel, a 14-year-old girl, carries the anger from one of The Mother's boyfriends raping Dorothy. Bad things happened to her, so she felt horrible and did terrible things to others. She's angry at the world and no longer likes herself.

Feeler*, a 10-year-old girl Fool, who helped carry the shame of what men did, wanted The Mother to love her.

Fenna*, an 8-year-old girl, helped absorb the horror of Anthony's satanic involvement.

Fern, a 10-year-old boy Fool, who looked down and away to avoid meeting another's gaze, helped bear the shame of what men did and wanted The Mother to love him.

Five, a 5-year-old girl, shared Ham's agony from seeing The Monster and breaking because she had the room.

Forgotten-One*, a 7-year-old boy, always asked first to avoid The Mother's wrath because that was The Mother's number one rule and went for everything.

Fluffy*, a non-gender 4-year-old alter, was made while living with Grandma by Half-Pint not to have emotion because feelings hurt and not to talk so he didn't have to lie. That way, he could still get love but not punishment.

Frank, a 7-year-old boy with a big head that held a lot, told it like it was because Dorothy needed honesty in her life.

Froggie was a 4-year-old boy from the Animal Cluster who croaked to be heard and helped the Little Ones hop from one to another.

Fur*, a 3-year-old girl Little One, expressed anger toward The Mother by growling and exposing her teeth, like a furry animal, but then The Mother only whipped her harder.

Gabby*, a confused talkative 6-year-old girl, was created because Dorothy liked to talk.

Genie, a 6-year-old girl named after Genie's magic lamp, which gave three wishes, has magical powers to make the pain disappear and push other alters to the background if they have too many bad memories.

George, a 10-year-old boy, displayed appropriate behavior so that people wouldn't be scared. He was attracted to guys and has terrible lungs.

Gina, a 15-year-old girl, helped absorb the hurt and terror from The Mother's beatings.

Glenn*, a 7-year-old boy, helped carry the pain and horror from The Mother stabbing Dorothy's hands with a fork when she reached across the dinner table.

Half-Pint, alter number 108, a 4-year-old girl from the Baby Cluster, helps endure the pain of knowing things The Mother did, like the broom and the burning.

Ham*, a 9-year-old boy named because Dorothy liked ham, saw The Monster and broke, so alter Five was created to help absorb Ham's resulting agony.

Heather*, a mid-teen girl created while living with Anthony, floated away to avoid trouble. She was needed for fairness because it was Anthony's way, or he abused us.

Heidi, a 10-year-old girl, Angry One, helped suffer the shame of having sex with one of The Mother's boyfriends. She had to be a mother, act grown-up, do grown-up things, and become an adult whore.

Holy Man is a Thinker, Wise One, Spirit, Helper, and Gatekeeper of the Sleepers.

Hope*, a 14-year-old girl from the Hope/Heart Cluster, helped provide hope for a better life.

Hurt, an 8-year-old boy, Taker, and Angry One from the Hurt Cluster, carried moderate pain over The Mother's brutality.

Hurter, a 7-year-old girl, helped us suffer shame from The Mother's scoldings and from having sex with one of The Mother's boyfriends.

Ice Queen, a 20-year-old female Nice One, was created while living with Anthony to do the satanic ceremonial tasks. She was firm, not abusive, but had emotions that could spiral out of control.

Intelligent One, a Spirit, Helper, Thinker, and Wise One, is an immortal man who learned from living, created to help make sense of life.

Iris (8) is a 10-year-old girl from the Hurt Cluster who's the color of a rainbow and focuses exclusively on drawing.

Isabelle* began as a 4-year-old girl but grew to age 12, carries the hurt and terror from The Mother putting Dorothy in a trashcan and beating her, and hid from Anthony but came out to teach Lynne's sons how to be kids while he was away.

Is-Is*, a 4-year-old girl, who helps bear severe childhood pain, resides in "lost land" and comes from the expression, "it is what it is, so just muddle through it." She explained Froggie and made Meme.

Ivy*, a 13-year-old girl, who attended junior high school, had no fear, so she talked to people.

I-See* was an ageless female angel alter from heaven who always watched over Dorothy and taught her to love.

JackJill, age 10, avoided sexual trauma by not having a gender.

James, made by Beth and Iris, began at age seven and grew into a 13-year-old boy Bad One from the Boy, Dark Secret Ones, and Hurt Clusters. He carried moderate anger over ruthlessness from The Mother and others and wanted to get back at them. James never cried. He was tough, so he didn't get hurt as girls did. He perceived hell as a dark place and always talked about death.

Janie, a 10-year-old girl, hid to make Dorothy not exist but later came out of hiding to help absorb the pain and horror of Dorothy's sexual exploitation and emotional wreckage.

Jan-the-Jelly-Jam, age seven, was non-sexual because Dorothy didn't like sex. She wanted to be invisible to go unnoticed by men and once became anorexic.

Jane, a 4-year-old bad girl, helped endure the horror of sex with The Mother and men.

Jay, a 7-year-old boy who aimed not to let anyone hurt us, claimed nothing was worth pain or crying.

Jennifer is a 10-year-old girl who carried great anger over The Mother's brutality, hated her, didn't give a crap, and wanted to hurt her because she injured others.

Jody*, age 10, helped endure the pain of abandonment by The Mother.

Joyce*, age 10, is neither boy nor girl, has different mannerisms, doesn't like getting shots in the butt, and is afraid of being locked up for being crazy.

Junior claimed to be a 10-year-old boy bitch because he grew tired of it.

Kara is a young woman Good One, and part of Sarah.

Katherine, a 1-year-old girl from the Kid Cluster, our second alter baby, was a crybaby who frequently cried in response to The Mother's neglect and abuse.

Katty*, a 6-year-old girl from the Kid Cluster, took on the horror of The Mother throwing a pot of hot water on Dorothy because Dorothy allowed the water to get too hot when warming the baby's bottle.

Kay was a 6-year-old girl who helped take on the excruciating pain, hate, and horror from The Mother's neglect and abuse and hurt herself when she became angry.

Ken (The Doorkeeper) is a 10-year-old boy who keeps track of the other alters comings and goings.

Knower was an immortal male Spirit, Helper, Thinker, and Wise One. He helped Dorothy determine what was happening and guided Dorothy through her vast darkness.

Lady Sophia, a 10-year-old girl Irish version of Sophia, is from the Goodie and Angry Clusters.

Leah (Shy One), a 12-year-old girl, wanted to be decent, so she wanted the bad about The Mother not to be true. She helped absorb the shame from The Mother and her boyfriends' continued sexual exploitation.

Lefty, a 7-year-old boy, was made because Dorothy threw balls with her left hand. He later told Mr. Clarke that he was made up and asked him for help to be authentic.

Liar*, who fabricated, was a 5-year-old half-boy and half-girl from the Sex Cluster.

Libby*, a 12-year-old girl, labeled emotions if there was a way to tell one from another.

Lilly (11) an 8-year-old girl, was trusting, caring, outgoing, and sane before suffering grave wreckage She frequently sat in a corner, banging her head against a wall.

Lisa*, originally Stupid-Head, a 12-year-old girl Taker from the Dummy and Hope/Heart Clusters, helped suffer the horror of being raped repeatedly.

Little*, a 3-year-old girl, Little One and Good One, helped carry the terror from The Mother setting fire to Dorothy's bed.

Liz Ann, an 11-year-old girl, created to take back our lives, likes crafts, drawing, writing stories, keyboard, reading, gardening, yard work, and her stuffie.

M, a 4-year-old girl from the Us Cluster, withdrew, blocked emotions, and rarely did or says anything for fear of feeling stupid and the unbearable shame it brought.

Magic* was a 10-year-old girl who hid to make Dorothy not exist but later came out of hiding to help bear the pain and horror of Dorothy's sexual exploitation and emotional wreckage.

Maria, an 8-year-old girl Gatekeeper of the Sleepers from the Faith and Hope/Heart Clusters, helped hold the key to the Sleepers.

Margie, a 10-year-old girl Gatekeeper of the Heart from the I's Cluster, carries the pain of encountering a man of the Church.

Mary (1), a 5-year-old girl from the Want-To-Bes, Baby, Angry, Hurt, We-Two Clusters, is one of the 12 Selves. She and Pam hold the agreeing in that she can ignore those inside who disagree, thereby promote moving forward with a decision.

Mary Jane, a 5-year-old girl, is Mary and Jane made into one and carries anger and horror from The Mother's abuses, including sexual exploitation by The Mother and men.

Mathew, a 5-year-old boy from the Nobody and Us Clusters, tried to convince The Mother he could be like other kids instead of taking care of the baby, cleaning the house, cooking, and selling his body.

May*, an 11-year-old girl protector, carries the betrayal experienced when hospital staff gave double messages.

Meana*, a 4-year-old mean girl, expressed anger over getting beaten up by men and The Mother.

Meme (Thumbelina) (15) is a 4-year-old teeny girl born of Is-Is, from the Baby, Strange Ones, and Happy Clusters. Meme started as an intelligent non-gender fairy with tiny wings that slept in a walnut shell but later became an alter.

Mickey, an 8-year-old boy, helped endure the fear of The Mother. He was so afraid to talk that he never learned.

Mike* was an 11-year-old boy from the Myself Cluster. Punky is in love with him.

Missy was a girl who began at age three but grew to age 12, initially created to help manage bewilderment from The Mother's crazy-making behavior. She later became an Evil One.

Misty*, a 5-year-old girl from the Baby Cluster, helps hold our pain from The Mother's abuse, like the broom and the burning, and helps soothe the four alter babies when they cry.

Morey*, an 8-year-old mean boy who helped carry Dorothy's anger toward herself, could have gotten rid of Dorothy by killing her and didn't feel bad when she got broken.

MR*, a 14-year-old girl, carries the pain of being described as mentally retarded for writing with her left hand, slanting her letters, or reading backward or upside down.

Neddie* is a 3-year-old girl who wants to be loved, not hated, and is connected to Carrie by love.

Nettie, an 8-year-old feral girl from the Crazy and We-Three Clusters, isolated and made the world disappear.

Nineteen, a 19-year-old male from the Anybody Cluster with superpowers when angry, lifted Anthony's car off Lynne's pinned legs and scared Anthony by tumbling a refrigerator on top of him.

Nina is a 6-year-old girl who helped us know what we were, why we existed, and how many we were.

Not So* was a 5-year-old who's half girl and half boy and helped suffer the shame from Dorothy's molestations and rapes.

Olive* was a 7-year-old girl who walked backward because she didn't want to be like others.

Overseer, a teenage boy made when Dorothy was four, was the spirit of and was a Gatekeeper of the Sleepers. With the help of the 12 Selves and the Great Ones, he balanced and hid the alters in that when they experienced too much confusion or pain, he made an alter to deal with it and created another if that alter became overwhelmed.

Pam (13), an 8-year-old girl who feels sad and helpless, helps carry the hate and pain from The Mother and men's abuse and, along with Mary, holds the key to agreeing.

Pamela Boy, "The Doorway to Hell," is a 12-year-old girl Thinker, Can-Be, "age slider," and Gatekeeper of Good and Evil.

Pam Peter, a 9-year-old boy in a girl's body, helped manage sadness, sat in a corner, cried, and banged his head against a wall.

Patty (20), an 8-year-old girl from the Me Cluster, can lock Dee away but can't permanently eliminate her. She helps carry the pain and humiliation from The Mother saying Dorothy was slow to grasp things, burning Dorothy, penetrating her with a broom handle, and allowing her boyfriends to rape Dorothy.

Paul, a 9-year-old boy who likes puppies, was made because boys are tough and don't cry or get hurt as girls do.

Paula* was a 16-year-old girl created while living with Anthony to help resolve Lynne's feelings about him. She helped kill Lynne's infant.

Paz, short for Topaz, was an 11-year-old girl who helped endure Dorothy's pain from The Mother's beatings.

Peacemaker*, a 13-year-old boy, tries to make peace inside with what happens outside.

Peaches-and-Cream*, an 8-year-old girl from the Bad and Sex Clusters, wanted what The Mother did not to be true so she could be a nice girl.

Penelope, a 6-year-old girl, who likes to paint, helps manage pain by disappearing.

Pennie (16), a 4-year-old girl Taker from the Us Cluster, helped bear the pain from The Mother not loving Dorothy, Dorothy's being an accident, and the agony and fear of lying between The Mother and men.

Peter, created for protection, was our oldest boy. He began as a 3-year-old "animal alter," "Dragon, Dear," but became a 3-year-old boy who grew to 13. He would change into a giant, robust, pinkish-purple dragon, scary to others but not us, to take The Mother's whippings.

Pink was a girl toddler from the We-Three Cluster who grew to age five. As a toddler, she helped endure the terror of the encounter with "The Monster."

PJ, a 3-year-old girl, helped carry our fear of The Mother. She was tiny and shy but feels better when discussing her painful memories.

Pollyanna (Polly), a 7-year-old, irrepressibly optimistic girl, finds the good in everyone because it's scary when everyone is terrible.

Pony, from the Animal Cluster, is one of the 12 Selves. He began as a pony. We rode him to fantasy locations to provide happiness. He later became a 4-year-old boy and eventually The Dream Machine.

Prissy* is a 4-year-old girl from the Baby Cluster.

Punk, a 12-year-old girl, one of the 12 Selves, likes rabbits and finger painting and carries much pain from The Mother's outrageous abuse.

Punky (9), a trusting tomboyish girl who grew from age 8 to 12, holds the key to unlocking happiness so life won't be horrible. She's a Helper and Good One from the Happy, Hope/Heart, and We-Two Clusters. To spread her responsibilities, Punky made three girls, Punky II, III, and IV, who grew from age 8 to 12.

Punky II* was the bad one.

Punky III* was the non-proper one.

Punky IV* lied and sat on men's laps.

Punky Lil (Grandma's Girl) is a 4-year-old girl made to help leave The Mother's ugliness behind and reconcile what The Mother said versus what Grandma said.

Rachel, a 6-year-old bull-headed girl soldier, carries the pain and humiliation of The Mother forcing Dorothy to lie in the yard nude facing the street with legs apart, holding a sign reading, "only 20 cents a pop."

Ripper*, a 10-year-old boy, helped relieve stress by ripping up paper.

Robot (The Dead One), an 11-year-old girl who feels nothing and has thoughts of being gay, came when Dorothy was traumatized in a mental ward.

Rock, a 3-year-old girl, Little One and Nobody, was bull-headed and didn't move when The Mother hurt Dorothy.

Rose was a 13-year-old female Angry One who helped bear moderate anger from The Mother's brutality.

Roxie, a 3-year-old girl, Little One, was emotionless because The Mother's continual torment was emotionally overwhelming.

Runner*, a girl who started at age five and grew to seven, broke running records at ages 5, 6, and 7.

Ruth, a 5-year-old girl from the Wronged, helped with anger caused by severe abuse and expressed it by being nasty.

Sad* a 12-year-old girl, who likes pigtails with ribbons, was made while living with Anthony to endure Lynne's sadness from that union.

Safe* is a 4-year-old girl who helps absorb our fear of everything.

Sam (19), a 7-year-old boy, holds the pain from The Mother forcing Dorothy to climb down an outdoor toilet hole, wants to give up, and doesn't know how to tell how things hurt him.

Samantha, a 6-year-old girl, helps take on the shame of being raped repeatedly. She shared with Mr. Clarke that she's a whore because she had lots of sex.

Sarah (2) is an immortal adult female who helped Dorothy know her inside alters, held the key to unlocking peace, saw the circle of nature, and applied it to Dorothy's life. She fought the demons that tried to turn Dorothy.

Sard was an 8-year-old boy Spirit and Gatekeeper of the Heart from the I's Cluster, who helped guide Dorothy through the vast darkness she endured and helped her read, write, and deal with people.

Seeker*, a 12-year-old girl Quiet One, seeks the truth and wants to live virtuously and help the bad. She doesn't wish for pain or to cause it.

Seer is an adult immortal female Wise One, Spirit, Helper, Thinker, and Gatekeeper of the Sleepers from the Me Cluster who sees the future and everything outside and keeps everything separated.

Seven-and-Three-Quarters, whose name is her age, is proud because she's almost eight. She's an Angry One from the Hurt Cluster and the 12 Selves. She carries tremendous hurt and terror from The Mother's outrageous mistreatment, including scrubbing Dorothy's privates.

Sexy, who was a 4-year-old girl from the Bad and Sex Clusters, a little whore, was fashioned like The Mother to get The Mother's love.

Shelby, an 11-year-old girl who likes celery, raw carrots, and apples, helps suffer the pain of The Mother killing Dorothy's baby bird.

Sherry was a 15-year-old girl leader from the Sex Cluster, was conceived by Cheri to con the psychiatric unit doctor.

Skeeter*, a 16-year-old boy Unreal One, got his name from mosquito bites that itched. He helped provide hope by believing life isn't so bad and will get better.

Silly Sally was a 12-year-old girl Evil One from the Happy and We-Two Clusters, initially created to be reasonable and stand up for Dorothy.

Sissie was a 6-year-old boy who liked dolls.

Six, whose name was her age, was an Angry One from the Us Cluster who wanted to be intelligent, have friends, and fit in to convince The Mother she could be like other kids instead of taking care of the baby, cleaning the house, cooking, and selling her body.

Sophia (15), a 10-year-old girl from the Goodie and Angry Clusters, dressed like a hippie, liking ruffled panties and dresses.

So-So*, a 9-year-old girl from the Unseen, once stuck under Dorothy's bed, was created to help suffer the horror from The Mother igniting it while Dorothy and her brother were underneath.

Spunky* is a 3-year-old girl who endures terrible feelings from The Mother putting Dorothy in a dog cage on the porch for the night as punishment for running away.

Star* (Hippy Girl) was a 13-year-old girl who liked peasant shirts and went to the stars when bad things happened.

Stuffy*, a non-gender 4-year-old alter, was made by Half-Pint not to have emotion or talk so as not to have to lie and so he wouldn't get punished but would still get love.

Susan, a 6-year-old girl, who became an Evil One with Anthony, was initially created to help absorb the pain from The Mother brushing Dorothy with hot water and Clorox or lye if she thought she was touching herself.

Sunshine (The One), a young adult female Nice One from the Hope/Heart Cluster, created while living with Anthony, was the only remaining righteous alter and returned from emotional death.

Suze, a girl who began at age five and became Suzie Q. at age 11, holds the horror from The Mother putting Dorothy in a dark attic for punishment.

Suzie Q. (Suzie), an 11-year-old girl from the Hurt Cluster, is a homemaker, likes to cook and fish, only eats ice cream and candy, and doesn't cause any hurt that can't be handled, so she's allowed to come and go freely.

T, a 5-year-old girl from the 12 Selves, cried for Dorothy because The Mother didn't allow it.

Tabatha, a 3-year-old girl whose afraid, helped hold the pain from The Mother's abuse, did dumb things, threw temper tantrums, worried about her soul, and was once waiting for something to happen because she was dead.

Tabby, a 15-year-old girl, helps us suffer the painful memories of our hospitalizations.

Tack*, a 14-year-old boy, carries the painful memory of being hit in the head with a pipe by one of The Mother's boyfriends.

Tamara, a 10-year-old girl, helps absorb the pain and humiliation of being raped repeatedly by The Mother and men.

Tami is a 6-year-old girl who The Mother called "The Little Bitch." She absorbed the humiliation and heartache from The Mother smacking Dorothy and forbidding her to be an angel with paper wings in a play.

Tara (5), a combination of Overseer, Sarah, and others, is a young adult immortal female Native American Wise One, Spirit, Helper, Thinker, Good One, and Gatekeeper of the Sleepers from the Hope/Heart Cluster.

Teach, a mid-teen girl, Strange One, held the pain of Lynne's having her bucket of hope broken so often that no hope remained.

Teresa*, a 3-year-old girl, helped bear the pain from The Mother forcing the choice between her and anyone else.

Terry*, a teenage boy, was conceived to tell Dorothy's teacher about being raped.

The Mom*, a 15-year-old girl from the Goodie Cluster, helped protect Dorothy from the mental hospital staff and The Mother.

Think*, a 3-year-old girl, didn't cry because The Mother became angry when Dorothy cried.

Tiffany, age four, Annie's daughter, helped carry the fear and belief that Dorothy was evil and kept people away.

Timothy A. Bradshaw (Charles II) (6), from the Boy and We-Two Clusters, is a 9-year-old second-grader who still prints, likes fast cars and fast women, and carries the shame from one of The Mother's boyfriend's deviant behavior.

Tina is an 8-year-old girl crybaby filled with hatred from absorbing The Mother's name-calling and beatings. She was so afraid to talk that she took a long time to learn.

Tinker, a 6-year-old girl, helped absorb evil and selfishness because Dorothy didn't want either.

Tommie, a 9-year-old girl who endured sexual confusion, wanted a girlfriend, but Mr. Clarke said she couldn't have one because she was nine and had a girl's body.

Toughie, a 12-year-old boy from the Bad Ones and Crazy Ones, helped others understand her world and helped Dorothy survive.

Twinkle*, a 5-year-old girl, saw stars when Dorothy got hit on the head.

Ugly, a 4-year-old girl Bad One, and Crazy One from the Us Cluster, helped endure the pain and horror of the evil and craziness heaped upon Dorothy.

Under*, a 9-year-old boy from the Unseen, once stuck under Dorothy's bed, was created to help suffer horror from The Mother igniting it while she and her brother were underneath.

Vicky* helped carry the fear of The Mother, but now just men. She began at age three and remains active. She's shy and leery of people, afraid of herself, and has irrational fears of lightning, bridges, and heights.

Wanda, a 3-year-old girl, who frequently ran away from home, helped bear our fear of The Mother but now just men.

Windy, from the Us Cluster, who started at age 11 and grew to age 13, lived in foster care sporadically and helped bear our hurt of life with The Mother.

Winter (3), a 20-year-old female intimidating Soldier, protector, robot, and Bad One, made when Anthony was killing animals and infants, isn't human in that she's emotionally rugged and has no physical sensations. She takes care of the evil stuff, holds the key to unlocking darkness and, along with others, holds the key to unlocking emotions.

Wisher, who started as a 2-year-old boy but grew to age 16, holds our pain of losing our dad.

Wizard is a 9-year-old boy who showed people they couldn't hurt him because he could turn his body into water or stone, so he mostly felt no pain.

Worker-of-the-Mind*, an adult female, keeps our many complicated matters separated, but that only helps a little.

ꝙꟽ (Dyslexia My), a 7-year-old girl, Evil One, was initially created to help carry the pain of being mistreated at school.

Zippy* was a 4-year-old boy Unreal One. Dorothy rode him to unique places like she did Rainbow and Pony. Having Zippy made her happy.

Zoe (17), Gatekeeper of the Vision, a 4-year-old girl, helps bear our pain from waves of abuse, including The Mother forcing us into parental roles at age four.

The 62 Clusters in This Story

Angry Cluster consisted of Adora, Amber, Jennifer, Lucy, Mary, Sophia, and Lady Sophia. They carried tremendous anger over The Mother's brutality, hated her, didn't give a crap, and wanted to hurt her because she injured others.

Angry Ones are Amanda, Angry, Bell, Heidi, Hurt, Mady, Rose, One, One-and-One-Half, Two, Three, Four, Six, Ten, Sixteen, 7 ¾, and Nineteen. They carry moderate anger over Dorothy's brutal mistreatment by The Mother and others and want revenge.

Animal Cluster, consisting of Froggie, Peter, Pony, Butterfly, and others, began as animal alters but grew into people alters.

Anybody Cluster, those whose minds were pre-set, for one thing, created for protection from Anthony, might have had names, but no one remembers them.

Baby Cluster, composed of Cathy, Crybaby, Katherine, Brooklyn, Angel, Mary, Punky Lil, Misty, Half-Pint, Meme, and Prissy, helps endure the pain from The Mother's many waves of abuse.

Bad Cluster consists of Andy, formerly Hater, Dee, Doer, Helpless, His-Self, Peaches-and-Cream, Rachel, Sexy, User, and the Bad Ones. They absorbed Dorothy's evil thoughts and emotions: anger, pain, humiliation, horror, hate, evil, killing self, and denial.

Bad Ones are Adora, Crystal, James, Sandy, Toughie, Ugly, Winter, and Winter-Two. They're rescuers who helped with survival by managing rage, as they had no emotions, but their ruthlessness could get us locked up.

Boy Cluster, comprised of Adam, Bobby, Charley, James, Paul, and Timothy A. Bradshaw, was made because boys are tough and don't cry or get hurt as girls do.

Can-Bes are Deon, Squirt, and Pamela Boy, who was a girl, and others, who copied alters needed for a job and replaced them if, for some reason, they couldn't remain out to finish it.

Crazy Ones are Ugly, Toughie, and the four Unreal Ones. They helped us suffer the pain and horror of the evil and craziness heaped upon us. They were feral alters, living in their unique world and wanting others to understand their world.

Dark Secret Ones, who perceived hell as a dark place, made up of Beth, Dee, Adam, and James, help endure the pain and horror of the wreckage caused by The Mother and men.

Dead Ones were babies who just cried, created while living with Anthony.

Dummy Cluster consisted of Lisa, originally Stupid-Head, Dummy-Two, Bo-Bo, originally Dummy, and non-alter, Dorothy. They bore the pain from The Mother frequently calling Dorothy stupid or a similar name.

Emotional Ones, unnamed children of various ages, fashioned to react without emotion to appear normal, had many feelings they never learned to hide.

Evil Ones were Curly, eB, yM, Missy, Silly Sally, Susan, and unnamed girls.

Faith Cluster consisted of Folly Farm, Maria, and Sarah, who believed in the Bible, God, and heaven and are part of our soul. Later in life, they learned to forgive and found some peace.

Fools are Feeler and Fern, who help bear the shame of what men did.

Gatekeepers of Good and Evil are Pamela Boy and Conrad, who help us know the difference between right and wrong and keep us safe by letting emotions come but stopping them when they become overwhelming and not allowing us to be used or pushed.

Gatekeepers of the Heart, composed of Abigail, Margie, Oneida, and spirits, Sard and Sender, were created to love and were thought to remove others' pain.

Gatekeepers of The Light, who are nameless, allow the "Light," goodness, to shine versus hiding it.

Gatekeepers of the Secrets, whose names aren't remembered, knew what happened but didn't tell the other alters, and they also kept good secrets to avoid trouble, like where toys were hidden from The Mother at Grandma's house.

Gatekeepers of the Sleepers were Overseer, Faith, Maria, Wise Ones, and others, who held the key to the sleeping children.

Gatekeepers of the Truth are unnamed alters holding the truth.

Goodie Cluster consists of Alice, Sophia, Lady Sophia, and The Mom. They represented what The Mother wanted Dorothy to be.

Good Ones are Cara, Little, Punky, Sarah, Tara, Kara, and Carrie, who believe in children, hope, angels, spirits, doing good, forgiveness, keeping safe, wisdom, dreams, wanting, and unconditional love, as do those from the Hope/Heart Cluster.

Great Ones, whose names and gender are unremembered, were four smart mid-teen alters made when Dorothy was four. With the help of the 12 Selves and Overseer, they created new alters when those present got filled with too many bad memories and emotional pain.

The Guys are Timothy A. Bradshaw, Bud, and some unnamed younger down-home dudes, who stick up for ladies.

Happy Cluster consists of Bunnie, Meme, Punky, and Silly Sally. They remember The Mother's abuse but don't judge her because they believe it isn't their place.

Helpers are Holy Man, Intelligent One, Knower, Sarah, Seer, Tara, Oneida, Annie, Punky, Punky Lil, Wise Ones, and unnamed others, who help us know what's happening.

Hidden Ones are Dee, Deon, Charlotte, Deand, D-Day, De-Death, De-de, and Dein, fragments except for Dee, who could remember up to 5 minutes of the feelings of a 15-minute whipping. Deand, three fragments, could remember all 15 minutes.

Hope/Heart Cluster is Beth, Hope, Carrie, Lisa, Maria, Sarah, Sunshine, and Tara. They believe in children, hope, angels, spirits, doing good, forgiveness, keeping safe, wanting, wisdom, dreams, and unconditional love, as do the Good Ones.

Hurt Cluster consists of Beth, Dee, Hurt, Iris, James, Mary, 7 ¾, and Suzie Q. They were markedly injured, spread their evil all around, and traded sex for a hug, smile, love, and to know the monster's location.

I's Cluster consists of Abigail, Peanut Butter, Sarah, and the Gatekeepers of the Heart, who help with reading, writing, and dealing with people.

Kids Cluster, alters under age 10, consisted of Art, Katherine, Katty, Ann, Kay, and three not included in the story, Kali, Kimberly, and Kable. They took care of others by helping take on the excruciating pain, hate, and horror from The Mother's neglect and abuse and hurt themselves when they became angry.

Killers were unnamed alters created while living with Anthony to drink Lynne to death or kill her somehow.

Little Ones, all under age four, are Fur, Rock, Roxie, Vicky, Little, Sky, David, Cathy, Katherine, Wanda, Child, Think, Teresa, Spunky, Neddie, PJ, Tabatha, and unnamed alters and "fragments." They came out when they thought it was safe and engaged in dangerous activities.

Me Cluster consisted of Amber, Bree, Candie, Dala, Patty, and Seer, who helped carry knowing what the system was, why it existed, and how many alters are in it. They don't give their names because doing so would've given away their power, as people could have called on them to provide a service. The Me Cluster has fewer alters than the Myself Cluster.

Myself Cluster was composed of Mike, Nancy, Nina, and unnamed others, differed from the Me Cluster in that it had more alters.

Nameless Ones are part of the system's unconscious.

Nice Ones were Ice Queen and Sunshine, who were also Want-To-Bes and weren't human because they had no emotions, except when near. When they got hurt emotionally, the system had to keep them safe by assigning the hurt to others, but they had to retain some pain if the system had to keep them safe by assigning the hurt to others, but they had to retain some pain if the system didn't have time to make room.

Nobodies were Baby, Big Joe, Dusty, Flower, Ivan, Mathew, Rock, and three unnamed alters. They weren't much of anything but helped determine what was happening.

Quiet Ones are Seeker and Sad, 12-year-old girls, and others mostly younger whose names aren't remembered. They whispered so as not to be heard to avoid The Mother's wrath, and because otherwise, people would know they did terrible things.

Sex Cluster is Cheri, Colet, Dirty, Peaches and Cream, Rachel, Sexy, Sherry, Two Bits, and Liar and Not So, each half boy and half girl, who help suffer the shame from the molestations and rapes.

Sleepers were unnamed sleeping boys and girls under the age of 10 who enabled locking away the painful experiences to forget them, and each needed to wake up and learn something different from Kristina.

Smart Ones are nameless and sit quietly to not be noticed by potential perpetrators. One watches documentaries.

Soldiers are Amanda, Belinda, Rachel, and Winter, made for protection while with Anthony.

Spirit Cluster, made up of Holy Man, Intelligent One, Knower, Sarah, Seer, Tara, Wise Ones, One, Two, Three, Sard, and Sender, guided the system through the vast darkness it endured.

Strange Ones were primarily ages 8 to 12, unnamed except for Meme and Teach, created when Dorothy heard voices while in the "crazy farm." They thought people on the radio could talk to them.

Takers were Angry, Hurt, Lisa, Pennie, and Dorothy, Anne, and Lynne. They were unlikable ones who took too much damage and harmed others though they preferred to stay hidden and not hurt anyone.

The 12 Selves were Amber, Am, Andy, Angry, Charles, Crybaby, Mary, Pony, Punk, 7 3/4, T, and Dorothy, the knights in shining armor, who protected the system by managing anything wrong or adverse that happened. They helped the Great Ones and Overseer create new alters when the existing ones got filled with too many painful memories and emotions.

Thinkers are Holy Man, Intelligent One, Knower, Pamela Boy, Seer, Sarah, and Tara. They're logical, rational, and analytical and have little to do with emotion because it interferes with thinking. Thinkers make sense of life and see the future.

Unnamed Ones were 27 unnamed alters, ages 4 to 12 for the most part, stuck in The Mother's bedroom wall, created to act adult because it wasn't safe to be a child.

Unreal Ones, who were part of the Crazy Ones, were Annie, Skeeter, Zippy, and one whose name isn't remembered. They lived in their private world and provided hope by wearing rose-colored glasses. They believed in forgiveness, everyone was good at heart and trustworthy, and that life wasn't as bad as it seemed and would get better.

Unseen was So-So and Under. They were stuck under Dorothy's bed. They were created to help her suffer the horror from The Mother igniting it while her brother, Ronald, and she were underneath.

Us Cluster, made up of Cindy, Dusty, Gypsy, Mathew, M., Melissa, Pennie, Six, Ugly, Windy, Willy, and many unnamed others, was sometimes referred to as "club 900." Their ages ranged from 3 to 15 years. They wanted to be intelligent, have friends, and fit in to convince The Mother they could be like other kids instead of taking care of the baby, cleaning the house, cooking, and selling their bodies. The more they accepted themselves, the more they allowed the emotions and ideas of others. They often spoke nearly in unison, sounding like a symphony of crickets; however, they sometimes talked as individuals. They wrote or printed as a group or individually. Some only spoke when spoken to and didn't do that very much. Many withdrew, blocked emotions, and rarely did or said anything due to the fear of feeling stupid and the accompanying unbearable shame.

Want-To-Bes were Alice, Carrie, Mary, Nice Ones, and non-alters: Anne, Lynne, and myself, Dorothy. They bore immense depression because they wanted to be kids, but The Mother didn't allow it.

Watchers were six alters whose names aren't remembered. They watched the behavior of other alters by transcending their bodies, floating to the ceiling, and observing and recalling without emotions. They learned how to behave by watching other people but they watched secretly because it would've been rude to stare.

We-One Cluster consists of Boo, Kali, Nora, Clara, and Tamara. There are three We Clusters. They help bear the hurt and terror of childhood wounding, including the humiliation of being raped repeatedly by The Mother and men. We Cluster alters are always out in groups and write or print in groups, but only one at a time speaks. The more they accept themselves, the more amenable they are to others' emotions and ideas.

We-Two Cluster consists of Deon, Charles, Kimberly, Punky, Silly Sally, Mary, and Timothy A. Bradshaw.

We-Three Cluster consists of Nettie, Annie, Amy, Pink, and Lilly.

Wise Ones, who are also Spirits, Thinkers, Helpers, and Gatekeepers of the Sleepers, are Holy Man, Intelligent One, Knower, Sarah, Seer, Tara, and three Nameless Ones, part of our unconscious. Wise Ones are immortal, enlightened, hold the key to power and knowledge, see the circle of nature, apply it to our lives, take care of the actual children and us by answering our questions, and are Pamela Boy's conscience.

Wronged was comprised of Max, Ruth, and unnamed others. They helped carry anger from severe abuse and expressed it by being nasty.

The 112 Named Alters and Fragments, Not in This Story

Albert, a 6-year-old playful boy, carries some of the pain from The Mother's years of abuse.

And-So-On, an 8-year-old boy, was made when we ran out of names, but we don't remember why we made him. He's likely in one of our hotels where we keep many inactive alters.

Andrew, a 3-year-old boy, was made when Dorothy lived with Grandma and met a 12-year-old neighbor boy named Andrew, who was courteous, played with Dorothy, treated her like regular people, and became part of her.

Ant, a tiny 3-year-old boy, wasn't noticeable or significant.

April, a 5-year-old girl, holds part of the secret about The Monster and a shed.

Asker, a 4-year-old girl, asked many questions like, "why is the sky blue" and got into trouble with The Mother, who told her to shut up because it just is.

Baa, a 2-year-old girl crybaby, carries pain from childhood abuse.

Baby, a 4-year-old girl preschooler Nobody, lives in "lost land" and helps bear childhood pain.

Barry, a bored 7-year-old boy, called Mary a brat, but we don't remember why we made him.

Bear, a 7-year-old boy, who might get angry but not furious, helps absorb pain from childhood abuse.

Be-Be, a baby girl, helps bear the pain from childhood abuse.

Betsy, a sweet 10-year-old girl who likes cooking and farming, came while living with Grandma to help leave behind the horror The Mother caused.

Big Joe, a 6-year-old boy Nobody, wasn't much of anything.

Blue* is a strong 8-year-old girl who takes some emotions and flies away.

Boo, a 5-year-old girl from the We-One Cluster, helps endure the pain and horror of childhood abuse.

Bud, one of The Guys, age eight, is a down-home guy who sticks up for ladies and likes chocolate chip cookies with little or no nuts.

Buffy is a sweet 4-year-old girl, but we don't remember why we made her.

Candie, a 6-year-old girl from the Me Cluster, helps suffer the shame of sexual abuse.

Charles IV, a 10-year-old boy, helps fear and other bad feelings go away.

Charlotte is a heartbroken 8-year-old girl fragment from the Hidden Ones.

Chatty, a 5-year-old girl, says everything on her mind because she likes to hear herself talk.

Chelsea, a 9-year-old girl who puts our minds at ease and represents peace, was made after hearing a seashell.

Colet, an 11-year-old girl teacher from the Sex Cluster, helps us suffer the pain and horror of being sexually abused multiple times.

Connie, an 8-year-old girl, helped take on the pain from The Mother's torment. She wanted to be a nice girl, so she wanted the stuff about The Mother to be untrue.

Crazy, a girl, age unknown, was made because we thought we were insane.

Cuddles, a 3-year-old girl created for cuddling, got her name from an unnamed wise Little One who liked to cuddle.

Curly, a 3-year-old boy from the Evil Ones, got his name from having curly hair.

David, a 3-year-old boy Little One, helped bear the pain and horror of The Mother's abuse.

Dean, a 4-year-old boy, is otherwise unremembered.

D-Day, whose name means the day of death, is a 5-year-old boy fragment from the Hidden Ones.

De-Death is a 6-year-old boy fragment from the Hidden Ones.

Dala, an 8-year-old girl from the Me Cluster, is otherwise unremembered.

Dein was a 6-year-old girl fragment from the Hidden Ones.

Dizzy Lizzie was an adolescent girl who carried anger from being raped by men.

Dog, a 5-year-old boy who carries anger toward The Mother, wanted to be a mean, vicious dog because The Mother put him in a cage.

Dolly, a 7-year-old loving girl, was made because everyone likes baby dolls.

Donna is a 5-year-old girl who carries happiness.

Dreamer is an unnamed meditator.

Ed, a 9-year-old boy, Adam's friend, was named after someone Dorothy liked. He was emotionally sensitive but had a rugged exterior and loved ice cream.

Eight, an 8-year-old boy, helps hold the pain and horror from The Mother's brutality.

Eva, a 7-year-old girl, stays good by not remembering anything.

Fairy/Bell, listed in Dorothy's "Knowing It's I" chart, may have been a fairy named Bell.

Faith was a teenage girl, Gatekeeper of the Sleepers.

Fear, a 10-year-old girl, helped suffer the horror of The Mother setting Dorothy's bed on fire to force her from under it.

Flower, a 5-year-old girl, was a Nobody.

Folly Farm, a 5-year-old girl from the Faith Cluster, helps us forgive and find peace.

Four, whose name is his age, is an Angry One.

Frolic, an 8-year-old playful girl, helps us suffer the pain of being raped.

Gypsy, an 11-year-old girl, is from the Us Cluster.

Healer was a mid-teen girl teacher and a Gatekeeper of the Sleepers.

Helpless is a 7-year-old girl from the Bad Cluster.

His-Self, an 8-year-old boy from the Bad Cluster whose purpose isn't remembered, was made when Dorothy ran out of names.

Ivan was a 6-year-old boy Nobody.

Jamey, a 6-year-old boy, helps us suppress our anger.

Jason is a 9-year-old boy who fished with Timothy and Paul.

Jimmie, an 8-year-old boy, helps us with fear.

Joanie, a 10-year-old girl, was made for reasons not remembered.

Joe, a 6-year-old boy, helped endure the pain and horror of The Mother's abusiveness. He became aware that he and 3-year-old Little Mary told a similar abuse history and blended with her into Mary Joe, a 6-year-old boy/girl.

Kable, a 7-year-old boy from the Kid Cluster, portrayed a grandma while playacting with Lynne's real grandson.

Kali is a 6-year-old girl from the Kid and We-One Clusters.

Kimberly is a 5-year-old girl from the We-Two and Kids Clusters who helped carry the fear of The Mother and men.

Kitty, a 5-year-old girl, helped Ted with the letter explaining Crystal.

Lane, a 9-year-old boy, helps bear the shame of people looking at us funny and veering away.

Little Lady (Lady), a 10-year-old girl, helps absorb the shame from people looking at us funny and veering away.

Little Mary, a 3-year-old girl made by Mary, helped endure the pain and horror of The Mother's abusiveness.

Lucas, a 2-year-old boy, helped us suffer the pain from The Mother insisting that Dorothy choose between her and anyone else.

Lucy is a 6-year-old girl from the Angry Cluster.

Mady, an 8-year-old boy Angry One, helped write that people give us a funny look and veer away. He's on the "Knowing It's I" chart.

Mallory, a 7-year-old girl, helped absorb the pain of many childhood waves of abuse.

Marsha, a 10-year-old girl, took care of one of Dorothy's younger siblings and played with her other siblings.

Marshall, a 10-year-old boy, hid to make us not exist but later came out of hiding. He wrote to Mr. Clarke that we were afraid because people were beginning to know we were not one.

Mary Joe, a 6-year-old boy/girl, a blend of Little Mary and Joe, was created when the two became aware they told a similar abuse history.

Max, a 5-year-old boy from the Wronged, helped carry anger from severe abuse and expressed it by being nasty.

Melissa is a 4-year-old girl from the Us Cluster.

Mona, a 3-year-old girl, had a Mona Lisa smile, which, according to Grandma, lit up the whole room.

Muffin is a 4-year-old girl who likes stuffies and whose name is sometimes made fun of.

Nancy, a 6-year-old girl from the Myself Cluster, was scared because Mr. Clarke didn't tell her what to do.

Nasty, a 6-year-old girl who helps carry the pain from The Mother calling us dirty, attended Leena's 39th birthday party.

No-No, an 8-year-old boy, helped write that people give us a funny look and veer away when we're in public and having fun.

Nora is a 7-year-old girl from the We-One Cluster.

One, whose name is his age, is a Spirit and Angry One.

One-and-One-Half, whose name is his age, is an Angry One.

Oneida is a 5-year-old girl, Helper, and Gatekeeper of the Heart.

Onwee, a 2-year-old girl, is bull-headed like Rock.

Peanut Butter, a 5-year-old girl from the I's Cluster, helped us read, write, and deal with people and wanted to play with Mr. Clarke.

Pewee, a 2-year-old boy, helped take Dorothy's whippings when Dorothy peed in her bed or pants.

Quinn, a 5-year-old girl who gets angry but not furious, helps relieve our pain by forgetting the bad stuff.

Rainbow, a non-gender 10-year-old, was ridden to beautiful places like Pony and Zippy were.

Ruby, an adult female, was conceived to help absorb the pain and humiliation of being exploited by men, made after Margie's encounter with a man of the Church.

Sag, a 10-year-old girl, likes bright colors.

Sandy is a 12-year-old girl, Bad One.

Sender is an 8-year-old boy Spirit from the I's Clusters.

Seven, a boy whose name is his age, is otherwise not remembered.

Shlet is an 8-year-old boy otherwise not remembered.

Skippy is an 8-year-old boy made because we liked to skip.

Sky, a non-gender 3-year-old, is a Little One who endeavors to keep us feeling peaceful.

Sleeper, a combination of Tara, Hidden Ones, and Sarah, was a female elder and Gatekeeper of the Sleepers.

Sixteen is an Angry One whose name is her age.

Smarty-Pants, a 5-year-old girl brat, asked our doctor if we had to stay in the hospital.

Squirt, a 3-year-old girl from the Can-Bes, is what Dorothy's grandparents called a little kid.

Ted, a 5-year-old boy, bore much of our pain from neglect and abuse. He felt sad and wished he were dead because he got so filled up with hurt.

Ten is a 10-year-old boy Angry One.

Three is a 3-year-old boy Spirit and Angry One.

Trevor is a 7-year-old boy who got to play with Lynne's real grandson.

Two is a 2-year-old boy Spirit and Angry One.

Two Bits, a 4-year-old girl from the Sex Cluster, wanted the stuff about The Mother not to be true so she could be a nice girl.

User is a 6-year-old girl from the Bad Cluster.

Whip is an 8-year-old boy whose purpose isn't remembered.

Willy is an 8-year-old boy from the Us Cluster.

Winter-Two, a 21-year-old woman, was once a fierce and growing Bad One.

Woody is a big, strong 13-year-old boy who once was in foster care and helped bear the hurt of life with The Mother.

Zero, The number "0" on the Knowing It's I chart, an 8-year-old boy, helped bear depression from The Mother telling Dorothy she was worthless.

Bibliography

Historically, renowned theorists described multiple personality states, including Pierre Janet, Sigmund Freud, Alfred Binet, William James, Benjamin Rush, Morton Prince, Boris Sidis, Enrico Morselli, and Sandor Ferenczi. The first published cases are those of Jeanne Fery, reported in 1586, and an example of exchanged personality that dates to Eberhardt Gmelin's account of 1791. Many individuals considered hysterics in the 19th century would today be diagnosed with "dissociative" disorders. Source: *Separating Fact from Fiction: An Empirical Examination of Six Myths About Dissociative Identity Disorder*, by Brand, Bethany L. Ph.D.; Sar, Vedat MD; Stavropoulos, Pam Ph.D.; Krüger, Christa MB, BCh, MMed (Psych), MD; Korzekwa, Marilyn MD; Martínez-Taboas, Alfonso Ph.D.; Middleton, Warwick MB, BS, Franzcp CP, MD. Harvard Review of Psychiatry: July/August 2016 - Volume 24 - Issue 4 - p 257-270.

According to the *Therapist's Guide to Clinical Intervention*, Johnson, Sharon L 1997, the central feature of Dissociative Identity Disorder (DID) is a disturbance in integrating identity, memory, or consciousness. It may have a sudden or gradual onset and may be temporary or chronic in its course. Depending on the disturbance (identity, memory, or consciousness), the individual's life experience is affected differently. Conceptually, the treatment course improves coping, maintains reality, and establishes normal integrative functions. The therapy goals are intact thought processes, maintenance of reality, enhanced coping, stress management, and personality integration. Treatment focus and objectives are identity thought processes, sensory/perceptual distortion, ineffective coping, ineffective stress management, and identity disturbance.

In 1994 The International Society for the Study of Dissociation, *Journal of Trauma and Dissociation,* adopted the guidelines for treating Dissociative Identity Disorder in adults, with the final revision occurring on June 12, 2010, copyright 2011. The Society doesn't recommend construing the Guidelines as a standard of clinical care. At present, however, the practice recommendations reflect the state-of-the-art in this field. The guidelines do not include all proper care methods or exclude other acceptable treatment interventions. Moreover, adhering to the Guidelines will not necessarily result in a successful treatment outcome in every case. Treatment should always be individualized. Clinicians must use their judgment concerning the appropriateness for a particular patient of a specific method of care in light of the clinical data presented by the patient and the options available at the time of treatment.

In the service of gradual "integration," the therapist may, at times, acknowledge that the patient experiences the identities, more commonly referred to as alters, as if they were separate. Nevertheless, a fundamental tenet of the psychotherapy of patients with DID is to increase communication and coordination among the alters.

Dissociative Identity Disorders are not rare conditions. In studies of the general population, a prevalence rate of 1% to 3% of the population has been described (Johnson, Cohen, Kasen, & Brook, 2006; Murphy, 1994; Ross, 1991; Sar, Akyüz, & Dog, 2007; Waller & Ross, 1997). Although DID is a relatively common disorder, R. P. Kluft (2009) observed that only 6% make their DID visible ongoing (p. 600).

Conceptual Issues and Physiological Manifestations

The DID patient is a single person who experiences having separate alters having relative psychological autonomy from one another. These subjective alters may take executive control of the person's body and behavior. They might influence their experience and behavior from within. Taken together, all alters make up the personality of the person with DID.

Literature has defined alters in several ways. For example, Putnam (1989) described them as highly discrete states of consciousness organized around a prevailing affect, sense of self (including body image), with a limited repertoire of behaviors and a set of state-dependent memories (p. 103).

Severe and prolonged traumatic experiences can lead to discrete, personified behavioral states, i.e., rudimentary alters. This encapsulates intolerable traumatic recollections, affects, sensations, beliefs, or behaviors and mitigates their impact on the child's overall development. Secondary structuring of these discrete behavioral states occurs over time through various developmental and symbolic mechanisms, resulting in the characteristics of the specific alters. The alters may develop in number, complexity, and sense of separateness as the child proceeds through latency, adolescence, and adulthood (R. P. Kluft, 1984; Putnam, 1997). DID develops during childhood, and clinicians have rarely encountered cases of DID that derive from adult-onset trauma. An exception is when adult-onset trauma superimposes on preexisting childhood trauma and preexisting latent or dormant "fragmentation."

Treatment Goals and Outcomes

Integrated functioning is the goal of treatment. Although the DID patient has the subjective experience of having separate alters, clinicians must remember that the patient is not a collection of different people sharing the same body. The DID patient should be seen as an entire adult, with the alters sharing responsibility for daily life. Clinicians working with DID patients generally must hold the whole person, i.e., the system of alters, responsible for the behavior of any constituent alters, even in amnesia or the sense of lack of control or agency over behavior (see Radden, 1996).

The Criteria for Dissociative Identity Disorder (DID) in the DSM-5

1. Two or more distinct identities or personality states are present, each with its own relatively enduring pattern of perceiving, relating to, and thinking about the environment and self.
    According to the DSM-5, personality states may be seen as an "experience of possession." These states involve a marked discontinuity in the sense of self and agency, accompanied by related alterations in affect, behavior, consciousness, memory, perception, cognition, and/or sensory-motor functioning. These signs and symptoms may be observed by others or reported by the individual."
    One important change from the fourth to the fifth edition of the DSM is that individuals may now report their perception of personality shifts rather than limiting diagnosis to shifts others must report.
2. Amnesia must occur, defined as gaps in remembering everyday events, important personal information, and/or traumatic events. (Dissociative Amnesia: Deeply Buried Memories) These new criteria for DID recognize that amnesia doesn't just occur for traumatic events but also for everyday events.
3. The person must be distressed by the disorder or have trouble functioning in one or more major life areas because of the disorder. This criterion is common among all serious mental illness diagnoses, as a diagnosis is not appropriate where the symptoms do not create distress and/or trouble functioning.
4. The disturbance is not part of normal cultural or religious practices. This DID criterion eliminates diagnosis in cultures or situations where multiplicity is appropriate. An example of this is in children, where an imaginary friend does not necessarily indicate mental illness.
5. The symptoms are not due to the direct physiological effects of a substance (such as blackouts or chaotic behavior during alcohol intoxication) or a general medical condition (such as complex partial seizures). This characteristic of dissociative identity disorder is important, as substance abuse or another medical condition is more appropriate to diagnose when present than DID.

Epilogue

This writer learned from Dorothy's youngest son that Dorothy lived to age 89 in semi-isolation on her small farm in Georgia. She continued to keep chickens for eggs and always delighted in having two dogs to pal with until her last few years. Her mood varied, but Dorothy was always happy to hear from or see her family. Her neighbors and handyman adored her, and she maintained contact with Mr. Hall.

David D. Yates was born in Drift, Kentucky, on April 9, 1944. He moved from town to town in Kentucky, West Virginia, and Ohio due to his father's employment in the mining and building industries. David has lived in California since 1962.

During his first year of college in 1963, he was president of the Sacramento County Youth for Mental Health Auxiliary. He earned a Bachelor of Science Degree in Psycholgy in 1966, Master of Science Degree in Counseling in 1980, and holds community college teaching and counseling credentials. Since then, he has completed thousands of hours of post-graduate education in mental illness, family dysfunction, and recovery from substances and other abuses.

David earned Parent Effectiveness Training and Shared Parenting certificates, wrote and taught a parent education program, and trained other instructors, before becoming a licensed Marriage, Family, and Child Therapist in 1981. He was also a Licensed Advanced Alcohol and Drug Counselor for several years.

David supervised counselors and graduate students at a nationally awarded crisis center for adolescents for eight years, in a domestic violence program for seven years, and a sexual offender program for two years. He has conducted and reported on hundreds of child custody and juvenile court investigations.

Presently he works part-time as a licensed therapist, primarily treating veterans suffering from post-traumatic stress. His approaches are Systemic, Cognitive-Behavioral, and Mindfulness-Based Counseling.

David currently lives in Shingle Springs, California, with his wife, Carol. His passions are golf and fishing.

David D. Yates

Dare to Reach Beyond Normal

License Information

You are free to:

Share – copy and redistribute the material in any medium or format
Adapt – remix, transform, and build upon the material.
The licensor cannot revoke these freedoms as long as you follow the license terms.

Under the following terms:
Attribution – You must give appropriate credit, provide a link to the license, and indicate if you make changes. You may do so reasonably but not in any way that suggests the licensor endorses you or your use.

You may not use the material for commercial purposes.

Share Alike
If you remix, transform, or build upon the material, you must distribute your contributions under the same license as the original.
No additional restrictions – You may not apply to legal terms or technological measures that legally restrict others from doing anything the license permits.

Notices:
You do not have to comply with the license for elements of the material in the public domain or where your use is permitted by an applicable exception or limitation.
No warranties are given. The license will not give you all the permissions necessary for your intended use. For example, other rights such as publicity, privacy, or moral rights may limit how you use the material.

Made in the USA
Monee, IL
05 March 2023

28674105R10168